Hsüan-tsang, Samuel Beal

Si-Yu-Ki

Buddhist Records of the Western World - Vol. 1

Hsüan-tsang, Samuel Beal

Si-Yu-Ki
Buddhist Records of the Western World - Vol. 1
ISBN/EAN: 9783337247928

Printed in Europe, USA, Canada, Australia, Japan

Cover: Foto ©Andreas Hilbeck / pixelio.de

More available books at **www.hansebooks.com**

TRÜBNER'S ORIENTAL SERIES.

"A knowledge of the commonplace, at least, of Oriental literature, philosophy, and religion is as necessary to the general reader of the present day as an acquaintance with the Latin and Greek classics was a generation or so ago. Immense strides have been made within the present century in these branches of learning; Sanskrit has been brought within the range of accurate philology, and its invaluable ancient literature thoroughly investigated; the language and sacred books of the Zoroastrians have been laid bare; Egyptian, Assyrian, and other records of the remote past have been deciphered, and a group of scholars speak of still more recondite Accadian and Hittite monuments; but the results of all the scholarship that has been devoted to these subjects have been almost inaccessible to the public because they were contained for the most part in learned or expensive works, or scattered throughout the numbers of scientific periodicals. Messrs. TRÜBNER & Co., in a spirit of enterprise which does them infinite credit, have determined to supply the constantly-increasing want, and to give in a popular, or, at least, a comprehensive form, all this mass of knowledge to the world."—*Times*.

NOW READY,

Post 8vo, pp. 568, with Map, cloth, price 16s.

THE INDIAN EMPIRE : ITS HISTORY, PEOPLE, AND PRODUCTS.

Being a revised form of the article "India," in the "Imperial Gazetteer,"
remodelled into chapters, brought up to date, and incorporating
the general results of the Census of 1881.

By W. W. HUNTER, C.I.E., LL.D.,

Director-General of Statistics to the Government of India.

"The article 'India,' in Volume IV., is the touchstone of the work, and proves clearly enough the sterling metal of which it is wrought. It represents the essence of the 100 volumes which contain the results of the statistical survey conducted by Dr. Hunter throughout each of the 240 districts of India. It is, moreover, the only attempt that has ever been made to show how the Indian people have been built up, and the evidence from the original materials has been for the first time sifted and examined by the light of the local research in which the author was for so long engaged."—*Times*.

THE FOLLOWING WORKS HAVE ALREADY APPEARED:—

Third Edition, post 8vo, cloth, pp. xvi.—428, price 16s.

ESSAYS ON THE SACRED LANGUAGE, WRITINGS, AND RELIGION OF THE PARSIS.

By MARTIN HAUG, Ph.D.,

Late of the Universities of Tübingen, Göttingen, and Bonn ; Superintendent of Sanskrit Studies, and Professor of Sanskrit in the Poona College.

EDITED AND ENLARGED BY DR. E. W. WEST.

To which is added a Biographical Memoir of the late Dr. HAUG by Prof. E. P. EVANS.

I. History of the Researches into the Sacred Writings and Religion of the Parsis, from the Earliest Times down to the Present.
II. Languages of the Parsi Scriptures.
III. The Zend-Avesta, or the Scripture of the Parsis.
IV. The Zoroastrian Religion, as to its Origin and Development.

"'Essays on the Sacred Language, Writings, and Religion of the Parsis,' by the late Dr. Martin Haug, edited by Dr. E. W. West. The author intended, on his return from India, to expand the materials contained in this work into a comprehensive account of the Zoroastrian religion, but the design was frustrated by his untimely death. We have, however, in a concise and readable form, a history of the researches into the sacred writings and religion of the Parsis from the earliest times down to the present—a dissertation on the languages of the Parsi Scriptures, a translation of the Zend-Avesta, or the Scripture of the Parsis, and a dissertation on the Zoroastrian religion, with especial reference to its origin and development."—*Times.*

Post 8vo, cloth, pp. viii.—176, price 7s. 6d.

TEXTS FROM THE BUDDHIST CANON

COMMONLY KNOWN AS "DHAMMAPADA."

With Accompanying Narratives.

Translated from the Chinese by S. BEAL, B.A., Professor of Chinese, University College, London.

The Dhammapada, as hitherto known by the Pali Text Edition, as edited by Fausböll, by Max Müller's English, and Albrecht Weber's German translations, consists only of twenty-six chapters or sections, whilst the Chinese version, or rather recension, as now translated by Mr. Beal, consists of thirty-nine sections. The students of Pali who possess Fausböll's text, or either of the above-named translations, will therefore needs want Mr. Beal's English rendering of the Chinese version ; the thirteen above-named additional sections not being accessible to them in any other form ; for, even if they understand Chinese, the Chinese original would be un-obtainable by them.

"Mr. Beal's rendering of the Chinese translation is a most valuable aid to the critical study of the work. It contains authentic texts gathered from ancient canonical books, and generally connected with some incident in the history of Buddha. Their great interest, however, consists in the light which they throw upon everyday life in India at the remote period at which they were written, and upon the method of teaching adopted by the founder of the religion. The method employed was principally parable, and the simplicity of the tales and the excellence of the morals inculcated, as well as the strange hold which they have retained upon the minds of millions of people, make them a very remarkable study."—*Times.*

"Mr. Beal, by making it accessible in an English dress, has added to the great services he has already rendered to the comparative study of religious history."—*Academy.*

"Valuable as exhibiting the doctrine of the Buddhists in its purest, least adulterated form, it brings the modern reader face to face with that simple creed and rule of conduct which won its way over the minds of myriads, and which is now nominally professed by 145 millions, who have overlaid its austere simplicity with innumerable ceremonies, forgotten its maxims, perverted its teaching, and so inverted its leading principle that a religion whose founder denied a God, now worships that founder as a god himself."—*Scotsman.*

Second Edition, post 8vo, cloth, pp. xxiv.—360, price 10s. 6d.

THE HISTORY OF INDIAN LITERATURE.

By ALBRECHT WEBER.

Translated from the Second German Edition by JOHN MANN, M.A., and THÉODOR ZACHARIAE, Ph.D., with the sanction of the Author.

Dr. BUHLER, Inspector of Schools in India, writes:—"When I was Professor of Oriental Languages in Elphinstone College, I frequently felt the want of such a work to which I could refer the students."

Professor COWELL, of Cambridge, writes:—"It will be especially useful to the students in our Indian colleges and universities. I used to long for such a book when I was teaching in Calcutta. Hindu students are intensely interested in the history of Sanskrit literature, and this volume will supply them with all they want on the subject."

Professor WHITNEY, Yale College, Newhaven, Conn., U.S.A., writes:—"I was one of the class to whom the work was originally given in the form of academic lectures. At their first appearance they were by far the most learned and able treatment of their subject; and with their recent additions they still maintain decidedly the same rank."

"Is perhaps the most comprehensive and lucid survey of Sanskrit literature extant. The essays contained in the volume were originally delivered as academic lectures, and at the time of their first publication were acknowledged to be by far the most learned and able treatment of the subject. They have now been brought up to date by the addition of all the most important results of recent research."—*Times.*

Post 8vo, cloth, pp. xii.—198, accompanied by Two Language Maps, price 12s.

A SKETCH OF THE MODERN LANGUAGES OF THE EAST INDIES.

By ROBERT N. CUST.

The Author has attempted to fill up a vacuum, the inconvenience of which pressed itself on his notice. Much had been written about the languages of the East Indies, but the extent of our present knowledge had not even been brought to a focus. It occurred to him that it might be of use to others to publish in an arranged form the notes which he had collected for his own edification.

"Supplies a deficiency which has long been felt."—*Times.*

"The book before us is then a valuable contribution to philological science. It passes under review a vast number of languages, and it gives, or professes to give, in every case the sum and substance of the opinions and judgments of the best-informed writers."—*Saturday Review.*

Second Corrected Edition, post 8vo, pp. xii.—116, cloth, price 5s.

THE BIRTH OF THE WAR-GOD.

A Poem. By KALIDASA.

Translated from the Sanskrit into English Verse by RALPH T. H. GRIFFITH, M.A.

"A very spirited rendering of the *Kumárasambhava*, which was first published twenty-six years ago, and which we are glad to see made once more accessible."—*Times.*

"Mr. Griffith's very spirited rendering is well known to most who are at all interested in Indian literature, or enjoy the tenderness of feeling and rich creative imagination of its author."—*Indian Antiquary.*

"We are very glad to welcome a second edition of Professor Griffith's admirable translation. Few translations deserve a second edition better."—*Athenæum.*

Post 8vo, pp. 432, cloth, price 16s.

A CLASSICAL DICTIONARY OF HINDU MYTHOLOGY AND RELIGION, GEOGRAPHY, HISTORY, AND LITERATURE.

By JOHN DOWSON, M.R.A.S.,
Late Professor of Hindustani, Staff College.

"This not only forms an indispensable book of reference to students of Indian literature, but is also of great general interest, as it gives in a concise and easily accessible form all that need be known about the personages of Hindu mythology whose names are so familiar, but of whom so little is known outside the limited circle of *savants.*"—*Times.*

"It is no slight gain when such subjects are treated fairly and fully in a moderate space; and we need only add that the few wants which we may hope to see supplied in new editions detract but little from the general excellence of Mr. Dowson's work."—*Saturday Review.*

Post 8vo, with View of Mecca, pp. cxii.—172, cloth, price 9s.

SELECTIONS FROM THE KORAN.

By EDWARD WILLIAM LANE,
Translator of "The Thousand and One Nights;" &c., &c.
A New Edition, Revised and Enlarged, with an Introduction by
STANLEY LANE POOLE.

". . . Has been long esteemed in this country as the compilation of one of the greatest Arabic scholars of the time, the late Mr. Lane, the well-known translator of the 'Arabian Nights.' . . . The present editor has enhanced the value of his relative's work by divesting the text of a great deal of extraneous matter introduced by way of comment, and prefixing an introduction."—*Times.*

"Mr. Poole is both a generous and a learned biographer. . . . Mr. Poole tells us the facts . . . so far as it is possible for industry and criticism to ascertain them, and for literary skill to present them in a condensed and readable form."—*Englishman, Calcutta.*

Post 8vo, pp. vi.—368, cloth, price 14s.

MODERN INDIA AND THE INDIANS,
BEING A SERIES OF IMPRESSIONS, NOTES, AND ESSAYS.
By MONIER WILLIAMS, D.C.L.,
Hon. LL.D. of the University of Calcutta, Hon. Member of the Bombay Asiatic Society, Boden Professor of Sanskrit in the University of Oxford.
Third Edition, revised and augmented by considerable Additions, with Illustrations and a Map.

"In this volume we have the thoughtful impressions of a thoughtful man on some of the most important questions connected with our Indian Empire. . . . An enlightened observant man, travelling among an enlightened observant people, Professor Monier Williams has brought before the public in a pleasant form more of the manners and customs of the Queen's Indian subjects than we ever remember to have seen in any one work. He not only deserves the thanks of every Englishman for this able contribution to the study of Modern India—a subject with which we should be specially familiar—but he deserves the thanks of every Indian, Parsee or Hindu, Buddhist and Moslem, for his clear exposition of their manners, their creeds, and their necessities."—*Times.*

Post 8vo, pp. xliv.—376, cloth, price 14s.

METRICAL TRANSLATIONS FROM SANSKRIT WRITERS.
With an Introduction, many Prose Versions, and Parallel Passages from Classical Authors.
By J. MUIR, C.I.E., D.C.L., LL.D., Ph.D.

". . . An agreeable introduction to Hindu poetry."—*Times.*

". . . A volume which may be taken as a fair illustration alike of the religious and moral sentiments and of the legendary lore of the best Sanskrit writers."—*Edinburgh Daily Review.*

Second Edition, post 8vo, pp. xxvi.—244, cloth, price 10s. 6d.

THE GULISTAN;

Or, ROSE GARDEN OF SHEKH MUSHLIU'D-DIN SADI OF SHIRAZ.

Translated for the First Time into Prose and Verse, with an Introductory Preface, and a Life of the Author, from the Atish Kadah,

By EDWARD B. EASTWICK, C.B., M.A., F.R.S., M.R.A.S.

"It is a very fair rendering of the original."—*Times.*

"The new edition has long been desired, and will be welcomed by all who t ke any interest in Oriental poetry. The *Gulistan* is a typical Persian verse-book of the highest order. Mr. Eastwick's rhymed translation . . . has long established itself in a secure position as the best version of Sadi's finest work."—*Academy.*

"It is both faithfully and gracefully executed."—*Tablet.*

In Two Volumes, post 8vo, pp. viii.—408 and viii.—348, cloth, price 28s.

MISCELLANEOUS ESSAYS RELATING TO INDIAN SUBJECTS.

By BRIAN HOUGHTON HODGSON, Esq., F.R.S.,

Late of the Bengal Civil Service; Corresponding Member of the Institute; Chevalier of the Legion of Honour; late British Minister at the Court of Nepál, &c., &c.

CONTENTS OF VOL. I.

Section I.—On the Kocch, Bódó, and Dhimál Tribes.—Part I. Vocabulary—Part II. Grammar.—Part III. Their Origin, Location, Numbers, Creed, Customs, Character, and Condition, with a General Description of the Climate they dwell in.—Appendix.

Section II.—On Himalayan Ethnology.—I. Comparative Vocabulary of the Languages of the Broken Tribes of Népál.—II. Vocabulary of the Dialects of the Kirant Language.—III. Grammatical Analysis of the Váyu Language. The Váyu Grammar.—IV. Analysis of the Báhing Dialect of the Kiranti Language. The Báhing Grammar.—V. On the Váyu or Háyu Tribe of the Central Himálaya.—VI. On the Kiranti Tribe of the Central Himálaya.

CONTENTS OF VOL. II.

Section III.—On the Aborigines of North-Eastern India. Comparative Vocabulary of the Tibetan, Bódó, and Gáró Tongues.

Section IV.—Aborigines of the North-Eastern Frontier.

Section V.—Aborigines of the Eastern Frontier.

Section VI.—The Indo-Chinese Borderers, and their connection with the Himalayans and Tibetans. Comparative Vocabulary of Indo-Chinese Borderers in Arakan. Comparative Vocabulary of Indo-Chinese Borderers in Tenasserim.

Section VII.—The Mongolian Affinities of the Caucasians.—Comparison and Analysis of Caucasian and Mongolian Words.

Section VIII.—Physical Type of Tibetans.

Section IX.—The Aborigines of Central India.—Comparative Vocabulary of the Aboriginal Languages of Central India.—Aborigines of the Eastern Ghats.—Vocabulary of some of the Dialects of the Hill and Wandering Tribes in the Northern Sircars.—Aborigines of the Nilgiris, with Remarks on their Affinities.—Supplement to the Nilgirian Vocabularies.—The Aborigines of Southern India and Ceylon.

Section X.—Route of Nepalese Mission to Pekin, with Remarks on the Watershed and Plateau of Tibet.

Section XI.—Route from Káthmándú, the Capital of Nepál, to Darjeeling in Sikim.—Memorandum relative to the Seven Cosis of Nepál.

Section XII.—Some Accounts of the Systems of Law and Police as recognised in the State of Nepál.

Section XIII.—The Native Method of making the Paper denominated Hindustan, Népálese.

Section XIV.—Pre-eminence of the Vernaculars; or, the Anglicists Answered; Being Letters on the Education of the People of India.

"For the study of the less-known races of India Mr. Brian Hodgson's 'Miscellaneous Essays' will be found very valuable both to the philologist and the ethnologist."—*Times.*

Third Edition, Two Vols., post 8vo, pp. viii.—268 and viii.—326, cloth, price 21s.

THE LIFE OR LEGEND OF GAUDAMA,

THE BUDDHA OF THE BURMESE. With Annotations.

The Ways to Neibban, and Notice on the Phongyies or Burmese Monks.

By THE RIGHT REV. P. BIGANDET,

Bishop of Ramatha, Vicar-Apostolic of Ava and Pegu.

"The work is furnished with copious notes, which not only illustrate the subject-matter, but form a perfect encyclopædia of Buddhist lore."—*Times.*

"A work which will furnish European students of Buddhism with a most valuable help in the prosecution of their investigations."—*Edinburgh Daily Review.*

"Bishop Bigandet's invaluable work."—*Indian Antiquary.*

"Viewed in this light, its importance is sufficient to place students of the subject under a deep obligation to its author."—*Calcutta Review.*

"This work is one of the greatest authorities upon Buddhism."—*Dublin Review.*

Post 8vo, pp. xxiv.—420, cloth, price 18s.

CHINESE BUDDHISM.

A VOLUME OF SKETCHES, HISTORICAL AND CRITICAL.

By J. EDKINS, D.D.

Author of "China's Place in Philology," "Religion in China," &c., &c.

"It contains a vast deal of important information on the subject, such as is only to be gained by long-continued study on the spot."—*Athenæum.*

"Upon the whole, we know of no work comparable to it for the extent of its original research, and the simplicity with which this complicated system of philosophy, religion, literature, and ritual is set forth."—*British Quarterly Review.*

The whole volume is replete with learning. . . . It deserves most careful study from all interested in the history of the religions of the world, and expressly of those who are concerned in the propagation of Christianity. Dr. Edkins notices in terms of just condemnation the exaggerated praise bestowed upon Buddhism by recent English writers."—*Record.*

Post 8vo, pp. 496, cloth, price 18s.

LINGUISTIC AND ORIENTAL ESSAYS.

WRITTEN FROM THE YEAR 1846 TO 1878.

By ROBERT NEEDHAM CUST,

Late Member of Her Majesty's Indian Civil Service; Hon. Secretary to the Royal Asiatic Society; and Author of "The Modern Languages of the East Indies."

"We know none who has described Indian life, especially the life of the natives, with so much learning, sympathy, and literary talent."—*Academy.*

"They seem to us to be full of suggestive and original remarks."—*St. James's Gazette.*

"His book contains a vast amount of information. The result of thirty-five years of inquiry, reflection, and speculation, and that on subjects as full of fascination as of food for thought."—*Tablet.*

"Exhibit such a thorough acquaintance with the history and antiquities of India as to entitle him to speak as one having authority."—*Edinburgh Daily Review.*

"The author speaks with the authority of personal experience. . . . . It is this constant association with the country and the people which gives such a vividness to many of the pages."—*Athenæum.*

Post 8vo, pp. civ.—348, cloth, price 18s.

BUDDHIST BIRTH STORIES; or, Jataka Tales.

The Oldest Collection of Folk-lore Extant:

BEING THE JATAKATTHAVANNANA,

For the first time Edited in the original Pâli.

By V. FAUSBOLL;

And Translated by T. W. RHYS DAVIDS.

Translation. Volume I.

"These are tales supposed to have been told by the Buddha of what he had seen and heard in his previous births. They are probably the nearest representatives of the original Aryan stories from which sprang the folk-lore of Europe as well as India. The introduction contains a most interesting disquisition on the migrations of these fables, tracing their reappearance in the various groups of folk-lore legends. Among other old friends, we meet with a version of the Judgment of Solomon."—*Times.*

"It is now some years since Mr. Rhys Davids asserted his right to be heard on this subject by his able article on Buddhism in the new edition of the 'Encyclopædia Britannica.'"—*Leeds Mercury.*

"All who are interested in Buddhist literature ought to feel deeply indebted to Mr. Rhys Davids. His well-established reputation as a Pali scholar is a sufficient guarantee for the fidelity of his version, and the style of his translations is deserving of high praise."—*Academy.*

"No more competent expositor of Buddhism could be found than Mr. Rhys Davids In the Jâtaka book we have, then, a priceless record of the earliest imaginative literature of our race; and . . . it presents to us a nearly complete picture of the social life and customs and popular beliefs of the common people of Aryan tribes, closely related to ourselves, just as they were passing through the first stages of civilisation."—*St. James's Gazette.*

Post 8vo, pp. xxviii.—362, cloth, price 14s.

A TALMUDIC MISCELLANY;

OR, A THOUSAND AND ONE EXTRACTS FROM THE TALMUD, THE MIDRASHIM, AND THE KABBALAH.

Compiled and Translated by PAUL ISAAC HERSHON,

Author of "Genesis According to the Talmud," &c.

With Notes and Copious Indexes.

"To obtain in so concise and handy a form as this volume a general idea of the Talmud is a boon to Christians at least."—*Times.*

"Its peculiar and popular character will make it attractive to general readers. Mr. Hershon is a very competent scholar. . . . Contains samples of the good, bad, and indifferent, and especially extracts that throw light upon the Scriptures."—*British Quarterly Review.*

"Will convey to English readers a more complete and truthful notion of the Talmud than any other work that has yet appeared."—*Daily News.*

"Without overlooking in the slightest the several attractions of the previous volumes of the 'Oriental Series,' we have no hesitation in saying that this surpasses them all in interest."—*Edinburgh Daily Review.*

"Mr. Hershon has . . . thus given English readers what is, we believe, a fair set of specimens which they can test for themselves."—*The Record.*

"This book is by far the best fitted in the present state of knowledge to enable the general reader to gain a fair and unbiassed conception of the multifarious contents of the wonderful miscellany which can only be truly understood—so Jewish pride asserts—by the life-long devotion of scholars of the Chosen People."—*Inquirer.*

"The value and importance of this volume consist in the fact that scarcely a single extract is given in its pages but throws some light, direct or refracted, upon those Scriptures which are the common heritage of Jew and Christian alike."—*John Bull.*

"It is a capital specimen of Hebrew scholarship; a monument of learned, loving, light-giving labour."—*Jewish Herald.*

Post 8vo, pp. xii.—228, cloth, price 7s. 6d.

THE CLASSICAL POETRY OF THE JAPANESE.

By BASIL HALL CHAMBERLAIN,

Author of "Yeigo Heñkaku Shirañ."

"A very curious volume. The author has manifestly devoted much labour to the task of studying the poetical literature of the Japanese, and rendering characteristic specimens into English verse."—*Daily News.*

"Mr. Chamberlain's volume is, so far as we are aware, the first attempt which has been made to interpret the literature of the Japanese to the Western world. It is to the classical poetry of Old Japan that we must turn for indigenous Japanese thought, and in the volume before us we have a selection from that poetry rendered into graceful English verse."—*Tablet.*

"It is undoubtedly one of the best translations of lyric literature which has appeared during the close of the last year."—*Celestial Empire.*

"Mr. Chamberlain set himself a difficult task when he undertook to reproduce Japanese poetry in an English form. But he has evidently laboured *con amore*, and his efforts are successful to a degree."—*London and China Express.*

Post 8vo, pp. xii.—164, cloth, price 10s. 6d.

THE HISTORY OF ESARHADDON (Son of Sennacherib),

KING OF ASSYRIA, B.C. 681–668.

Translated from the Cuneiform Inscriptions upon Cylinders and Tablets in the British Museum Collection; together with a Grammatical Analysis of each Word, Explanations of the Ideographs by Extracts from the Bi-Lingual Syllabaries, and List of Eponyms, &c.

By ERNEST A. BUDGE, B.A., M.R.A.S.,

Assyrian Exhibitioner, Christ's College, Cambridge.

"Students of scriptural archæology will also appreciate the 'History of Esarhaddon.'"—*Times.*

"There is much to attract the scholar in this volume. It does not pretend to popularise studies which are yet in their infancy. Its primary object is to translate, but it does not assume to be more than tentative, and it offers both to the professed Assyriologist and to the ordinary non-Assyriological Semitic scholar the means of controlling its results."—*Academy.*

"Mr. Budge's book is, of course, mainly addressed to Assyrian scholars and students. They are not, it is to be feared, a very numerous class. But the more thanks are due to him on that account for the way in which he has acquitted himself in his laborious task."—*Tablet.*

Post 8vo, pp. 448, cloth, price 21s.

THE MESNEVI

(Usually known as THE MESNEVIYI SHERIF, or HOLY MESNEVI)

OF

MEVLANA (OUR LORD) JELALU 'D-DIN MUHAMMED ER-RUMI.

Book the First.

Together with some Account of the Life and Acts of the Author, of his Ancestors, and of his Descendants.

Illustrated by a Selection of Characteristic Anecdotes, as Collected by their Historian,

MEVLANA SHEMSU-'D-DIN AHMED, EL EFLAKI, EL 'ARIFI.

Translated, and the Poetry Versified, in English,

By JAMES W. REDHOUSE, M.R.A.S., &c.

"A complete treasury of occult Oriental lore."—*Saturday Review.*

"This book will be a very valuable help to the reader ignorant of Persia, who is desirous of obtaining an insight into a very important department of the literature extant in that language."—*Tablet.*

Post 8vo, pp. xvi.—280, cloth, price 6s.

EASTERN PROVERBS AND EMBLEMS

ILLUSTRATING OLD TRUTHS.

BY REV. J. LONG,

Member of the Bengal Asiatic Society, F.R.G.S.

" We regard the book as valuable, and wish for it a wide circulation and attentive reading."—*Record.*

" Altogether, it is quite a feast of good things."—*Globe.*

" It is full of interesting matter."—*Antiquary.*

Post 8vo, pp. viii.—270, cloth, price 7s. 6d.

INDIAN POETRY;

Containing a New Edition of the "Indian Song of Songs," from the Sanscrit of the "Gita Govinda" of Jayadeva; Two Books from "The Iliad of India" (Mahabharata), "Proverbial Wisdom" from the Shlokas of the Hitopadesa, and other Oriental Poems.

BY EDWIN ARNOLD, C.S.I., Author of "The Light of Asia."

" In this new volume of Messrs. Trübner's Oriental Series, Mr. Edwin Arnold does good service by illustrating, through the medium of his musical English melodies, the power of Indian poetry to stir European emotions. The 'Indian Song of Songs' is not unknown to scholars. Mr. Arnold will have introduced it among popular English poems. Nothing could be more graceful and delicate than the shades by which Krishna is portrayed in the gradual process of being weaned by the love of

' Beautiful Radha, jasmine-bosomed Radha,'

from the allurements of the forest nymphs, in whom the five senses are typified."—*Times.*

" No other English poet has ever thrown his genius and his art so thoroughly into the work of translating Eastern ideas as Mr. Arnold has done in his splendid paraphrases of language contained in these mighty epics."—*Daily Telegraph.*

" The poem abounds with imagery of Eastern luxuriousness and sensuousness; the air seems laden with the spicy odours of the tropics, and the verse has a richness and a melody sufficient to captivate the senses of the dullest."—*Standard.*

" The translator, while producing a very enjoyable poem, has adhered with tolerable fidelity to the original text."—*Overland Mail.*

" We certainly wish Mr. Arnold success in his attempt 'to popularise Indian classics,' that being, as his preface tells us, the goal towards which he bends his efforts."—*Allen's Indian Mail.*

Post 8vo, pp. xvi.—296, cloth, price 10s. 6d.

THE MIND OF MENCIUS;

OR, POLITICAL ECONOMY FOUNDED UPON MORAL PHILOSOPHY.

A SYSTEMATIC DIGEST OF THE DOCTRINES OF THE CHINESE PHILOSOPHER MENCIUS.

Translated from the Original Text and Classified, with Comments and Explanations,

By the REV. ERNST FABER, Rhenish Mission Society.

Translated from the German, with Additional Notes,

By the REV. A. B. HUTCHINSON, C.M.S., Church Mission, Hong Kong.

" Mr. Faber is already well known in the field of Chinese studies by his digest of the doctrines of Confucius. The value of this work will be perceived when it is remembered that at no time since relations commenced between China and the West has the former been so powerful—we had almost said aggressive—as now. For those who will give it careful study, Mr. Faber's work is one of the most valuable of the excellent series to which it belongs."—*Nature.*

Post 8vo, pp. 336, cloth, price 16s.

THE RELIGIONS OF INDIA.

By A. BARTH.

Translated from the French with the authority and assistance of the Author.

The author has, at the request of the publishers, considerably enlarged the work for the translator, and has added the literature of the subject to date ; the translation may, therefore, be looked upon as an equivalent of a new and improved edition of the original.

"Is not only a valuable manual of the religions of India, which marks a distinct step in the treatment of the subject, but also a useful work of reference."—*Academy.*

"This volume is a reproduction, with corrections and additions, of an article contributed by the learned author two years ago to the 'Encyclopédie des Sciences Religieuses.' It attracted much notice when it first appeared, and is generally admitted to present the best summary extant of the vast subject with which it deals."—*Tablet.*

"This is not only on the whole the best but the only manual of the religions of India, apart from Buddhism, which we have in English. The present work . . . shows not only great knowledge of the facts and power of clear exposition, but also great insight into the inner history and the deeper meaning of the great religion, for it is in reality only one, which it proposes to describe."—*Modern Review.*

"The merit of the work has been emphatically recognised by the most authoritative Orientalists, both in this country and on the continent of Europe. But probably there are few Indianists (if we may use the word) who would not derive a good deal of information from it, and especially from the extensive bibliography provided in the notes."—*Dublin Review.*

"Such a sketch M. Barth has drawn with a master-hand."—*Critic (New York).*

Post 8vo, pp. viii.—152, cloth, price 6s.

HINDU PHILOSOPHY.

The SĀNKHYA KĀRIKA of IS'WARA KRISHNA.

An Exposition of the System of Kapila, with an Appendix on the Nyāya and Vais'eshika Systems.

By JOHN DAVIES, M.A. (Cantab.), M.R.A.S.

The system of Kapila contains nearly all that India has produced in the department of pure philosophy.

"The non-Orientalist . . . finds in Mr. Davies a patient and learned guide who leads him into the intricacies of the philosophy of India, and supplies him with a clue, that he may not be lost in them. In the preface he states that the system of Kapila is the 'earliest attempt on record to give an answer, from reason alone, to the mysterious questions which arise in every thoughtful mind about the origin of the world, the nature and relations of man and his future destiny,' and in his learned and able notes he exhibits 'the connection of the Sankhya system with the philosophy of Spinoza,' and 'the connection of the system of Kapila with that of Schopenhauer and Von Hartmann.'"—*Foreign Church Chronicle.*

"Mr. Davies's volume on Hindu Philosophy is an undoubted gain to all students of the development of thought. The system of Kapila, which is here given in a translation from the Sânkhya Kârikâ, is the only contribution of India to pure philosophy. . . . Presents many points of deep interest to the student of comparative philosophy, and without Mr. Davies's lucid interpretation it would be difficult to appreciate these points in any adequate manner."—*Saturday Review.*

"We welcome Mr. Davies's book as a valuable addition to our philosophical library."—*Notes and Queries.*

Post 8vo, pp. x.—130, cloth, price 6s.

A MANUAL OF HINDU PANTHEISM. VEDÂNTASÂRA.

Translated, with copious Annotations, by MAJOR G. A. JACOB,
Bombay Staff Corps; Inspector of Army Schools.

The design of this little work is to provide for missionaries, and for others who, like them, have little leisure for original research, an accurate summary of the doctrines of the Vedânta.

"There can be no question that the religious doctrines most widely held by the people of India are mainly Pantheistic. And of Hindu Pantheism, at all events in its most modern phases, its Vedântasâra presents the best summary. But then this work is a mere summary: a skeleton, the dry bones of which require to be clothed with skin and bones, and to be animated by vital breath before the ordinary reader will discern in it a living reality. Major Jacob, therefore, has wisely added to his translation of the Vedântasâra copious notes from the writings of well-known Oriental scholars, in which he has, we think, elucidated all that required elucidation. So that the work, as here presented to us, presents no difficulties which a very moderate amount of application will not overcome."—*Tablet.*

"The modest title of Major Jacob's work conveys but an inadequate idea of the vast amount of research embodied in his notes to the text of the Vedantasara. So copious, indeed, are these, and so much collateral matter do they bring to bear on the subject, that the diligent student will rise from their perusal with a fairly adequate view of Hindù philosophy generally. His work . . . is one of the best of its kind that we have seen."—*Calcutta Review.*

Post 8vo, pp. xii.—154, cloth, price 7s. 6d.

TSUNI—‖GOAM :

The Supreme Being of the Khoi-Khoi.

By THEOPHILUS HAHN, Ph.D.,

Custodian of the Grey Collection, Cape Town; Corresponding Member
of the Geogr. Society, Dresden; Corresponding Member of the
Anthropological Society, Vienna, &c., &c.

"The first instalment of Dr. Hahn's labours will be of interest, not at the Cape only, but in every University of Europe. It is, in fact, a most valuable contribution to the comparative study of religion and mythology. Accounts of their religion and mythology were scattered about in various books; these have been carefully collected by Dr. Hahn and printed in his second chapter, enriched and improved by what he has been able to collect himself."—*Prof. Max Müller in the Nineteenth Century.*

"Dr. Hahn's book is that of a man who is both a philologist and believer in philological methods, and a close student of savage manners and customs."—*Saturday Review.*

"It is full of good things."—*St. James's Gazette.*

In Four Volumes. Post 8vo, Vol. I., pp. xii.—392, cloth, price 12s. 6d.,
and Vol. II., pp. vi.—408, cloth, price 12s. 6d.

A COMPREHENSIVE COMMENTARY TO THE QURAN.

To which is prefixed Sale's Preliminary Discourse, with Additional Notes and Emendations.

Together with a Complete Index to the Text, Preliminary Discourse, and Notes.

By Rev. E. M. WHERRY, M.A., Lodiana.

"As Mr. Wherry's book is intended for missionaries in India, it is no doubt well that they should be prepared to meet, if they can, the ordinary arguments and interpretations, and for this purpose Mr. Wherry's additions will prove useful."—*Saturday Review.*

Post 8vo, pp. vi.—208, cloth, price 8s. 6d.

THE BHAGAVAD-GÎTÂ.

Translated, with Introduction and Notes

By JOHN DAVIES, M.A. (Cantab.)

"Let us add that his translation of the Bhagavad Gîtâ is, as we judge, the best that has as yet appeared in English, and that his Philological Notes are of quite peculiar value."—*Dublin Review.*

Post 8vo, pp. 96, cloth, price 5s.

THE QUATRAINS OF OMAR KHAYYAM.

Translated by E. H. WHINFIELD, M.A.,
Barrister-at-Law, late H.M. Bengal Civil Service.

Omar Khayyám (the tent-maker) was born about the middle of the fifth century of the Hejirah, corresponding to the eleventh of the Christian era, in the neighbourhood of Naishapur, the capital of Khorasán, and died in 517 A.H. (=1122 A.D.)

"Mr. Whinfield has executed a difficult task with considerable success, and his version contains much that will be new to those who only know Mr. Fitzgerald's delightful selection."—*Academy.*

"There are several editions of the Quatrains, varying greatly in their readings. Mr. Whinfield has used three of these for his excellent translation. The most prominent features in the Quatrains are their profound agnosticism, combined with a fatalism based more on philosophic than religious grounds, their Epicureanism and the spirit of universal tolerance and charity which animates them."—*Calcutta Review.*

Post 8vo, pp. xxiv.—268, cloth, price 9s.

THE PHILOSOPHY OF THE UPANISHADS AND ANCIENT INDIAN METAPHYSICS.

As exhibited in a series of Articles contributed to the *Calcutta Review.*

By ARCHIBALD EDWARD GOUGH, M.A., Lincoln College, Oxford; Principal of the Calcutta Madrasa.

"For practical purposes this is perhaps the most important of the works that have thus far appeared in 'Trübner's Oriental Series.' . . . We cannot doubt that for all who may take it up the work must be one of profound interest."—*Saturday Review.*

In Two Volumes. Vol. I., post 8vo, pp. xxiv.—230, cloth, price 7s. 6d.

A COMPARATIVE HISTORY OF THE EGYPTIAN AND MESOPOTAMIAN RELIGIONS.

By Dr. C. P. TIELE.

Vol. I.—HISTORY OF THE EGYPTIAN RELIGION.

Translated from the Dutch with the Assistance of the Author.

By JAMES BALLINGAL.

"It places in the hands of the English readers a history of Egyptian Religion which is very complete, which is based on the best materials, and which has been illustrated by the latest results of research. In this volume there is a great deal of information, as well as independent investigation, for the trustworthiness of which Dr. Tiele's name is in itself a guarantee; and the description of the successive religion under the Old Kingdom, the Middle Kingdom, and the New Kingdom, is given in a manner which is scholarly and minute."—*Scotsman.*

Post 8vo, pp. xii.—302, cloth, price 8s. 6d.
YUSUF AND ZULAIKHA.
A POEM BY JAMI.
Translated from the Persian into English Verse.
BY RALPH T. H. GRIFFITH.

" Mr. Griffith, who has done already good service as translator into verse from the Sanskrit, has done further good work in this translation from the Persian, and he has evidently shown not a little skill in his rendering the quaint and very oriental style of his author into our more prosaic, less figurative, language. . . . The work, besides its intrinsic merits, is of importance as being one of the most popular and famous poems of Persia, and that which is read in all the independent native schools of India where Persian is taught. It is interesting, also, as a striking instance of the manner in which the stories of the Jews have been transformed and added to by tradition among the Mahometans, who look upon Joseph as ' the ideal of manly beauty and more than manly virtue ;' and, indeed, in this poem he seems to be endowed with almost divine, or at any rate angelic, gifts and excellence."—*Scotsman.*

Post 8vo, pp. viii.—266, cloth, price 9s.
LINGUISTIC ESSAYS.
BY CARL ABEL.
CONTENTS.

Language as the Expression of National Modes of Thought.	The Connection between Dictionary and Grammar.
The Conception of Love in some Ancient and Modern Languages.	The Possibility of a Common Literary Language for all Slavs.
The English Verbs of Command.	The Order and Position of Words in the Latin Sentence.
Semariology.	The Coptic Language.
Philological Methods.	

The Origin of Language.

" All these essays of Dr. Abel's are so thoughtful, so full of happy illustrations, and so admirably put together, that we hardly know to which we should specially turn to select for our readers a sample of his workmanship."—*Tablet.*

" An entirely novel method of dealing with philosophical questions and impart a real human interest to the otherwise dry technicalities of the science."—*Standard.*

" Dr. Abel is an opponent from whom it is pleasant to differ, for he writes with enthusiasm and temper, and his mastery over the English language fits him to be a champion of unpopular doctrines."—*Athenæum.*

" Dr. Abel writes very good English, and much of his book will prove entertaining to the general reader. It may give some useful hints, and suggest some subjects for profitable investigation, even to philologists."—*Nation (New York).*

Post 8vo, pp. ix.—281, cloth, price 10s. 6d.
THE SARVA-DARSANA-SAMGRAHA ;
OR, REVIEW OF THE DIFFERENT SYSTEMS OF HINDU PHILOSOPHY.
BY MADHAVA ACHARYA.
Translated by E. B. COWELL, M.A., Professor of Sanskrit in the University of Cambridge, and A. E. GOUGH, M.A., Professor of Philosophy in the Presidency College, Calcutta.

This work is an interesting specimen of Hindu critical ability. The author successively passes in review the sixteen philosophical systems current in the fourteenth century in the South of India ; and he gives what appears to him to be their most important tenets.

" The translation is trustworthy throughout. A protracted sojourn in India, where there is a living tradition, has familiarised the translators with Indian thought."—*Athenæum.*

Post 8vo, pp. xxxii.—336, cloth, price 10s. 6d.
THE QUATRAINS OF OMAR KHAYYAM.
The Persian Text, with an English Verse Translation.
BY E. H. WHINFIELD, late of the Bengal Civil Service.

Post 8vo, pp. lxv.—368, cloth, price 14s.

TIBETAN TALES DERIVED FROM INDIAN SOURCES.

Translated from the Tibetan of the KAH-GYUR.

By F. ANTON VON SCHIEFNER.

Done into English from the German, with an Introduction,

By W. R. S. RALSTON, M.A.

"Mr. Ralston adds an introduction, which even the most persevering children of Mother Goose will probably find infinitely the most interesting portion of the work."—*Saturday Review.*

"Mr. Ralston, whose name is so familiar to all lovers of Russian folk-lore, has supplied some interesting Western analogies and parallels, drawn, for the most part, from Slavonic sources, to the Eastern folk-tales, culled from the Kahgyur, one of the divisions of the Tibetan sacred books."—*Academy.*

"The translation . . . could scarcely have fallen into better hands. An Introduction . . . gives the leading facts in the lives of those scholars who have given their attention to gaining a knowledge of the Tibetan literature and language."—*Calcutta Review.*

"Ought to interest all who care for the East, for amusing stories, or for comparative folk-lore. Mr. Ralston . . . is an expert in story-telling, and in knowledge of the comparative history of popular tales he has few rivals in England."—*Pall Mall Gazette.*

Post 8vo, pp. xvi.—224, cloth, price 9s.

UDÂNAVARGA.

A COLLECTION OF VERSES FROM THE BUDDHIST CANON.

Compiled by DHARMATRÂTA.

BEING THE NORTHERN BUDDHIST VERSION OF DHAMMAPADA.

Translated from the Tibetan of Bkah-hgyur, with Notes, and Extracts from the Commentary of Pradjnavarman,

By W. WOODVILLE ROCKHILL.

"Mr. Rockhill's present work is the first from which assistance will be gained for a more accurate understanding of the Pali text; it is, in fact, as yet the only term of comparison available to us. The 'Udanavarga,' the Thibetan version, was originally discovered by the late M. Schiefner, who published the Tibetan text, and had intended adding a translation, an intention frustrated by his death, but which has been carried out by Mr. Rockhill. . . . Mr. Rockhill may be congratulated for having well accomplished a difficult task."—*Saturday Review.*

"There is no need to look far into this book to be assured of its value."—*Athenæum.*

"The Tibetan verses in Mr. Woodville Rockhill's translation have all the simple directness and force which belong to the sayings of Gautama, when they have not been adorned and spoiled by enthusiastic disciples and commentators."—*St. James's Gazette.*

In Two Volumes, post 8vo, pp. xxiv.—566, cloth, accompanied by a Language Map, price 25s.

A SKETCH OF THE MODERN LANGUAGES OF AFRICA.

By ROBERT NEEDHAM CUST,

Barrister-at-Law, and late of Her Majesty's Indian Civil Service.

"Any one at all interested in African languages cannot do better than get Mr. Cust's book. It is encyclopædic in its scope, and the reader gets a start clear away in any particular language, and is left free to add to the initial sum of knowledge there collected."—*Natal Mercury.*

"Mr. Cust has contrived to produce a work of value to linguistic students."—*Nature.*

"Mr. Cust's experience in the preparation of his previous work on the indigenous tongues of the East Indies was, of course, of great help to him in the attempt to map out the still more thorny and tangled brake of the African languages. His great support, however, in what must have been a task of immense labour and care has been the unflagging enthusiasm and gusto with which he has flung himself into his subject."—*Scotsman.*

Post 8vo, pp. xii.—312, with Maps and Plan, cloth, price 14s.

A HISTORY OF BURMA.

Including Burma Proper, Pegu, Taungu, Tenasserim, and Arakan. From
the Earliest Time to the End of the First War with British India.
By LIEUT.-GEN. SIR ARTHUR P. PHAYRE, G.C.M.G., K.C.S.I., and C.B.,
Membre Correspondant de la Société Académique Indo-Chinoise
de France.

"Sir Arthur Phayre's contribntion to Trübner's Oriental Series supplies a recognised want, and its appearance has been looked forward to for many years. . . . .
General Phayre deserves great credit for the patience and industry which has resulted
in this History of Burma."—*Saturday Review.*

"A laborious work, carefully performed, which supplies a blank in the long list of
histories of countries, and records the annals, unknown to literature, of a nation
which is likely to be more prominent in the commerce of the future."—*Scotsman.*

Third Edition. Post 8vo, pp. 276, cloth, price 7s. 6d.

RELIGION IN CHINA.

By JOSEPH EDKINS, D.D., PEKING.

Containing a Brief Account of the Three Religions of the Chinese, with
Observations on the Prospects of Christian Conversion amongst that
People.

"Dr. Edkins has been most careful in noting the varied and often complex phases
of opinion, so as to give an account of considerable value of the subject."—*Scotsman.*

"As a missionary, it has been part of Dr. Edkins' duty to study the existing
religions in China, and his long residence in the country has enabled him to acquire
an intimate knowledge of them as they at present exist."—*Saturday Review.*

"Dr. Edkins' valuable work, of which this is a second and revised edition, has,
from the time that it was published, been the standard authority upon the subject
of which it treats."—*Nonconformist.*

"Dr. Edkins . . . may now be fairly regarded as among the first authorities on
Chinese religion and language."—*British Quarterly Review.*

Third Edition. Post 8vo, pp. xv.-250, cloth, price 7s. 6d.

OUTLINES OF THE HISTORY OF RELIGION TO THE SPREAD OF THE UNIVERSAL RELIGIONS.

By C. P. TIELE,

Doctor of Theology, Professor of the History of Religions in the
University of Leyden.
Translated from the Dutch by J. ESTLIN CARPENTER, M.A.

"Few books of its size contain the result of so much wide thinking, able and laborious study, or enable the reader to gain a better bird's-eye view of the latest results
of investigations into the religious history of nations. As Professor Tiele modestly
says, 'In this little book are outlines—pencil sketches, I might say—nothing more.'
But there are some men whose sketches from a thumb-nail are of far more worth
than an enormous canvas covered with the crude painting of others, and it is easy to
see that these pages, full of information, these sentences, cut and perhaps also dry,
short and clear, condense the fruits of long and thorough research."—*Scotsman.*

Post 8vo, pp. x.-274, cloth, price 9s.

THE LIFE OF THE BUDDHA AND THE EARLY HISTORY OF HIS ORDER.

Derived from Tibetan Works in the Bkah-hgyur and Bstan-hgyur.
Followed by notices on the Early History of Tibet and Khoten.
Translated by W. W. ROCKHILL, Second Secretary U.S. Legation in China.

"The volume bears testimony to the diligence and fulness with which the author
has consulted and tested the ancient documents bearing upon his remarkable subject."—*Times.*

"Will be appreciated by those who devote themselves to those Buddhist studies
which have of late years taken in these Western regions so remarkable a development. Its matter possesses a special interest as being derived from ancient Tibetan
works, some portions of which, here analysed and translated, have not yet attracted
the attention of scholars. The volume is rich in ancient stories bearing upon the
world's renovation and the origin of castes, as recorded in these venerable authorities."—*Daily News.*

In Two Volumes, post 8vo, pp. cviii.-242, and viii.-370, cloth, price 24s.
Dedicated by permission to H.R.H. the Prince of Wales.

BUDDHIST RECORDS OF THE WESTERN WORLD,

Translated from the Chinese of Hiuen Tsiang (A.D. 629).

By SAMUEL BEAL, B.A.,

Trin. Coll., Camb.); R.N. (Retired Chaplain and N.I.); Professor of Chinese, University College, London; Rector of Wark, Northumberland, &c.

An eminent Indian authority writes respecting this work:—"Nothing more can be done in elucidating the History of India until Mr. Beal's translation of the 'Si-yu-ki' appears."

"It is a strange freak of historical preservation that the best account of the condition of India at that ancient period has come down to us in the books of travel written by the Chinese pilgrims, of whom Hwen Thsang is the best known."—*Times.*

"We are compelled at this stage to close our brief and inadequate notice of a book for easy access to which Orientalists will be deeply grateful to the able translator."—*Literary World.*

"Full of interesting revelations of the religious feelings, fables, and superstitions, manners and habits of peoples inhabiting a vast region, comprising North and North-Western India and contiguous countries in that remote and obscure period."—*Daily News.*

Third Edition. Post 8vo, pp. viii.-464, cloth, price 16s.

THE SANKHYA APHORISMS OF KAPILA,

With Illustrative Extracts from the Commentaries.

Translated by J. R. BALLANTYNE, LL.D., late Principal of the Benares College.

Edited by FITZEDWARD HALL.

Post 8vo, pp. xlviii.-398, cloth, price 12s.

THE ORDINANCES OF MANU.

Translated from the Sanskrit, with an Introduction.

By the late A. C. BURNELL, Ph.D., C.I.E.

Completed and Edited by E. W. HOPKINS, Ph.D., of Columbia College, N.Y.

"This work is full of interest; while for the student of sociology and the science of religion it is full of importance. It is a great boon to get so notable a work in so accessible a form, admirably edited, and competently translated."—*Scotsman.*

"Few men were more competent than Burnell to give us a really good translation of this well-known law book, first rendered into English by Sir William Jones. Burnell was not only an independent Sanskrit scholar, but an experienced lawyer, and he joined to these two important qualifications the rare faculty of being able to express his thoughts in clear and trenchant English. . . . We ought to feel very grateful to Dr. Hopkins for having given us all that could be published of the translation left by Burnell."—F. Max Müller in the *Academy.*

TRÜBNER'S
ORIENTAL SERIES.

SI-YU-KI.

BUDDHIST RECORDS

OF

THE WESTERN WORLD.

TRANSLATED FROM THE CHINESE

OF (HIUEN TSIANG) (A.D. 629).

BY

SAMUEL BEAL,

B.A. (TRIN. COL. CAMB.), R.N. (RETIRED CHAPLAIN AND N.I.), PROFESSOR OF CHINESE,
UNIVERSITY COLLEGE, LONDON ; RECTOR OF WARK, NORTHUMBERLAND, ETC.

IN TWO VOLUMES.

VOL. I.

LONDON:

TRÜBNER & CO., LUDGATE HILL.

1884.

[All rights reserved.]

Ballantyne Press
BALLANTYNE, HANSON AND CO.
EDINBURGH AND LONDON

These Volumes

ARE DEDICATED

(BY GRACIOUS PERMISSION)

TO

H.R.H. ALBERT EDWARD

PRINCE OF WALES.

CONTENTS.

INTRODUCTION.

THE progress which has been made in our knowledge of Northern Buddhism during the last few years is due very considerably to the discovery of the Buddhist literature of China. This literature (now well known to us through the catalogues already published)[1] contains, amongst other valuable works, the records of the travels of various Chinese Buddhist pilgrims who visited India during the early centuries of our era. These records embody the testimony of independent eye-witnesses as to the facts related in them, and having been faithfully preserved and allotted a place in the collection of the sacred books of the country, their evidence is entirely trustworthy.

It would be impossible to mention *seriatim* the various points of interest in these works, as they refer to the geography, history, manners, and religion of the people of India. The reader who looks into the pages that follow will find ample material for study on all these questions. But there is one particular that gives a more than usual interest to the records under notice, and that is the evident sincerity and enthusiasm of the travellers themselves. Never did more devoted pilgrims leave their native country to encounter the perils of travel in foreign and distant lands; never did disciples more ardently desire to gaze on the sacred vestiges of their religion; never did men endure greater sufferings by desert, mountain,

---

[1] *Catalogue of the Chinese Buddhist Tripiṭaka,* by Samuel Beal; *Catalogue of the Buddhist Tripiṭaka,* by Bunyiu Nanjio.

and sea than these simple - minded earnest Buddhist priests. And that such courage, religious devotion, and power of endurance should be exhibited by men so sluggish, as we think, in their very nature as the Chinese, this is very surprising, and may perhaps arouse some consideration.

Buddhist books began to be imported into China during the closing period of the first century of our era. From these books the Chinese learned the history of the founder of the new religion, and became familiar with the names of the sacred spots he had consecrated by his presence. As time went on, and strangers from India and the neighbourhood still flocked into the Eastern Empire, some of the new converts (whose names have been lost) were urged by curiosity or a sincere desire to gaze on the mementoes of the religion they had learned to adopt, to risk the perils of travel and visit the western region. We are told by I-tsing (one of the writers of these Buddhist records), who lived about 670 A.D., that 500 years before his time twenty men, or about that number, had found their way through the province of Sz'chuen to the Mahâbôdhi tree in India, and for them and their fellow-countrymen a Mahârâja called Śrîgupta built a temple. The establishment was called the "Tchina Temple." In I-tsing's days it was in ruins. In the year 290 A.D. we find another Chinese pilgrim called Chu Si-hing visiting Khotan; another called Fa-ling shortly afterwards proceeded to North India, and we can hardly doubt that others unknown to fame followed their example. At any rate, the recent accidental discovery of several stone tablets with Chinese inscriptions at Buddha Gayâ,[2] on two of which we find the names of the pilgrims Chi-I and Ho-yun, the former in company "with some other priests," shows plainly that the sacred spots were visited from time to time by priests from China, whose names indeed are unknown to us from any other source, but who were

---

[2] See *J. R. A. S.*, N.S., vol. xiii. pp. 552-572.

impelled to leave their home by the same spirit of religious devotion and enthusiasm which actuated those with whom we are better acquainted.

The first Chinese traveller whose name and writings have come down to us is the Śâkyaputra Fa-hian. He is the author of the records which follow in the pages of the present Introduction. His work, the *Fo-kwŏ-ki*, was first known in Europe through a translation[3] made by M. Abel Rémusat. But Klaproth claimed the discovery of the book itself from the year 1816,[4] and it was he who shaped the rough draft of Rémusat's translation from chap. xxi. of the work in question to the end. Of this translation nothing need be said in this place; it has been dealt with elsewhere. It will be enough, therefore, to give some few particulars respecting the life and travels of the pilgrim, and for the rest to refer the reader to the translation which follows.

SHIH FA-HIAN.

A.D. 400.

In agreement with early custom, the Chinese mendicant priests who adopted the Buddhist faith changed their names at the time of their leaving their homes (ordination), and assumed the title of Śâkyaputras, sons or mendicants of Śâkya. So we find amongst the inscriptions at Mathurâ[5] the title Śâkya Bhikshunyaka or Śâkya Bhîkshor added to the religious names of the different benefactors there mentioned. The pilgrim Fa-hian, therefore, whose original name was Kung, when he assumed the religious title by which he is known to us, took also the appellation of Shih or the Śâkyaputra, the disciple or son of Śâkya. He was a native of Wu-Yang, of the district of Ping-Yang, in the province of Shan-si. He left his home and became a Śrâmaṇêra at three years of age. His

---

[3] *Fŏ koŭ ki*, Paris, 1836.
[4] Julien's Preface to the *Vie de Hiouen Thsang*, p. ix. n. 2.
[5] *Arch. Survey of India*, vol. iii pp. 37, 48; also Professor Dowson, *J. R. A. S.*, N.S., vol. v. pp. 182 ff.

early history is recorded in the work called *Ko-săng-chuen*, written during the time of the Liang dynasty, belonging to the Suh family (502–507 A.D.) But so far as we are now concerned, we need only mention that he was moved by a desire to obtain books not known in China, and with that aim set out in company with other priests (some of whom are named in the records) from Chang'an, A.D. 399, and after an absence of fourteen years returned to Nankin, where, in connection with Buddhabhadra (an Indian Śramaṇa, descended from the family of the founder of the Buddhist religion), he translated various works and composed the history of his travels. He died at the age of eighty-six.

Fa-hian's point of departure was the city of Chang'an in Shen-si; from this place he advanced across the Lung district (or mountains) to the fortified town of Chang-yeh in Kan-suh; here he met with some other priests, and with them proceeded to Tun-hwang, a town situated to the south of the Bulunghir river, lat. 39° 30′ N., long. 95° E. Thence with four companions he pushed forward, under the guidance, as it seems, of an official, across the desert of Lop to Shen-shen, the probable site of which is marked in the map accompanying the account of Prejevalsky's journey through the same district; according to this map, it is situated in lat. 38° N., and long. 87° E. It corresponds with the Cherchen of Marco Polo. Fa-hian tells us that Buddhism prevailed in this country, and that there were about 4000 priests. The country itself was rugged and barren. So Marco Polo says, " The whole of this province is sandy, but there are numerous towns and villages."[6] The Venetian traveller makes the distance from the town of Lop five days' journey. Probably Fa-hian did not visit the town of Cherchen, but after a month in the kingdom turned to the north-west, apparently following the course of the Tarim, and after fifteen days arrived in the kingdom of Wu-i or Wu-ki. This kingdom seems

[6] *Marco Polo*, cap. xxxviii.

to correspond to Karshar or Karasharh, near the Lake Tenghiz or Bagarash, and is the same as the 'O-ki-ni of Hiuen Tsiang.[7]   Prejevalsky took three days in travelling from Kara-moto to Korla, a distance of about 42 miles,[8] so that the fifteen days of Fa-hian might well represent in point of time the distance from Lake Lob to Karasharh. Our pilgrims would here strike on the outward route of Hiuen Tsiang.   It was at this spot they fell in with their companions Pao-yun and the rest, whom they had left at Tun-hwang.   These had probably travelled to Karasharh by the northern route, as it is called, through Kamil or Kamul to Pidshan and Turfan; for we read that whilst Fa-hian remained at Karasharh, under the protection of an important official, some of the others went back to Kao-chang (Turfan), showing that they had come that way.

From Karasharh Fa-hian and the others, favoured by the liberality of Kung sün (who was in some way connected with the Prince of Ts'in), proceeded south-west to Khotan. The route they took is not well ascertained; but probably they followed the course of the Tarim and of the Khotan rivers. There were no dwellings or people on the road, and the difficulties of the journey and of crossing the rivers "exceeded power of comparison."   After a month and five days they reached Khotan.   This country has been identified with Li-yul of the Tibetan writers.[9]   There is some reason for connecting this "land of Li" with the Lichchhavis of Vaiśâli.   It is said by Csoma Korösi "that the Tibetan writers derive their first king (about 250 B.C.) from the Litsabyis or Lichavyis."[10]   The chief prince or ruler of the Lichchhavis was called the "great lion" or "the noble lion."[11]   This is probably the explanation of Maha-li, used by Spence Hardy as "the name of the king of the Lichawis."[12]   Khotan would thus be the land of the

---

[7] *Vol.* i. p. 17.
[8] *Prejevalsky's Kulja,* p. 50.
[9] Rockhill.
[10] *Manual of Buddhism,* p. 236, n.

[11] *Sac. Bks. of the East,* vol. xix. p. 258.
[12] *Manual of Buddhism,* p. 282.

lion-people (*Siṁhas*). Whether this be so or not, the
polished condition of the people and their religious zeal
indicate close connection with India, more probably with
Baktria. The name of the great temple, a mile or two to
the west of the city, called the Nava-saṅghârâma, or royal
"new temple," is the same as that on the south-west of
Balkh, described by Hiuen Tsiang;[13] and the introduction of Vaiśravaṇa as the protector of this convent, and
his connection with Khotan, the kings of that country
being descended from him,[14] indicate a relationship, if
not of race, at least of intercourse between the two
kingdoms.

After witnessing the car procession of Khotan, Fa-hian
and some others (for the pilgrims had now separated for a
time), advanced for twenty-five days towards the country
of Tseu-ho, which, according to Klaproth, corresponds with
the district of Yangi-hissar, from which there is a caravan
route due south into the mountain region of the Tsung-
ling. It was by this road they pursued their journey for
four days to a station named Yu-hwui, or, as it may also
be read, Yu-fai; here they kept their religious fast, after
which, journeying for twenty-five days, they reached the
country of Kie-sha. I cannot understand how either of
the last-named places can be identified with Ladakh.[15]
Yu-hwui is four days south of Tseu-ho;[16] and twenty-five
days beyond this brings the pilgrims to the country of
Kie-sha, in the centre of the Tsung-ling mountains.

Nor can we, on the other hand, identify this kingdom of
Kie-sha (the symbols are entirely different from those
used by Hiuen Tsiang, ii. p. 306, for Kashgâr) with that
of the Kossaioi of Ptolemy, the Khaśas of Manu, and the
Khaśâkas of the *Vishṇu Purâṇa*.[17] These appear to have
been related to the Cushites of Holy Scripture.

---

[13] Vol. i. p. 44.

[14] *Inf.*, vol. ii. p. 309.

[15] See Laidlay's note, *Fa-hian*, p.
26, n. 6, and Wood's *Oxus* (Yule's
introduction), p. xl. n. 2.

[16] So we read in Fa-hian's text.

[17] See Eitel, *Handbook*, s.v. *K'hacha*;
Laidlay's *Fa-hian*, p. 31.

Advancing for a month across the Tsung-ling range towards India, the pilgrims reached the little country of To-li, that is, the valley of Dârail in the Dard country. This valley is on the right or western bank of the Indus, long. 73° 44′ E., and is watered by a river Daril.[18] Still advancing south-west for fifteen days, they strike the Indus (or probably the Swât river), crossing which, they enter on the kingdom of Udyâna, where they found Buddhism in a flourishing condition. Concerning this country and its traditions, we have ample records in Hiuen Tsiang, Book iii. (p. 119). Here then we may leave Fa-hian; his farther travels may be followed by the details given in his own writings, and to these we refer the reader.

Sung Yun.

A.D. 518.

This pilgrim was a native of Tun-hwang, in what is sometimes called Little Tibet, lat. 39° 30′ N., long. 95° E. He seems to have lived in a suburb of the city of Lo-yang (Honan-fu) called Wan-I. He was sent, A.D. 518, by the Empress of the Northern Wei dynasty, in company with Hwui Săng, a Bhikshu of the Shung-li temple of Lo-yang, to the western countries to seek for books. They brought back altogether one hundred and seventy volumes or sets of the Great Development series. They seem to have taken the southern route from Tun-hwang to Khotan, and thence by the same route as Fa-hian and his companion across the Tsung-ling mountains. The Ye-tha (Ephthalites) were now in possession of the old country of the Yue-chi, and had recently conquered Gandhâra. They are described as having no walled towns, but keeping order by means of a standing army that moved here and there. They used felt (leather) garments, had no written character, nor any knowledge

---

[8] *Vide infra,* p. 134, n. 37.

of the heavenly bodies.   On all hands it is plain the
Ye-tha were a rude horde of Turks who had followed in
the steps of the Hiung-nu; they were, in fact, the Ephthalites or Huns of the Byzantine writers.   "In the
early part of the sixth century their power extended
over Western India, and Cosmas tells us of their king
Gollas who domineered there with a thousand elephants
and a vast force of horsemen."[19]   Sung-yun also names
the power of the king whom the Ye-tha had set up over
Gandhâra.   He was of the Lae-lih dynasty, or a man of
Lae-lih, which may perhaps be restored to Lâra.   Accòrding
to Hiuen Tsiang,[20] the northern Lâra people belonged to
Valabhî, and the southern Lâras to Mâlava.   It was one
of these Lâra princes the Ye-tha had set over the kingdom of Gandhâra.   It may have been with the Gollas
of Cosmas that the Chinese pilgrims had their interview.   At any rate, he was lording it over the people
with seven hundred war-elephants, and was evidently a
fierce and oppressive potentate.

The Ye-tha, according to Sung-yun, had conquered
or received tribute from more than forty countries in all,
from Tieh-lo in the south to Lae-lih in the north, eastward to Khotan, westward to Persia.   The symbols
Tieh-lo probably represent Tîrabhukti, the present Tirhut,
the old land of the Vṛijjis.   The Vṛijjis themselves were
in all probability Skythian invaders, whose power had
reached so far as the borders of the Ganges at Patna,
but had there been checked by Ajâtaśatru.   They had
afterwards been driven north-east to the mountains
bordering on Nêpâl.[21]   The Ye-tha also extended their
power so far as this, and northward to Lae-lih, *i.e.*,
Mâlava.   As these conquests had been achieved two generations before Sung-yun's time, we may place this invasion of India therefore about A.D. 460.

The notices of the country of Udyâna by Sung-yun

[19] Yule, Wood's *Oxus,* xxvii.   [20] Vol. ii. pp. 260, 266, notes 56, 71.
[21] V. de St. Martin, *Mémoire,* p. 368.

vie with those found in Hiuen Tsiang for abundance of
detail and legendary interest. It is singular that the
supposed scene of the history of Vessantara, "the giving
king" of Hiuen Tsiang and the Pi-lo of Sung-yun, should
be placed in this remote district. The *Vessantara Jâtaka*
(so called) was well known in Ceylon in Fa-hian's time;[22]
it forms part of the sculptured scenes at Amarâvatî and
Sânchi; it is still one of the most popular stories amongst
the Mongols. How does the site of the history come to
be placed in Udyâna? There are some obscure notices
connected with the succession of the Maurya or Môriya
sovereigns from the Śâkya youths who fled to this district
of Udyâna ·which may throw a little light on this subject.
The Buddhists affirm that Aśôka belonged to the same
family as Buddha, because he was descended from Chandragupta, who was the child of the queen of one of the
sovereigns of Môriyanagara. This Môriyanagara was
the city founded by the Śâkya youths who fled from Kapilavastu; so that whatever old legends were connected
with the Śâkya family were probably referred to Udyâna
by the direct or indirect influence of Aśôka, or by his
popularity as a Buddhist sovereign. But, in any case,
the history of Udyâna is mixed up with that of the
Śâkya family, and Buddha himself is made to acknowledge Uttarasêna as one of his own kinsmen.[23] We may
suppose then that these tales did actually take their rise
from some local or family association connected with
Udyâna, and found their way thence into the legends of
other countries. Hence while we have in the Southern
account mention made of the elephant that could bring
rain from heaven, which was the cause of Vessantara's
banishment, in the Northern accounts this is, apparently,
identified with the peacock (*mayûra*) that brought water
from the rock.[24] But the subject need not be pursued
farther in this place; it is sufficient to note the fact that

[21] *Fa-hian,* cap. 38. [23] *Inf.,* vol. i. pp. 131 f.
[24] *Inf.,* vol. i. p. 126.

many of the stories found in the Northern legends are somehow or other localised in this pleasant district of Udyâna. Sung-yun, after reaching so far as Peshâwar and Nagarahâra, returned to China in the year A.D. 521.

HIUEN TSIANG.
A.D. 629.

This illustrious pilgrim was born in the year 603 A.D., at Ch'in Liu, in the province of Ho-nan, close to the provincial city. He was the youngest of four brothers. At an early age he was taken by his second brother, Chang-tsi, to the eastern capital, Lo-yang. His brother was a monk belonging to the Tsing-tu temple, and in this community Hiuen Tsiang was ordained at the age of thirteen years.[25] On account of the troubles which occurred at the end of the dynasty of Sui, the pilgrim in company with his brother sought refuge in the city of Shing-tu, the capital of the province of Sz'chuen, and here at the age of twenty he was fully ordained as a Bhikshu or priest. After some time he began to travel through the provinces in search of the best instructor he could get, and so came at length to Chang'an. It was here, stirred up by the recollection of Fa-hian and Chi-yen, that he resolved to go to the western regions to question the sages on points that troubled his mind. He was now twenty-six years of age. He accordingly set out from Chang'an in company with a priest of Tsing-chau of Kan-suh, and having reached that city, rested there. Thence he proceeded to Lan-chau, the provincial city of Kan-suh. He then advanced with a magistrate's escort to Liang-chau, a prefecture of Kan-suh, beyond the river. This city was the entrepôt for merchants from Tibet and the countries east of the Tsung-ling mountains; and to these Hiuen Tsiang explained the sacred books and revealed his purpose of going to the kingdom of the Brâhmans to seek for the law. By them

---

[25] That is, became a novice or Srâmaṇêra.

he was amply provided with means for his expedition, and, notwithstanding the expostulation of the governor of the city, by the connivance of two priests he was able to proceed westward as far as Kwa-chau, a town about ten miles to the south of the Hu-lu river, which seems to be the same as the Bulunghir.

From this spot, going north in company with a young man who had offered to act as his guide, he crossed the river by night, and after escaping the treachery of his guide, came alone to the first watch-tower. Five of these towers, at intervals of 100 li, stretched towards the country of I-gu (Kamul). We need not recount the way in which the pilgrim prevailed on the keepers of the first and fourth tower to let him proceed; nor is it necessary to recount the fervent prayers to Kwan-yin and his incessant invocation of the name of this divinity. Suffice it to say, he at last reached the confines of I-gu, and there halted. From this place he was summoned by the prince of Kao-chang (Turfan), who, after vainly attempting to keep him in his territory, remitted him to 'O-ki-ni, that is, Kara-sharh, from which he advanced to Kuché. Here the narrative in the pages following carries us on through the territory of Kuché to Bâlukâ, or Bai, in the Aksu district, from whence the pilgrim proceeds in a northerly direction across the Icy Mountains (Muzart) into the well-watered plains bordering on the Tsing Lake (Issyk-kul); he then proceeded along the fertile valley of the Su-yeh river (the Chu or Chui) to the town of Taras, and thence to Nujkend and Tâshkand.

It is not necessary to follow the pilgrim's route farther than this, as the particulars given in the translation following, and the notes thereto, will sufficiently set forth the line of his advance.

Hiuen Tsiang returned from his Indian travels across the Pâmîr and through Kashgâr and the Khotan districts. He had been away from China since A.D. 629; he returned A.D. 645. He brought back with him—

1. Five hundred grains of relics belonging to the body (flesh) of Tathâgata.

2. A golden statue of Buddha on a transparent pedestal.

3. A statue of Buddha carved out of sandal-wood on a transparent pedestal. This figure is a copy of the statue which Udâyana, king of Kauśâmbî, had made.

4. A similar statue of sandal-wood, copy of the figure made after Buddha descended from the Trayastriṁśas heaven.

5. A silver statue of Buddha on a transparent pedestal.

6. A golden statue of Buddha on a transparent pedestal.

7. A sandal-wood figure of Buddha on a transparent pedestal.

8. One hundred and twenty-four works (*sûtras*) of the Great Vehicle.

9. Other works, amounting in the whole to 520 fasciculi, carried by twenty-two horses.

There are many interesting particulars given in the "Life of Hiuen Tsiang" by Hwui-lih, which need not be named here, respecting the work of translation and the pilgrim's death at the age of sixty-five. They will be fully set forth in the translation of that memoir, which it is hoped will follow the present volumes.

We will simply add, that of all the books translated by Hiuen Tsiang, there are still seventy-five included in the collection of the Chinese *Tripiṭaka.* The titles of these books may be seen in the catalogue prepared by Mr. Bun-yiu Nanjio, coll. 435, 436.

BUDDHIST LITERATURE IN CHINA.

Although it was known that there were copies of translations of the Buddhist *Tripiṭaka* in the great monasteries in China, no complete set of these books had been brought to England until the Japanese Government furnished us with the copy now in the India Office Library in the year

1875. Respecting these books I will extract one passage from the report which was drawn up by direction of the Secretary of State for India :—

"The value of the records of the 'Chinese pilgrims' who visited India in the early centuries of our era, and the account of whose travels is contained in this collection, is too well understood to need any remark. I regret that none of the books referred to by M. Stas. Julien, in his introduction to the '*Vie de Hiouen Thsang*,' and which he thought might be found in Japan, are contained in this collection; but there is still some hope that they may be found in a separate form in some of the remote monasteries of that country, or more probably in China itself." [26]

To that opinion I still adhere. I think that if searching inquiry were made at Honan-fu and its neighbourhood, we might learn something of books supposed to be lost. And my opinion is grounded on this circumstance, that efforts which have been made to get copies (in the ordinary way) of books found in the collection of the Tripiṭaka have failed, and reports furnished that such works are lost. M. Stas. Julien himself tells us that Dr. Morrison, senior, reported that the *Si-yu-ki* (the work here translated) could not be procured in China. And such is the listlessness of the Chinese literati about Buddhist books, and such the seclusion and isolation of many of the Buddhist establishments in China, that I believe books may still exist, or even original manuscripts, of which we know nothing at present. It would be strange if such were not the case, considering what has taken place in respect of fresh discoveries of fragments or entire copies of MSS. of our own sacred scriptures in remote monasteries of Christendom.

In conclusion, I desire to express the debt I owe, in the execution of this and other works, to the learning and

[26] Beal's Catalogue, p. 1.

intimate knowledge of the Chinese language possessed by M. Stas. Julien.

I should not have attempted to follow in his steps had his own translation of the *Si-yu-ki* been still procurable. But as it had long been out of print, and the demand for the book continued to be urgent, I have attempted to furnish an independent translation in English of the Chinese pilgrim's travels.

I am very largely indebted to James Burgess, LL.D., for assistance in carrying these volumes through the press. His close acquaintance with Buddhist archæology and literature will give value to many of the notes which appear on the pages following, and his kind supervision of the text and preparation of the index attached to it demand my thanks and sincere acknowledgments.

I am also under great obligations to Colonel Yule, C.B., and to Dr. R. Rost, for their ever-ready help and advice, especially during my visits to the Library of the India Office.

I have not overlooked the remarks of various writers who have honoured me by noticing my little book (*Buddhist Pilgrims*), published in 1869. I venture, however, to hope that I have by this time established my claim to be regarded as an independent worker in this field of literature. I have not therefore quoted instances of agreement or disagreement with the writers referred to; in fact, I have purposely avoided doing so, as my object is not to write a chapter of grammar, but to contribute towards the history of a religion; but I have suffered no prejudice to interfere with the honesty of my work.

I shall now proceed to the translation of the travels of Fa-hian and Sung-yun, referring the student to the original edition of my *Buddhist Pilgrims* for many notes and explanations of the text, which want of space forbids me to reproduce in these volumes.

THE TRAVELS OF FA-HIAN.

BUDDHIST-COUNTRY-RECORDS.

By Fa-hian, the S'âkya of the Sung (Dynasty).

[DATE, 400 A.D.]

I. FA-HIAN, when formerly residing at Ch'ang-an,[1] regretted the imperfect condition of the *Vinaya piṭaka*. Whereupon, afterwards, in the second year of Hung-shi, the cyclic year being *Chi-hai*,[2] he agreed with Hwui-king, Tao-ching, Hwui-ying, Hwui-wu, and others, to go to India for the purpose of seeking the rules and regulations (*of the Vinaya*).

Starting on their way from Ch'ang-an, they crossed the Lung (*district*) and reached the country of K'ien-kwei;[3] here they rested during the rains. The season of the rains being over, going forward, they came to the country of Niu-t'an;[4] crossing the Yang-lu hills, they reached Chang-yeh,[5] a military station. Chang-yeh at this time was much disturbed, and the roadways were not open. The king[6] of Chang-yeh being anxious, kept them there, himself entertaining them. Thus they met Chi-yen, Hwui-kin, Sang-shau, Pao-yun, Sang-king, and others; pleased that they were like-minded, they kept the rainy

---

[1] The former capital of the province of Shenrsi, now called Si-gan-fu.

[2] There is an error here of one year. It should be the cyclical characters *Kang tsze*, *i.e.*, A.D. 400–401 (*Ch. Ed.*)

[3] This is the name of the prince who ruled the country. The capital town is, according to Klaproth, to the north-east of Kin, a *hian* town close to Lan-chau.

[4] This is also the name of a prince, and not of a country. He ruled over a district called Ho-si, "the country to the west of the (Yellow) River" (Tangut).

[5] Chang Yeh is still marked on the Chinese maps just within the north-west extremity of the Great Wall.

[6] Called Tün-nich, who died A.D. 401 (*Ch. Ed.*)

season together. The rainy season being over, they again pressed on to reach Tun-hwang.[7] The fortifications here are perhaps 80 li in extent from east to west, and 40 li from north to south. They all stopped here a month and some days, when Fa-hian and others, five men in all, set out first, in the train of an official, and so again parted with Pao-yun and the rest. The prefect of Tun-hwang, called Li-ho, provided them with means to cross the desert (*sand-river*).[8] In this desert are many evil demons and hot winds; when encountered, then all die without exception. There are no flying birds above, no roaming beasts below, but everywhere gazing as far as the eye can reach in search of the onward route, it would be impossible to know the way but for dead men's decaying bones, which show the direction.

Going on for seventeen days about 1500 li, they reached the country of Shen-shen.[9]

II. This land is rugged and barren. The clothing of the common people is coarse, and like that of the Chinese people; only they differ in respect to the serge and felt. The king of this country honours the law (of Buddha). There are some 4000 priests, all of the Little Vehicle belief (*learning*). The laity and the Śramaṇas of this country wholly practise the religion of India, only some are refined and some coarse (in their observances). From this proceeding westward, the countries passed through are all alike in this respect, only the people differ in their language (*Hu words*). The professed disciples of Buddha, however, all use Indian books and the Indian language. Remaining here a month or more, again they went northwest for fifteen days and reached the country of Wu-i (Wu-ki?).[10] The priests of Wu-i also are about 4000 men;

[7] A frontier town of considerable military importance, 39° 30′ N. lat., 95° E. long. (Prejevalsky's Map). This town was wrested from Tün-nieh in the third month of this year by Li Ho, or more properly Li Ko, who ruled as the "illustrious warrior king of the Liang dynasty" (*Ch. Ed.*)

[8] The desert of Lop (Marco Polo).

[9] The kingdom of Shen-shen or Leu-lan (conf. Richtofen in Prejevalsky's *Kulja*, p. 144, and *passim*).

[10] The pilgrims probably followed

all (*belong to*) the Little Vehicle (*school of*) learning;
their religious rules are very precise (*arranged methodi-
cally*). When Śramaṇas of the Ts'in land arrive here, they
are unprepared for the rules of the priests. Fa-hian
obtaining the protection of Kung-sün, an official (*hing
t'ang*) of the Fu (*family*), remained here two months and
some days. Then he returned to Pao-yun and the
others.[11] In the end, because of the want of courtesy
and propriety on the part of the Wu-i people, and because their treatment of their guests was very cool,
Chi-yen, Hwui-kin, and Hwui-wu forthwith went back
towards Kao-chang, in order to procure necessaries for
the journey. Fa-hian and the others, grateful for the
presents they received of Fu Kung-sün, forthwith journeyed to the south-west. On the road there were no
dwellings or people. The sufferings of their journey on
account of the difficulties of the road and the rivers
(*water*) exceed human power of comparison. They were
on the road a month and five days, and then managed to
reach Khotan.[12]

III. This country is prosperous and rich (*happy*); the
people are very wealthy, and all without exception honour
the law (*of Buddha*). They use religious music for mutual
entertainment. The body of priests number even several
myriads, principally belonging to the Great Vehicle. They
all have food provided for them (*church-food, commons*);
the people live here and there. Before their house
doors they raise little towers, the least about twenty feet
high. There are priests' houses for the entertainment of
foreign priests and for providing them with what they
need. The ruler of the country lodged Fa-hian and the
rest in a *saṅgháráma*. The name of the *saṅgháráma* was

the course of the river Tarim. (For
Wu-ki see *infra*, p. 17, n. 52.)

[11] It would appear from this that
Fa-hian had reached Wu-i by the
route of Lake Lop and the river
Tarim; the others had gone from
Tun-hwang by another route.

[12] Called in Tibetan works Li-yul,
or the land of Li. It is possible that
the word Li (which means *bell-metal*
in Tibetan) may be connected with
li in *Lichchhavis*. (Compare Spence
Hardy, *M. B.*, p. 282, and *ante*, p.
v.)

Gômati. This is a temple of the Great Vehicle with three thousand priests, who assemble to eat at the sound of the *ghanṭâ*. On entering the dining-hall, their carriage is grave and demure, and they take their seats in regular order. All of them keep silence; there is no noise with their eating-bowls; when the attendants (*pure men*) give more food, they are not allowed to speak to one another, but only to make signs with the hand. Hwui-king, Tao-ching, Hwui-ta set out in advance towards the Kie-sha country, but Fa-hian and the rest, desiring to see the image-procession, remained three months and some days. In this country there are fourteen great *sanghârâmas*, not counting the little ones. From the first day of the fourth month they sweep and water the thoroughfares within the city and decorate the streets. Above the city gate they stretch a great awning and use every kind of adornment. This is where the king and the queen and court ladies take their place. The Gômati priests, as they belong to the Great Vehicle, which is principally honoured by the king, first of all take their images in procession. About three or four li from the city they make a four-wheeled image-car about thirty feet high, in appearance like a moving palace, adorned with the seven precious substances. They fix upon it streamers of silk and canopy curtains. The figure is placed in the car [13] with two Bôdhisattvas as companions, whilst the Dêvas attend on them; all kinds of polished ornaments made of gold and silver hang suspended in the air. When the image is a hundred paces from the gate, the king takes off his royal cap, and changing his clothes for new ones, proceeds barefooted, with flowers and incense in his hand, from the city, followed by his attendants. On meeting the image, he bows down his head and worships at its feet, scattering the flowers and burning the incense. On entering the city, the queen and court ladies from above the gate-tower

---

[13] For some curious details about the *Rath-yâtrâs*, or car-festivals, see Simpson, *J. R. A. S.*, N. S., vol. xvi. pp. 13 ff.

scatter about all kinds of flowers and throw them down in wild profusion. So splendid are the arrangements for worship.

The cars are all different, and each *sanghârâma* has a day for its image-procession. They begin on the first day of the fourth month and go on to the fourteenth day, when the processions end. The processions ended, the king and queen then return to the palace.

Seven or eight li to the west of the city there is a *sanghârâma* called the Royal-new-temple. It was eighty years in finishing, and only after three kings (*reigns*) was it completed. It is perhaps twenty *chang* in height (290 *feet*). It is adorned with carving and inlaid work, and covered with gold and silver. Above the roof all kinds of jewels combine to perfect it. Behind the tower there is a hall of Buddha, magnificent and very beautiful. The beams, pillars, doors, and window-frames are all gold-plated. Moreover, there are priests' apartments, also very splendid, and elegantly adorned beyond power of description. The kings of the six countries east of the Ling give many of their most valuable precious jewels (*to this monastery*), being seldom used (for personal adornment), [*or*, they seldom give things of common use].

IV. After the image-procession of the fourth month, Sang-shau, one of the company, set out with a Tartar (Hu) pilgrim towards Ki-pin.[14] Fa-hian and the others pressed on towards the Tseu-ho country.[15] They were twenty-five days on the road, and then they arrived at this kingdom. The king of the country is earnest (in his piety). There are a thousand priests and more, principally belonging to the Great Vehicle. Having stopped here fifteen days, they then went south for four days[16] and entered the Tsung-ling mountains. Arriving at Yu-hwui, they kept their religious rest; the religious rest being over, they

---

[14] Kábul.

[15] Probably the Yárkand district.

[16] They probably followed the Yárkand river.

journeyed on twenty-five days to the Kie-sha [17] country, where they rejoined Hwui-king and the rest.

V. The king of this country keeps the *Pan-che-yue-sse.* The *Pan-che-yue-sse* (*Pañchavarshá,* parishad) in Chinese words is "the great five-yearly assembly:" At the time of the assembly he asks Śramaṇas from the four quarters, who come together like clouds. Being assembled, he decorates the priests' session place; he suspends silken flags and spreads out canopies; he makes gold and silver lotus flowers; he spreads silk behind the throne, and arranges the paraphernalia of the priests' seats. The king and the ministers offer their religious presents for one, two, or three months, generally during spring-time. The king-made assembly being over, he further exhorts his ministers to arrange their offerings; they then offer for one day, two days, three days, or five days. The offerings being finished, the king, taking from the chief officer of the embassy and from the great ministers of the country the horse he rides, with its saddle and bridle, mounts it, and then (taking) white taffeta, jewels of various kinds, and things required by the Śramaṇas, in union with his ministers he vows to give them all to the priests; having thus given them, they are redeemed at a price from the priests.

The country is hilly and cold; it produces no variety of grain; only wheat will ripen. After the priests have received their yearly dues the mornings become frosty; the king, therefore, every year induces the priests to make the wheat ripen, and after that to receive their yearly portion. There is a stone spitting-vessel in this country belonging to Buddha, of the same colour as his alms-dish. There is also a tooth of Buddha; the people of the country have built a *stúpa* on account of this tooth. There are a thousand priests and more, all belong-

---

[17] For some remarks on this country see vol. ii. p. 298, n. 46. As stated on p. xiv., a people called Kossaioi are noticed by Ptolemy. But they seem to be Cushites. Concerning the Kossaioi or Kassai, as a very ancient people, see Mr. T. G. Pinches' remarks, *J. R. A. S., N.S.,* vol. xvi. p. 302.

ing to the Little Vehicle.   From the mountains eastward the common people wear garments made of coarse stuff, as in the Ts'in country, but with respect to felt and serge they are different.   The religious practices of the Śramaṇas are so various and have increased so, that they cannot be recorded.   This country is in the middle of the Ts'ung-ling range; from the Ts'ung-ling onwards the plants, trees, and fruits are all different (*from those before met with*), except the bamboo, the *an-shih-lau* (pomegranate ?), and the sugar-cane.

VI. From this going onwards towards North India, after being a month on the road, we managed to cross Ts'ung-ling.   In Ts'ung-ling there is snow both in winter and summer.   Moreover there are poison-dragons, who when evil-purposed spit poison, winds, rain, snow, drifting sand, and gravel-stones; not one of ten thousand meeting these calamities, escapes.   The people of that land are also called Snowy-mountain men (Tukhâras ?).   Having crossed (Ts'ung)-ling, we arrive at North India.   On entering the borders there is a little country called To-li,[18] where there is again a society of priests all belonging to the Little Vehicle.   There was formerly an Arhat in this country who by magic power took up to the Tuśita heaven a skilful carver of wood to observe the length and breadth (*size*), the colour and look, of Maitrêya Bôdhisattva, that returning below he might carve wood and make his image (*that is*, carve a wooden image of him).   First and last he made three ascents for observation, and at last finished the figure.   Its length is 80 feet, and its upturned foot 8 feet; on fast-days it ever shines brightly.   The kings of the countries round vie with each other in their religious offerings to it.   Now, as of yore, it is in this country.[19]

VII. Keeping along (Ts'ung)-ling, they journeyed southwest for fifteen days.   The road was difficult and broken,

---

[18] Called the valley of Ta-li-lo by Hiuen Tsiang, *infra*, p. 134, n. 37.

[19] For an account of this image see *infra*, p. 134.

with steep crags and precipices in the way. The mountain-side is simply a stone wall standing up 10,000 feet. Looking down, the sight is confused, and on going forward there is no sure foothold. Below is a river called Sint'u-ho. In old days men bored through the rocks to make a way, and spread out side-ladders, of which there are seven hundred (*steps?*) in all to pass. Having passed the ladders, we proceed by a hanging rope-bridge and cross the river. The two sides of the river are something less than 80 paces apart, as recorded by the *Kiu-yi*;[20] but neither Chang-kin nor Kan-ying of the Han arrived here. The body of priests asked Fa-hian whether it was known when the eastward passage of the religion of Buddha began. Hian replied, "When I asked the men of that land, they all said there was an old tradition that from the time of setting up the image of Maitrêya Bôdhisattva, and afterwards, there were Śramaṇas from India who dispatched the dharma-vinaya beyond this river." The setting up of the image took place rather more than three hundred years after the *Nirvâṇa* of Buddha, in the time of Ping-wang of the Chau family.[21] According to this, we may say that the extension of the great doctrine began from this image. If, then, Maitrêya Mahâsattva be not the successor of Sâkya, who is there could cause the three gems to spread everywhere, and frontier men to understand the law? As we certainly know that the origin of the opening of the mysterious revolution is not man's work, so the dream of Ming Ti was from this also.

VIII. Crossing the river, we come to the country of Wu-chang.[22] The country of Wu-chang commences North India. The language of Mid-India is used by all. Mid-India is what they call the middle country. The dress of the people, their food and drink, are also the same as in the middle country. The religion of Buddha is very flourishing. The places where the priests stop and lodge

---

[20] A topographical description of the empire.
[21] 770 A.D.   [22] Udyâna.

they call *sanghârâmas.* In all there are five hundred *sang-hârâmas;* they belong to the Little Vehicle without exception. If a strange Bhikshu arrives here, they give him full entertainment for three days; the three days being over, then they bid him seek for himself a place to rest permanently.

Tradition says : When Buddha came to North India, he then visited this country. Buddha left here as a bequest the impression of his foot. The footprint is sometimes long and sometimes short, according to the thoughtfulness of a man's heart: it is still so, even now. Moreover, the drying-robe-stone in connection with the place where he converted the wicked dragon still remains. The stone is a *chang* and four-tenths high, and more than two *chang* across. It is smooth on one side. Three of the pilgrims, Hwui-king, Tao-ching, and Hwui-ta, went on ahead towards Buddha's shadow and Nagarahâra. Fa-hian and the rest stopped in this country during the rains ; when over, they went down south to the country of Su-ho-to.[23]

IX. In this country also the law of Buddha flourishes. This is the place where, in old days, Śakra, ruler of Dêvas, made apparitionally the hawk and dove, in order to try Bôdhisattva, who cut off his flesh to ransom the dove. Buddha, when he perfected wisdom, going about with his disciples, spoke thus: "This is the place where, in a former birth, I cut my flesh to ransom the dove." From this the people of the country getting to know the fact, built a *stûpa* on the spot, and adorned it with gold and silver.

X. From this, descending eastward, journeying for five days, we arrive at the country of Gandhâra (Kien-to-wei). This is the place which Dharmavarddhana, the son of Aśôka, governed. Buddha also in this country, when he was a Bôdhisattva, gave his eyes in charity for the sake of a man. On this spot also they have raised a great *stûpa*, adorned with silver and gold. The people of this country mostly study the Little Vehicle.

XI. From this going east seven days, there is a country

<hr>

[23] Swât.

called Chu-ch'a-shi-lo.[24] Chu-ch'a-shi-lo in Chinese words is "cut-off head." Buddha, when he was a Bôdhisattva, gave his head in charity to a man in this place, and hence comes the name. Again going eastwards for two days, we come to the place where he gave his body to feed the starving tiger. On these two spots again are built great *stûpas*, both adorned with every kind of precious jewel. The kings, ministers, and people of the neighbouring countries vie with one another in their offerings, scattering flowers and lighting lamps without intermission. These and the two *stûpas* before named the men of that district call " the four great *stûpas*."

XII. From the country of Gandhâra going south for four days, we come to the country of Fo-lu-sha.[25] Buddha in former days, whilst travelling with his disciples here and there, coming to this country, addressed Ânanda thus : " After my death (*parinirvâna*), a king of the country called Ki-ni-kia (Kanika or Kanishka) will raise on this spot a *stûpa*." After Kanishka's birth, he was going round on a tour of observation. At this time Śakra, king of Dêvas, wishing to open out his purpose of mind, took the form of a little shepherd-boy building by the roadside a tower. The king asked and said, " What are you doing ? " Replying, he said, " Making a Buddha-tower." The king said, " Very good." On this the king built over the little boy's tower another tower, in height 40 *chang* and more, adorned with all precious substances. Of all *stûpas* and temples seen by the travellers, none can compare with this for beauty of form and strength. Tradition says this is the highest of the towers in Jambudvîpa. When the king had completed his tower, the little tower forthwith came out from the side on the south of the great tower more than three feet high.

The alms-bowl of Buddha is still in this country. Formerly a king of the Yue-chi, swelling[26] with his army, came

[24] Takshaśilâ, vid. *infra*, p. 138.

[25] Purushapura (Peshâwar).

[26] This is a forced translation. I think the symbol *ta* should be placed before Yue-chi ; it would thus refer to the Great Yue-chi.

to attack this country, wishing to carry off Buddha's alms-bowl. Having subdued the country, the king of the Yue-chi, deeply reverencing the law of Buddha, wished to take the bowl and go; therefore he began his religious offer-ings. The offerings made to the three precious ones being finished, he then caparisoned a great elephant and placed the bowl on it. The elephant then fell to the ground and was unable to advance. Then he made a four-wheeled carriage on which the dish was placed; eight elephants were yoked to draw it, but were again unable to advance. The king then knew that the time of his bowl-relationship was not come. So filled with shame and regrets, he built on this place a *stûpa* and also a *sanghârâma;* moreover, he left a guard to keep up every kind of religious offer-ing.

There are perhaps 700 priests. At the approach of noon the priests bring out the alms-bowl, and with the Upâsakas make all kinds of offerings to it; they then eat their mid-day meal. At even, when they burn incense, they again do so. It is capable of holding two pecks and more. It is of mixed colour, but yet chiefly black. The four divisions are quite clear, each of them being about two-tenths thick. It is glistening and bright. Poor people with few flowers cast into it, fill it; but some very rich people, wishful with many flowers to make their offerings, though they present a hundred thousand myriad of pecks, yet in the end fail to fill it. Pao-yun and Sang-king only made their offerings to the alms-dish of Buddha and then went back. Hwui-king, Hwui-ta, and Tao-ching had previously gone on to the Nagarahâra country to offer their common worship to the Buddha - shadow, his tooth and skull - bone. Hwui-king fell sick, and Tao-ching remained to look after him. Hwui-ta alone went back to Fo-lu-sha, where he met with the others, and then Hwui-ta, Pao-yun, and Sang-king returned together to the Ts'in land. Hwui-ying, dwelling in the temple of Buddha's alms-bowl, died there.

From this Fa-hian went on alone to the place of Buddha's skull-bone.

XIII. Going west 16 *yôjanas*, (Fa-hian) reached the country of Na-kie (Nagarahâra). On the borders, in the city of Hi-lo,[27] is the *vihâra* of the skull-bone of Buddha ; it is gilded throughout and adorned with the seven precious substances.

The king of the country profoundly reverences the skull-bone. Fearing lest some one should steal it, he appoints eight men of the first families of the country, each man having a seal to seal (*the door*) for its safe keeping. In the morning, the eight men having come, each one inspects his seal, and then they open the door. The door being opened, using scented water, they wash their hands and bring out the skull-bone of Buddha. They place it outside the *vihâra* on a high throne; taking a circular stand of the seven precious substances, the stand is placed below (*it*), and a glass bell as a cover over it. All these are adorned with pearls and gems. The bone is of a yellowish-white colour, four inches across and raised in the middle. Each day after its exit men of the *vihâra* at once mount a high tower, beat a large drum, blow the conch, and sound the cymbal. Hearing these, the king goes to the *vihâra* to offer flowers and incense. The offerings finished, each one in order puts it on his head (worships it) and departs. Entering by the east door and leaving by the west, the king every morning thus offers and worships, after which he attends to state affairs. Householders and elder-men also first offer worship and then attend to family affairs. Every day thus begins, without neglect from idleness. The offerings being all done, they take back the skull-bone. In the *vihâra* there is a final-emancipation tower (*a tower shaped like a dâgaba*) which opens and shuts, made of the seven precious substances, more than five feet high, to receive it.

Before the gate of the *vihâra* every morning regularly,

---

[27] Hiḍḍa.

there are sellers of flowers and incense; all who wish to make offerings may buy of every sort. The kings of the countries round also regularly send deputies to make offerings. The site of the *vihára* is forty paces square. Though heaven should quake and the earth open, this spot would not move.

Going from this one *yôjana* north, we come to the capital of Nagarahára. This is the place where Bôdhisattva, in one of his births, gave money in exchange for five flowers[28] to offer to Dipankara Buddha. In the city there is, moreover, a Buddha-tooth tower, to which religious offerings are made in the same way as to the skull-bone.

North-east of the city one *yôjana* we come to the opening of a valley in which is Buddha's religious staff, where they have built a *vihára* for making offerings to it. The staff is made of ox-head sandal-wood; its length is a *chang* and six or seven tenths; it is enclosed in a wooden sheath, from which a hundred or a thousand men could not move it. Entering the valley and going west four days, there is the *vihára* of Buddha's *sanghátí*, to which they make religious offerings. When there is a drought in that country, the magistrates and people of the country, coming together, bring out the robe for worship and offerings, then Heaven gives abundant rain. Half a *yôjana* to the south of the city of Nagarahára there is a cavern (*stone dwelling*); it is on the south-west side of a high mountain. Buddha left his shadow here. At a distance of ten paces or so we see it, like the true form of Buddha, of a gold colour, with the marks and signs perfectly clear and shining. On going nearer to it or farther off, it becomes less and less like the reality. The kings of the bordering countries have sent able artists to copy the likeness, but they have not been able (*to do so*). Moreover, those people have a tradition according to which the

[28] These flowers are generally represented as growing on one stalk or stem (*Tree and Serpent Worship*, pl. l.)

thousand Buddhas will here leave their shadows. About five hundred paces to the west of the shadow, when Buddha was alone, he cut his hair and pared his nails. Then Buddha himself with his disciples together built a tower about seven or eight *chang* high, as a model for all towers of the future. It still exists. Beside it is a temple; in the temple are 700 priests or so. In this district there are as many as a thousand towers in honour of Arhats and Pratyêka Buddhas.

XIV. After remaining here during two months of winter, Fa-hian and two companions went south across the Little Snowy Mountains. The Snowy Mountains, both in summer and winter, are covered (*heaped*) with snow. On the north side of the mountains, in the shade, excessive cold came on suddenly, and all the men were struck mute with dread; Hwui-king alone was unable to proceed onwards. The white froth came from his mouth as he addressed Fa-hian and said, "I too have no power of life left; but whilst there is opportunity, do you press on, lest you all perish." Thus he died. Fa-hian, caressing him, exclaimed in piteous voice, "Our purpose was not to produce fortune!"[29] Submitting, he again exerted himself, and pressing forward, they so crossed the range; on the south side they reached the Lo-i[30] country. In this vicinity there are 3000 priests, belonging both to the Great and Little Vehicle. Here they kept the rainy season. The season past, descending south and journeying for ten days, they reached the Po-na[31] country, where there are also some 3000 priests or more, all belonging to the Little Vehicle. From this journeying eastward for three days, they again crossed the Sin-tu river. Both sides of it are now level.

XV. The other side of the river there is a country named Pi-t'u.[32] The law of Buddha is very flourishing; they belong both to the Great and Little Vehicle. When they

---

[29] Or, to be a fortunate one.
[30] Rohi, *i.e.*, Afghanistan.
[31] Bannu.
[32] Bhida.

saw pilgrims from China arrive, they were much affected
and spoke thus, "How is it that men from the frontiers
are able to know the religion of family-renunciation and
come from far to seek the law of Buddha?" They liber-
ally provided necessary entertainment according to the
rules of religion.

XVI. Going south-east from this somewhat less than
80 *yôjanas*, we passed very many temples one after
another, with some myriad of priests in them. Having
passed these places, we arrived at a certain country. This
country is called Mo-tu-lo.[33] Once more we followed
the Pu-na[34] river. On the sides of the river, both right and
left, are twenty *sanghârâmas*, with perhaps 3000 priests.
The law of Buddha is progressing and flourishing. Beyond
the deserts are the countries of Western India. The kings
of these countries are all firm believers in the law of
Buddha. They remove their caps of state when they
make offerings to the priests. The members of the royal
household and the chief ministers personally direct the
food-giving; when the distribution of food is over, they
spread a carpet on the ground opposite the chief seat (the
president's seat) and sit down before it. They dare not
sit on couches in the presence of the priests. The rules
relating to the almsgiving of kings have been handed
down from the time of Buddha till now. Southward
from this is the so-called middle-country (Mâdhyadeśa).
The climate of this country is warm and equable, without
frost or snow. The people are very well off, without poll-
tax or official restrictions. Only those who till the royal
lands return a portion of profit of the land. If they
desire to go, they go; if they like to stop, they stop.
The kings govern without corporal punishment; criminals
are fined, according to circumstances, lightly or heavily.
Even in cases of repeated rebellion they only cut off the
right hand. The king's personal attendants, who guard
him on the right and left, have fixed salaries. Through-

[33] Mathurâ.   [34] Jumnâ or Yamunâ river.

out the country the people kill no living thing nor drink
wine, nor do they eat garlic or onions, with the exception of Chandâlas only. The Chandâlas are named "evil
men" and dwell apart from others; if they enter a town
or market, they sound a piece of wood in order to separate themselves; then men, knowing who they are, avoid
coming in contact with them. In this country they do
not keep swine nor fowls, and do not deal in cattle; they
have no shambles or wine-shops in their market-places.
In selling they use cowrie shells. The Chandâlas only
hunt and sell flesh. Down from the time of Buddha's
Nirvâna, the kings of these countries, the chief men and
householders, have raised *vihâras* for the priests, and
provided for their support by bestowing on them fields,
houses, and gardens, with men and oxen. Engraved title-
deeds were prepared and handed down from one reign to
another; no one has ventured to withdraw them, so that
till now there has been no interruption. All the resident
priests having chambers (*in these vihâras*) have their
beds, mats, food, drink, and clothes provided without
stint; in all places this is the case. The priests ever
engage themselves in doing meritorious works for the
purpose of religious advancement (*karma*—building up
their religious character), or in reciting the scriptures, or
in meditation. When a strange priest arrives, the senior
priests go out to meet him, carrying for him his clothes
and alms-bowl. They offer him water for washing his
feet and oil for rubbing them; they provide untimely
(*vikâla*) food. Having rested awhile, they again ask him
as to his seniority in the priesthood, and according to this
they give him a chamber and sleeping materials, arranging everything according to the *dharma*. In places where
priests reside they make towers in honour of Śâriputra,
of Mudgalaputra, of Ânanda, also in honour of the *Abhidharma*, *Vinaya*, and *Sûtra*. During a month after the
season of rest the most pious families urge a collection for
an offering to the priests; they prepare an untimely meal

for them, and the priests in a great assembly preach the law. The preaching over, they offer to Sâriputra's tower all kinds of scents and flowers; through the night they burn lamps provided by different persons. Sâriputra originally was a Brâhman; on a certain occasion he went to Buddha and requested ordination. The great Mudgala and the great Kâśyapa did likewise. The Bhikshunîs principally honour the tower of Ânanda, because it was Ânanda who requested the lord of the world to let women take orders; Srâmanêras mostly offer to Râhula; the masters of the *Abhidharma* offer to the *Abhidharma;* the masters of the *Vinaya* offer to the *Vinaya.* Every year there is one offering, each according to his own day. Men attached to the Mahâyâna offer to *Prajña-pâramitâ*, Mañjuśrî, and Avalôkitêśvara. When the priests have received their yearly dues, then the chief men and householders and Brâhmans bring every kind of robe and other things needed by the priests to offer them; the priests also make offerings one to another. Down from the time of Buddha's death the rules of conduct for the holy priesthood have been (thus) handed down without interruption.

After crossing the Indus, the distance to the Southern Sea of South India is from four to five myriads of li; the land is level throughout, without great mountains or valleys, but still there are rivers.

XVII. South-east from this, after going 18 *yôjanas*, there is a country called Saṁkâśya. This is the place where Buddha descended after going up to the Trayastriṁśas heaven to preach the law during three months for his mother's benefit. When Buddha went up to the Trayastriṁśas heaven by the exercise of his miraculous power (*spiritual power of miracle*), he contrived that his disciples should not know (*of his proceeding*). Seven days before the completion (*of the three months*) he broke the spell, so that Aniruddha, using his divine sight, beheld the Lord of the world afar, and forthwith addressed the venerable (Ârya) Mahâmudgalaputra, "You can go and salute the

Lord of the world." Mudgalyâyana accordingly went, and bowing down, worshipped the foot and exchanged friendly greetings. The friendly meeting over, Buddha said to Mudgalyâyana, " After seven days are over I shall descend to Jambudvîpa." Mudgalyâyana then returned. On this the great kings of the eight kingdoms, the ministers and people, not having seen Buddha for a long time, were all desirous to meet him. They assembled like clouds in this country to meet the Lord of the world. At this time Utpalâ Bhikshuṇî thought thus with herself: " To-day the kings of the countries and the ministers and people are going to worship and meet Buddha. I am but a woman ; how can I get to see him first ?" Buddha forthwith by his miraculous power made her, by transformation, into a holy Chakravartti king, and as such she was the very first to worship him. Buddha being now about to come down from the Trayastriṁśas heaven, there appeared a threefold precious ladder. The middle ladder was made of the seven precious substances, standing above which Buddha began to descend. Then the king of the Brahmâ heavens (Brahmakâyikas) caused a silver ladder to appear, on which he took his place on Buddha's right hand, holding a white chauri. Then Śakra, king of Dêvas, caused a bright golden ladder to appear, on which he took his place on the left, holding in his hand a precious parasol. Innumerable Dêvas were in attendance whilst Buddha descended. After he had come down, the three ladders disappeared in the earth, except seven steps, which remained visible. In after times Aśôka, wishing to discover the utmost depths to which these ladders went, employed men to dig down and examine into it. They went on digging till they came to the yellow spring (the earth's foundation), but yet had not come to the bottom. The king, deriving from this an increase of faith and reverence, forthwith built over the ladders a *vihâra*, and facing the middle flight he placed a standing figure (of Buddha) sixteen feet high. Behind the *vihâra* he erected a stone pillar thirty cubits high, and on the top placed the figure of a lion. Within the pillar on the four sides are figures of Buddha; both within and without it is shining and bright as glass. It happened once that some heretical doctors had a contention with the Śramaṇas respecting this as a place of residence. Then the argument of the Śramaṇas failing, they all agreed to the following compact: " If this place properly belongs to the Śramaṇas, then there will be some supernatural proof given of it." Immediately on this the lion on the top of the pillar uttered a loud roar. Witnessing this testimony, the unbelievers, abashed, withdrew from the dispute and submitted.

The body of Buddha, in consequence of his having partaken of divine food during three months, emitted a divine fragrance, unlike that of men. Immediately after his descent he bathed himself. Men of after ages erected in this place a bath-house, which yet remains. There is also a tower erected on the spot where the Bhikshuṇî Utpalâ was the first to adore Buddha. There is also a tower on the spot where Buddha when in the world cut his hair and his nails, and also on the following spots, viz., where the three former Buddhas, as well as Śâkyamuni Buddha, sat down, and also where they walked for exercise, and also where there are certain marks and impressions of the different Buddhas. These towers still remain. There is also one erected where Brahmâ, Śakra, and the Dêvas attended Buddha when he came down from heaven. There are perhaps a thousand male and female disciples who have their meals in common. They belong promiscuously to the systems of the Great and Little Vehicle, and dwell together. A white-eared dragon is the patron of this body of priests. He causes fertilising and seasonable showers of rain to fall within their country, and preserves it from plagues and calamities, and so causes the priesthood to dwell in security. The priests, in gratitude for these favours, have erected a dragon-chapel, and within it placed a resting-place (*seat*) for his accommodation.

Moreover, they make special contributions, in the shape of religious offerings, to provide the dragon with food. The body of priests every day select from their midst three men to go and take their meal in this chapel. At the end of each season of rain, the dragon suddenly assumes the form of a little serpent, both of whose ears are edged with white. The body of priests, recognising him, place in the midst of his lair a copper vessel full of cream; and then, from the highest to the lowest, they walk past him in procession as if to pay him greeting all round. He then suddenly disappears. He makes his appearance once every year. This country is very productive: the people are very prosperous, and exceedingly rich beyond comparison. Men of all countries coming here are well taken care of and obtain what they require. Fifty *yôjanas* to the north of this temple there is a temple called " Fire Limit," which is the name of an evil spirit. Buddha himself converted this evil spirit, whereupon men in after ages raised a *vihâra* on the spot. At the time of the dedication of the *vihâra* an Arhat spilt some of the sacred water, poured on his hands, and let it fall on the earth, and the place where it fell is still visible; though they have often swept the place to remove the mark, yet it still remains and cannot be destroyed. There is, besides, in this place a tower of Buddha which a benevolent spirit ever keeps clean and waters, and which (*was built*) without a human architect. There was once an heretical king who said, " Since you can do this, I will bring a great army and quarter it here, which shall accumulate much filth and refuse. Will you be able to clear all this away, I wonder ? " The spirit immediately caused a great tempest to rise and blow over the place, as a proof that he could do it. In this district there are a hundred small towers; a man might pass the day in trying to count them without succeeding. If any one is very anxious to discover the right number, then he places a man by the side of each tower and afterwards numbers the men;

but, even in this case, it can never be known how many or how few men will be required. There is also a *sanghârâma* here containing about 600 or 700 priests. In this is a place where a Pratyêka Buddha ate [35] (*the fruit*); the spot of ground where he died is just in size like a chariot-wheel; all the ground around it is covered with grass, but this spot produces none. The ground also where he dried his clothes is bare of vegetation; the traces of the impress of the clothes remain to this day.

XVIII. Fa-Hian resided in the dragon *vihâra* during the summer rest. After this was over, going south-east seven *yôjanas*, he arrived at the city of Ki-jou-i (Kanauj). This city borders on the Ganges. There are two *sanghârâmas* here, both belonging to the system of the Little Vehicle. Going from the city six or seven li in a westerly direction, on the north bank of the river Ganges, is the place where Buddha preached for the good of his disciples. Tradition says that he preached on impermanency and sorrow, and also on the body being like a bubble and foam. On this spot they have raised a tower, which still remains. Crossing the Ganges and going south three *yôjanas*, we arrive at a forest called A-lo. Here also Buddha preached the law. They have raised towers on this spot, and also where he sat down and walked for exercise.

XIX. Going south-east from this place ten *yôjanas*, we arrive at the great country of Sha-chi. Leaving the southern gate of the capital city, on the east side of the road is a place where Buddha once dwelt. Whilst here he bit (*a piece from*) the willow stick and fixed it in the earth; immediately it grew up seven feet high, neither more or less. The unbelievers and Brâhmans, filled with jealousy, cut it down and scattered the leaves far and wide, but yet it always sprung up again in the same place as before. Here also they raised towers on places where the four Buddhas walked for exercise and sat down. The ruins still exist.

[35] Probably the text is corrupt. There is a common phrase, "to drink the draught of sweet dew," a euphemism for "*died.*" It may be so in the present instance.

XX. Going eight *yôjanas* southwards from this place, we arrive at the country of Kiu-sa-lo (Kôsala) and its chief town She-wei (Śrâvastî). There are very few inhabitants in this city, altogether perhaps about 200 families. This is the city which King Prasênajit governed. Towers have been built in after times on the site of the ruined *vihâra* of Mahâprajâpatî, also on the foundations (*of the house*) of the lord Sudatta, also on the spot where the Angulimâlya was burnt, who was converted and entered nirvâna; all these towers are erected in the city. The unbelieving Brâhmans, from jealousy, desired to destroy these various buildings, but on attempting to do so, the heavens thundered and the lightnings flashed, so that they were unable to carry out their design. Leaving the city by the south gate and proceeding 1200 paces on the road, on the west side of it is the place where the lord Sudatta built a *vihâra*. This chapel opens towards the east. The principal door is flanked by two side chambers, in front of which stand two stone pillars; on the top of the left-hand one is the figure of a wheel, and on the right-hand one the image of an ox. The clear water of the tanks, the luxuriant groves, and numberless flowers of variegated hues combine to produce the picture of what is called a Jêtavana *vihâra*. When Buddha ascended into the Trayastriṁshas heavens to preach for the sake of his mother, after ninety days' absence, King Prasênajit desiring to see him again, carved out of the sandal-wood called Gôśîrshachandana (*ox-head*) an image of the Buddha and placed it on Buddha's throne. When Buddha returned and entered the *vihâra*, the image, immediately quitting its place, went forward to meet him. On this Buddha addressed these words to it: " Return, I pray you, to your seat. After my *Nirvâna* you will be the model from which my followers (*four schools or classes*) shall carve their images." On this the figure returned to its seat. This image, as it was the very first made of all the figures of Buddha, is the one which all subsequent ages have followed as a model. Buddha then removed and dwelt in a small *vihâra* on the south side of the greater one, in a place quite separated from that occupied by the image, and about twenty paces from it. The Jêtavana *vihâra* originally had seven stages. The monarchs of the surrounding countries and the people vied with each other in presenting religious offerings at this spot. They decked the place with flags and silken canopies; they offered flowers and burnt incense, whilst the lamps shone continually from evening till daylight with unfading splendour. A rat taking in his mouth the wick of a lamp caused it to set fire to one · of the hanging canopies, and this resulted in a general conflagration and the entire destruction of the seven storeys of the *vihâra.* The kings and people of the surrounding countries were deeply grieved, thinking that the sandal-wood figure had also been consumed. Four or five days afterwards, on opening the door of the eastern little chapel, they were surprised to behold the original figure there. The people were filled with joy, and they agreed to rebuild the chapel. Having completed two stages, they removed the image from its new situation back to where it was before. When Fa-Hian and To-Ching arrived at this chapel of the Jêtavana, they reflected that this was the spot in which the Lord of men had passed twenty-five years of his life; they themselves, at the risk of their lives, were now dwelling amongst foreigners; of those who had with like purpose travelled through a succession of countries with them, some had returned home, some were dead; and now, gazing on the place where Buddha once dwelt but was no longer to be seen, their hearts were affected with very lively regret. Whereupon the priests belonging to that community came forward and addressed (Fa)-Hian and To-(Ching) thus: "From what country have you come?" To which they replied, "We come from the land of Han." Then those priests, in astonishment, exclaimed, "Wonderful! to think that men from the frontiers of the earth should come so far as this from a desire to search for the law;" and then talking between themselves they said, "Our various superiors and brethren, who have succeeded one another in this place from the earliest time till now, have none of them seen men of Han come so far as this before."

Four li to the north-west of the *vihâra* is a copse called "Recovered-sight." Originally there were 500 blind men dwelling on this spot beside the chapel. On one occasion Buddha declared the law on their account; after listening to his sermon they immediately recovered their sight. The blind men, overcome with joy, drove their staves into the earth and fell down on their faces in adoration. The staves forthwith took root and grew up to be great trees. The people, from a feeling of reverence, did not presume to cut them down, and so they grew and formed a grove, to which this name of "Recovered-sight"[36] was given. The priests of the chapel of the Jêtavana resort in great numbers to this shady copse to meditate after their mid-day meal. Six or seven li to the north-east of the Jêtavana *vihâra* is the site of the chapel which Mother Viśâkhâ built,[37] and invited Buddha and the priests to occupy. The ruins are still there. The great garden enclosure of the Jêtavana *vihâra* has two gates, one opening towards the east, the other towards the north. This garden is the plot of ground which the noble Sudatta bought after covering it with gold coins. The chapel is in the middle of it; it was here Buddha resided for a very long time, and expounded the law for the salvation of men. Towers have been erected on the various spots where he walked for exercise or sat down. These towers have all distinctive names given them, as, for example, the place where Buddha was accused of murdering (*the harlot*) Sundarî.[38] Leaving the Jêtavana

---

[36] Restored by Stan. Julien to Âptanêtravana (tome ii. p. 308), and by Cunningham to Âptâkshivana (*Arch. Surv.*, vol. i. p. 344, n.) Cf. vol. ii. p. 12.

[37] This chapel of Mother Viśâkhâ is placed by Cunningham south-east from the Jêtavana (*Arch. Surv.*, vol. i. p. 345, n.) The text may be wrong.

[38] See vol. ii. p. 7.

by the eastern gate, and going north seventy paces, on the
west side of the road is the place where Buddha formerly
held a discussion with the followers of the ninety-six
heretical schools. The king of the country, the chief
ministers, the landowners and people, all came in great
numbers to hear him. At this time a woman who was
an unbeliever, called Chiñchimanâ,[39] being filled with jealousy, gathered up her clothes in a heap round her person
so as to appear with child, and then accused Buddha in a
meeting of priests of unrighteous conduct. On this Śakra,
the king of Dêvas, taking the appearance of a white mouse,
came and gnawed through her sash; on this the whole
fell down, and then the earth opened and she herself went
down alive into hell. Here also is the place where Dêvadatta, having poisoned his nails for the purpose of destroying Buddha, went down alive into hell. Men in after
times noted these various places for recognition. Where the
discussion took place they raised a chapel more than six
chang (70 feet) high, with a sitting figure of Buddha in it.
To the east of the road is a temple (*Dêvâlaya*) belonging
to the heretics, which is named " Shadow-covered." It is
opposite the *vihâra* erected on the place of the discussion,
and of the same height. It has received the name of
"Shadow-covered" because when the sun is in the west, the
shadow of the *vihâra* of the Lord of the World covers the
temple of the heretics; but when the sun is in the east, the
shadow of the latter is bent to the north, and does not over-
shadow the chapel of Buddha.[40] The heretics constantly appointed persons to take care of their temple, to sweep and
water it, to burn incense and light lamps for religious
worship; towards the approach of morning their lamps disappeared, and were discovered in the middle of the Buddhist
chapel. On this the Brâhmans, being angry, said, "These
Śramaṇas take our lamps for their own religious worship;"
whereupon the Brâhmans set a night-watch, and then they
saw their own gods take the lamps and move round Buddha's

[39] Vol. ii. p. 9, n. 23.   [40] Vol. ii. p. 10.

chapel three times, after which they offered the lamps and suddenly disappeared. On this the Brâhmans, recognising the greatness of Buddha's spiritual power, forsook their families and became his disciples. Tradition says that about the time when these things happened there were ninety *sanghârâmas* surrounding the Jêtavana chapel, all of which, with one exception, were occupied by priests. In this country of Mid-India there are ninety-six heretical sects, all of whom allow the reality of worldly phenomena. Each sect has its disciples, who beg their food, but do not carry alms-dishes. They also piously build hospices by the side of solitary roads for the shelter of travellers, where they may rest, sleep, eat and drink, and are supplied with all necessaries. The followers of Buddha, also, as they pass to and fro, are entertained by them, only different arrangements are made for their convenience. Dêvadatta also has a body of disciples still existing; they pay religious reverence to the three past Buddhas, but not to Śâkyamuni Buddha.[41]

Four li to the south-east of Śrâvastî is the place where the Lord of men stood by the side of the road when King Virûdhaka [42] (Liu-li) wished to destroy the country of the Śâkya family; on this spot there is a tower built. Fifty li to the west of the city we arrive at a town called To-wai;[43] this was the birthplace of Kâśyapa Buddha. Towers are erected on the spot where he had an interview with his father and also where he entered *Nirvâna*. A great tower has also been erected over the relics of the entire body of Kâśyapa Tathâgata.

XXI. Leaving the city of Śrâvastî, and going twelve *yôjanas* to the south-east, we arrived at a town called Na-pi-ka. This is the birthplace of Krakuchchhanda [44] Buddha. There are towers erected on the spots where the interview between the father and son took place, and also where he

---

[41] This is an important notice, as it indicates the character of Devadatta's position with reference to Buddha.

[42] See vol. ii. p. 11.

[43] Tadwa, see vol. ii. p. 13.

[44] See vol. ii. p. 18.

entered *Nirvâna.* Going north from this place less than one *yôjana,* we arrive at a town where Kanakamuni Buddha was born ;[45] there are towers also erected here over similar places as the last.

XXII. Going eastward from this less than a *yôjana,* we arrive at the city of Kapilavastu. In this city there is neither king nor people; it is like a great desert.[46] There is simply a congregation of priests and about ten families of lay people. On the site of the ruined palace of Suddhôdana there is a picture of the prince's mother, whilst the prince, riding on a white elephant, is entering the womb. Towers have been erected on the following spots : where the royal prince left the city by the eastern gate ; where he saw the sick man ; and where he caused his chariot to turn and take him back to his palace. There are also towers erected on the following spots : at the place where Asita observed the marks of the royal prince ; where Ânanda and the others struck the elephant, drew it out of the way, and hurled it ; where the arrow, going south-east 30 li, entered the earth, from which bubbled up a fountain of water, which in after generations was used as a well for travellers to drink at ; also on the spot where Buddha, after arriving at supreme wisdom, met his father ; where the 500 Śâkyas, having embraced the faith, paid reverence to Upâli ; at the place where the earth shook six times ; at the place where Buddha expounded the law on behalf of all the Dêvas, whilst the four heavenly kings guarded the four gates of the hall, so that his father could not enter : at the place where Mahâprajâpatî presented Buddha with a *sanghâtî* whilst he was sitting under a Nyagrôdha tree with his face to the east, which tree still exists ; at the place where Virûdhaka-râja killed the offspring of the Śâkyas who had previously entered on the path *Srôtâpanna.* All these towers are still in existence.[47] A few li to the north-

<hr>

[45] Vol. ii. p. 19.

[46] Vol. ii. p. 14 ; and conf. Fergusson's *Archæology in India,* p. 110.

[47] Compare the accounts given by Hiuen Tsiang, Book vi.

east of the city is the royal field where the prince, sitting underneath a tree, watched a ploughing-match. Fifty li to the east of the city is the royal garden called Lumbinî; it was here the queen entered the bath to wash herself, and, having come out on the northern side, advanced twenty paces, and then holding a branch of the tree in her hand, as she looked to the east, brought forth the prince. When born he walked seven steps; two dragon-kings washed the prince's body,—the place where this occurred was afterwards converted into a well, and here, as likewise at the pool, the water of which came down from above for washing (the child), the priests draw their drinking water. All the Buddhas have four places universally determined for them:—(1.) The place for arriving at supreme wisdom; (2.) The place for turning the wheel of the law; (3.) The place for expounding the true principles of the law and refuting the heretics; (4.) The place for descending to earth after going into the Trayastriṁśas heaven to explain the law to their mothers. Other places are chosen according to existing circumstances. The country of Kapilavastu is now a great desert; you seldom meet any people on the roads for fear of the white elephants and the lions. It is impossible to travel negligently. Going east five *yôjanas* from the place where Buddha was born, there is a country called La n-m o (Râmagrâma).[48]

XXIII. The king of this country obtained one share of the relics of Buddha's body. On his return home he built a tower, which is the same as the tower of Râmagrâma. By the side of it is a tank in which lives a dragon, who constantly guards and protects the tower and worships there morning and night. When King Aśôka was living he wished to destroy the eight towers and to build eightyfour thousand others. Having destroyed seven, he next proceeded to treat this one in the same way.[49] The dragon therefore assumed a body and conducted the king within

[48] Vol. ii. p. 26. Cf. Fah-hian, p. 89, n. 1.

[49] Cf. *Fo-sho-hing-tsan-king,* v. 2298; also *infra,* vol. ii. p. 27.

his abode, and having shown him all the vessels and appliances he used in his religious services, he addressed the king and said : " If you can worship better than this, then you may destroy the tower. Let me take you out ; I will have no quarrel with you." King Aśôka, knowing that these vessels were of no human workmanship, immediately returned to his home. This place having become desert, there was no one either to water it or sweep, but ever and anon a herd of elephants carrying water in their trunks piously watered the ground, and also brought all sorts of flowers and perfumes to pay religious worship at the tower. Some pilgrims from different countries used to come here to worship at the tower. On one occasion some of these met the elephants, and being much frightened, concealed themselves amongst the trees. Seeing the elephants perform their service according to the law, they were greatly affected. They grieved to think that there was no temple here or priests to perform religious service, so that the very elephants had to water and sweep. On this they gave up the great precepts and took upon them the duties of Śrâmanêras. They began to pluck up the brushwood and level the ground, and arrange the place so that it became neat and clean. They urged the king of the country to help make residences for the priests. Moreover, they built a temple in which priests still reside. These things occurred recently, since which there has been a regular succession (of priests), only the superior of the temple has always been a Śrâman êra.[50] Three *yôjanas* east of this place is the spot where the royal prince dismissed his charioteer Chandaka and the royal horse, previous to their return. Here also is erected a tower.

XXIV. Going eastward from this place four *yôjanas*, we arrive at the Ashes-tower.[51] Here also is a *sanghârâma*. Again going twelve *yôjanas* eastward, we arrive at the town of Kuśinagara. To the north of this town, where the Lord

---

[50] Vol. ii. p. 27. [51] Vol. ii. p. 31.

of the World, lying by the side of the Hiraṇyavatî river, with his head to the north and a *sal* tree on either side of him, entered *Nirvâṇa;* also in the place where Subhadra[52] was converted, the very last of all his disciples; also where for seven days they paid reverence to the Lord of the World lying in his golden coffin; also where Vajrapâṇi[53] threw down his golden mace, and where the eight kings divided the relics; in each of the above places towers have been raised and *sânghârâmâs* built, which still exist.   In this city also there are but few inhabitants; such families as there are, are connected with the resident congregation of priests.   Going south-east twelve *yôjanas*[54] from this place, we arrive at the spot where the Lichchhavis, desiring to follow Buddha to the scene of his *Nirvâṇa,* were forbidden to do so.   On account of their affection for Buddha they were unwilling to go back, on which Buddha caused to appear between them and him a great and deeply-scarped river, which they could not cross.   He then left with them his alms-bowl as a memorial, and exhorted them to return to their houses.   On this they went back and erected a stone pillar, on which this account is engraved.

XXV. From this going five *yôjanas* eastward, we arrive at the country of Vaiśâlî.[55] To the north of the city of Vaiśâlî there is the *vihâra* of the great forest,[56] which has a two-storied tower.   This chapel was once occupied by Buddha. Here also is the tower which was built over half the body of Ânanda.   Within this city dwelt the lady Âmrapâlî,[57] (*who*

[52] Cf. *Fo-sho.,* p. 290.

[53] Or does this refer to the Mallas throwing down their maces (hammers)?

[54] Laidlay has by mistake translated the French S.W. instead of S.E.   But the French editors have also mistranslated the distance, which is twelve *yôjanas,* and not twenty.   We have thus nineteen *yôjanas* between Kuśinagara (Kasia) and Vaiśâlî (Besarh), which is as nearly correct as possible.

[55] Vaiśâlî, a very famous city in the Buddhist records.   Cunning-

ham identifies it with the present Besarh, twenty miles north of Hajipûr.

[56] This chapel was situated in the neighbourhood of the present village of Bakhra, about two miles N.N.W. of Besarh.   It is alluded to in the Singhalese records as the Mahâvano Vihâro.   From Burnouf we find it was built by the side of a tank known as the Markaṭahrada, or Monkey tank (*Introd. Buddh. Indien,* p. 74), (*Man. Bud.,* p. 356).

[57] Cf. *Fo-sho.,* p. 253.

built) a tower for Buddha; the ruins still exist. Three li to the south of the city, on the west side of the road, is the garden which the lady Âmrapâlî gave to Buddha as a resting-place. When Buddha was about to enter *Nirvâṇa*, accompanied by his disciples, he left Vaiśâlî by the western gate, and turning his body to the right,[58] he beheld the city and thus addressed his followers: " In this place I have performed the last religious act of my earthly career." Men afterwards raised a tower on this spot. Three li to the north-west of the city is a tower called " the tower of the deposited bows and clubs." The origin of this name was as follows:[59]—On one of the upper streams of the Ganges there was a certain country ruled by a king. One of his concubines gave birth to an unformed fœtus, whereupon the queen being jealous, said, " Your conception is one of bad omen." So they closed it up in a box of wood and cast it into the Ganges. Lower down the stream there was another king, who, taking a tour of observation, caught sight of the wooden box floating on the stream. On bringing it to shore and opening it, he found inside a thousand children very fair, well formed, and most unique. The king hereupon took them and brought them up. When they grew up they turned out to be very brave and warlike, and were victorious over all whom they went to attack. In process of time they marched against the kingdom of the monarch, their father, at which he was filled with consternation. On this his concubine asked the king why he was so terrified; to whom he replied, " The king of that country has a thousand sons, brave and warlike beyond compare, and they are coming to attack my country; this is why I am alarmed." To this the concubine replied, " Fear not! but erect on the east of the city a high tower, and when the rebels come, place me on it; I will restrain them." The king did so, and when the invaders arrived, the concubine addressed them

[58] Cf. *Fo-sho.*, v. 1930 and n. 3.
[59] For another account of this fable, cf. vol. ii. p. 71.

from the tower, saying, "You are my children. Then why are you rebellious?" They replied, "Who are you that say you are our mother?" The concubine replied, "If ye will not believe me, all of you look up and open your mouths." On this the concubine, with both her hands, pressed her breasts, and from each breast proceeded five hundred jets of milk, which fell into the mouths of her thousand sons. On this the rebels, perceiving that she was indeed their mother, immediately laid down their bows and clubs. The two royal fathers, by a consideration of these circumstances, were able to arrive at the condition of Pratyêka Buddhas, and the tower erected in their honour remains to this day. In after times, when the Lord of the World arrived at supreme reason, he addressed his disciples in these words, "This is the place where I formerly laid aside my bow and my club." Men in after times, coming to know this, founded a tower in this place, and hence the name. The thousand children are in truth the thousand Buddhas of this Bhadra-kalpa. Buddha, when standing beside this tower, addressed Ânanda thus, "After three months I must enter *Nirvâṇa*," on which occasion Mâra-râja so fascinated the mind of Ânanda that he did not request Buddha to remain in the world. Going east from this point three or four li there is a tower. One hundred years after the *Nirvâṇa* of Buddha there were at Vaiśâlî certain Bhikshus who broke the rules of the *Vinaya* in ten particulars,[60] saying that Buddha had said it was so, at which time the Arhats and the orthodox Bhikshus, making an assembly of 700 ecclesiastics, compared and collated the *Vinaya Piṭaka* afresh. Afterwards men erected a tower on this spot, which still exists.

XXVI. Going four *yôjanas* east, we arrive at the confluence of the five rivers. When Ânanda was going from the country of Magadha towards Vaiśâlî, desiring to enter *Nir-*

---

[60] For an account of this council see *Abstract of Four Lectures*, Lect. ii. There is an expression *fan fu* after the words "orthodox Bhikshus" (rule-holding Bhikshus), which may either be enclitic, or mean "a mixed multitude."

vána, the Dêvas acquainted King Ajâtaśatru of it. The king immediately set out after him at the head of his troops, and arrived at the banks of the river. The Lichchhavis of Vaiśâlî, hearing that Ânanda was coming, likewise set out to meet him and arrived at the side of the river. Ânanda then reflected that if he were to advance, King Ajâtaśatru would be much grieved, and if he should go back, then the Lichchhavis would be indignant. Being perplexed, he forthwith entered the *Samádhi* called the " brilliancy of flame," consuming his body, and entered *Nirvána* in the midst of the river. His body was divided into two parts; one part was found on either side of the river; so the two kings, taking the relics of half his body, returned and erected towers over them.[61]

XXVII. Crossing the river, and going south one *yôjana,* we arrive at Magadha and the town of Pâṭaliputra (Palin-fu). This is the town in which King Aśôka reigned. In the city is the royal palace, the different parts of which he commissioned the genii (*demons*) to construct by piling up the stones. The walls, doorways, and the sculptured designs are no human work. The ruins still exist. The younger brother of King Aśôka having arrived at the dignity of an Arhat, was in the habit of residing in the hill Grîdhrakûṭa, finding his chief delight in silent contemplation. The king respectfully requested him to come to his house to receive his religious offerings. His brother, pleased with his tranquillity in the mountain, declined the invitation. The king then addressed his brother, saying, " If you will only accept my invitation, I will make for you a hill within the city." Then the king, providing all sorts of meat and drink, invited the genii, and addressed them thus, " I beg you to accept my invitation for to-morrow; but as there are no seats, I must request you each to bring his own." On the morrow the great genii came, each one bringing with him a great stone, four

<hr>

[61] For this account and generally about Vaiśâlî, cf. vol. ii. book vii. p. 66.

or five paces square. After the feast (*the session*), he deputed the genii to pile up (their seats) and make a great stone mountain; and at the base of the mountain with five great square stones to make a rock chamber, in length about 35 feet and in breadth 22 feet and in height 11 feet or so.

In this city (*i.e.*, of Pâṭaliputra or Patna) once lived a certain Brâhman called Râdha-Svâmi (?) (Lo-tai-sz-pi-mi), of large mind and extensive knowledge, and attached to the Great Vehicle. There was nothing with which he was unacquainted, and he lived apart occupied in silent meditation. The king of the country honoured and respected him as his religious superior. If he went to salute him, he did not dare to sit down in his presence. If the king, from a feeling of esteem, took him by the hand, the Brâhman thoroughly washed himself. For something like fifty years the whole country looked up to this man and placed its confidence on him alone. He mightily extended the influence of the law of Buddha, so that the heretics were unable to obtain any advantage at all over the priesthood.

By the side of the tower of King Aśôka is built a *sanghârâma* belonging to the Great Vehicle, very imposing and elegant. There is also a temple belonging to the Little Vehicle. Together they contain about 600 or 700 priests; their behaviour is decorous and orderly. Here one may see eminent priests from every quarter of the world; Śramaṇas and scholars who seek for instruction all flock to this temple. The Brâhman teacher is called Mañjuśrî. The great Śramaṇas of the country, and all the Bhikshus attached to the Great Vehicle, esteem and reverence him; moreover he resides in this *sanghârâma.* Of all the kingdoms of Mid-India, the towns of this country are especially large. The people are rich and prosperous; they practise virtue and justice. Every year on the eighth day of the second month there is a procession of images. On this occasion they construct a four-wheeled car, and erect upon it a tower of five stages, composed of bamboos lashed together, the whole being supported by a centre-post resembling a large spear with three points, in height twenty-two feet and more. So it looks like a pagoda. They then cover it over with fine white linen, which they afterwards paint with gaudy colours. Having made figures of the dêvas, and decorated them with gold, silver, and glass, they place them under canopies of embroidered silk. Then at the four corners (of the car) they construct niches (*shrines*), in which they place figures of Buddha in a sitting posture, with a Bôdhisattva standing in attendance. There are perhaps twenty cars thus prepared and differently decorated. During the day of the procession both priests and laymen assemble in great numbers. There are games and music, whilst they offer flowers and incense. The Brahmâchârîs come forth to offer their invitations. The Buddhas, then, one after the other, enter the city. After coming into the town again they halt. Then all night long they burn lamps, indulge in games and music, and make religious offerings. Such is the custom of all those who assemble on this occasion from the different countries round about. The nobles and householders of this country have founded hospitals within the city, to which the poor of all countries, the destitute, cripples, and the diseased, may repair. They receive every kind of requisite help gratuitously. Physicians inspect their diseases, and according to their cases order them food and drink, medicine or decoctions, everything in fact that may contribute to their ease. When cured they depart at their convenience. King Aśôka having destroyed seven (of the original) pagodas, constructed 84,000 others. The very first which he built is the great tower which stands about three li to the south of this city. In front of this pagoda is an impression of Buddha's foot, (*over which*) they have raised a chapel, the gate of which faces the north. To the south of the tower is a stone pillar, about a *chang* and a half in girth (18 *feet*), and three *chang* or so in height (35 *feet*). On the surface of this pillar is an inscription to the following effect: " King Aśôka

c

presented the whole of Jambudvîpa to the priests of the four quarters, and redeemed it again with money, and this he did three times." Three or four hundred paces to the north of the pagoda is the spot where Aśôka was born (*or resided*). On this spot he raised the city of Ni-li, and in the midst of it erected a stone pillar, also about 35 feet in height, on the top of which he placed the figure of a lion, and also engraved an historical record on the pillar giving an account of the successive events connected with Ni-li, with the corresponding year, day, and month.[62]

XXVIII. From this city proceeding in a south-easterly direction nine *yôjanas*, we arrive at a small solitary stone hill, on the top of which is a stone cell.[63] The stone cell faces the south. On one occasion, when Buddha was sitting in this cell, Śakra Dêva, taking the divine musician Pañchaśikha,[64] caused him to sound a strain in the place where Buddha was. Then Śakra Dêva proposed forty-two questions to Buddha, drawing some traces upon a stone with his finger. The remains of the structure and tracings yet exist. There is a *sanghârâma* built here. Going south-west from this one *yôjana*, we arrive at the village of Na-lo.[65] This was the place of Śâriputra's birth. Śâriputra returned here to enter *Nirvâṇa*. A tower therefore was erected here, which is still in existence. Going west from this one *yôjana*, we arrive at the new Râja-gṛiha. This was the town which King Ajâtaśatru built. There are two *sanghârâmas* in it. Leaving this town by the west gate and proceeding 300 paces, (we arrive at) the tower which King Ajâtaśatru raised over the share of Buddha's relics which he obtained. Its height is very imposing. Leaving the south side of the city and proceeding southwards four li, we enter a valley

[62] For an account of Magadha, cf. vol. ii. p. 82 ff.

[63] The Indra-śila-gṛihâ of Hiuen Tsiang, see vol. ii. p. 180.

[64] For an account of this event, see *Manual of Buddhism*, pp. 289, 290; also Childers' *Pâli Dict.*, sub voc. *Pañcasikho*.

[65] The Kâlapinâka of Hiuen Tsiang, vol. ii. p. 177.

situated between five hills. These hills encircle it completely like the walls of a town. This is the site of
the old town of King Bimbisâra. From east to west
it is about five or six li, from north to south seven or
eight li. Here Śâriputra and Mudgalyâyana first met
Aśvajit.[66] Here also the Nirgrantha made a pit with fire
in it, and poisoned the food which he invited Buddha
to eat. Here also is the spot where King Ajâtaśatru,
intoxicating a black elephant, desired to destroy Buddha.[67]
To the north-east of the city, in a crooked defile, (*the
physician*) Jîvaka[68] erected a *vihâra* in the garden of Amba-
pâlî, and invited Buddha and his 1250 disciples to receive
her religious offerings. The ruins still exist. Within the
city all is desolate and without inhabitants.

XXIX. Entering the valley and striking the mountains
towards the south-east, ascending 15 li we arrive at the
hill called Grïdhrakûṭa. Three li from the top is a stone
cavern facing the south. Buddha used in this place to
sit in meditation.[69] Thirty paces to the north-west is
another stone cell in which Ânanda practised meditation.
The Dêva Mâra Piśuna, having assumed the form of a
vulture, took his place before the cavern and terrified
Ânanda. Buddha by his spiritual power pierced the
rock, and with his outstretched hand patted Ânanda's
shoulder.[70] On this his fear was allayed. The traces of
the bird and of the hand-hole are still quite plain; on
this account the hill is called "The Hill of the Vulture
Cave." In front of the cave is the place where the four
Buddhâs sat down. Each of the Arhats likewise has a
cave where he sat in meditation. Altogether there are
several hundreds of these. Here also, when Buddha was
walking to and fro from east to west in front of his cell,
Dévadatta, from between the northern eminences of the

[66] For this incident see vol. ii. p. 178.

[67] For this incident see *Fo sho.*, pp. 246-247.

[68] See vol. ii. p. 152.

[69] For these places see vol. ii. p. 153 ff.

[70] Hiuen Tsiang says "*his head*," vol. ii. p. 154.

mountain, rolled down athwart his path a stone which wounded Buddha's toe. The stone is still there. The hall in which Buddha preached has been destroyed; the foundations of the brick walls [71] still exist, however. The peaks of this mountain are picturesque and imposing; it is the loftiest of the five mountains. Fa-Hian having bought flowers, incense, and oil and lamps in the new town, procured the assistance of two aged Bhikshus as guides. Fa-Hian, ascending the Grĭdhrakûṭa mountain, offered his flowers and incense and lit his lamps for the night. Being deeply moved, he could scarcely restrain his tears as he said, " Here it was in bygone days Buddha dwelt and delivered the *Suraṅgama Sûtra.* Fa-Hian, not privileged to be born when Buddha lived, can but gaze on the traces of his presence and the place which he occupied." Then he recited the Śuraṅgama [72] in front of the cave, and remaining there all night, he returned to the new town.

XXX. Some 300 paces north of the old town, on the west side of the road, is the Kalaṇḍavêṇuvana *vihâra.* It still exists, and a congregation of priests sweep and water it. Two or three li to the north of the chapel is the Shi-mo-she-na (Śamaśâna), which signifies " the field of tombs for laying the dead." Striking the southern hill and proceeding westward 300 paces, there is a stone cell called the Pippala [73] cave, where Buddha was accustomed to sit in meditation after his mid-day meal. Still west five or six li there is a stone cave situated in the northern shade of the mountain and called Che-ti.[74] This is the place where 500 Arhats assembled after the *Nirvâṇa* of Buddha to arrange the collection of sacred books. At the time when the books were recited three vacant seats

[71] It was, therefore, a structural building, not a cave.

[72] This *Sûtra* must not be confused with the expanded one of the same name. There is a full account of this perilous visit of Fa-hian to the top of the Grĭdhrakûṭa hill, and how he was attacked by tigers, in the "history of the high priests" (*K'o-sang-chuen*).

[73] Vol. ii. p. 156.

[74] Vol. ii. p. 161.

were specially prepared and adorned. The one on the left was for Śâriputra, the one on the right for Mudgalyâyana. The assembly was yet short of 500 by one Arhat; and already the great Kâśyapa was ascending the throne when Ânanda stood without the gate unable to find admission;[75] on this spot they have raised a tower which still exists. Still skirting the mountain, we find very many other stone cells used by the Arhats for the purpose of meditation. Leaving the old city and going north-east three li, we arrive at the stone cell of Dêvadatta, fifty paces from which there is a great square black stone. Some time ago there was a Bhikshu who walked forward and backward on this stone meditating on the impermanency, the sorrow, and vanity of his body (*life*). Thus realising the character of impurity, loathing himself, he drew his knife and would have killed himself. But then he reflected that the Lord of the World had forbidden self-murder. But then again he thought, "Although that is so, yet I am simply anxious to destroy the three poisonous thieves (*evil desire, hatred, ignorance*)." Then again he drew his knife and cut his throat. On the first gash he obtained the degree of Srôtâpanna; when he had half done the work he arrived at the condition of Anâgâmin, and after completing the deed he obtained the position of an Arhat and entered *Nirvâna.*

XXXI. Going west from this four *yôjanas*, we arrive at the town of Gayâ. All within this city likewise is desolate and desert. Going south 20 li, we arrive at the place where Bôdhisattva, when alive, passed six years in self-inflicted austerities. This place is well wooded. From this place westward three li, is the spot where Buddha entered the water to bathe and the dêva lowered the branch of a tree to help him out of the water. Again, going north two li, we arrive at the place where the village girls[76] gave the milk and rice to Buddha. From this going north

[75] Cf. *Abstract of Four Lectures,* p. 72.

[76] Mi-kia for Grâmika, or Grâmikî; as *Ni-kia,* for Ka-ni-kia.

two li is the spot where Buddha, seated on a stone under a great tree, and looking towards the east, ate the rice and milk. The tree and the stone still remain. The stone is about six feet square and two in height. In Mid-India the heat and cold are so equalised that trees will live for thousands of years, and even so many as ten thousand. Going north-east from this half a *yôjana*, we arrive at a stone cell, into which Bôdhisattva entering, sat down with his legs crossed, and as he faced the west he reflected with himself, " If I am to arrive at the condition of perfect wisdom, let there be some spiritual manifestation." Immediately on the stone wall there appeared the shadow of Buddha, in length somewhat about three feet. This shadow is still distinctly visible. Then the heavens and the earth were shaken, and all the dêvas in space cried out and said, " This is not the place appointed for the Buddhas (*past* or *those to come*) to arrive at perfect wisdom; at a distance less than half a *yôjana* south-west from this, beneath the Pei-to tree, is the spot where all the Buddhas (*past* or *yet to come*) should arrive at that condition." The dêvas having thus spoken, immediately went before him, singing and leading the way with a view to induce him to follow. Then Bôdhisattva, rising up, followed them. When distant thirty paces from the tree, a dêva gave him some grass of good omen.[77] Bôdhisattva having accepted it, advanced fifteen paces. Then 500 blue birds[78] came flying towards him, and having encircled Bôdhisattva three times, departed. Bôdhisattva, then going forward, arrived under the Pei-to tree, and spreading out the grass of good omen, sat down with his face towards the east. Then it was that Mâra-râja dispatched three pleasure-girls from the northern quarter to come and tempt him, whilst Mâra himself coming from the south, assailed him likewise. Then Bôdhisattva letting the toe of his foot down to the earth, the whole army of Mâra was scat-

[77] Kuśa grass.
[78] For this and other incidents, see vol. ii. p. 124. Consult also the notes in Fah-hian (Beal's *Bud. Pilg.*, p. 123).

tered, and the three women were changed into hags. On the place above mentioned, where he inflicted on himself mortification for six years, and on each spot subsequently mentioned, men in after times raised towers and placed figures (*of Buddha*), which still remain. Buddha having arrived at supreme wisdom, for seven days sat contemplating the tree, experiencing the joys of emancipation. On this spot they have raised a tower, as well as on the following, viz., where he walked for seven days under the Pei-to tree, from east to west; where all the dêvas, having caused the appearance of a hall composed of the seven precious substances, for seven days paid religious worship to Buddha; where the blind dragon Muchilinda for seven days encircled Buddha in token of respect; also where Buddha, seated on a square stone beneath a Nyagrôdha tree, and with his face to the east, received the respectful salutation of Brahmâ; also where the four heavenly kings respectfully offered him his alms-bowl; also where the 500 merchants presented him with parched corn and honey; also where he converted the Kâśyapas, elder and younger brothers, and their thousand disciples. In the place where Buddha arrived at perfect reason there are three *sanghârâmas*, in all of which priests are located. The dependants of the congregation of priests supply them with all necessaries, so that there is no lack of anything. They scrupulously observe the rules of the Vinaya with respect to decorum, which relate to sitting down, rising up, or entering the assembly; and the rules which the holy congregation observed during Buddha's lifetime are still observed by these priests. The sites of the four great pagodas have always been associated together from the time of the *Nirvâna*. The four great pagodas are those erected on the place where he was born, where he obtained emancipation, where he began to preach, and where he entered *Nirvâna*.

XXXII. Formerly, when King Aśôka was a lad,[79] playing

<hr>

[79] That is, in a previous birth.

on the road, he met Sâkya Buddha going begging. The little boy, rejoiced at the chance, gave him a handful of earth as an offering. Buddha received it, and on his return sprinkled it on the ground where he took his exercise. In return for this act of charity the lad became an iron-wheel king and ruled over Jambudvîpa. On assuming the iron-wheel he was on a certain occasion going through Jambudvîpa on a tour of inspection, at which time he saw one of the places of torment for the punishment of wicked men situated between the two iron-circle mountains. He immediately asked his attendant ministers, " What is this place ? " To this they replied and said, " This is the place where Yâma-râja, the infernal king, inflicts punishment on wicked men for their crimes." The king then began to reflect and said, " If the demon king, in the exercise of his function, requires to have a place of punishment for wicked men, why should not I, who rule men (*on earth*), have a place of punishment likewise for the guilty ? " On this he asked his ministers, " Who is there that I can appoint to make for me a hell,[80] and to exercise authority therein for the punishment of wicked men ? " In reply they said, " None but a very wicked man can fulfil such an office." The king forthwith dispatched his ministers in every direction to seek for such a man. In the course of their search they saw, by the side of a running stream, a lusty great fellow of a black colour, with red hair and light eyes ; with the talons of his feet he caught the fish, and when he whistled to the birds and beasts, they came to him ; and as they approached he mercilessly shot them through, so that none escaped. Having caught this man, he was brought before the king. The king then gave him these secret orders, " You must enclose a square space with high walls, and with this enclosure plant every kind of flower and fruit (*tree*), and make beautiful alcoves, and arrange everything with such taste as to make people anxious to look within.

[80] For this incident see vol. ii. p. 85.

Make a wide gate to it, and then when any one enters, seize him at once and subject him to every kind of torture. Let no one (*who has once entered*) ever go out again. And I strictly enjoin you, that if I even should enter, that you torture me also and spare not. Now, then, I appoint you lord of this place of torment!" It happened that a certain Bhikshu, as he was going his rounds begging for food, entered the gate. The infernal keeper seeing him, made preparations to put him to torture. The Bhikshu, being much frightened, suppliantly begged a moment's respite. "Permit me, at least, to partake of my mid-day meal," he said. It so happened that just then another man entered the place, on which the keeper directly seized him, and, putting him in a stone mortar, began to. pound his body to atoms till a red froth formed. The Bhikshu having witnessed this spectacle, began to reflect on the impermanency, the sorrow, the vanity of bodily existence, that it is like a bubble and froth of the sea, and so he arrived at the condition of an Arhat. This having transpired, the infernal keeper laid hold of him and thrust him into a caldron of boiling water. The heart of the Bhikshu and his countenance were full of joy. The fire was extinguished and the water became cold, whilst in the middle of it there sprang up a lotus, on the top of which the Bhikshu took his seat. The keeper forthwith proceeded to the king and said, "A wonderful miracle has occurred in the place of torture; would that your majesty would come and see it." The king said, "I dare not come, in consideration of my former agreement with you." The keeper replied, "This matter is one of great moment: it is only right you should come; let us consider your former agreement changed." The king then directly followed him and entered the prison; on which the Bhikshu, for his sake, delivered a religious discourse, so that the king believed and was converted. Then he ordered the place of torture to be destroyed, and repented of all the evil he had formerly committed. From the time of his conversion he exceedingly honoured the three precious ones (*i.e.*, Buddha, Dharma, Saṅgha), and went continually to the spot underneath the Pei-to tree for the purpose of repentance, self-examination, and fasting. In consequence of this, the queen on one occasion asked, " Where does the king go so constantly ? " The ministers replied, " He continually resides under the Pei-to tree." The queen hereupon, awaiting an opportunity when the king was not there, sent men to cut the tree down. The king repairing as usual to the spot, and seeing what had happened, was so overpowered with grief that he fell down senseless on the ground. The ministers, bathing his face with water, after a long time restored him to consciousness. Then the king piled up the earth on the four sides of the stump of the tree, and commanded the roots to be moistened with a hundred pitchers of milk. Then prostrating himself at full length on the ground, he made the following vow, " If the tree does not revive I will never rise up again." No sooner had he done this than the tree began to force up small branches from the root, and so it continued to grow until it arrived at its present height, which is somewhat less than 120 feet.

XXXIII. From this place going south three li, we arrive at a mountain called the Cock's-foot. The great Kâśyapa is at present within this mountain.[81] He divided the mountain at its base, so as to open a passage (*for himself*). This entrance is now closed up (*impassable*). At a considerable distance from this spot there is a side chasm; it is in this the entire body of Kâśyapa is now preserved. Outside this chasm is the place where Kâśyapa, when alive, washed his hands. The people of that region who are afflicted with headaches use the earth brought from the place as an ointment, and this immediately cures them. As soon as the sun begins to decline [82] the Arhats come and take

[81] For an account of this mountain see vol. ii. p. 144.

[82] Or, it may be translated, "Therefore, since then, there have been Arhats," &c. ; but this is not so agreeable with the context as the translation I have given. .

their abode in this hill. Buddhist pilgrims of that and other countries come year by year to pay religious worship to Kâśyapa; if any should happen to be distressed with doubts, directly the sun goes down the Arhats arrive and begin to discourse with (*the pilgrims*) and explain their doubts and difficulties; and, having done so, forthwith they disappear. The thickets about this hill are dense and tangled. There are, moreover, many lions, tigers, and wolves prowling about, so that it is not possible to travel without great care.

XXXIV. Fa-Hian returning towards Pâṭaliputra, kept along the course of the Ganges, and after going ten *yôjanas* in a westerly direction, arrived at a *vihâra* called "Desert" (Kwang-ye), in which Buddha resided. Priests still dwell in it. Still keeping along the course of the Ganges and going west twelve *yôjanas*, we arrive at the country of Kâśi and the city of Bânâras. About ten li or so to the north-east of this city is the chapel of the deer park of the Ṛishis. This garden was once occupied by a Pratyêka Buddha. There are always wild deer reposing in it for shelter. When the Lord of the World was about to arrive at supreme wisdom, all the dêvas in space began to chant a hymn and say, " The son of Śuddhôdana-râja, who has left his home to acquire supreme wisdom, after seven days will arrive at the condition of Buddha." The Pratyêka Buddha hearing this, immediately entered *Nirvâna*. Therefore the name of this place is the deer park of the Ṛishi. The world-honoured Buddha having arrived at complete knowledge, men in after ages erected a *vihâra* on this spot. Buddha being desirous to convert Âjñâtâ Kaundinya and his companions, known as the five men, they communed one with another and said, " This Śramana Gautama having for six years practised mortifications, reducing himself to the daily use of but one grain of hemp and one of rice, and in spite of this having failed to obtain supreme wisdom, how much less shall he now obtain that condition by entering into men's society and removing the checks he placed upon his words and thoughts and actions! To-day when he comes here, let us carefully avoid all conversation with him." On Buddha's arrival the five men rose and saluted him, and here they have erected a tower; also on the following spots, viz., on a site sixty paces to the north of the former place, where Buddha, seated with his face to the east, began to turn the wheel of the law (to preach) for the purpose of converting Kauṇḍinya and his companions (*known as*) "the five men;" also on a spot twenty paces to the north of this, where Buddha delivered his prediction concerning Maitrêya; also on a spot fifty paces to the south of this, where the dragon Êlâpatra asked Buddha at what time he should be delivered from his dragon-form; in all these places towers have been erected which still exist. In the midst (*of the park*) there are two *sanghârâmas* which still have priests dwelling in them. Proceeding north-west thirteen *yôjanas* from the park of the deer, there is a country called Kauśâmbî. There is a *vihâra* there called Ghôshira-vana (*the garden of Ghôshira*), in which Buddha formerly dwelt; it is now in ruins. There are congregations here, principally belonging to the system known as the Little Vehicle. Eight *yôjanas* east of this place is a place where Buddha once took up his residence and converted an evil demon. They have also erected towers on various spots where he sat or walked for exercise when he was resident in this neighbourhood. There are *san-ghârâmas* still existing here, and perhaps a hundred priests.

XXXV. Going 200 *yôjanas* south from this, there is a country called Ta-Thsin (Dakshiṇa). Here is a *sanghâ-râma* of the former Buddha Kâśyapa.[83] It is constructed out of a great mountain of rock, hollowed to the proper shape.

---

[83] This convent is described by Hiuen Tsiang in Book x. It was probably dedicated to Pârvatî (the Po-lo-yu of Fa-hian, which he translates "pigeon"—*pârâvata*) or Chandâ, and is situated in the Chanda district of the Dekhan. The King Sadvaha, a friend of Nâgârjuna, was probably the same as the Sindhuka of the *Vayu-Purâṇa.* He is called Shi-în-teh-kia by I-tsing.

This building has altogether five stages. The lowest is made with elephant figures, and has five hundred stone cells in it. The second is made with lion shapes, and has four hundred chambers. The third is made with horse shapes, and has three hundred chambers. The fourth is made with ox shapes, and has two hundred chambers. The fifth is made with dove shapes, and has one hundred chambers in it. At the very top of all is a spring of water, which, flowing in a stream before the rooms, encircles each tier, and so, running in a circuitous course, at last arrives at the very lowest stage of all, where, flowing past the chambers, it finally issues through the door. Throughout the consecutive tiers, in various parts of the building, windows have been pierced through the solid rock for the admission of light, so that every chamber is quite illuminated and there is no darkness. At the four corners of this edifice they have hewn out the rock into steps, as means for ascending. Men of the present time, being small of stature, ascend the ladder and thus reach the top in the usual way; but men of old reached it with one foot.[84] The reason· why they name this building Po-lo-yu is from an Indian word signifying " pigeon." There are always Arhats abiding here. This land is barren and without inhabitants. At a considerable distance from the hill there are villages, but all of them are inhabited by heretics. They know nothing of the law of Buddha, or Śramaṇas, or Brâhmaṇas, or of any of the different schools of learning. The men of that country continually see persons come flying to the temple. On a certain occasion there were some Buddhist pilgrims from different countries who came here to pay religious worship. Then the men of the villages above alluded to asked them, saying, " Why do you not fly ? All the religious persons hereabouts that we see (*are able to*) fly." These men then answered by way of excuse, " Because our wings are not yet perfectly formed." The country of Ta-Thsin (Dekhan) is precipitous and the roads

[84] Referring perhaps to the *one-footed men* of Ktesias. It may possibly be, "*at one bound.*"

dangerous. Those who wish to go there, even if they know the place, ought to give a present to the king of the country, either money or goods. The king then deputes certain men to accompany them as guides, and so they pass the travellers from one place to another, each party pointing out their own roads and intricate bypaths. Fa-Hian finding himself in the end unable to proceed to that country, reports in the above passages merely what he has heard.

XXXVI. From Bânâras going eastward we arrive at the town of Pâṭaliputra again. The purpose of Fa-Hian was to seek for copies of the *Vinaya Piṭaka;* but throughout the whole of Northern India the various masters trusted to tradition only for their knowledge of the precepts, and had no originals to copy from. Wherefore Fa-Hian had come even so far as Mid-India. But here in the *sanghârâma* of the Great Vehicle he obtained one collection of the precepts, viz., the collection used by the Mahâsanghika assembly. This was that used by the first great assembly of priests during Buddha's lifetime. It is reported that this was the one used in the Jêtavana *vihâra.* Except that the eighteen sects have each their own private rules of conduct,[85] they are agreed in essentials. In some minor details they differ, as well as in a more or less exact attention to matters of practice. But the collection (*of this sect*) is regarded as the most correct and complete. Moreover, he obtained one copy of precepts from dictation, comprising about *7000 gâthâs.* This version was that used by the assembly belonging to the school of the Sarvâstivâdas; the same, in fact, as is generally used in China. The masters of this school also hand down the precepts by word of mouth, and do not commit them to writing. Moreover, in this assembly he obtained a copy of the *Samyuktâbhidharma-hṛidaya Śâstra,* including altogether about 6000 *gâthâs.* Moreover, he obtained a copy of the *Nirvâṇa Sûtra,* consisting altogether of 2500 verses.

[85] *Vide* I-tsing, *Nan-hai,* § 25.

Moreover, he obtained in one volume the *Vâipulya-pari-nirvâna Sûtra*, containing about 5000 verses. Moreover, he procured a copy of the *Abhidharma* according to the school of the Mahâsaṅghikas. On this account Fa-Hian abode in this place for the space of three years engaged in learning to read the Sanskṛit[86] books, and to converse in that language, and in copying the precepts. When To-ching arrived in Mid-India and saw the customary behaviour of the Śramaṇas, and the strict decorum observed by the assembly of priests, and their religious deportment, even to the smallest matters, then, sorrowfully reflecting on the meagre character of the precepts known to the different assemblies of priests in the border-land of China, he bound himself by a vow and said, " From the present time for ever till I obtain the condition of Buddha, may I never again be born in a frontier country." And in accordance with this expression of his wish, he took up his permanent abode in this place, and did not return. And so Fa-Hian, desiring, according to his original purpose, to spread the knowledge of the precepts throughout the land of Han (China), returned alone.

XXXVII. Following down the river Ganges in an easterly direction for eighteen *yôjanas*, we come to the great king-dom of Chen-po (Champâ) on its southern shore. In the place where Buddha once dwelt, and where he moved to and fro for exercise, also where the four previous Buddhas sat down, in all these places towers have been erected, and there are still resident priests. From this continuing to go eastward nearly fifty *yôjanas*, we arrive at the kingdom of Tâmralipti. This is at the sea-mouth. There are twenty-four *saṅghârâmas* in this country; all of them have resident priests, and the law of Buddha is generally respected. Fa-Hian remained here for two years, writing out copies of the sacred books (*sûtras*) and drawing image-pictures. He then shipped himself on board a great merchant vessel. Putting to sea, they pro-

86 Fan.

ceeded in a south-westerly direction, catching the first fair wind of the winter season. They sailed for fourteen days and nights, and arrived at the country of the lions (Siṁhala, Ceylon). Men of that country (Tâmralipti) say that the distance between the two is about 700 *yôjanas.* This kingdom (*of lions*) is situated on a great island. From east to west it is fifty *yôjanas*, and from north to south thirty *yôjanas.* On every side of it are small islands, perhaps amounting to a hundred in number. They are distant from one another ten or twenty li and as much as 200 li. All of them depend on the great island. Most of them produce precious stones and pearls. The *mâni*-gem is also found in one district, embracing a surface perhaps of ten li. The king sends a guard to protect the place. If any gems are found, the king claims three out of every ten.

XXXVIII. This kingdom had originally no inhabitants, but only demons and dragons dwelt in it. Merchants of different countries (*however*) came here to trade. At the time of traffic, the demons did not appear in person, but only exposed their valuable commodities with the value affixed. Then the merchantmen, according to the prices marked, purchased the goods and took them away. But in consequence of these visits (*coming, going, and stopping*), men of other countries, hearing of the delightful character of the place, flocked there in great numbers, and so a great kingdom was formed. This country enjoys an agreeable climate, without any differences in winter or summer. The plants and trees are always verdant. The fields are sown just according to men's inclination; there are no fixed seasons. Buddha came to this country from a desire to convert a malevolent dragon. By his spiritual power he planted one foot to the north of the royal city, and one on the top of a mountain, the distance between the two being fifteen *yôjanas.* Over the foot-impression (*on the hill*) to the north of the royal city, is erected a great tower, in height 470 feet. It is adorned with gold and silver, and perfected with every precious substance. By the side of this tower, moreover, is erected a *saṅghârâma*, which is called Abhayagiri, containing 5000 priests. They have also built here a hall of Buddha, which is covered with gold and silver engraved work, conjoined with all precious substances. In the midst of this hall is a jasper figure (*of Buddha*), in height about 22 feet. The entire body glitters and sparkles with the seven precious substances, whilst the various characteristic marks are so gloriously portrayed that no words can describe the effect. In the right hand it holds a pearl of inestimable value. Fa-Hian had now been absent many years from the land of Han ; the manners and customs of the people with whom he had intercourse were entirely strange to him. The towns, people, mountains, valleys, and plants and trees which met his eyes, were unlike those of old times. Moreover, his fellow-travellers were now separated from him—some had remained behind, and some were dead. To consider the shadow (*of the past*) was all that was left him ; and so his heart was continually saddened. All at once, as he was standing by the side of this jasper figure, he beheld a merchant present to it as a religious offering a white taffeta fan of Chinese manufacture. Unwittingly (Fa-Hian) gave way to his sorrowful feelings, and the tears flowing down · filled his eyes. A former king of this country sent an embassy to Mid-India to procure a slip of the Pei-to tree. This they planted by the side of the Hall of Buddha. When it was about 220 feet high, the tree began to lean towards the south-east. The king, fearing it would fall, placed eight or nine surrounding props to support the tree. Just in the place where the tree was thus supported it put forth a branch which pierced through the props, and, descending to the earth, took root. This branch is about twenty inches round. The props, although pierced through the centre, still surround (*the tree*), which stands now without their support, yet men have not removed them.

Under the tree is erected a chapel, in the middle of which

is a figure (*of Buddha*) in a sitting posture. Both the clergy and laity pay reverence to this figure with little intermission. Within the capital, moreover, is erected the chapel of the tooth of Buddha, in the construction of which all the seven precious substances have been employed. The king purifies himself according to the strictest Brâhmaṇical rules, whilst those men within the city who reverence (*this relic*) from a principle of belief also compose their passions according to strict rule. This kingdom, from the time it has been so governed, has suffered neither from famine, calamity, nor revolution. The treasury of this congregation of priests contains numerous gems and a *mâni*-jewel of inestimable value. Their king once entered the treasury, and, going round it for the purpose of inspection, he saw there this *mâni*-gem. On beholding it, a covetous feeling sprung up in his heart, and he desired to take it away with him. For three days this thought afflicted him, but then he came to his right mind. He directly repaired to the assembly of the priests, and bowing down his head, he repented of his former wicked purpose, and addressing them, said, " Would that you would make a rule from this time forth and for ever, on no account to allow a king to enter your treasury, and no Bhikshu except he is of forty years' seniority—after that time he may be permitted to enter." There are many noblemen and rich householders within the city. The houses of the Sa-poh (Sabæan) merchants are very beautifully adorned. The streets and passages are smooth and level. At the head of the four principal streets there are preaching halls. On the 8th, 14th, and 15th day of the month they prepare a lofty throne within each of these buildings, and the religious members of the community of the four classes all congregate to hear the preaching of the law. The men of this country say that there are in the country altogether fifty or sixty thousand priests, all of whom live in community (*have their food* [commons] *provided*). Besides these, the king supplies five or six thousand persons within the city with food in common (*or*, with common food (*commons*)). These persons, when they require, take their alms-bowls and go (*to the appointed place*), and, according to the measure of the bowls, fill them and return. They always bring out the tooth of Buddha in the middle of the third month. Ten days beforehand, the king magnificently caparisons a great elephant, and commissions a man of eloquence and ability to clothe himself in royal apparel, and, riding on the elephant, to sound a drum and proclaim as follows:— " Bôdhisattva during three *Asañkhyéya kalpas* underwent every kind of austerity; he spared himself no personal sufferings; he left his country, wife, and child; moreover, he tore out his eyes to bestow them on another, he mangled his flesh to deliver a dove (*from the hawk*), he sacrificed his head in alms, he gave his body to a famishing tiger, he grudged not his marrow or brain. Thus he endured every sort of agony for the sake of all flesh. Moreover, when he became perfect Buddha, he lived in the world forty-nine years preaching the law and teaching and converting men. He gave rest to the wretched, he saved the lost. Having passed through countless births, he then entered *Nirvâna*. Since that event is 1497 years. The eyes of the world were then put out, and all flesh deeply grieved. After ten days the tooth of (*this same*) Buddha will be brought forth and taken to the Abhayagiri *vihâra*. Let all ecclesiastical and lay persons within the kingdom, who wish to lay up a store of merit, prepare and smooth the roads, adorn the streets and highways; let them scatter every kind of flower, and offer incense in religious reverence to the relic." This proclamation being finished, the king next causes to be placed on both sides of the procession-road representations of the five hundred bodily forms which Bôdhisattva assumed during his successive births. For instance, his birth as Sudâna;[87] his appearance

---

[87] The *Sudâna Jâtaka*, the same as the *Vesantara Jâtaka*; both this and the *Sâma Jâtaka* are among the Sânchi sculptures.

as Sâma ; his birth as the king of the elephants, and as an antelope. These figures are all beautifully painted in divers colours, and have a very life-like appearance. At length the tooth of Buddha is brought forth and conducted along the principal road. As they proceed on the way, religious offerings are made to it. When they arrive at the Abhaya *vihâra* they place it in the Hall of Buddha, where the clergy and laity all assemble in vast crowds and burn incense, and light lamps, and perform every kind of religious ceremony, both night and day, without ceasing. After ninety complete days they again return it to the *vihâra* within the city. This chapel is thrown open on fast days for the purpose of religious worship, as the law (of Buddha) directs. Forty li to the east of the Abhaya *vihâra* is a mountain, on which is built a chapel called Po-ti (*Bôdhi*) ; there are about 2000 priests in it. Amongst them is a very distinguished Shaman called Ta-mo-kiu-ti (Dharmakôti or Dharmagupta). The people of this country greatly respect and reverence him. He resides in a cell, where he has lived for about forty years. By the constant practice of benevolence he has been able to tame the serpents and mice, so that they stop together in one cell, and do not hurt one another.

XXXIX. Seven li to the south of the capital is a chapel called Mahâvihâra, in which there are 3000 priests. Amongst them was a very eminent Śramaṇa, whose life was so pure that the men of the country generally gave him credit for being an Arhat. At the time of his approaching death, the king, having come to inspect and inquire, according to the custom of the law, assembled the priests and asked the Bhikshu, "Hast thou attained reason?" On which he made reply in truth, "I am an Arhat." After his death, the king immediately examined the sacred books, with a view to perform the funeral obsequies according to the rules for such as are Arhats. Accordingly, about four or five li to the east of the *vihâra* they raised a very great pyre of wood, about 34 feet square and of the same height.　Near the top they placed tiers of sandal-wood, aloe, and all kinds of scented wood.　On the four sides they constructed steps.　Then, taking some clean and very white camlet cloth, they bound it around and above the pyre.　They then constructed above a funeral carriage, like the hearses used in this country, except that there are no dragon-ear handles (cf. *ting urh*).　Then, at the time of the cremation (*dāva*), the king, accompanied by the four classes of the people, assembled in great numbers, came to the spot provided with flowers and incense for religious offerings, and followed the hearse till it arrived at the place of the funeral ceremony.　The king, then, in his own person, offered religious worship with flowers and incense.　This being over, the hearse was placed on the pyre, and oil of cinnamon poured over it in all directions.　Then they set light to the whole.　At the time of kindling the fire, the whole assembly occupied their minds with solemn thoughts.　Then removing their upper garments, and taking their wing-like fans, which they use as sun-shades, and approaching as near as possible to the pyre, they flung them into the midst of the fire in order to assist the cremation.　When all was over, they diligently searched for the bones and collected them together, in order to raise a tower over them.　Fa-Hian did not arrive in time to see this celebrated person alive, but only to witness his funeral obsequies.　At this time, the king, being an earnest believer in the law of Buddha, desired to build a new *vihâra* for this congregation of priests.　First of all he provided for them a great feast, after which he selected a pair of strong working oxen and ornamented their horns with gold, silver, and precious things.　Then providing himself with a beautiful gilded plough, the king himself ploughed round the four sides of the allotted space;[88] after which, ceding all personal right over the land, houses, or people within the area thus enclosed, he presented (*the whole to the*

---

[88] A *king*, or 15$\frac{14}{16}$ acres.

priests).   Then he caused to be engraved on a metal plate (*the following inscription*):—"From this time and for all generations hereafter, let this property be handed down from one (*body of priests*) to the other, and let no one dare to alienate it, or change (*the character of*) the grant."   When Fa-Hian was residing in this country, he heard a religious brother from India, seated on a high throne, reciting a sacred book and saying, " The Pâtra (*alms-bowl*) of Buddha originally was preserved in Vaiśâlî, but now it is in the borders of Gandhâra.   After an uncertain period of years [Fa-Hian, at the time of the recital, heard the exact number of years, but he has now forgotten it], it will go on to the country of the western Yu-chi. After another period it will go to the country of Khotan. After a similar period it will be transported to Kouché. In about the same period it will come back to the land of Han ; after the same period it will return to the land of lions (Simhala, Ceylon); after the same period it will return to Mid-India; after which it will be taken up into the Tushta heaven.   Then Maitrêya Bôdhisattva will exclaim with a sigh, ' The alms-dish of Śâkyamuni Buddha has come.'   Then all the Dêvas will pay religious worship to it with flowers and incense for seven days.   After this it will return to Jambudvîpa, and a sea-dragon, taking it, will carry it within his palace, awaiting till Maitrêya is about to arrive at complete wisdom, at which time the bowl, again dividing itself into four as it was at first, will re-ascend the Pin-na[89] mountain.   After Maitrêya has arrived at supreme wisdom, the four heavenly Kings will once more come and respectfully salute him as Buddha, after the same manner as they have done to the former Buddhas.   The thousand Buddhas of this Bhadra-kalpa will all of them use this same alms-dish ; when the bowl has disappeared, then the law of Buddha will gradually perish ; after which the years of man's life will begin to contract until it be no more than five years in duration.

[89] In some places this is written An-na, as though for (Sum)ana.

At the time of its being ten years in length, rice and butter will disappear from the world, and men will become extremely wicked. The sticks they grasp will then transform themselves into knives and clubs, with which they will attack one another, and wound and kill each other. In the midst of this, men who have acquired religious merit will escape and seek refuge in the mountains; and when the wicked have finished the work of mutual destruction, they will come from their hiding-places, and will converse together and say, ' Men of old lived to a very advanced age, but now, because wicked men have indulged without restraint in every transgression of the law, our years have dwindled down to their present short span, even to the space of ten years. Now, therefore, let us practise every kind of good deed, encouraging within ourselves a kind and loving spirit; let us enter on a course of virtue and righteousness.' Thus, as each one practises faith and justice, their years will begin to increase in double ratio till they reach 80,000 years of life. At the time when Maitrêya is born, when he first begins to declare his doctrine (turn the wheel of the law), his earliest converts will be the followers of the bequeathed law of Sâkya Buddha, those who have forsaken their families, those who have sought refuge in the three sacred names, those who have kept the five great commandments, and attended to their religious duties in making continued offerings to the three precious objects of worship. His second and third body of converts shall be those who, by their previous conduct, have put themselves in a condition for salvation." Fa-Hian, on hearing this discourse, wished to copy it down, on which the man said, " This has no Scripture-original; I only repeat by word of mouth (*what I have learned*)."

XL. Fa-Hian resided in this country for two years. Continuing his search, he obtained a copy of the *Vinaya Piṭaka* according to the school of the Mahîsâsakas. He also obtained a copy of the Great *Âgama* (*Dîrghâgama*), and of the Miscellaneous *Âgama* (*Saṃyuktâgama*), and also a collection of the Miscellaneous *Piṭaka* (*Sannipâta*). All these were hitherto unknown in the land of Han. Having obtained these works in the original language (*Fan*), he forthwith shipped himself on board a great merchant vessel, which carried about two hundred men. Astern of the great ship was a smaller one, in case the larger vessel should be injured or wrecked. Having got a fair wind, they sailed eastward for two days, when suddenly a tempest (*typhoon*) arose, and the ship sprung a leak. The merchants then desired to haul up the smaller vessel, but the crew of that ship, fearing that a crowd of men would rush into her and sink her, cut the towing cable and she fell off. The merchantmen were greatly terrified, expecting their death momentarily. Then dreading lest the leak should gain upon them, they forthwith took their heavy goods and merchandise and cast them overboard. Fa-Hian also flung overboard his water-pitcher (*kuṇḍikâ*) and his washing-basin, and also other portions of his property. He was only afraid lest the merchants should fling into the sea his sacred books and images. And so with earnestness of heart he invoked Avalôkitêśvara, and paid reverence to the Buddhist saints (*the priesthood*) of the land of Han, speaking thus: " I indeed have wandered far and wide in search of the law. Oh, bring me back again, by your spiritual power, to reach some resting-place." And so the hurricane blew on for thirteen days and nights; they then arrived at the shore of a small island, and on the tide going out they found the place of the leak. Having forthwith stopped it up, they again put to sea on their onward voyage. In this ocean there are many pirates, who, coming on you suddenly, destroy everything. The sea itself is boundless in extent ; it is impossible to know east or west except by observing the sun, moon, or stars, and so progress. If it is dark, rainy weather, the only plan is to steer by the wind without guide. During the darkness of night we only see the great waves beating one against the other and shining like fire, whilst shoals of

sea-monsters of every description (*surround the ship*).
The merchants, perplexed, knew not towards what land
they were steering. The sea was bottomless and no
soundings could be found, so that there was no chance
of anchoring. At length, the weather clearing up, they
got their right bearings, and once more shaped a correct
course and proceeded onwards; but if (*during the bad
weather*) they had happened to have struck on a hidden
rock, there could have been no escape. Thus they voyaged
for ninety days and more, when they arrived at a country
called Ye-po-ti (Java, *or, perhaps*, Sumatra). In this
country heretics and Brâhmaṇs flourish, but the law
of Buddha is not much known. Stopping here the
best portion of five months, Fa-Hian again embarked on
board another merchant vessel, having also a crew of two
hundred men or so. They took with them fifty days'
provisions, and set sail on the 16th day of the fourth
month. Fa-Hian kept his "rest" on board this ship.
They shaped a course north-east for Kwang-chow. After
a month and some days, when sounding the middle
watch of the night, a black squall suddenly came on,
accompanied with pelting rain. The merchantmen and
passengers were all terrified. Fa-Hian at this time also,
with great earnestness of mind, again entreated Avalôkitêśvara and all the priesthood of China to exert their
divine power in their favour, and protect them till daylight.[90]
When the day broke, all the Brâhmaṇs, consulting together,
said, " It is because we have got this Śramaṇa on board we
have no luck, and have incurred this great mischief. Come,
let us land this Bhikshu on any island we meet, and let
us not all perish for the sake of one man." The religious
patron (*Dânapati*) of Fa-Hian then said, " If you land this
Bhikshu, you shall also land me with him; and if not,
you had better kill me: for if you put this Śramaṇa on
shore, then, when I arrive in China, I will go straight to
the king and report you; and the king of that country

90 Cf. ἤχοντο ἡμέραν γενέσθαι, Acts xxiii. 29.

is a firm believer in the law of Buddha, and greatly honours the Bhikshus and priests." The merchantmen on this hesitated, and (*in the end*) did not dare to land him. The weather continuing very dark, the pilot's observations were perversely wrong.[91] Nearly seventy days had now elapsed. The rice for food and the water for congee were nearly all done. They had to use salt water for cooking, whilst they gave out to every man about two pints of fresh water. And now, when this was just exhausted, the merchants held a conversation and said, " The proper time for the voyage to Kwang-Chow is about fifty days, but now we have exceeded that time these many days—shall we be perverse?" On this they put the ship on a north-west course to look for land. After twelve days' continuous sailing, they arrived at the southern coast of Lau-Shan which borders on the prefecture of Chang-Kwang. They then obtained good fresh water and vegetables ; and so, after passing through so many dangers and difficulties and such a succession of anxious days, (*the pilgrim*) suddenly arrived at this shore. On seeing the Lí-ho vegetable (*a sort of reed*), he was confident that this was indeed the land of Han. But not seeing any men or traces of life, they knew not what place it was. Some said they had not yet arrived at Kwang-chow, others maintained they had passed it. In their uncertainty, therefore, they put off in a little boat, and entered a creek to look for some one to ask where they were. Meeting with two hunters, they got them to go back with them, making Fa-Hian interpret their words and question them. Fa-Hian having first tried to inspire them with confidence, then leisurely asked them, " What men are you ? " They replied, " We are disciples of Buddha." Then he asked, " What do you look for in these mountains here ? " They prevaricated, and said, " To-morrow is the 15th day of the seventh month, and we were anxious to catch some-

[91] That is, he was perverse in following his wrong observations, or calculations.

thing to sacrifice to Buddha." Again he asked, "What country is this?" They replied, "This is Tsing-Chow, on the borders of the prefecture of Chang-Kwang, dependent on the house of Lin." Having heard this, the merchants were very glad, and immediately begging that their goods might be landed, they deputed men to go with them to Chang-Kwang. The prefect, Li-I, who was a faithful follower of the law of Buddha, hearing that there was a Śramaṇa arrived with sacred books and images in a ship from beyond the seas, immediately proceeded to the shore with his followers to escort the books and sacred figures to the seat of his government. After this the merchants returned towards Yang-Chow. Meanwhile Liu arriving at Tsing-Chow,[92] entertained Fa-Hian for the whole winter and summer. The summer period of rest being over, Fa-Hian, removed from the society of his fellow-priests for so long, was anxious to get back to Chang'an. But as his plans were important, he directed his course first towards the southern capital. Having met the priests, he exhibited the sacred books he had brought back.

Fa-Hian, leaving Chang'an, was five years in arriving at Mid-India. He resided there during six years, and was three years more before he arrived at Tsing-Chow. He had successively passed through nearly thirty different countries. In all the countries of India, after passing the sandy desert, the dignified carriage of the priesthood and the surprising influence of religion cannot be adequately described. But because our learned doctors had not heard of these things, he was induced, regardless of personal risk, to cross the seas, and to encounter every kind of danger in returning home. Having been preserved by divine power (*by the three honourable ones*), and brought through all dangers safely, he was further induced to commit to writing these records of his travels, desiring that honourable readers might be informed of them as well as himself.

[92] *Fă* for *chi* (?).

THE MISSION

OF

SUNG-YUN[1] AND HWEI SĂNG

TO OBTAIN

BUDDHIST BOOKS IN THE WEST.[2]   (518 A.D.)

*[Translated from the 5th Section of the History of the
Temples of Lo-Yang (Honan Fu).]*

IN the suburb Wen-I, to the north-east of the city of
Lo-Yang, was the dwelling of Sung-Yun of Tun-hwang,[3]
who, in company with the Bhikshu Hwei Săng, was sent
on an embassy to the western countries by the Empress
Dowager (Tai-Hau) of the Great Wei dynasty[4] to obtain
Buddhist books. This occurred in the eleventh month
of the first year of the period *Shén kwei* (517–518 A.D.)
They procured altogether 170 volumes, all standard works,
belonging to the Great Vehicle.

First of all, having repaired to the capital, they proceeded in a westerly direction forty days, and arrived at
the Chíh-Ling (Barren Ridge), which is the western frontier of the country. On this ridge is the fortified outpost
of the Wei territory. The Chíh-Ling produces no trees or
shrubs, and hence its name (*Barren*). Here is the common
resort (*cave*) of the rat-bird. These two animals being
of different species (*chung*), but the same genus (*lui*), live
and breed together. The bird is the male, the rat the

---

[1] Called by Rémusat Sung-Yun tse
(*Fa-hian*, cap. viii. n. 1); but the word
" tse " is no component part of the
name. The passage in the original
is this : " In the Wan-I suburb (*li*)
is the house (*tsc*) of Sun Yun of
Tun-hwang."

[2] Western countries (*si yu*).

[3] Tun-hwang, situated on a branch
of the Bulunghir river, vide *antc*,
p. xxiv. n.

[4] At the fall of the Tsin dynasty
(420 A.D.), the northern provinces of
China became the possession of a
powerful Tartar tribe known as the
Wei. A native dynasty (the South-

female. From their cohabiting in this manner, the name rat-bird cave is derived.

Ascending the Chîh-Ling and proceeding westward twenty-three days, having crossed the Drifting Sands, they arrived at the country of the Tuh-kiueh-'hun.[5] Along the road the cold was very severe, whilst the high winds, and the driving snow, and the pelting sand and gravel were so bad, that it was impossible to raise one's eyes without getting them filled. The chief city of the Tuh-kiueh-'hun and the neighbourhood is agreeably warm. The written character of this country is nearly the same as that of the Wei. The customs and regulations observed by these people are mostly barbarous in character (after the rules of the outside barbarians or foreigners). From this country going west 3500 li, we arrive at the city of Shen-Shen.[6] This city, from the time it set up a king, was seized by the Tuh-kiueh-'hun, and at present there resides in it a military officer (the second general) for subjugating (pacifying) the west. The entire cantonment[7] amounts to 3000 men, who are employed in withstanding the western Hu.

From Shen-Shen going west 1640 li, we arrive at the city of Tso-moh.[8] In this town there are, perhaps, a hundred families resident. The country is not visited with rain, but they irrigate their crops from the streams of water. They know not the use of oxen or ploughs in their husbandry.

In the town is a representation of Buddha with a Bôdhisattva, but certainly not in face like a Tartar. On questioning an old man about it, he said, " This was done by Lu-Kwong, who subdued the Tartars." From

ern Sung) ruled in the southern provinces, and has been regarded by subsequent writers as the legitimate one (Edkins).

[5] The Eastern Turks. The 'Hun were a southern horde of the 'Tieh lei Turks. *Vide* Doolittle's *Vocab. and Handbook*, vol. ii. p. 206.

[6] Shen-shen or Leu-lan (Beal's *Bud. Pilg.*, p. 4, n.), probably the Charchan of Marco Polo; Mayers (*Manual*, 536) places it near Pidjan; but for remarks on its situation *vide* Yule's *Marco Polo*, vol. i. p. 179, n. 1 ; vol. ii. p. 475; *vide* also Prejevalsky's *Kulja*, Remarks by Barou Richto-pen, p. 144, &c.

[7] *P'u lo* [bulak ?].

[8] Probably the Ni - mo of Hiuen Tsiang.

this city going westward 1275 li, we arrive at the city of Moh.   The flowers and fruits here are just like those of Lo-Yang, but the native buildings and the foreign officials are different in appearance.

From the city Moh going west 22 li, we arrive at the city of Han-Mo.[9]   Fifteen li to the south of this city is a large temple, with about 300 priests in it.   These priests possess a golden full-length figure of Buddha, in height a *chang* and $\frac{6}{10}$ths (about 18 feet).   Its appearance is very imposing, and all the characteristic marks of the body are bright and distinct.   Its face was placed repeatedly looking eastward ; but the figure, not approving of that, turned about and looked to the west.   The old men have the following tradition respecting this figure :—They say that originally it came from the south, transporting itself through the air.   The king of Khotan himself seeing it, paid it worship, and attempted to convey it to his city, but in the middle of the route, when they halted at night the figure suddenly disappeared.   On dispatching men to look after it, they found it had returned to its old place. Immediately, therefore, (the king) raised a tower, and appointed 400 attendants to sweep and water (the tower). If any of these servitors receive a hurt of any kind, they place some gold leaf on this figure according to the injured part, and so are directly cured.   Men in after ages built towers around this image of 18 feet, and the other image-towers, all of which are ornamented with many thou-sand flags and streamers of variegated silk.   There are perhaps as many as 10,000 of these, and more than half of them belonging to the Wei country.[10]   Over the flags are inscriptions in the square character, recording the several dates when they were presented; the greater number are of the nineteenth year of *T'ai Ho*, the second year of King

<hr>

[9] This is probably the Pi-mo of Hiuen Tsiang (Pein, iii. 243), the Pein of Marco Polo. The figure described in the text is also alluded to by Hiuen Tsiang, and is identi-fied with the sandal-wood image of Udyâna, king of Kauśâmbî.

[10] That is, were presented by sove-reigns of the Wei dynasty, or during their reign.

Ming, and the second year of Yen Chang.[11] There was only one flag with the name of the reigning monarch on it, and this was a flag of the period *Yaou Tsin* (A.D. 406).

From the town of Han-Mo going west 878 li, we arrive at the country of Khotan. The king of this country wears a golden cap on his head, in shape like the comb of a cock; the appendages of the head-dress hang down behind him two feet, and they are made of taffeta (*kün*), about five inches wide. On state occasions, for the purpose of imposing effect, there is music performed, consisting of drums, horns, and golden cymbals. The king is also attended by one chief bowman, two spearmen, five halberdiers, and, on his right and left, swordsmen, not exceeding a hundred men. The poorer sort of women here wear trousers, and ride on horseback just as well as their husbands. They burn their dead, and, collecting the ashes, erect towers (*fau t'u*) over them. In token of mourning they cut their hair and disfigure their faces, as though with grief. Their hair is cut to a length of four inches, and kept so all round. When the king dies, they do not burn his body, but enclose it in a coffin and carry it far off and bury it in the desert. They found a temple to his memory, and, at proper times, pay religious service to his manes.

The king of Khotan[12] was no believer in the law of Buddha. A certain foreign merchantman on a time brought a Bhikshu called Pi-lu-shan (Vairôchana) to this neighbourhood, and located him under a plum-tree to the south of this city. On this an informer approached the king and said, " A strange Śramaṇa has come (*to your majesty's dominions*) without permission, and is now

---

[11] The period *T'ai-Ho* began 477 A.D. and ended 500 A.D., so that there could be no nineteenth year of this period : either the text is faulty or it may possibly refer to the nineteenth year of the reign of Hiao Wén Ti, which would be 490 A.D. The other dates named correspond to 502 A.D. and 514 A.D.

[12] One hundred and sixty-five years after the establishment of the kingdom of Li-yul (Khotan), the King Vijayasambhava, son of Yeula, ascended the throne, and in the fifth year of his reign the dharma was first introduced into Li-yul (Rockhill).

residing to the south of the city under the plum-tree." The king, hearing this, was angry, and forthwith went to see Vairôchana. The Bhikshu then addressed the king as follows: " Ju-lai (Tathâgata) has commissioned me to come here to request your majesty to build for him a perfectly finished pagoda (lit. *a pagoda with a surmounting spire or dish*), and thus secure to yourself perpetual felicity." The king said, " Let me see Buddha, and then I will obey him." Vairôchana then sounded a gong;[13] on which Buddha commissioned Râhula to assume his appearance, and manifest himself in his true likeness in the air. The king prostrated himself on the ground in adoration, and at once made arrangements for founding a temple and *vihâra* under the tree. Then he caused to be carved a figure of Râhula; and, lest suddenly it should perish, the king afterwards constructed a chapel for its special preservation. At present it is carefully protected by a sort of shade (*jar*) that covers it; but, notwithstanding this, the shadow of the figure constantly removes itself outside the building, so that those who behold it cannot help paying it religious service (*by circumambulating it*). In this place (*or* chapel) are the shoes of a Pratyêka Buddha, which have up to the present time resisted decay. They are made neither of leather or silk,—in fact, it is impossible to determine what the material is. The extreme limits of the kingdom of Khotan reach about 3000 li or so from east to west.

In the second year of Shau Kwai (519 A.D.) and the 7th month, 29th day, we entered the kingdom of Chü-ku-po (Chakuka—Yerkiang). The people of that country are mountain-dwellers. The five kinds of cereals grow in abundance. In eating these, they make them into cakes. They do not permit the slaughter of animals, and such of them as eat flesh only use that which dies of itself. The customs and spoken language are like those of the people of

---

[13] The expression in the original implies the use of some magical influence to constrain Buddha to send Râhula.

Khotan, but the written character in use is that of the Brâhmaṇs. The limits of this country can be traversed in about five days.

During the first decade of the 8th month we entered the limits of the country of Han-Pan-to (Kabhanda),[14] and going west six days, we ascended the Tsung-ling mountains; advancing yet three days to the west, we arrived at the city of Kiueh-Yu;[15] and after three days more, to the Puh-ho-i mountains.[16] This spot is extremely cold. The snow accumulates both by winter and summer. In the midst of the mountain is a lake in which dwells a mischievous dragon. Formerly there was a merchant who halted at night by the side of the lake. The dragon just then happened to be very cross, and forthwith pronounced a spell and killed the merchant. The king of Pan-to,[17] hearing of it, gave up the succession to his son, and went to the kingdom of U-chang[18] to acquire knowledge of the spells used by the Brâhmaṇs. After four years, having procured these secrets, he came back to his throne, and, ensconced by the lake, he enchanted the dragon, and, lo! the dragon was changed into a man, who, deeply sensible of his wickedness, approached the king. The king immediately banished him from the Tsung-ling mountains more than 1000 li from the lake. The king of the present time is of the thirteenth generation (*from these events*). From this spot westward the road is one continuous ascent of the most precipitous character; for a thousand li there are over-hanging crags, 10,000 fathoms high, towering up to the very heavens. Compared with this road, the ruggedness of the great pass known as the Mang-men is as nothing, and the eminences of the celebrated Hian mountains (*in Honan*) are like level country. After entering the Tsung-ling mountains, step by step, we crept upwards for four days,

---

[14] Kabhanda is identified by Yule with Sarikkul and Tash Kurghan. *Yule* infra, vol. ii. p. 298, n. 40.

[15] Or, Kong-yu.

[16] This phrase Puh-ho-i may also be translated the "Untrustworthy Mountains."

[17] That is, Kavandha or, Kabhanda or, Sarikkul.

[18] Udyâna in Northern India.

and then reached the highest part of the range. From this point as a centre, looking downwards, it seems just as though one was poised in mid-air. The kingdom of Han-pan-to stretches as far as the crest of these mountains.[19] Men say that this is the middle point of heaven and earth. The people of this region use the water of the rivers for irrigating their lands ; and when they were told that in the middle country (*China*) the fields were watered by the rain, they laughed and said, " How could heaven provide enough for all?" To the eastward of the capital of this country there is a rapid river[20] (or a river, Mang-tsin) flowing to the north-east towards Sha-leh[21] (Kashgâr). The high lands of the Tsung-ling mountains do not produce trees or shrubs. At this time, viz., the 8th month, the air is icy cold, and the north wind carries along with it the drifting snow for a thousand li. At last, in the middle decade of the 9th month, we entered the kingdom of Poh-ho (Bolor?). The mountains here are as lofty and the gorges deep as ever. The king of the country has built a town, where he resides, for the sake of being in the mountains. The people of the country dress handsomely, only they use some leathern garments. The land is extremely cold—so much so, that the people occupy the caves of the mountains as dwelling-places, and the driving wind and snow often compel both men and beasts to herd together. To the south of this country are the great Snowy Mountains, which, in the morning and evening vapours, rise up like gem-spires.

In the first decade of the 10th month we arrived at the country of the Ye-tha (Ephthalites). The lands of this country are abundantly watered by the mountain streams, which fertilise them, and flow in front of all the dwellings. They have no walled towns, but they keep order by means

[19] To the west of the Tsung-ling mountains all the rivers flow to the westward, and enter the sea (*Ch. Ed.*)

[20] That is, perhaps, the Karâ-Sou of Klaproth, which flows into the Tiz-âb, an affluent of the Yerkiang river ; or it may be the Si-to river, on which Yarkand stands, and which empties itself into Lake Lob, in the Sandy Desert.

[21] Sha-leh, perhaps for Su-leh, *i.c.*, Kashgâr.

of a standing army that constantly moves here and there. These people also use felt garments. The course of the rivers is marked by the verdant shrubs. In the summer the people seek the cool of the mountains; in the winter they disperse themselves through the villages. They have no written character. Their rules of politeness are very defective. They have no knowledge at all of the movements of the heavenly bodies; and, in measuring the year, they have no intercalary month, or any long and short months; but they merely divide the year into twelve parts, and that is all. They receive tribute from all surrounding nations: on the south as far as Tieh-lo;[22] on the north, the entire country of Lae-leh,[23] eastward to Khotan, and west to Persia—more than forty countries in all. When they come to the court with their presents for the king, there is spread out a large carpet about forty paces square, which they surround with a sort of rug hung up as a screen. The king puts on his robes of state and takes his seat upon a gilt couch, which is supported by four golden phœnix birds. When the ambassadors of the Great Wei dynasty were presented, (*the king*), after repeated prostrations, received their letters of instruction. On entering the assembly, one man announces your name and title; then each stranger advances and retires. After the several announcements are over, they break up the assembly. This is the only rule they have; there are no instruments of music visible at all. The royal ladies of the Ye-tha[24] country also wear state robes, which trail on the ground three feet and more; they have special train-bearers for carrying these lengthy robes. They also wear on their heads a horn, in length eight feet[25] and more, three feet of its length being red

---

[22] This may possibly be Tira-bhukti, the present Tirhut. But see *ante*, p. xvi.

[23] The Lá-la or Lára people occupied Málava or Valabhi; vide *infra*, vol. ii. p. 266, n. 71. See also note at the end of this Introduction.

[24] The Ye-tha were probably the White Huns, or Ephthalites.

[25] I see no other way of translating this passage, although it seems puzzling to know how these royal ladies could carry such an ornament as this upon their heads.

coral. This they ornamented with all sorts of gay colours, and such is their head-dress. When the royal ladies go abroad, then they are carried; when at home, then they seat themselves on a gilded couch, which is made (*from the ivory of?*) a six-tusked white elephant, with four lions (*for supporters*).[26] Except in this particular, the wives of the great ministers are like the royal ladies; they in like manner cover their heads, using horns, from which hang down veils all round, like precious canopies. Both the rich and poor have their distinctive modes of dress. These people are of all the four tribes of barbarians the most powerful. The majority of them do not believe in Buddha. Most of them worship false gods. They kill living creatures and eat their flesh. They use the seven precious substances, which all the neighbouring countries bring as tribute, and gems in great abundance. It is reckoned that the distance of the country of the Yetha from our capital is upwards of 20,000 li.

On the first decade of the 11th month we entered the confines of the country of Po-sse[27] (Persia). This territory (*ground*) is very contracted. Seven days farther on we come to a people who dwell in the mountains and are exceedingly impoverished. Their manners are rough and ill-favoured. On seeing their king, they pay him no honour; and when the king goes out or comes in, his attendants are few. This country has a river which formerly was very shallow; but afterwards, the mountains having subsided, the course of the stream was altered and two lakes were formed. A mischievous dragon took up his residence here and caused many calamities. In the summer he rejoiced to dry up the rain, and in the winter

---

[26] Literally the passage is, "They make the seat from a six-tusked white elephant and four lions."

[27] The name of Persia or Eastern Persia extended at this time even to the base of the Tsung-ling mountains (*vide* Elphinstone's *India*). The Parthians assumed the Persian name and affected Persian manners, "διασώζουσι καὶ ἀπομιμοῦνται τὰ Περσικὰ ὀυκ ἀξιοῦντες, ἐμοὶ δοκει, Παρθυαῖοι νομίζεσθαι, Πέρσαι δὲ εἶναι προσποιούμενοι," says the Emperor Julian (*Or. de Constantin.*, gest. ii. p. 63; Rawlinson's *Herod.*, i. 534, n.)

to pile up the snow.   Travellers by his influence are subjected to all sorts of inconveniences.   The snow is so brilliant that it dazzles the sight; men have to cover their eyes, or they would be blinded by it; but if they pay some religious service to the dragon, they find less difficulty afterwards.

In the middle decade of the 11th month we entered the country of Shie-Mi (Sâmbî ?).   This country is just beyond the Tsung-ling mountains.   The aspect of the land is still rugged; the people are very poor; the rugged narrow road is dangerous—a traveller and his horse can hardly pass along it one at a time.   From the country of Po-lu-lai (Bolor) to the country of U-chang (Udyâna) they use iron chains for bridges.   These are suspended in the air for the purpose of crossing (over the mountain chasms).   On looking downwards no bottom can be perceived; there is nothing on the side to grasp at in case of a slip, but in a moment the body is hurled down 10,000 fathoms.   On this account travellers will not cross over in case of high winds.

On the first decade of the 12th month we entered the U-chang country (Udyâna).   On the north this country borders on the Tsung-ling mountains; on the south it joins India.   The climate is agreeably warm.   The territory contains several thousand li.[28]   The people and productions are very abundant.   The fertility of the soil is equal to that of the plateau of Lin-tsze[29] in China and the climate more equable.   This is the place where Pe-lo[30] (Vessantara) gave his child as alms, and where Bôdhisattva gave his body (*to the tigress*).   Though these old stories relate to things so distant, yet they are preserved among the local legends (?).   The king of the country religiously observes a vegetable diet; on the great fast-days[31] he pays adoration to Buddha, both morning and evening, with sound of drum, conch, *vîṇa* (*a sort of lute*), flute, and

---

[28] There is no word for *li* in the text.

[29] In Shan-tung.

[30] Pe-lo, the first and last syllable in Vessantara.

[31] *Vide* Jul. ii. 6, n.

all kinds of wind instruments. After mid-day he devotes himself to the affairs of government. Supposing a man has committed murder, they do not suffer him to be killed; they only banish him to the desert mountains, affording him just food enough to keep him alive (lit. a bit and a sup). In investigating doubtful cases,[32] they rely on the pure or foul effect of drastic medicines; then, after examination, the punishment is adjusted according to the circumstances. At the proper time they let the streams overflow the land, by which the soil is rendered loamy and fertile. All provisions necessary for man are very abundant, cereals of every kind (lit. of a hundred sorts) flourish, and the different fruits (lit. the five fruits) ripen in great numbers. In the evening the sound of the (convent) bells may be heard on every side, filling the air (world); the earth is covered with flowers of different hues, which succeed each other winter and summer, and are gathered by clergy and laity alike as offerings for Buddha.

The king of the country seeing Sung-Yun (*inquired respecting him, and*) on their saying that the ambassadors of the Great Wei (*dynasty*) had come, he courteously received their letters of introduction. On understanding that the Empress Dowager was devotedly attached to the law of Buddha, he immediately turned his face to the east, and, with closed hands and meditative heart, bowed his head; then, sending for a man who could interpret the Wei language, he questioned Sung Yun and said, "Are my honourable visitors men from the region of sun-rising?" Sung-Yun answered and said, "Our country is bounded on the east by the great sea; from this the sun rises according to the divine will (*the command of Tathâgata*)." The king again asked, "Does that country produce holy men?" Sung-Yun then proceeded to enlarge upon the virtues of Confucius, of the Chow and Laou

<hr>

[32] This passage is translated by (R.) thus: "When any matter is involved in doubt, they appeal to drugs, and decide upon the evidence of these" (*Fah-hian*, c. viii. n. 1).

(Tseu), of the Chwang (*period*), and then of the silver walls and golden palaces of Fairy Land (P'eng lai Shan),[33] and then of the spirits, genii, and sages who dwell there; he further dilated on the divination of Kwan-lo, the medicinal art of Hwa-to, and .the magical power of Tso-ts'ze;[34] descanting on these various subjects, and properly distinguishing their several properties, he finished his address. Then the king said, "If these things are really as your worship says, then truly yours is the land of Buddha, and I ought to pray at the end of my life that I may be born in that country."

After this, Sung-Yun with Hwei Săng left the city for the purpose of inspecting the traces which exist of the teaching (or religion) of Tathâgata. To the east of the river is the place where Buddha dried his clothes. When first Tathâgata came to the country of U-chang, he went to convert a dragon-king. He, being angry with Buddha, raised a violent storm with rain. The *sanghâṭî* of Buddha was soaked through and through with the wet. After the rain was over, Buddha stopped on a rock, and, with his face to the east, sat down whilst he dried his robe (*kashâya*). Although many years have elapsed since then, the traces of the stripes of the garment are as visible as if newly done, and not merely the seams and bare outline, but one can see the marks of the very tissue itself, so that in looking at it, it appears as if the garment had not been removed, and, if one were asked to do it, as if the traces might be lifted up (*as the garment itself*). There are memorial towers erected on the spot where Buddha sat, and also where he dried his robe. To the west of the river is a tank occupied by a nâga-râja. By the side of the tank is a temple served by fifty priests and more. The Nâga-râja ever and anon assumes supernatural appearances. The king of the country propitiates

---

him with gold and jewels, and other precious offerings, which he casts into the middle of the tank; such of these as find their way out through a back exit, the priests are permitted to retain. Because the dragon thus provides for the necessary expenses of this temple (clothes and food), therefore men call it the Nâga-râja Temple.

Eighty li to the north of the royal city there is the trace of the shoe of Buddha on a rock. They have raised a tower to cover it. The place where the print of the shoe is left on the rock is as if the foot had trodden on soft mud. Its length is undetermined, as at one time it is long, and at another time short. They have now founded a temple on the spot, capable of accommodating seventy priests and more. Twenty paces to the south of the tower is a spring of water issuing from a rock. Buddha once purifying (*his mouth*), planted a piece of his chewing-stick [35] in the ground; it immediately took root, and is at present a great tree, which the Tartars call Po-lu.[36] To the north of the city is the To-lo [37] temple, in which there are very numerous appliances for the worship of Buddha. The pagoda is high and large. The priests' chambers are ranged in order round the temple (*or* tower). There are sixty full-length golden figures (*herein*). The king, when-ever he convenes (*or* convening yearly) a great assembly, collects the priests in this temple. On these occasions the Śramaṇas within the country flock together in great crowds (*like clouds*). Sung-Yun and Hwei Săng, remark-ing the strict rules and eminent piety (*extreme austerities*) of those Bhikshus, and from a sense that the example of these priests singularly conduced to increase (their own) religious feelings, remitted two servants for the use of the convent to present the offerings and to water and sweep. From the royal city going south-east over a mountainous district eight days' journey, we come to the place where Tathâgata, practising austerities, gave up his body to feed

---

[35] Dantakâshṭa.　　[36] The Pilu tree—*Salvadora Persica.*　　[37] Târa (?).

a starving tiger. It is a high mountain, with scarped precipices and towering peaks that pierce the clouds. The fortunate tree [38] and the Ling-chi grow here, whilst the groves and fountains (*or* the forest rivulets), the docile stags, and the variegated hues of the flowers, all delight the eye. Sung-Yun and Hwei Săng devoted a portion of their travelling funds to erect a pagoda on the crest of the hill, and they inscribed on a stone, in the square character, an account of the great merits of the Wei dynasty. This mountain possesses a temple called "Collected Bones," [39] with 300 priests and more. One hundred and odd li to the south of the royal city is the place where Buddha (Julai), formerly residing in the Mo-hiu country, peeled off his skin for the purpose of writing upon it, and extracted (*broke off*) a bone of his body for the purpose of writing with it. [40] Aśôka-râja raised a pagoda on this spot for the purpose of enclosing these sacred relics. It is about ten *chang* high (120 *feet*). On the spot where he broke off his bone, the marrow ran out and covered the surface of a rock, which yet retains the colour of it, and is unctuous as though it had only recently been done.

To the south-west of the royal city 500 li is the Shen-shi [41] hill (*or* the hill of (*the Prince*) Sudâna). The sweet waters and delicious fruits (*of this place*) are spoken of in the sacred books. [42] The mountain dells are agreeably warm; the trees and shrubs retain a perpetual verdure. At the time when the pilgrims arrived (*ta'i tsuh*), the gentle breeze which fanned the air, the songs of the birds, the trees in their spring-tide beauty, the butterflies that fluttered over the numerous flowers, all this caused Sung-Yun, as he gazed on this lovely scenery in a distant

---

[38] Remusat translates it the tree *kalpa daru*.

[39] Remusat gives "collected gold."

[40] The text is corrupt. I have substituted *chu* for *tso*. Mo-hiu is the *Margus*; the country would therefore be Margiana. But probably it refers to the Oxus country.

[41] *Shen-shi*, "illustrious resolution;" evidently a mistake for *shen-shi*, "illustrious charity" (Sudâna).

[42] That is, in the *Jâtaka* book, where the history of Vessantara is recorded.

land, to revert to home thoughts; and so melancholy were
his reflections, that he brought on a severe attack of ill-
ness; after a month, however, he obtained some charms
of the Brâhmans, which gave him ease.

To the south-east of the crest of the hill Shen-shi is a
rock-cave of the prince,[43] with two chambers to it. Ten
paces in front of this cave is a great square stone on
which it is said the prince was accustomed to sit; above
this Aśôka raised a memorial tower.

One li to the south of the tower is the place of the
Paññasâlâ (*leafy hut*) of the prince. One li north-east
of the tower, fifty paces down the mountain, is the place
where the son and daughter of the prince persisted in
going round a tree, and would not depart (*with the Brâhman*). On this the Brâhman beat them with rods till
the blood flowed down and moistened the earth. This
tree still exists, and the ground, stained with blood, now
produces a sweet fountain of water. Three li to the west
of the cave is the place where the heavenly king Śakra,
assuming the appearance of a lion sitting coiled up in the
road, intercepted Man-köa.[44] On the stone are yet traces
of his hair and claws: the spot also where Ajitakûṭa[45]
(O-chou-to-kiu) and his disciples nourished the father and
mother (*i.e.*, the prince and princess). All these have memorial towers. In this mountain formerly were the beds of 500

[43] That is, of the Prince Sudatta
or the Bountiful Prince. The whole
of the history alluded to in the text
may be found in Spence Hardy's
Manual of Buddhism under the
Wessantara Jútaka, p. 116. The
account states that Wessantara (the
prince alluded to in the text, called
"the Bountiful," because of his extreme charity) gave to the king of
Kâliṅga a white elephant that had
the power to compel rain to fall.
On this the subjects of the prince's
father (who was called Sanda) forced
him to banish the prince, with his
wife (Madri-dêwi) and his two
children, to the rock Wankagiri,
where the events alluded to in the
text occurred. See *Tree and Serpent Worship*, pl. lxv. fig. 1.

[44] This may possibly allude to
Madri-dêwi; the symbol *kea* denotes "a lady." We read that
Śakra caused some wild beasts to
appear to keep Madri-dêwi from
coming back. See Spence Hardy,
loc. cit.; and also the lions in the
Sânchi sculpture, *Tree and Serpent
Worship*, pl. xxxii. fig. 2.

[45] Called Achchhuta in the Singhalese accounts. He was an ascetic
who resided in the neighbourhood
of the hill.

Arhats, ranged north and south in a double row ; their seats also were placed opposite one to another.   There is now a great temple here with about 200 priests.   To the north of the fountain which supplied the prince with water is a temple.   A herd of wild asses frequent this spot for grazing.   No one drives them here, but they resort here of their own accord.   Daily at early morn they arrive ; they take their food at noon, and so they protect the temple. These are spirits who protect the tower (protecting-tower-spirits), commissioned for this purpose by the Rĭshi Uh-po.[46]   In this temple there formerly dwelt a Shami (Srâmaṇêra), who, being constantly occupied in sifting ashes (*belonging to the convent*), fell into a state of spiritual ecstasy (*Samâdhi*).   The Karmadâna[47] of the convent had his funeral obsequies performed, and drew him about, without his perceiving it, whilst his skin hung on his shrunken bones.   The Rĭshi Uh-po continued to take the office of the Srâmaṇêra in the sifting of the ashes.   On this the king of the country founded a chapel to the Rĭshi, and placed in it a figure of him as he appeared, and ornamented it with much gold leaf.

Close to the peak of this hill is a temple of Po-keen, built by the Yakshas.   There are about eighty priests in it. They say that the Arhats and Yakshas continually come to offer religious services, to water and sweep the temple, and to gather wood for it.   Ordinary priests are not allowed to occupy this temple.   The Shaman To-Ying, of the Great Wei dynasty, came to this temple to pay religious worship ; but having done so, he departed, without daring to take up his quarters there.   During the middle decade of the 4th month of the first year of Ching-Kwong (520 A.D.), we entered the kingdom of Gandhâra.   This country closely resembles the territory of U-chang.   It was formerly called the country of Ye-po-lo.[48]   This is the country which

---

[46] The symbol for "*Uh*" is doubtful.
[47] The steward.
[48] Referring, in all probability, to the dragon Apalâla, whose fountain to the N.E. of Mungali (the capital of U-chang) gave rise to the river Subhavastu or Swêti, that flows through this territory.

the Ye-thas[49] destroyed, and afterwards set up Lae-lih to be king[50] over the country; since which events two generations have passed. The disposition of this king (*or* dynasty) was cruel and vindictive, and he practised the most barbarous atrocities. He did not believe the law of Buddha, but loved to worship demons. The people of the country belonged entirely to the Brâhmaṇ caste; they had a great respect for the law of Buddha, and loved to read the sacred books, when suddenly this king came into power, who was strongly opposed to anything of the sort. Entirely self-reliant on his own strength, he had entered on a war with 'the country of Ki-pin (Cophene),[51] disputing the boundaries of their kingdom, and his troops had been already engaged in it for three years.

The king has 700 war-elephants, each of which carries ten men armed with sword and spear, while the elephants. are armed with swords attached to their trunks, with which to fight when at close quarters. The king continually abode with his troops on the frontier, and never returned to his kingdom, in consequence of which the old men had to labour and the common people were oppressed. Sung-Yun repaired to the royal camp to deliver his credentials. The king[52] was very rough with him, and failed to salute him. He sat still whilst receiving the letters. Sung-Yun perceived that these remote barbarians were unfit for exercising public duties, and that their arrogancy refused to be checked. The king now sent for interpreters, and addressed Sung-Yun as follows: "Has your worship not suffered much inconvenience in traversing all these countries and encountering so many dangers

---

[49] Alluding perhaps to the conquest of Kitolo, at the beginning of the fifth century. The king conquered Gandhâra, and made Peshâwar his capital.

[50] Or, set up a Lâra dynasty, but the whole of the context is obscure.

[51] Then in the possession of the Great Yuchi, whose capital was Kâbul.

[52] This king was probably the one called Onowei, who reigned under the title "So-lin-teu-pim-teu-fa Khan," or, "the prince who seizes and holds firmly." We are told that he refused homage to the Wei Tartars, alluding probably to the circumstance recorded in this account of Sung-Yun (C.)

on the road ? " Sung-Yun replied, " We have been sent by our royal mistress to search for works of the great translation through distant regions. It is true the difficulties of the road are great, yet we cannot (*dare not*) say we are fatigued ; but your majesty and your forces (*three armies*), as you sojourn here on the frontier of your kingdom, enduring all the changes of heat and cold, are not you also nearly worn out ? " The king, replying, said, " It is impossible to submit to such a little country as this, and I am sorry that you should ask such a question." Sung-Yun, on first speaking with the king, (*thought*), " This barbarian is unable to discharge with courtesy his official duties; he sits still whilst receiving diplomatic papers; " and now being about to reply to him again, he determined to reprove him as a fellow-man (*or* having the feelings of a man); and so he said, " Mountains are high and low—rivers are great and small—amongst men also there are distinctions, some being noble and others ignoble. The sovereign of the Ye-tha, and also of U-chang, when they received our credentials, did so respectfully; but your majesty alone has paid us no respect." The king, replying, said, " When I see the king of the Wei, then I will pay my respects; but to receive and read his letters whilst seated, what fault can be found with this? When men receive a letter from father or mother, they don't rise from their seats to read it. The Great Wei sovereign is to me (for the nonce) both father and mother, and so, without being unreasonable, I will read the letters you bring me still sitting down." Sung-Yun then took his departure without any official salutation. He took up his quarters in a temple, in which his entertainment was very poor. At this time the country of Po-tai[53] sent two young lions to the king of Gandhâra as a present. Sung-Yun had an opportunity

[53] Perhaps the same as the Fa-ti (Betik) of Hiuen Tsiang, 400 li to the west of Bokhara (Jul. tome iii. p. 282). But the character of the text is so unfinished, that Po-tai may stand for Badakshân.

of seeing them; he noticed their fiery temper and courageous mien. The pictures of these animals common in China are not at all good resemblances of them.

After this, going west five days, they arrived at the place where Tathâgata made an offering of his head for the sake of a man, where there is both a tower and temple, with about twenty priests. Going west three days, we arrive at the great river Sin-tu. On the west bank of this river is the place where Tathâgata took the form of (*or* became) a great fish called Ma-kie (*Makara*), and came out of the river, and for twelve years supported the people with his flesh. On this spot is raised a memorial tower. On the rock are still to be seen the traces of the scales of the fish.

Again going west thirteen days' journey, we arrived at the city of Fo-sha-fu.[54] The river valley (*in which this city is built*) is a rich loamy soil. The city walls have gate-defences. The houses are thick, and there are very many groves (*around the city*), whilst fountains of water enrich the soil; and as for the rest, there are costly jewels and gems in abundance. The customs of the people are honest and virtuous. Within this city there is an heretical temple [55] of ancient date called "Sang-teh" (Sânti?). All religious persons frequent it and highly venerate it. To the north of the city one li is the temple of the White Elephant Palace.[56] Within the temple all is devoted to the service of Buddha. There are here stone images highly adorned and very beautiful, very many in number, and covered with gold sufficient to dazzle the eyes. Before the temple and belonging to it is a tree called the White Elephant Tree, from which, in fact, this temple took its origin and name.

[54] The Varusha (Po-lou-sha) of Hiuen Tsiang.

[55] In this passage I take the word *fan* (all) to be a misprint for *Fan* (Brâhman), in which case the expression *Wei fan* would mean "heretical Brâhmans." If this be not the correct translation of the passage, then it may perhaps be rendered thus: "Within and without this city there are very many old temples, which are named 'Sang-teh' (*sandi*, union or assembly?)."

[56] This is probably the Pilusâra *stûpa* of Hiuen Tsiang (Jul. tome ii. p. 54).

Its leaves and flowers are like those of the Chinese date-tree, and its fruit begins to ripen in the winter quarter. The tradition common amongst the old people is this: "That when this tree is destroyed, then the old law of Buddha will also perish." Within the temple is a picture of the prince [57] and his wife, and the figure of the Brâhman begging the boy and the girl. The Tartars, seeing this picture, could not refrain from tears.

Again going west one day's journey, we arrive at the place where Tathâgata plucked out his eyes to give in charity. Here also is a tower and a temple. On a stone of the temple is the impress of the foot of Kâśyapa Buddha. Again going west one day, we crossed a deep river,[58] more than 300 paces broad. Sixty li south-west of this we arrive at the capital of the country of Gandhâra.[59] Seven li to the south-east of this city there is a Tsioh-li Feou-thou[60] (*a pagoda with a surmounting pole*). [The record of Tao-Yung says, "Four li to the east of the city."] Investigating the origin of this tower, we find that when Tathâgata was in the world he was passing once through this country with his disciples on his mission of instruction; on which occasion, when delivering a discourse on the east side of the city, he said, "Three hundred years after my *Nirvâna*, there will be a king of this country called Ka-ni-si-ka (Kanishka). On this spot he will raise a pagoda (*Feou-thou*). Accordingly, 300 years after that event, there was a king of this country so called. On one occasion, when going out to the east of the city, he saw four children engaged in making a Buddhist tower out of cows' dung. They had raised it about three feet high, when suddenly they disappeared (*or*, it fell). [The record states, "One of the children, raising himself in the air and turning towards the king, repeated a verse (*gâthâ*).] The king, surprised at this miraculous event,

---

[57] That is, of the Bountiful Prince (Wessantara) referred to before.

[58] The Indus.

[59] That is, Peshâwar.

[60] *Tsioh-li* means "a sparrow," but it is phonetic for *tila*, a surmounting spear or trident.

immediately erected a tower for the purpose of enclosing
(*the small pagoda*), but gradually the small tower grew
higher and higher, and at last went outside and removed
itself 400 feet off, and there stationed itself. Then the king
proceeded to widen the foundation of the great tower 300
paces and more.[61] [The record of Tao-Yung says 390 paces.]
To crown all, he placed a roof-pole upright and even.
[The record of Tao-Yung says it was 35 feet high.]
Throughout the building he used carved wood; he constructed stairs to lead to the top. The roof consisted
of every kind of wood. Altogether there were thirteen
storeys; above which there was an iron pillar, three feet
high,[62] with thirteen gilded circlets. Altogether the height
from the ground was 700 feet. [Tao-Yung says the iron
pillar was $88\frac{8}{10}$ feet (*high*), with fifteen encircling discs,
and $63\frac{2}{10}$ *changs* from the ground (743 *feet*).] This meritorious work being finished, the dung pagoda, as at first,
remained three paces south of the great tower. The
Brâhmans, not believing that it was really made of dung,
dug a hole in it to see. Although years have elapsed
since these events, this tower has not corrupted; and
although they have tried to fill up the hole with scented
earth, they have not been able to do so. It is now
enclosed with a protecting canopy. The Tsioh-li pagoda,
since its erection, has been three times destroyed by lightning, but the kings of the country have each time restored
it. The old men say, "When this pagoda is finally destroyed by lightning, then the law of Buddha also will
perish."

The record of Tao-Yung says, "When the king had
finished all the work except getting the iron pillar up
to the top, he found that he could not raise this heavy
weight. He proceeded, therefore, to erect at the four
corners a lofty stage; he expended in the work large trea-

---

[61] Hiuen Tsiang says it was a li
and a half in circumference.
[62] Most likely there is a mistake
in the text; the height of the iron
pillar should be 30 feet.

sures, and then he with his queen and princes ascending on to it, burnt incense and scattered flowers, with all their hearts and power of soul; then, with one turn of the windlass, they raised the weight, and so succeeded in elevating it to its place. The Tartars say, therefore, that the four heavenly kings lent their aid in this work, and that, if they had not done so, no human strength would have been of any avail. Within the pagoda there is contained every sort of Buddhist utensil; here are gold and jewelled (vessels) of a thousand forms and vast variety, to name which even would be no easy task. At sunrise the gilded discs of the vane are lit up with dazzling glory, whilst the gentle breeze of morning causes the precious bells (that are suspended from the roof) to tinkle with a pleasing sound. Of all the pagodas of the western world, this one is by far the first (in size and importance). At the first completion of this tower they used true pearls in making the network covering over the top; but after some years, the king, reflecting on the enormous value of this ornamental work, thought thus with himself: "After my decease (*funeral*) I fear some invader may carry it off"—or "supposing the pagoda should fall, there will be no one with means sufficient to re-build it;" on which he removed the pearl work and placed it in a copper vase, which he removed to the north-west of the pagoda 100 paces, and buried it in the earth. Above the spot he planted a tree, which is called Po-tai (*Bôdhi*), the branches of which, spreading out on each side, with their thick foliage, completely shade the spot from the sun. Underneath the tree on each side there are sitting figures (*of Buddha*) of the same height, viz., a *chang* and a half (17 *feet*). There are always four dragons in attendance to protect these jewels; if a man (*only in his heart*) covets them, calamities immediately befall him. There is also a stone tablet erected on the spot, and engraved on it are these words of direction: "Hereafter, if this tower is destroyed, after long search, the virtuous man may find here pearls (*of value sufficient*) to help him restore it."

Fifty paces to the south of the Tsioh-li pagoda there is a stone tower, in shape perfectly round, and two *chang* high (27 *feet*). There are many spiritual indications (*shown by it*); so that men, by touching it, can find out if they are lucky or unlucky. If they are lucky, then by touching it the golden bells will tinkle; but if unlucky, then, though a man should violently push the tower, no sound would be given out. Hwei Săng, having travelled from his country, and fearing that he might not have a fortunate return, paid worship to this sacred tower, and sought a sign from it. On this, he did but touch it with his finger, and immediately the bells rang out. Obtaining this omen, he comforted his heart. And the result proved[63] the truth of the augury. When Hwei Săng first went up to the capital, the Empress had conferred upon him a thousand streamers of a hundred feet in length and of the five colours, and five hundred variegated silk (*mats ?*) of scented grass. The princes, dukes, and nobility had given him two thousand flags. Hwei Săng, in his journey from Khotan to Gandhâra,—wherever there was a disposition to Buddhism—had freely distributed these in charity; so that when he arrived here, he had only left one flag of 100 feet in length, given him by the Empress. This he decided to offer as a present to the tower of Śivika-râja, whilst Sung-Yun gave two servants to the Tsioh-li pagoda in perpetuity, to sweep it and water it. Hwei Săng, out of the little travelling funds he had left, employed a skilful artist to depict on copper the Tsioh-li pagoda and also the four principal pagodas of Śâkyamuni.

After this, going north-west seven days' journey, they crossed a great river (Indus), and arrived at the place where Tathâgata, when he was Śivika-râja,[64] delivered the

---

[63] Or, he consoled himself by the thought that after his undertaking he would have a safe return.

[64] *Vide* Jul., tome ii. p. 137 (*infra*, p. 125, n. 20), and *Abstract of Four Lectures*, p. 31.

dove; here there is a temple and a tower also. There was formerly here a large storehouse of Śivika-râja, which was burnt down. The grain which was in it was parched with the heat, and is still to be found in the neighbourhood (*of the ruins*). If a man take but a single grain of this, he never suffers from fever; the people of the country also take it to prevent the power of[65] the sun hurting them.

[The records of Tao-Yung say, " At Na-ka-lo-ho[66] there is a skull-bone of Buddha, four inches round, of a yellowish-white colour, hollow underneath, (*sufficient*) to receive a man's finger, shining, and in appearance like a wasp-nest.]

We then visited the Ki-ka-lam[67] temple. This contains the robe (*kashâya*) of Buddha in thirteen pieces. In measurement this garment is as long as it is broad (or, when measured, it is sometimes long and sometimes broad). Here also is the staff of Buddha, in length a *chang* and seven-tenths (*about* 18 *feet*), in a wooden case, which is covered with gold leaf. The weight of this staff is very uncertain; sometimes it is so heavy that a hundred men cannot raise it, and at other times it is so light that one man can lift it. In the city of Na-kie (Nagarahâra) is a tooth of Buddha and also some of his hair, both of which are contained in precious caskets; morning and evening religious offerings are made to them.

We next arrive at the cave of Gôpâla,[68] where is the shadow of Buddha. Entering the mountain cavern fifteen feet, and looking for a long time (*or*, at a long distance) at the western[69] side of it opposite the door, then at length the figure, with its characteristic marks, appears; on going nearer to look at it, it gradually grows fainter

[65] Or, to enable them to bear the power of the sun.

[66] Nagarahâra.

[67] The Khakkharam Temple, or the Temple of the Religious Staff (vide *Fa-hian*, cap. xiii.)

[68] The text is here, as in various other parts, corrupt. I have substituted *po* for *lo* in Gôpâla; and *kuh* for *luh*, *i.e.*, "cave" for "deer."

[69] The text has *sz'* (four) for *si* (west).

and then disappears. On touching the place where it was with the hand, there is nothing but the bare wall. Gradually retreating, the figure begins to come in view again, and foremost is conspicuous that peculiar mark between the eyebrows [70] (*úrṇa*), which is so rare among men. Before the cave is a square stone, on which is a trace of Buddha's foot.

One hundred paces south-west of the cave is the place where Buddha washed his robe. One li to the north of the cave is the stone cell of Mudgalyâyana; to the north of which is a mountain, at the foot of which the great Buddha with his own hand made a pagoda ten *chang* high (115 *feet*). They say that when this tower sinks down and enters the earth, then the law of Buddha will perish. There are, moreover, seven towers here, to the south of which is a stone with an inscription on it; they say Buddha himself wrote it. The foreign letters are distinctly legible even to the present time.

Hwei Săng abode in the country of U-chang two years. The customs of the western foreigners (Tartars) are, to a great extent, similar (*with ours*); the minor differences we cannot fully detail. When it came to the second month of the second year of Ching-un (521 A.D.) he began to return.

The foregoing account is principally drawn from the private records of Tao-Yung and Sung-Yun. The details given by Hwei Săng were never wholly recorded.

[70] I think this is the meaning of the passage, "We begin to see the mark, face-distinguishing, so rare among men."

Note, p. xci.—With reference to Lâla or Lâra, it seems from Cunningham's remark (*Arch. Survey*, vol. ii. p. 31) that this term is equivalent to "lord." The Lâras, according to Hiuen Tsiang, dwelt in Mâlava and Valabhî. It was from this region that the ancestors of Vijaya came (*Ind. Antiq.*), vol. xiii. p. 35, n. 25 ; see also *Journ. of Páli Text Soc.*, 1883, p. 59). It is worth consideration whether these Lâras or Lords were akin to the Vṛijjis of Vaisâli, who were also "lords" (Gothic, *Fraujas*) (?), and whether they were not both Northern invaders allied to the Yue-chi. The fable of the daughter of the king of Vanga cohabiting with a wild lion (*Dîparamsa*, chap. ix.) may simply mean that one of these Northerners (who were called *Lions*) carried off a native girl and cohabited with her. From this union sprang the thirty-two brothers, of whom the eldest were Vijaya and Sumeta (*vide Dîparamsa, loc. cit.*)

BUDDHIST RECORDS OF THE WESTERN WORLD.

TA-T'ANG-SI-YU-KI.

Records of the Western World[1] (compiled during) the Great T'ang[2] dynasty (A.D. 618–907); translated by Imperial command by Hiuen Tsiang,[3] a Doctor of the three Piṭakas, and edited by Pien Ki, a Shaman of the Ta-tsung-chi Temple.

PREFACE.[4]

WHEN of yore *the precious hair-circle*[5] shed forth its flood of light, the sweet dew was poured upon the great thousand (*worlds*),[6] the *golden mirror*[7] displayed its brightness, and a fragrant wind was spread over the earth; then it was known that he had appeared in the three worlds[8]

[1] The "Western World." This expression denotes generally the countries west of China. Mr. Mayers, in his note on Chang K'ien (*Reader's Manual*, No. 18), confines the meaning to Turkistân.

[2] That is, during the reign of T'ai Tsung (Chĕng Kwan) of the Great T'ang dynasty, A.D. 646.

[3] Hiuen Tsiang: in spelling Chinese names, the method of Dr. Wells Williams in his *Tonic Dictionary* has been generally followed. See note 10.

[4] This preface was written by Chang Yueh, who flourished as minister of state under T'ang Hüan Tsung (A.D. 713-756). He is called Tchang-choue by Stan. Julien. It is written in the usual ornate style of such compositions. I have mostly followed Julien's rendering

and refer the reader to his explanatory notes for fuller information.

[5] This phrase designates one of the thirty-two marks (viz. the *ûrṇa*) which characterise a great man, and which were recognised on the Buddha. See Burnouf, *Lotus de la Bonne Loi*, pp. 30, 543, 553, and 616; *Introd. Buddh.* (2d ed.), p. 308; Foucaux, *Lalita Vistara*, p. 286; Beal, *Fo-sho-hing-tsan-king*, I. i. 83, 84, 114, &c.; Hodgson, *Essays* (Serampore edit.), p. 129, or (Lond. 1874) pt. i. p. 90; Hardy, *Manual of Buddhism* (2d ed.), p. 150, &c.

[6] Julien explains this as "the great chiliocosm," and refers to Reinusat, *Melang. Post.*, p. 94.

[7] The moon.

[8] Buddha had appeared in the world of desires (*Kâmadhâtu*), the

who is rightly named the lord of the earth. His brightness, indeed, dwells in the four limits (*of the universe*), but his sublime model was fixed in the middle of the world. Whereupon, as the sun of wisdom declined, the shadow of his doctrine spread to the East, the grand rules of the emperor [9] diffused themselves afar, and his imposing laws reached to the extremities of the West.

There was in the temple of "great benevolence" a doctor of the three *Piṭakas* called Hiuen Tsiang.[10] His common name was Chin-shi. His ancestors came from Ing-chuen;[11] the emperor Hien [12] held the sceptre; reigning at Hwa-chau,[13] he opened the source. The great Shun entertained the messengers as he laid on Li-shan [14] the foundation of his renown. · The three venerable ones distinguished themselves during the years of *Ki*.[15] The six extraordinary (*events*) shone during the Han period. In penning odes there was one who equalled the clear moon; in wandering by the way there was one who resembled the brilliant stars—(*his illustrious ancestors*) like fishes in the lake, or as birds assembled before the wind, by their choice services in the world served to produce as their result an illustrious descendant.

The master of the law under these fortunate influences came into the world. In him were joined sweetness and virtue. These roots, combined and deeply planted, produced their fruits rapidly. The source of his wisdom (*reason*) was deep, and wonderfully it increased. At his opening life he was rosy as the evening vapours and

world of forms (*Rûpadhâtu*), the world without forms (*Arûpadhâtu*). —Julien. But here it simply means "in the world."

[9] The emperor T'ai-tsung of the T'áng dynasty (A.D. 627–649).

[10] I adopt this mode of spelling for reasons stated in the introduction. He is generally known from Julien's French version as "Hiouen Thsang." Mr. Mayers (*Reader's Manual*, p. 290) calls him Huan Chwan; Mr. Wylie, Yuén-Chwàng; and the name is also represented by Hhüen-Chwâng.

[11] Yu-cheu, in the province of Honan.—Jul.

[12] That is, Hwang Ti (B.C. 2697), otherwise called Hien-yuen-shi.

[13] Hwa-chau was an island of the kingdom of Hwa-siu, where Fo-hi fixed his court.—Jul.

[14] For Shun and Li-shan consult Mayers under *Shun* (*op. cit.* No. 617).

[15] *I.e.*, under the reign of the Chau, whose family name was K'i.—Jul.

(*round*) as the rising moon. As a boy (*collecting-sand age*) he was sweet as the odour of cinnamon or the vanilla tree. When he grew up he thoroughly mastered the *Fan* and *Su*;[16] the nine borders [17] were filled with (*bore*) his renown, the five prefectures (*or* palaces) together resounded his praise.

At early dawn he studied the true and the false, and through the night shone forth his goodness; the mirror of his wisdom, fixed on the true receptacle, remained stationary. He considered the limits of life, and was permanently at rest (*in the persuasion that*) the vermilion ribbon and the violet silken tassels are the pleasing bonds that keep one attached to the world; but the precious car and the red pillow, these are the means of crossing the ford and escaping the world. Wherefore he put away from him the pleasures of sense, and spoke of finding refuge in some hermit retreat. His noble brother Chang-tsi was a master of the law, a pillar and support of the school of Buddha. He was as a dragon or an elephant (*or* a dragon-elephant) in his own generation, and, as a falcon or a crane, he mounted above those to come. In the court and the wilderness was his fame exalted; within and without was his renown spread. Being deeply affectionate, they loved one another, and so fulfilled the harmony of mutual relationship (*parentage*). The master of the law was diligent in his labour as a student; he lost not a moment of time, and by his studies he rendered his teachers illustrious, and was an ornament to his place of study. His virtuous qualities were rightly balanced, and he caused the perfume of his fame to extend through the home of his adoption. Whip raised, he travelled on his even way; he mastered the nine divisions of the books, and swallowed (*the lake*) Mong;[18] he worked his paddles across the dark ford; he gave his attention to

---

[16] That is, the books of the legendary period of Chinese history, from 2852 B.C. to 2697 B.C.

[17] Or *the nine islands* (*Khiu-kao-tsai-in*), concerning which there is a passage in the *Shi King.*—Jul. p. lii.

[18] To swallow the lake Mong is a metaphorical way of saying he had acquired a vast erudition.—Jul.

(*looked down upon*) the four *Védas*, whilst finding *Lu* small.[19]

From this time he travelled forth and frequented places of discussion, and so passed many years, his merit completed, even as his ability was perfected. Reaching back to the beginning, when the sun and moon first lit up with their brightness the spiritually (*created*) world, or, as Tseu-yun, with his kerchief suspended at his girdle, startled into life (*developed*) his spiritual powers, so in his case the golden writing gradually unfolded itself. He waited for the autumn car, yet hastened as the clouds; he moved the handle of jade[20] for a moment, and the mist-crowds were dispersed as the heaped-up waves. As the occasion required, he could use the force of the flying discus or understand the delicate sounds of the lute used in worship.[21]

With all the fame of these acquirements, he yet embarked in the boat of humility and departed alone. In the land of Hwan-yuen he first broke down the boasting of the iron-clad stomach;[22] in the village of Ping-lo in a moment he exhibited the wonder of the floating wood.[23] Men near and afar beheld him with admiration as they said one to another, "Long ago we heard of the eight dragons of the family of Sun, but now we see the double wonder (*ke*) of the gate of Chin. Wonderful are the men of Ju and Ing."[24] This is true indeed! The master

---

[19] To find "Lu small" is an allusion to a passage in Mencius : "Confucius mounted on the mountain of the East, and found that the king of Lu (*i.e.*, his own country) was small." (Jul.) The meaning of the expression in the text seems to be that Hiuen Tsiang found his own studies contracted and small, so he bent down his head to examine the *Védas*.

[20] The fly-flap of the orator has a jade handle.

[21] So I have ventured to translate the word *pai*, although in the addenda at the end of Book I. the word is considered corrupt.

[22] This probably refers to some minor encounter or discussion which Hiuen Tsiang had in his own country. The expression "iron-clad stomach" refers to the story told of one he met with in his travels in India who wore an iron corslet lest his learning should burst open his body.—*Si-yu-ki*, book x. fol. 9.

[23] I cannot but think this refers to the ability of Hiuen Tsiang in hitting on the solution of a difficult question, as the blind tortoise with difficulty finds the hole in a floating piece of wood.

[24] The rivers Ju and Ing are in the province of Honan. The saying in the text is quoted from a letter addressed

of the law, from his early days till he grew up, pondered in heart the mysterious principles (*of religion*). His fame spread wide among eminent men.

At this time the schools were mutually contentious; they hastened to grasp the end without regarding the beginning; they seized the flower and rejected the reality; so there followed the contradictory teaching of the North and South, and the confused sounds of " Yes " and " No," perpetual words! On this he was afflicted at heart, and fearing lest he should be unable to find out completely the errors of translations, he purposed to examine thoroughly the literature of the *perfume elephant*,[25] and to copy throughout the list of the dragon palace.[26]

With a virtue of unequalled character, and at a time favourable in its indications, he took his staff, dusted his clothes, and set off for distant regions. On this he left behind him the dark waters of the Pa river;[27] he bent his gaze forwards; he then advanced right on to the T"sungling mountains. In following the courses of rivers and crossing the plains he encountered constant dangers. Compared with him Po-wang[28] went but a little way, and the journey of Fa-hien[29] was short indeed. In all the districts through which he journeyed he learnt thoroughly the dialects; he investigated throughout the deep secrets (*of religion*) and penetrated to the very source of the stream. Thus he was able to correct the books and trans-

by Siun-yu to the emperor during the eastern Han dynasty.—Jul.

[25] If we may venture to give a meaning to this expression, the " perfume elephant " (*Gandhahasti*), which so. frequently occurs in Buddhist books, it may refer to the solitary elephant (bull elephant) when in rut. A perfume then flows from his ears. The word is also applied to an elephant of the very best class.

[26] The books carried (as the fable says) to the palace of the Nāgas to be kept in safety.

[27] It rises in the Lan-thien district of the department of Si-'gan-fu in the province of Shen-si.—Jul.

[28] The celebrated general Chang K'ien, who lived in the second century B.C., was the first Chinese who penetrated to the extreme regions of the west. " In B.C. 122 he was sent to negotiate treaties with the kingdom of Si-yu, the present Turkistân " (Mayers). He was ennobled as the Marquis Po-Wang. Beal, *Travels of Fah-hian*, &c., pp. xvii, xviii; Pauthier, *Jour. Asiat.*, ser. iii. 1839, p. 260; Julien, *Jour. Asiat.*, ser. iv. tom. x. (1847), or *Ind. Ant.*, vol. iv. pp. 14, 15.

[29] The well-known Chinese Buddhist traveller, A.D. 399-414.

cend (*the writers of*) India. The texts being transcribed on palm leaves, he then returned to China.

The Emperor T'ai Tsung, surnamed Wen-wang-ti, who held the golden wheel and was seated royally on the throne, waited with impatience for that eminent man. He summoned him therefore to the green enclosure,[30] and, impressed by his past acquirements, he knelt before him in the yellow palace. With his hand he wrote proclamations full of affectionate sentiments; the officers of the interior attended him constantly; condescending to exhibit his illustrious thoughts, he wrote a preface to the sacred doctrine of the *Tripiṭaka*, consisting of 780 words. The present emperor (Kao Tsung) had composed in the spring pavilion a sacred record consisting of 579 words, in which he sounded to the bottom the stream of deep mystery and expressed himself in lofty utterances. But now, if he (*Hiuen Tsiang*) had not displayed his wisdom in the wood of the cock,[31] nor scattered his brightness on the peak of the vulture,[32] how could he (*the emperor*) have been able to abase his sacred composition in the praise of the ornament of his time?

In virtue of a royal mandate, he (*Hiuen Tsiang*) translated 657 works from the original Sanskrit (*Fan*). Having thoroughly examined the different manners of distant countries, the diverse customs of separate people, the various products of the soil and the class divisions of the people, the regions where the royal calendar is received[33] and where the sounds of moral instruction have come, he has composed in twelve books the *Ta-t'ang-si-yu-ki*. Herein he has collected and written down the most secret principles of the religion of Buddha, couched in language plain and precise. It may be said, indeed, of him, that his works perish not.

[30] The green enclosure surrounding the imperial seat or throne.

[31] The *Kukkuṭa saṅghârâma* near Pâtna.

[32] The Vulture Peak (*Gṛidhrakûṭa parvata*), near Râjagṛiha.

[33] The royal calendar is the work distributed annually throughout the empire, containing all information as to the seasons, &c.—Jul.

BOOK I.

(1) *O-ki-ni;* (2) *K'iu-chi;* (3) *Poh-luh-kia;* (4) *Nu-chih-kien;* (5) *Che-shi;* (6) *Fei-han;* (7) *Su-tu-li-sse-na;* (8) *Să-mo-kien;* (9) *Mi-mo-kia;* (10) *K'ie-po-ta-na;* (11) *K'iuh-shwang-ni-kia;* (12) *Tu-mi;* (13) *Ho-han;* (14) *Pu-ho;* (15) *Fa-ti;* (16) *Ho-li-sih-mi-kia;* (17) *Ki-shwang-na;* (18) *Ch'i-ngoh-yen-na;* (19) *Hwŭh-lo-mo;* (20) *Su-man;* (21) *Kio-ho-yen-na;* (22) *Hu-sha;* (23) *Kho-to-lo;* (24) *Kiu-mi-to;* (25) *Po-kia-lang;* (26) *Hi-lu-sih-min-kien;* (27) *Ho-lin;* (28) *Po-ho;* (29) *Jui-mo-to;* (30) *Hu-shi-kien;* (31) *Ta-la-kien;* (32) *Kie-chi;* (33) *Fan-yen-na;* (34) *Kia-pi-shi.*

INTRODUCTION.[1]

IF we examine in succession the rules of the emperors,[2] or look into the records of the monarchs,[3] when P'au I[4] began to adjust matters[5] and Hien-yuen[6] began to let

---

[1] The beginning of this Book consists of an introduction, written by Chang Yueh, the author of the preface.—Jul.

[2] That is, of the "three sovereigns" called (by some) Fuh-hi, Shĕn-nung, and Hwang-ti; others substitute Chuh Yung for Hwang-ti.—Mayers, *op. cit.*, p. 367 n.

[3] That is, the five kings (*Ti*) who followed Hwang-ti. The records of these kings and monarchs are, of course, mostly apocryphal.

[4] P'au I is the same as Fuh-hi or T'ai Hao; the name is interpreted as "the slaughterer of beasts."—Mayers.

[5] To "adjust matters," so it seems the expression *chuh chan* must be interpreted. The symbol *chan* occupies the place of the East in Wan's arrangement of the Trigrams, and symbolises "movement." It is also used for "wood," because, as some say, "the East symbolises spring, when the growth of vegetation begins." Others say that the symbol "wood" as the analogue of *chan* is a misprint for *yî*, signifying increase (vid. Legge, *Yî King*, p. 248). But in any case, in the text the idea is of "movement towards order." Fuh-hi, like his sister Nu-kwa, is said to have reigned "under wood."

[6] Hien Yuen is the same as Hwang-ti; it is the name of the hill near which the emperor dwelt.

fall his robes,[7] we see how they administered the affairs, and first divided the limits of the empire.[8]

When T'ang(-ti) Yao[9] received the call of heaven (*to rule*), his glory reached to the four quarters; when Yu(-ti) Shun[10] had received his map of the earth, his virtue flowed throughout the nine provinces. From that time there have come down clear[11] records, annals of events; though distant, we may hear the previous doings (*of eminent men*), or gather their words from the records of their disciples. How much rather when we live under a renowned government, and depend on those without partial aims.[12] Now then our great T'ang emperor (*or* dynasty), conformed in the highest degree to the heavenly pattern,[13] now holds the reins of government, and unites in one the six parts of the world, and is gloriously established. Like a fourth august monarch, he illustriously administers the empire. His mysterious controlling power flows afar; his auspicious influence (*fame* or *instruction*) widely extends: like the heaven and the earth, he covers and sustains (*his subjects*), or like the resounding wind or the fertilising rain. The eastern barbarians bring him tribute;[14] the western frontiers are brought to submission. He has secured and hands down the succession, appeasing tumult, restoring order.[15] He certainly surpasses the previous kings; he

---

[7] Hwang-ti, among other things, "regulated costume." It is probably to this the text refers.

[8] Hwang-ti "mapped out his empire in provinces, and divided the land into regular portions."—Mayers.

[9] The great emperor Yao, with his successor Shun, stand at the dawn of Chinese history. His date is 2356 B.C. He was called the Marquis or Lord (*hau*) of T'ang, because he moved from the principality of T'ao to the region of T'ang.

[10] That is, Shun, of the family of Yeou-yu: he succeeded Yao, by whom he was adopted after he had disinherited his son Tan Chu, B.C. 2258. He is said to have received the "map of the earth," an expres-

sion derived from "the map of the empire into provinces," by Hwang-ti.

[11] I have so translated this passage, although Julien takes the opposite sense. I suppose *hung* to mean "clear" or "plain."

[12] "Without partial aims," rendered by Julien "qui pratique le *non-agir*." The expression *wou-wei* generally means "absence of self" or "selfish aims."

[13] Julien renders this "*gouverne à l'instar du ciel*," which no doubt is the meaning of the text.

[14] Are enrolled as tribute-bearers.

[15] Referring to the troubles of the last years of the Sui dynasty, which was followed by the T'ang.—Jul.

embraces in himself the virtues of former generations. Using the same currency [16] (*or* literature), all acknowledge his supreme rule. If his sacred merit be not recorded in history, then it is vain to exalt the great (*or* his greatness); if it be not to illumine the world, why then shine so brilliantly his mighty deeds? [17]

Hiuen Tsiang, wherever he bent his steps, has described the character of each country. Although he has not examined the country or distinguished the customs (*in every case*), he has shown himself trustworthy. [18] With respect to the emperor who transcends the five and surpasses the three, we read how all creatures enjoy his benefits, and all who can declare it utter his praises. From the royal city throughout the (*five*) Indies, men who inhabit the savage wilds, those whose customs are diverse from ours, through the most remote lands, all have received the royal calendar, all have accepted the imperial instructions; alike they praise his warlike merit and sing of his exalted virtues and his true grace of utterance. This is the first thing to be declared. In searching through previous annals no such thing has been seen or heard of. In all the records of biography no such an account has been found. It was necessary first to declare the benefits arising from the imperial rule: now we proceed to narrate facts, which have been gathered either by report or sight, as follows:—

This Sahalôka [19] (Soh-ho) world is the three-thousand-

---

[16] The symbol *wan* probably refers to the literature used alike by all the subjects of the Great T'ang. It can hardly mean that they all spoke the same language.

[17] This at least appears to be the meaning of the passage. Julien translates as follows: "Si les effets merveilleux de cette administration sublime n'étaient point consignés dans l'histoire, comment pourrait-on célébrer dignement les grandes vues (de l'empereur)? Si on ne les publiait par avec éclat, comment pourrait-on mettre en lumière un règne aussi florissant?"

[18] I do not like this translation; I should prefer to suppose Chang Yueh's meaning to be that Hiuen Tsiang wherever he went exalted the name of China (*Fung t'u*; *Fung* being the name of Fuh-hi), and that he left this impression respecting the emperor who transcends the five and excels the three, &c.

[19] The Soh-ho (*or* So-ho) world is thus defined by Jin-Ch'au (*Fa-kiai-lih-t'u*, part i. fol. 2): "The region

great-thousand system of worlds (*chiliocosm*), over which one
Buddha exercises spiritual authority (*converts and controls*).
In the middle of the great chiliocosm, illuminated by one
sun and moon, are the four continents,[20] in which all the
Buddhas, lords of the world,[21] appear by apparitional
birth,[22] and here also die, for the purpose of guiding holy
men and worldly men.

The mountain called Sumêru stands up in the midst of
the great sea firmly fixed on a circle of gold, around which
mountain the sun and moon revolve; this mountain is
perfected by (*composed of*) four precious substances, and is
the abode of the Dêvas.[23]   Around this are seven mountain-ranges and seven seas; between each range a flowing
sea of the eight peculiar qualities.[24]   Outside the seven

(*t'u*) over which Buddha reigns is
called Soh-ho-shi-kiai; the old *Sûtras* change it into Sha-po, *i.e.*, *sarva.*
It is called in the *Sûtras* 'the patient
land;' it is surrounded by an iron
wall, within which are a thousand
myriad worlds (*four empires*)." It
seems from this that (*in later times at
least*) the Soh-ho world is the same
as the "great chiliocosm of worlds."
The subject of the expansion of the
Buddhist universe from one world
(*four empires*) to an infinite number
of worlds is fully treated by Jin-
ch'au in the work above named and
in the first part of my *Catena of
Buddhist Scriptures.*   There is an
expression, "tolerant like the earth,"
in the *Dhammapada*, vii. 95; from this
idea of "patience" attributed to the
earth was probably first derived the
idea of the "patient people or beings" inhabiting the earth; and
hence the lord of the world is called
Sahâmpati, referred first to Mahâ-
brahma, afterwards to Buddha.
Childers says (*Pâli Dict.* sub voc.):
"I have never met with Sahaloka or
Sahalokadhâtu in Pâli."   Dr. Eitel
in his *Handbook* translates a passage
quoted as if the Saha world were
the *capital* of the great chiliocosm
(sub voc. *Saha*).   I should take the
passage to mean that the Saha world

is the *collection* of all the worlds of
the great chiliocosm.

[20] The four continents or empires
are the four divisions or quarters of
the world. — *Catena of Buddhist
Scriptures*, p. 35.

[21] Lords of the world, or honourable of the age, a title corresponding to *lôkanâtha*, or (in Pâli) *lôka-
nâtho*, "protector or saviour of the
world."—Childers, *sub voc.*

[22] I cannot think Julien is right
in translating this passage by "y
répandent l'influence de leurs vertus."
The expression "*fa-in-sǎng*" must
refer to the apparitional mode of
birth known as *anupapâdaka*; and
the body assumed by the Buddhas
when thus born is called *Nirmâna-
kâya.*

[23] The abode of the Dêvas, or
rather, "where the Dêvas wander
to and fro and live."   The idea of
Sumêru corresponds with Olympus.
On the top of each is placed the
"abodes of the gods."   In the case
of Sumêru, there are thirty-three
gods or palaces.   Buddhist books
frequently explain this number
thirty-three as referring to the year,
the four seasons or quarters, and the
twenty-eight days of the month.

[24] For the *eight* distinctive qualities, see *Catena*, p. 379.

golden mountain-ranges is the salt sea. There are four lands (countries or islands, *dvîpas*) in the salt sea, which are inhabited. On the east, (Pûrva)vidêha ; on the south, Jambudvîpa ; on the west, Gôdhanya ; on the north, Kurudvîpa.

A golden-wheel monarch rules righteously the four ; a silver-wheel monarch rules the three (excepting Kuru) ; a copper-wheel monarch rules over two (excepting Kuru and Gôdhanya) ; and an iron-wheel monarch rules over Jambudvîpa only. When first a wheel-king[25] is established in power a great wheel-gem appears floating in space, and coming towards him ; its character—whether gold, silver, copper, or iron—determines the king's destiny[26] and his name.[27]

In the middle of Jambudvîpa there is a lake called Anavatapta,[28] to the south of the Fragrant Mountains and to the north of the great Snowy Mountains ; it is 800 li and more in circuit ; its sides are composed of gold, silver, lapis-lazuli, and crystal ; golden sands lie at the bottom, and its waters are clear as a mirror. The great earth Bôdhisattva,[29] by the power of his vow, transforms himself into a Nâga-râja and dwells therein ; from his dwelling the cool waters proceed forth and enrich Jambudvîpa (Shen-pu-chau).[30]

From the eastern side of the lake, through the mouth of a silver ox, flows the Ganges (King-kia)[31] river ; encircling the lake once, it enters the south-eastern sea.

---

[25] A *wheel-king* is a king who holds the wheel or discus of authority or power—*Chakravarttî Râja.*

[26] That is, as the text says, whether he is to rule over four, three, two, or one of the divisions of the earth.

[27] His name (*i.e.*, gold-wheel-king, silver-wheel-king, &c.) is derived from this first sign or miraculous event.

[28] Defined in a note as "without the annoyance of heat," *i.e.*, cool ; *an* + *avatapta. As. Res.*, vol. vi. p. 488.

[29] I have translated *tai-ti-p'u-sa* as "the great earth Bôdhisattva," although Julien renders it "the Bôdhisattva of the great universe,"

because there is such a Bôdhisattva, viz., Kshitigarbha, who was invoked by Buddha at the time of his temptation by Mâra ; and because I do not think that *tai ti* can be rendered *universe.* The reference appears to be to one Nâga, viz., Anavatapta Nâga-râja.

[30] In the Chinese Jambudvîpa is represented by three symbols, *Shen-pu-chau ;* the last symbol means an "isle" or "islet," and therefore the compound is equivalent to Jambudvîpa.

[31] The *King-kia* or Ganges river was anciently written *Hang-ho* or

From the south of the lake, through a golden elephant's mouth, proceeds the Sindhu (Sin-to) [32] river; encircling the lake once, it flows into the south-western sea.

From the western side of the lake, from the mouth of a horse of lapis-lazuli, proceeds the river Vakshu (Po-tsu), [33] and encircling the lake once, it falls into the north-western sea. From the north side of the lake, through the mouth of a crystal lion, proceeds the river Sîtâ (Si-to), [34] and encircling the lake once, it falls into the north-eastern sea.

River Hang. It was also written *Hang-kia* (Ch. Ed.)

[32] Sin-to, the Sindhu or Indus; formerly written *Sin-t'au* (Ch. Ed.)

[33] The Vakshu (*Po-tsu,* formerly written *Poh-ch'a*) is the Oxus or Amu-Daria (Idrisi calls it the Wakhsh-ab), which flows from the Sarik-kul lake in the Pamir plateau, lat. 37° 27′ N., long. 73° 40′ E., at an elevation of about 13,950 feet. It is supplied by the melting snows of the mountains, which rise some 3500 feet higher along its southern shores. It is well called, therefore, "the cool lake" (Anavatapta). The Oxus issues from the western end of the lake, and after "a course of upwards of a thousand miles, in a direction generally north-west, it falls into the southern end of the lake Aral" (Wood). This lake Lieut. Wood intended to call Lake Victoria. Its name, Sarik-kul,— "the yellow valley"—is not recognised by later travellers, some of whom call it Kul-i-Pâmir-kulân, "the lake of the Great Pamir." Wood's *Oxus*, pp. 232, 233, note 1; *Jour. R. Geog. Soc.*, vol. xL (1870), pp. 122, 123, 449, 450, vol. xlii. p. 507, vol. xlvi. pp. 390ff., vol. xlvii. p. 34, vol. xlviii. p. 221; Bretschneider, *Med. Geog.*, pp. 166 n, 167.

[34] The Sîtâ (*Si-to,* formerly written *Si-t'o*) is probably the Yarkand river (the Zarafshan). This river rises (according to Prejevalsky) in the Karakorum mountains, at an elevation of 18,850 feet (lat. 35°30′ N. long. 77°45′ E.) It takes a north and then a westerly course, and passing to the eastward of Lake Sarik-kul, bends to the north and finally to the east. It unites with the Kashgar and Khotan rivers, and they conjointly form the Tarim, which flows on to Lake Lob, and is there lost. The Sîtâ is sometimes referred to the Jaxartes or the Sarik-kul river (*Jour. Roy. As. Soc.*, N.S., vol. vi. p. 120). In this case it is identified with the Silis of the ancients (Ukert, *Geographie der Griechen und Römer*, vol. iii. 2, p. 238). It is probably the Side named by Ktesias,—"stagnum in India in quo nihil innatet, omnia mergantur" (Pliny, *H. N.*, lib. xxxi. 2, 18). This agrees with the Chinese account that the Yellow River flows from the "weak water" (*Joshwai*), which is a river "fabled to issue from the foot of the Kwên-lun mountain." "It owes its name to the peculiar nature of the water, which is incapable of supporting even the weight of a feather" (Mayers, *sub voc.*) This last remark agrees curiously with the comment on *Jâtaka* xxi., referred to by Minayef in his *Pâli Grammar* (p. ix. Guyard's translation), which derives the name of Sîtâ from *sad + ara*, adding that "the water is so subtle that the feather of a peacock cannot be supported by it, but is *swallowed up*" (Pâli, *sîditi*, from root *sad*, "to sink") A river Sîlâ is mentioned in the *Mahâbhârata* (vi. 6, sl. 219). north of Mêru. Megasthenês mentions both a fountain and river Silas which had the same peculiarity.

They also say that the streams of this river Sîtâ, entering the earth, flow out beneath the Tsih[35] rock mountain, and give rise to the river of the middle country (China).[36]

At the time when there is no paramount wheel-monarch, then the land of Jambudvîpa has four rulers.[37]

On the south "the lord of elephants;"[38] the land here is warm and humid, suitable for elephants.

On the west "the lord of treasures;"[39] the land borders on the sea, and abounds in gems.

On the north "the lord of horses;"[40] the country is cold and hard, suitable for horses.

On the east "the lord of men;"[41] the climate is soft and

Conf. Schwanbeck, *Megasthenēs*, pp. 37, 88, 109; *Ind. Ant.*, vol. vi. pp. 121, 130, vol. v. pp. 88, 334, vol. x. pp. 313, 319; Diodorus, lib. ii. 37; Arrian, *Indika*, c. vi., 2; Strabo. lib. xv. c. i. 38; Boissonade, *Anecd. Græc.*, vol. i. p. 419; Antigonus, *Mirab.*, c. 161; Isidorus Hisp., *Origg.*, xiii. 13; Lassen, *Zeitschrift f. Kunde des Morgenl.*, vol. ii. p. 63, and *Ind. Alterth.* (2d edit.), vol. i. p. 1017, vol. ii. p. 657; *Asiat. Res.*, vol. viii. pp. 313, 322, 327; Humboldt, *Asie Cent.*, tom. ii. pp. 404-412; *Jour. R. Geog. Soc.*, vol. xxxviii. p. 435, vol. xlii. pp. 490, 503 n.

[35] The Tsih rock, or the mountain of "piled up stones" (*tsih-shih-shan*). This mountain is placed in my native map close to the "blue sea," in the "blue sea" district (the region of Koko-nor). It may probably correspond with the Khadatu-bulak (*rock fountain*) or the Tsaghan Ashibantu (*white rock*) in Prejevalsky's map. Both of these are spurs of the Altyn-Tâgh range of mountains. Dr. Eitel, in his *Handbook* (sub voc. *Sîtâ*), says that "the eastern outflux of the Anavatapta lake . . . loses itself in the earth, but reappears again on the Aśmakûṭâ mountains, as the source of the river Hoangho." Here, I assume, the Aśmakûṭa mountains correspond with the *Tsih-shih-shan* of the text.

[36] The "River of China" is the Yellow River. Concerning its source consult Baron Richthofen's remarks on Prejevalsky's Lob Nor (p. 137, seq.) The old Chinese opinion was that the source of the river was from the Milky Way—*Tin-ho*) Mayers, p. 311). It was found afterwards that the source was in the *Sing-suh-hai*, *i.e.*, the "starry sea," which is marked on the Chinese map, and is probably the same as the Oring-nor.

[37] This clause might also be rendered "when there is no wheel-king allotted to rule over Jambudvîpa, then the earth (*is divided between*) four lords."

[38] Gajapati, a name given to kings; also the name of an old king of the south of Jambudvîpa (Monier Williams, *Sansk. Dict.* sub voc,) Abu Zaid al Hassan says this was the title given by the Chinese to the "king of the Indies" (Renaudot, *Mohamm. Trav.* (Eng. edit., 1733), p. 53.

[39] Chattrapati or Chattrapa, "lord of the umbrella," a title of an ancient king in Jambudvîpa (hence *Satrap*). Julien, p. lxxv. n.; Monier Williams, *sub voc.*

[40] Aśvapati (Jul.) I have translated *king* by "hard." Julien has omitted it.

[41] Narapati, one of the four mythical kings of Jambudvîpa (Mon. Williams, *sub voc.*) It was assumed

agreeable (*exhilarating*), and therefore [42] there are many men.

In the country of "the lord of elephants" the people are quick and enthusiastic, and entirely given to learning. They cultivate especially magical arts. They wear a robe [43] thrown across them, with their right shoulder bare; their hair is done up in a ball on the top, and left undressed on the four sides. Their various tribes occupy different towns; their houses are built stage over stage.

In the country of "the lord of treasures" the people have no politeness or justice. They accumulate wealth. Their dress is short, with a left skirt. [44] They cut their hair and cultivate their moustache. They dwell in walled towns and are eager in profiting by trade.

The people of the country of "the lord of horses" are naturally (*t'ien tsz'*) wild and fierce. They are cruel in disposition; they slaughter (*animals*) [45] and live under large felt tents; they divide like birds (*going here and there*) attending their flocks.

The land of "the lord of men" is distinguished for the wisdom and virtue and justice of the people. They wear a head-covering and a girdle; the end of their dress

---

the dynasty ruling at Vijayanagara by in the fifteenth and sixteenth centuries. The Arab travellers of the ninth century say the Chinese gave this title to the emperor of China, and also to "the king of Greece" (Renaudot, *u. s.*, p. 53). Compare the Homeric epithet, Ἄναξ ἀνδρῶν.

[42] I have taken the "therefore" to be part of this sentence, not of the next.

[43] This seems to me to be the meaning—"they wear a cross-scarf." Julien translates, they wear a bonnet, "posé en travers."

[44] This passage seems to mean that their clothes, which are cut short, overlap to the left—literally, "short, fashion, left, overlapping" (*jin*, the place where garments overlap.— Medhurst, *Ch. Dict.*, sub voc.)

[45] So I take it. The expression *shă lŭh* means "to slaughter." I do not understand Julien's "et tuent leurs semblables." There is a passage, however, quoted by Dr. Bretschneider (*Notices of the Mediæval Geography, &c., of Western Asia*, p. 114), from Rubruquis, which alludes to a custom among the Tibetans corresponding to that in Julien's translation—"post hos sunt Tebet, homines solentes comedere parentes suos defunctus." But, which is not the case in the text, the barbarians are made to slay their kin in order to eat them. *Conf.* Reinaud, *Relat.*, tom. i. p. 52; Renaudot, *Moham. Trav.* (Eng. ed., 1733), pp. 33, 46, and Remarks, p. 53; Rennie, *Peking*, vol. ii. p. 244; Yule's *Marco Polo*, vol. i. pp. 292, 302.

(*girdle*) hangs to the right.   They have carriages and robes according to rank;[46] they cling to the soil and hardly ever change their abode; they are very earnest in work, and divided into classes.

With respect to the people belonging to these three rulers, the eastern region is considered the best; the doors of their dwellings open towards the east, and when the sun rises in the morning they turn towards it and salute it.   In this country the south side is considered the most honourable.   Such are the leading characteristics in respect of manners and customs relating to these regions.

But with regard to the rules of politeness observed between the prince and his subjects, between superiors and inferiors, and with respect to laws and literature, the land of "the lord of men" is greatly in advance.   The country of "the lord of elephants" is distinguished for rules which relate to purifying the heart and release from the ties of life and death; this is its leading excellency. With these things the sacred books and the royal decrees are occupied.   Hearing the reports of the native races and diligently searching out things old and new, and examining those things which came before his eyes and ears, it is thus he (*i.e.*, Hiuen Tsiang) obtained information.

Now Buddha having been born in the western region and his religion having spread eastwards, the sounds of the words translated have been often mistaken, the phrases of the different regions have been misunderstood on account of the wrong sounds, and thus the sense has been lost. The words being wrong, the idea has been perverted. Therefore, as it is said, "it is indispensable to have the right names, in order that there be no mistakes."

Now, men differ according to the firmness or weakness of their nature, and so the words and the sounds (*of their languages*) are unlike.   This may be the result either of

---

[46] Literally, carriages and robes have order or rank.   It might also, without violence, be translated "(they possess) carriages and robes, and schools."

climate or usage. The produce of the soil differs in the same way, according to the mountains and valleys. With respect to the difference in manners and customs, and also as to the character of the people in the country of "the lord of men," the annals sufficiently explain this. In the country of "the lord of horses" and of "the lord of treasures" the (*local*) records and the proclamations explain the customs faithfully, so that a brief account can be given of them.

In the country of "the lord of elephants" the previous history of the people is little known. The country is said to be in general wet and warm, and it is also said that the people are virtuous and benevolent. With respect to the history of the country, so far as it has been preserved, we cannot cite it in detail; whether it be that the roads are difficult of access, or on account of the revolutions which have occurred, such is the case. In this way we see at least that the people only await instruction to be brought to submission, and when they have received benefit they will enjoy the blessing of civilization (*pay homage*). How difficult to recount the list of those who, coming from far, after encountering the greatest perils (*difficulties*), knock at the gem-gate [47] with the choice tribute of their country and pay their reverence to the emperor Wherefore, after he (*Hiuen Tsiang*) had travelled afar in search of the law, in his moments of leisure he has preserved these records of the character of the lands (*visited*). After leaving the black ridge, the manners of the people are savage (*barbarous*). Although the barbarous tribes are intermixed one with the other, yet the different races are distinguishable, and their territories have well-defined boundaries. Generally speaking, as the land suits, [48] they build walled towns and devote themselves to agriculture and raising cattle. They

---

[47] The *gem-gate*, I should think, is the *Yuh-mun*, the western frontier of the empire, not the gate of the emperor's palace.

[48] Julien translates this "generally speaking they are sedentary."

naturally hoard wealth and hold virtue and justice in light esteem. They have no marriage decorum, and no distinction of high or low. The women say, "I consent to use you as a husband and live in submission, (*and that is all*)." [49] When dead, they burn the body, and there is no determined period for mourning. They scar their faces and cut their ears. They crop their hair and tear their clothes.[50] They slay their herds and offer them in sacrifice to the manes of the dead. When rejoicing, they wear white garments; when in mourning, they clothe themselves in black. Thus we have described briefly points of agreement in the manners and customs of these people. The differences of administration depend on the different countries. With respect to the customs of India, they are contained in the following records.

Leaving the old country of Kau-chang,[51] from this neighbourhood there begins what is called the 'O-ki-ni country.

'O-KI-NI.

(Anciently called Wu-ki.)[52]

The kingdom of 'O-ki-ni (Akni or Agni) is about 500 li from east to west, and about 400 li from north to south.

---

[49] This sentence appears to allude to the custom of polyandry, or rather to the custom of the province of Kamul (Yule's *Marco Polo*, bk. i. ch. xli. vol. i. pp. 212, 214). It amounts to this: the woman says, "I consent whilst using you as a husband to submit," or "I consent to use you as a husband whilst dwelling under the roof." Julien translates it: "Ce sont les paroles des femmes qu'on suit; les hommes sont placés au-dessus d'elles."

[50] They do all this when bereaved, that is, of their relatives, and when they mourn.

[51] Leaving the ancient land of Kau-chang, i.e., the land which had long been occupied by the Uïgurs or Turks. The route of Hiuen Tsiang up to this point is detailed in his life. Leaving Liang-chau (a prefecture in Kansuh), he proceeded to Kwa-chau; he then crossed the Hulu river (Bulunghir) and advanced northward and westward through the desert. Having passed Hami and Pidshan, keeping westward, he comes to Turfan, the capital of the Uïgur country. He then advances to 'O-ki-ni.

[52] 'O-ki-ni. This may otherwise be written Wu-ki. Julien writes Yen-ki. The symbol ïcu is said sometimes to have the sound yen. This country corresponds to Karshar, or Kara-shahr, near the lake Tenghiz (Bagarach).

The chief town of the realm is in circuit 6 or 7 li.   On all sides it is girt with hills.   The roads are precipitous and easy of defence.   Numerous streams unite, and are led [53] in channels to irrigate the fields.   The soil is suitable for red millet, winter wheat, scented dates, grapes, pears, and plums, and other fruits.   The air is soft and agreeable; the manners of the people are sincere and upright.   The written character is, with few differences, like that of India. The clothing (*of the people*) is of cotton or wool.   They go with shorn locks and without head-dress.   In commerce they use gold coins, silver coins, and little copper coins. The king is a native of the country ; he is brave, but little attentive to (*military*) plans, yet he loves to speak of his own conquests.   This country has no annals.   The laws are not settled.   There are some ten or more *Sanghârâmas* with two thousand priests or so, belonging to the Little Vehicle, of the school of the Sarvâstivâdas (Shwo-yih-tsai-yu-po). The doctrine of the *Sûtras* and the requirements of the *Vinaya* are in agreement with those of India, and the books from which they study are the same.   The professors of religion read their books and observe the rules and regulations with purity and strictness.   They only eat the three pure aliments, and observe the method known as the "gradual" one.[54]

Going south-west from this country 200 li or so, surmounting a small mountain range and crossing two large rivers, passing westwards through a level valley some 700 li or so, we come to the country of K'iu-chi[55] [*anciently written* Kuei-tzŭ].

<hr>

[53] *Tai yin*, to carry off or lead here and there.   The text means they lead the water in channels from reservoirs.

[54] The transition doctrine between the Little and Great Vehicle.

[55] The route here described to Kuchâ would agree tolerably well with that laid down on Prejevalsky's map, viz., 200 li south-west to Korla, passing two rivers (for the Balgaktai-'ol and the Kaidu-gol, after uniting,

appear to bifurcate before reaching Karashahr), crossing a spur of the Kurugh-tagh range, and then keeping westward for about 150 miles across a level valley-plain to Kuchâ.   See Bretschneider, *Not. Med. Geog.*, p. 149.   I may observe that the pronunciation of *k'iu* in *K'iu-chi* is determined in a note, as equal to *k*(*u*) and (*w*)*uh*, that is *kuh*.

KINGDOM OF K'IU-CHI (KUCHÉ).

The country of K'iu-chi is from east to west some thousand li or so; from north to south about 600 li. The capital of the realm is from 17 to 18 li in circuit. The soil is suitable for rice and corn, also (*a kind of rice called*) *keng-t'ao;*[56] it produces grapes,[57] pomegranates, and numerous species of plums, pears, peaches, and almonds, also grow here. The ground is rich in minerals—gold, copper, iron, and lead, and tin.[58] The air is soft, and the manners of the people honest. The style of writing (*literature*) is Indian, with some differences. They excel other countries in their skill in playing on the lute and pipe. They clothe themselves with ornamental garments of silk and embroidery.[59] They cut their hair and wear a flowing covering (*over their heads*). In commerce they use gold, silver, and copper coins. The king is of the K'iu-chi race; his wisdom being small, he is ruled by a powerful minister. The children born of common parents have their heads flattened by the pressure of a wooden board.[60]

There are about one hundred convents (*sanghârâmas*) in this country, with five thousand and more disciples. These belong to the Little Vehicle of the school of the Sarvâstivâdas (Shwo-yih-tsai-yu-po). Their doctrine (*teaching of Sûtras*) and their rules of discipline (*principles of the Vinaya*) are like those of India, and those who read them use the same (*originals*). They especially hold to the

---

[56] A rice which is not glutinous (Jul.), *i.e.*, common rice.

[57] The grape in Chinese is *pu-ta'u;* this is one of the products which the earth is said to have produced naturally, and on which men (*all flesh*) fed for a period; those who took little retaining their whiteness of colour, those who ate greedily turning dark-coloured. (See in the *Chung-hu-mo-ho-ti-king*, k. i. fol. 3). The similarity between this word *pu-ta'u* and the Greek βότρυς has been pointed out by Mr. Kingsmill.

[58] The mistake in the text of *ming* for *yuen* is pointed out by M. Julien.

[59] The symbol *hǒ* sometimes means "embroidered work done by puncturing leather"—Medhurst. This seems more applicable to the passage than the other meaning of *felt* or *coarse-wool*.

[60] This is a well-known custom among some tribes of North American Indians.

customs of the "gradual doctrine," and partake only of the three pure kinds of food. They live purely, and provoke others (*by their conduct*) to a religious life.

To the north of a city on the eastern borders of the country, in front of a Dêva temple, there is a great dragon-lake. The dragons, changing their form, couple with mares. The offspring is a wild species of horse (*dragon-horse*), difficult to tame and of a fierce nature. The breed of these dragon-horses became docile. This country consequently became famous for its many excellent[61] horses. Former records (*of this country*) say : " In late times there was a king called ' Gold Flower,' who exhibited rare intelligence in the doctrines (*of religion*). He was able to yoke the dragons to his chariot. When the king wished to disappear, he touched the ears of the dragons with his whip, and forthwith he became invisible."

From very early time till now there have been no wells in the town, so that the inhabitants have been accustomed to get water from the dragon lake. On these occasions the dragons, changing themselves into the likeness of men, had intercourse with the women. Their children, when born, were powerful and courageous, and swift of foot as the horse. Thus gradually corrupting themselves, the men all became of the dragon breed, and relying on their strength, they became rebellious and disobedient to the royal authority. Then the king, forming an alliance with the Tuh-kiueh (Turks),[62] massacred the men of the city ; young and old, all were

---

[61] The word for "excellent" in the original is *shen*. There is a good deal said about these horses (called *shen*) in the account of the early intercourse of China with Turkestan (*circ.* 105 B.C.) See a paper by Mr. Kingsmill in the *J. R. A. S.*, N.S., vol. xiv. p. 99 n. Compare Marco Polo, bk. i. cap. 2, "*excellent* horses known as Turquans." &c. ; also Yule's note 2, and what is said about the *white* mares.—Yule's *Marco Polo*, vol. i. chap. 61, pp. 45, 46, 291.

[62] The Tuh-kiueh, or Turks, are the same as the Hiung-nû or Kara-nirûs, who drove the Yueh-chi or Yueh-ti (Viddhals) from the neighbourhood of the Chinese frontier (*J. R. A. S.* loc. cit. p. 77) ; they are to be distinguished from the Tokhâri, who overran the Græco-Baktrian kingdom and were driven thence by the Viddhals, who had fled before the Hiung-nû, and attacked the Tokhâri from the *west* (p. 81). See note 121 *infra*.

destroyed, so that there was no remnant left; the city is now a waste and uninhabited.

About 40 li to the north of this desert city there are two convents close together on the slope of a mountain, but separated by a stream of water,[63] both named Chau-hu-li, being situated east and west of one another, and accordingly so called.[64] (*Here there is*) a statue of Buddha,[65] richly adorned and carved with skill surpassing that of men. The occupants of the convents are pure and truthful, and diligent in the discharge of their duties. In (*the hall of*) the eastern convent, called the Buddha pavilion, there is a jade stone, with a surface of about two feet in width, and of a yellowish white colour; in shape it is like a sea-shell; on its surface is a foot trace of Buddha, 1 foot 8 inches long, and eight inches or so in breadth; at the expiration of every fast-day it emits a bright and sparkling light.

Outside the western gate of the chief city, on the right and left side of the road, there are (*two*) erect figures of Buddha, about 90 feet high. In the space in front of these statues there is a place erected for the quinquennial[66] assembly. Every year at the autumnal equinox, during ten several days, the priests assemble from all the country in this place. The king and all his people, from the highest to the lowest, on this occasion abstain from public business, and observe a religious fast; they listen to the

---

[63] So I think the passage must be translated. It is not the mountain that is divided by a stream, but the convents which stand on the slope of the mountain. The mountain, therefore, would slope to the north or south, and the convents stand east and west of one another, with a stream between them.

[64] That is, called the Eastern "Chau-hu-li" and the Western "Chau-hu-li." The expression *chau-hu-li*, although perfectly intelligible, is difficult to translate. The symbol *li* probably means a "pair" or "couple;" *chau-hu* means "supported, or dependent on, the brightness of the sun." The title, therefore, would be "bright-supported pair," referring, of course, to their receiving the eastern and western light of the sun respectively.

[65] I do not think there are two images; the text says, "the image of Buddha exquisitely adorned," &c.

[66] Called Panchavarsha or Panchavarshika, and instituted by Asoka.—Jul. See note 178 *inf.*

sacred teachings of the law, and pass the days without weariness.

In all the convents there are highly adorned images of Buddha, decorated with precious substances and covered with silken stuffs. These they carry (*on stated occasions*) in idol-cars, which they call the " procession of images." On these occasions the people flock by thousands to the place of assembly.

On the fifteenth and last day of the month the king. of the country and his ministers always consult together respecting affairs of state, and after taking counsel of the chief priests, they publish their decrees.

To the north-west of the meeting-place we cross a river and arrive at a convent called 'O-she-li-ni.[67] The hall of this temple is open and spacious. The image of Buddha is beautifully carved. The disciples (*religious*) are grave and decorous and very diligent in their duties; rude and rough (*men*)[68] come here together; the aged priests are learned and of great talent, and so from distant spots the most eminent men who desire to acquire just principles - come here and fix their abode. The king and his ministers and the great men of the realm offer to these priests the four sorts of provision, and their celebrity spreads farther and farther.

The old records say : " A former[69] king of this country worshipped the ' three precious ' ones.[70] Wishing to pay homage to the sacred relics of the outer world, he in-trusted the affairs of the empire to his younger brother on the mother's side. The younger brother having received such orders, mutilated himself in order to prevent any evil risings[71] (*of passion*). He enclosed the mutilated

---

[67] 'O-*she-li-ni*, according to the Ch. text, means "extraordinary" or "unique;" it may possibly be intended for Asâdhâraṇa.

[68] So it seems to mean, *fei tae ping shi*, " criminals and rude (*men*) come together here."

[69] I translate the symbol *sien* by "former" or "previous;" not by "first" or "the first." It appears to refer to a past king, indefinite as to time.

[70] Buddha, the law, the community.

[71] Or, " evil suspicions."

parts in a golden casket, and laid it before the king. 'What is this?' inquired the king. In reply he said, 'On the day of your majesty's return home, I pray you open it and see.' The king gave it to the manager of his affairs, who intrusted the casket to a portion of the king's bodyguard to keep. And now, in the end, there were certain mischief-making people who said, 'The king's deputy, in his absence, has been debauching himself in the inner rooms of the women.' The king hearing this, was very angry, and would have subjected his brother to cruel punishment. The brother said, 'I dare not flee from punishment, but I pray you open the golden casket.' The king accordingly opened it, and saw that it contained a mutilated member. Seeing it, he said, 'What strange thing is this, and what does it signify?' Replying, the brother said, 'Formerly, when the king proposed to go abroad, he ordered me to undertake the affairs of the government. Fearing the slanderous reports that might arise, I mutilated myself. You now have the proof of my foresight. Let the king look benignantly on me.' The king was filled with the deepest reverence and strangely moved with affection ; in consequence, he permitted him free ingress and egress throughout his palace.[72]

"After this it happened that the younger brother, going abroad, met by the way a herdsman who was arranging to geld five hundred oxen. On seeing this, he gave himself to reflection, and taking himself as an example of what they were to suffer, he was moved with increased compassion, (*and said*), 'Are not my present sufferings [73] the consequence of my conduct in some former condition of life?' He forthwith desired with money and precious jewels to redeem this herd of oxen. In consequence of this act of love, he recovered by degrees from mutilation, and on this account he ceased to enter the apartments of the women. The king, filled with wonder, asked him the

---

[72] Inner palace, palace of the women, "the harem."

[73] My present mutilated form.

reason of this, and having heard the matter from beginning to end, looked on him as a 'prodigy' (*khi-teh*), and from this circumstance the convent took its name, which he built to honour the conduct of his brother and perpetuate his name."

After quitting this country and going about 600 li to the west, traversing a small sandy desert, we come to the country of Poh-luh-kia.

POH-LUH-KIA [BÂLUKÂ OR AKSU].

(*Formerly called Che-meh or Kih-meh.*)[74]

The kingdom of Poh-luh-kia is about 600 li from east to west, and 300 li or so from north to south. The chief town is 5 or 6 li in circuit. With regard to the soil, climate, character of the people, the customs, and literature (laws of composition), these are the same as in the country of K'iu-chi. The language (*spoken language*) differs however a little. It produces a fine sort of cotton and hair-cloth, which are highly valued by neighbouring (frontier) countries.

There are some ten *saṅghârâmas* here; the number of priests (priests and followers) is about one thousand. These follow the teaching of the "Little Vehicle," and belong to the school of the Sarvâstivâdas (Shwo-yih-tsai-yu-po).[75]

---

[74] *Kih-meh* doubtless represents the *Kou-mé* of Julien (see the *Mémoire Analytique* by V. St. Martin, *Mem. s. l. Contr. Occid,* tom. ii. p. 265); it was formerly the eastern portion of the kingdom of Aksu. The name Poh-lu-kia or Bâlukâ is said to be derived from a Turkish tribe which "in the fourth century of our era occupied the north-western parts of Kansu."—*Ibid.* p. 266. The modern town of Aksu is 56 geog. miles E. from Ush-turfan, in lat. 41° 12′ N., long. 79° 30′ E. Aksu is 156 Eng. miles in a direct line W.S.W. from Kuchâ, which is in lat. 41° 38′ N., long. 83° 25′ E. on Col. Walker's map.

[75] The school of the Sarvâstivâdas; one of the early schools of Buddhism, belonging to the Little Vehicle, *i.e.*, the Hînayâna, or the imperfect mode of conveyance. This early form of Buddhism, according to Chinese accounts, contemplated only the deliverance of a portion of the world, viz., the Saṅgha or society; the Mahâyâna or complete (*great*) mode of conveyance, on the other hand, taught a universal deliverance. The Sarvâstivâdas believed in "the existence of things," opposed to idealism. Burnouf, *Introd.* (2d edit.), p. 397; Vassilief, *Bouddh.,* pp. 57, 78, 113, 243, 245.

Going 300 li or so to the north-west of this country, crossing a stony desert, we come to Ling-shan[76] (*ice-mountain*). This is, in fact, the northern plateau of the T'sung-ling range,[77] and from this point the waters mostly have an eastern flow. Both hills and valleys are filled with snowpiles, and it freezes both in spring and summer; if it should thaw for a time, the ice soon forms again. The roads are steep and dangerous, the cold wind is extremely biting, and frequently fierce dragons impede and molest travellers with their inflictions.[78] Those who travel this road should not wear red garments nor carry loud-sounding[79] calabashes. The least forgetfulness of these precautions entails certain misfortune. A violent wind suddenly rises with storms of flying sand and gravel; those who encounter them, sinking through exhaustion, are almost sure to die.

Going 400 li or so, we come to the great Tsing lake.[80]

---

[76] Ling-shan, called by the Mongols "Musur-aola," with the same meaning. —V. de St. Martin, p. 266.

[77] I translate it thus, because it agrees with Hwui-lih's account in the Life of Hiuen Tsiang, although it may also be rendered "this is (*or*, these mountains are) to the north of the T'sung-ling. The waters of the plateau," &c. The T'sung-ling mountains are referred to in the Twelfth Book; they are called T'sung, either because the land produces a great quantity of onions (*t'sung*), or because of the blue (*green !*) colour of the mountain sides. On the south they join the great Snowy Mountains; on the north they reach to the "hot-sea," *i.e.*, the Tsing lake, of which he next speaks. So that the Icy Mountains form the northern plateau of the range. The rivers which feed the Tarim do, in fact, take their rise here. Conf. *Jour. R. Geog. Soc.*, vol. xl. p. 344 ; Wood's *Oxus*, p. xl.

[78] The inflictions or calamities alluded to are the sand and gravel storms, referred to below.

[79] Or, it may be 'ought not to carry calabashes nor shout loudly." Perhaps the reason why calabashes are forbidden is that the water freezing in them might cause them to burst with a loud sound, which would cause the "snow piles" to fall. Why "red garments" should be interdicted is not so plain, unless dragons are enraged by that colour.

[80] The Tsing (limpid) lake is the same as Issyk-kul, or Temurtu. It is 5200 feet above the sea-level. It is called *Jo-hai*, "the hot sea," not because its waters are warm, but because when viewed from the Ice Mountain, it appears hot by comparison (note in the *Life* of Hiuen Tsiang). The direction is not given here ; but from Aksu to Issyk-kul is about 110 English miles to the north-east. Conf. Bretschneider, *Med. Geog.*, note 57, p. 37 ; *Jour. R. Geog. Soc.*, vol. xxxix. pp. 318 ff., vol. xl. pp. 250, 344, 375-399, 449.

This lake is about 1000 li in circuit, extended from east to west, and narrow from north to south. On all sides it is enclosed by mountains, and various streams empty themselves into it and are lost. The colour of the water is a bluish-black, its taste is bitter and salt. The waves of this lake roll along tumultuously as they expend themselves (*on the shores*). Dragons and fishes inhabit it together. At certain (*portentous*) occasions scaly mousters rise to the surface, on which travellers passing by put up their prayers for good fortune. Although the water animals are numerous, no one dares (*or ventures*) to catch them by fishing.

Going 500 li or so to the north-west of the Tsing lake, we arrive at the town of the Su-yeh river.[81] This town is about 6 or 7 li in circuit; here the merchants from surrounding countries congregate and dwell.

The soil is favourable for red millet and for grapes; the woods are not thick, the climate is windy and cold; the people wear garments of twilled wool.

Passing on from Su-yeh westward, there are a great number[82] of deserted towns; in each there is a chieftain (*or* over each there is established a chief); these are not dependent on one another, but all are in submission to the Tuh-kiueh.

From the town of the Su-yeh river as far as the Ki-shwang-na[83] country the land is called Su-li, and the people are called by the same name. The literature (*written characters*) and the spoken language are likewise so called. The primary characters are few; in the begin-

---

ning they were thirty[84] or so in number: the words are composed by the combination of these; these combinations have produced a large and varied vocabulary.[85] They have some literature,[86] which the common sort read together; their mode of writing is handed down from one master to another without interruption, and is thus preserved. Their inner clothing is made of a fine hair-cloth (linen); their outer garments are of skin, their lower garments of linen, short and tight.[87] They adjust their hair so as to leave the top of the head exposed (*that is,* they shave the top of their heads). Sometimes they shave their hair completely. They wear a silken band round their foreheads. They are tall of stature, but their wills are weak and pusillanimous. They are as a rule crafty and deceitful in their conduct and extremely covetous. Both parent and child plan how to get wealth; and the more they get the more they esteem each other; but the well-to-do and the poor are not distinguished; even when immensely rich, they feed and clothe themselves meanly. The strong bodied cultivate the land; the rest (*half*) engage in money-getting (*business*).

Going west from the town Su-yeh 400 li or so, we come to the " Thousand springs."[88] This territory is about 200 li square. On the south are the Snowy Mountains, on the other sides (*three boundaries*) is level tableland. The soil is well watered; the trees afford a grateful shade, and the flowers in the spring months are varied and like

[84] So my copy has it: Julien translates it *thirty-two.*

[85] Literally, "the flowing forth from these has gradually become large and varied."

[86] "Some historical records" (*Shu-ki*); or, it may be, "they have books and records."

[87] This difficult passage seems to mean that they use linen as an article of clothing; that their upper garments (jackets or jerkins) are of leather; their breeches are of linen, made short and tight.

[88] That is, Myn-bulak (Bingheul), a country with innumerable lakes —Eitel. Myn-bulak lies to the north of the road from Aulié-ata to Tersa; the high mountains to which it clings are the Urtak-taù. "The Kirghizes, even now, consider Myn-bulak to be the best place for summer encampment between the Chu and the Syr-Daria." " Here there is good pasturage, with a dense and succulent herbage, and there are numerous clear springs."—Severtsof, *J. R. G. Soc.,* vol. xl. pp. 367-369.

tapestry.   There are a thousand springs of water and lakes here, and hence the name.   The Khân of the Tuh-kiueh comes to this place every (*year*) to avoid the heat. There are a number of deer here, many of which are ornamented with bells and rings;[89] they are tame and not afraid of the people, nor do they run away.   The Khân is very fond of them, and has forbidden them to be killed on pain of death without remission; hence they are preserved and live out their days.

Going from the Thousand springs westward 140 or 150 li, we come to the town of Ta-lo-sse (Taras).[90]   This town is 8 or 9 li in circuit; merchants from all parts assemble and live here with the natives (Tartars).   The products and the climate are about the same as Su-yeh.

Going 10 li or so to the south, there is a little deserted town.   It had once about 300 houses, occupied by people of China.   Some time ago the inhabitants were violently carried off by the Tuh-kiueh, but afterwards assembling a number of their countrymen, they occupied this place in common.[91]   Their clothes being worn out, they adopted the Turkish mode of dress, but they have preserved their own native language and customs.

[89] Probably the "rings" (*hwan*) refer to neck-collars.

[90] M. Viv. de St. Martin has remarked, in his *Mémoire Analytique* (Jul., *Mém.*, tom. ii. pp. 267–273), that the distance from Lake Issyk-kul to Taras or Talas (which he places at the town of Turkistân, by the Jaxartes river), is too short by 1000 li; or, in other words, that from Su-yeh to the "Thousand springs" (Bingheul or Myn-bulak), instead of 400 li, should be 1400 li.   The same writer explains that in Kiepert's map of Turkistân there is a locality called Myn-bulak in the heights above the town of Turkistân, about a dozen leagues east from it.   This would agree with the 140 or 150 li of Hiuen Tsiang.   But see notes 93 and 95 below, and conf. Bretschneider's valuable note, *Med. Geog.*, p. 37, and *Notes on Chin. Med. Trav.*, pp. 34, 75, 114; Klaproth, *Nouv. Jour. Asiat.*, tom. xii. p. 283; Deguignes, *Hist. des Huns*, tom. ii. p. 500, tom. iii. pp. 219, 229; Yule's *Cathay*, p. clxv.; Wood's *Oxus*, p. xlii.; Rubruquis, in *Rec. de Voy. et de Mém.*, tom. iv. pp. 279, 280.

[91] The little deserted town alluded to in the text is named elsewhere (St. Martin, *Mémoires sur l'Arménie*, tom. ii. p. 118).   We gather from Hiuen Tsiang that the inhabitants were originally captives, carried off from China by the Turks, who assembled and formed a community in this place.

Going 200 li or so south-west from this, we come to the town called Peh-shwui ("White Water.") [92] This town is 6 or 7 li in circuit. The products of the earth and the climate are very superior to those of Ta-lo-sse.

Going 200 li or so to the south-west, we arrive at the town of Kong-yu, [93] which is about 5 or 6 li in circuit. The plain on which it stands is well watered and fertile, and the verdure of the trees grateful and pleasing. From this going south 40 or 50 li, we come to the country of Nu-chih-kien.

NU-CHIH-KIEN [NUJKEND].

The country of Nu-chih-kien [94] is about 1000 li in circuit; the land is fertile, the harvests are abundant, the plants and trees are rich in vegetation, the flowers and

[91] The town called "White Water" is the Isfijab of Persian writers according to V. de St. Martin, p. 274.

[93] The bearing *south-west* in this and the preceding case from Turkistân (if, with Julien, we identified that town with Taras) would take us over the Jaxartes and away from Tâshkand (Che-shi). In the tabular statement given by St. Martin (p. 274) the bearings and distances are as follows :—From Ta-lo-sse to Peh-shwui, 200 li to the south ; Peh-shwui to Kong-yu, 200 li southerly ; Kong-yu to Nu-chih-kien, 50 li south ; Nu-chih-kien to Chè-shi, 200 li west. But the bearing from Taras to the "White Water" (Peh-shwui) is south-west, and from the "White Water" to Kong-yu is again south-west. We have then a short distance of 50 li to the south to Nu-chih-kien, after which there are 200 li west to Tâshkand. Working back from Tâshkand, which appears to be a *certain* point according to the distances and bearings given, wo reach to about the River Talas, far to the eastward of Turkistân. If Aulié-ata on the Talas (lat. 43° 55′ N., long. 71° 24′ E., and 110 geog. miles from the river Chu)

be his Ta-lo-sse, then his route would lie across the head waters of the Karagati—a feeder of the Chu, and of the Jar-su—an affluent of the Talas, where we should place the Thousand Springs. But Myn-bulak is to the west of the Talas on the way to Tersa (35 miles west of Aulié-ata), which *may* be Ta-lo-sse. From Tersa, on a river of the same name which flows between Myn-bulak and the Urtak-taü hills, his route must have been to the south-west, either by Chemkent to Tâshkand — the same route as was afterwards followed by Chenghiz Khân ; or he must have gone over the Aksai hills, on the road to Namangan, into the valley of the Chatkal or Upper Chirchik, and so south-west and then west to Tâshkand. Myn-bulak, however, is north-east of Tersa, not east. See Severtsof's account of the country from Lake Issyk-kul to Tâshkand in *Jour. R. Geog. Soc.*, vol. xl. pp. 353–358, 363–370, &c., also p. 410. The site of Kong-yu has not been ascertained.

[94] Called Nejkath by Edrisi.— V. St. Martin, p. 276. Conf. Quatremère, *Not. et Extr. des MSS.*, tom. xiii. p. 259. But the identification

fruit plentiful and agreeable in character. This country is famous for its grapes. There are some hundred towns which are governed by their own separate rulers. They are independent in all their movements. But though they are so distinctly divided one from the other, they are all called by the general name of Nu-chih-kien.

Going hence about 200 li west, we come to the country of Che-shi (*stony country*).

CHE-SHI [CHÂJ].

The country of Che-shi[95] is 1000 or so li in circuit. On the west it borders on the river Yeh.[96] It is contracted towards the east and west, and extended towards the north and south. The products and climate are like those of Nu-chih-kien.

There are some ten towns in the country, each governed by its own chief; as there is no common sovereign over them, they are all under the yoke of the Tuh-kiueh. From this in a south-easterly direction some 1000 li or so, there is a country called Fei-han.

FEI-HAN [FERGHÂNAH].[97]

This kingdom is about 4000 li in circuit. It is enclosed by mountains on every side. The soil is rich and fertile,

of Taras in note 93 leads us to seek Nu-chih-kien on the Chatkal, to the east of Tâshkand.

[95] That is, Tâshkand, which means in Turkish the "tower" or "residence of (*tash*) stone" (V. St. Martin, p. 276 n.), corresponding with the explanation in the text. Compare Λίθινος πύργος of Ptolemy, *Geog.*, I. xi. 4, 6, xii. 1, 3, 9, 10 ; VL xiii. 2 ; Ouseley, *Orient. Geog.*, p. 269 ; Leyden and Erskine's *Memoirs of Baber* (edit. 1826), pp. xl. 99, 102 ; Deguignes, *Hist. G. des Huns*, tom. ii. p. 497, tom. v. pp. 26, 31 ; Ritter, *Asien*, vol. v. p. 570 ; Klaproth, *Magaz. Asiat.*, tom. i. p. 31 ; and Bretschneider, *Med. Geog.*, pp. 159, 160. It is in lat. 41° 19′ N., long. 69° 15′ E., and in H. Moll's map (1702) is called Al-Chach, and placed 155 miles south-west from "Taras or Dahalan." Rawlinson identifies Λίθινος πύργος with Tâsh-kurghân and with Kie-cha of Fahien.—*Jour. R. Geog. Soc.*, vol. xlii. p. 503. Yule, however, doubts this : Wood's *Oxus*, int. pp. xxxix., xl.

[96] The River Yeh, *i.e.*, the Sihun, Syr-daria, or Jaxartes.

[97] The distance, about 200 miles south-east of Tâshkand, takes us to the upper waters of the Jaxartes, the actual Khanate of Khokand. The pilgrim did not himself go there, but writes from report.

it produces many harvests, and abundance of flowers and fruits. It is favourable for breeding sheep and horses. The climate is windy and cold. The character of the people is one of firmness and courage. Their language differs from that of the neighbouring countries. Their form is rather poor and mean. For ten years or so the country has had no supreme ruler. The strongest rule by force, and are independent one of another. They divide their separate possessions according to the run of the valleys and mountain barriers. Going from this country [98] westward for 1000 li or so, we come to the kingdom of Su-tu-li-sse-na.

Su-tu-li-sse-na [Sutrishna].

The country of Su-tu-li-sse-na [99] is some 1400 or 1500 li in circuit. On the east it borders on the Yeh river (Jaxartes). This river has its source in the northern plateau of the Tsung-ling range, and flows to the north-west; sometimes it rolls its muddy waters along in quiet, at other times with turbulence. The products and cus-

---

[98] Hiuen Tsiang did not go to Ferghânah. The symbol used is *chi*, not *hing*. This will explain why the writer of the *Life* of Hiuen Tsiang (Hwui-lih) omits all mention of Ferghânah, and takes the pilgrim west from Tâshkand to Su-tu-li-sse-na, 1000 li. So that in the text we are to reckon 1000 li (200 miles approximately) not from Khokand, but from Tâshkand. It must be remembered that the kingdom or country of Su-tu-li-sse-na is spoken of, not a town.

[99] Sutrishna (Satrughna), also called Ustrûsh, Ustrûshṭa, Setrû-shṭa, and Isterûshân) or Usrûshna is a country "well known to Arabian geographers, situated between Ferghânah and Samarkand."—V. St. Martin, p. 278. It is described in the text as bordering on the Jaxartes on the east; we may sup-

pose, therefore, that this river was its eastern boundary. It is said to be 1500 li in circuit; we may place the western boundary, therefore, some 500 li to the west of Khojend. This limit would meet the requirements of the text, where the country is described as reaching 1000 li west from Tâshkand. Of course west means to the west of south-west. The town of Sutrishna is now represented by Ura-Tape, Uratippa or Ura-tiubé, which is some 40 miles south-west from Khojend and 100 miles south-south-west from Tâshkand (lat. 39.57 N., long. 69.57 E.) The Syr-daria, Sihun or Jaxartes, however, is to the north of Uratiubé. Ouseley, *Orient. Geog.*, p. 261; *Ariana Antiq.*, p. 162; Edrisi (Joubert's *transl.*), tom. ii. pp. 203, 206; Baber's *Memoirs*, pp. xlii, 9.

toms of the people are like those of Che-shi. Since it has had a king, it has been under the rule of the Turks.

North-west [100] from this we enter on a great sandy desert, where there is neither water nor grass. The road is lost in the waste, which appears boundless, and only by looking in the direction of some great mountain, and following the guidance of the bones which lie scattered about, can we know the way in which we ought to go.

SĂ-MO-KIEN (SAMARKAND).

The country of Să-mo-kien [101] is about 1600 or 1700 li in circuit. From east to west it is extended, from north to south it is contracted. The capital of the country is 20 li or so in circuit. It is completely enclosed by rugged land and very populous. The precious merchandise of many foreign countries is stored up here. The soil is rich and productive, and yields abundant harvests. The forest trees afford a thick vegetation, and flowers and fruits are plentiful. The *Shen* horses are bred here. The inhabitants are skilful in the arts and trades beyond those of other countries. The climate is agreeable and temperate. The people are brave and energetic. This country is in the middle of the Hu people (*or* this is the middle

[100] Here again there is no intimation that Hiuen Tsiang traversed this desert. It is merely stated that there is such a desert on the north-west of the kingdom of Sutrishna. It is the desert of Kizil-kûm. There is no occasion, therefore, to change the direction given in the text. (See Julien's note *in loco*). Conf. *Jour. R. Geog. Soc.*, vol. xxxviii. pp. 435, 438, 445.

[101] Called in Chinese the Kang country, *i.e.*, the peaceful or blessed country. Samarkand (lat. 39° 49′ N., long. 67° 18′ E.) is probably the Μαρδκανδα of Arrian, *Anab. Alex.*, lib. iii. c. 30, and iv. c. 5 ; Q. Curtius, lib. viii. c. 1, 20; Ptol. *Geog.* lib. vi. c. 11, 9 ; viii. 23, 10 ; Strabo, lib. xi. c. 11, 4 ; conf. Bretschneider, *Med. Geog.*, pp. 27, 60, 162–165 ; *Chin. Med. Trav.*, pp. 23, 38, 48, 76, 116 ; Palladius, *Chinese Recorder*, vol. vi. p. 108 ; D'Herbelot, *Bibl. Orient.*, p. 738 ; Wilson's *Ariana Antiq.*, p. 165 ; Yule, *Marco Polo*, vol. i. pp. 191 f., ii. pp. 456, 460 ; *Cathay*, pp. cxxx, ccxliv, and 192 ; *Jour. Roy. As. Soc.*, N.S., vol. vi. p. 93 ; *Jour. Asiat.*, ser. vi. tom. ix. pp. 47, 70 ; Deguignes, *Hist. des Huns*, tom. iv. p. 49; Gaubil, *H. de Gentchiscan*, p. 37 ; Sprenger, *Post und Reise Routen*, p. 20 ; Baber's *Mem.*, p. xxxvi. ; Ouseley, *Orient. Geog.*, pp. 232–238, 248–278 ; *Jour. R. Geog. Soc.*, vol. xl. pp. 453–462. Conf. the " Kang-dez " of the *Vindidad* and *Bundahis*.

of the Hu).[102]   They are copied by all surrounding people
in point of politeness and propriety.   The king is full of
courage, and the neighbouring countries obey his commands.
The soldiers and the horses (*cavalry*) are strong and numerous, and principally men of Chih-kia.[103]   These men of
Chih-kia are naturally brave and fierce, and meet death as a
refuge (*escape* or *salvation*).   When they attack, no enemy
can stand before them.   From this going south-east, there
is a country called Mi-mo-ho.[104]

MI-MO-HO [MAGHIÂN].

The country Mi-mo-ho[105] is about 400 or 500 li in circuit.   It lies in the midst of a valley.   From east to west
it is narrow, and broad from north to south.   It is like
Sa-mo-kien in point of the customs of the people and products.   From this going north, we arrive at the country
K'ie-po-ta-na.[106]

K'IE-PO-TA-NA [KEBÛD].

The country of K'ie-po-ta-na[107] is about 1400 or 1500
li in circuit.   It is broad from east to west, and narrow

[102] A term applied to the foreign-speaking (Tartar) people by some Chinese authors.

[103] These Chakas would seem to be the people of Chaghâniân, who were evidently a warlike people.—*Jour. Roy. As. Soc.*, N.S., vol. vi. p. 102.

[104] The rice country.—Ch. Ed.

[105] Here we observe again that Hiuen Tsiang did not visit Mi-mo-ho, but simply gives a report of it. This place probably corresponds with the district of Maghiân (lat. 39° 16′ N., long. 67° 42′ E.), 50 miles south-east of Samarkand. — Meyendorf, *Voyage à Boukhara*, pp. 161, 493; *Jour. Roy. Geog. Soc.*, vol. xl. pp. 449-451, 460, 461; and vol. xliii. pp. 263 ff., with Fedchenko's map of the district.

[106] The country of people in numbers.—Ch. Ed.

[107] This district of Kêbûd-Mêhê-kêt, Kêbûd, or Kêshbûd, is named by the Arabian geographers (*vid.* V. de St. Martin, *Mémoire Analytique*, p. 281), but its situation is not given.   M. V. de St. Martin places it in a north-westerly direction from Samarkand (*vid.* Jul. note *in loco*), but his calculation is founded on a misconception.   Hiuen Tsiang does not reckon from this place to K'iuh-shwang-ni-kia, but from Samarkand.   This is plain from the use of the word *hing*, and also from Hwui-lih (p. 60).—Ouseley, *Orient. Geog.*, p. 279; Baber's *Memoirs*, p. 85.

from north to south.　It is like Sa-mo-kien in point of customs and products.　Going about 300 li to the west (*of Samarkand*), we arrive at K'iuh-shwang-ni-kia.

K'IUH-SHWANG-NI-KIA [KASHANIA].

The kingdom of K'iuh-shwang-ni-kia[108] is 1400 or 1500 li in circuit; narrow from east to west, broad from north to south.　It resembles Sa-mo-kien in point of customs and products.　Going 200 li or so west from this country, we arrive at the Ho-han country.[109]

HO-HAN [KUAN].[110]

This country is about 1000 li in circuit; in point of customs and products it resembles Sa-mo-kien.　Going west from here, we come, after 400 li or so, to the country of Pu-ho.[111]

PU-HO [BOKHÂRA].

The Pu-ho[112] country is 1600 or 1700 li in circuit; it is broad from east to west, and narrow from north to south. In point of climate and products it is like Sa-mo-kien, Going west from this 400 li or so, we come to the country Fa-ti.[113]

[108] In Chinese "What country?" Kashania, described as a beautiful and important town of Sogdh, half way between Samarkand and Bokhâra.　This exactly suits the text, which places it 300 li (60 miles) west of Samarkand.—Istakhri, Mordtmann's *Transl.*, p. 131; Edrisi, tom. ii. pp. 199, 201; Ouseley, *Orient. Geog.*, p. 258; Abu'lfeda, *Choras. et Marar. Desc.*, p. 48.

[109] Eastern repose.—*Ch. Ed.*

[110] The part of the river of Sogdh (Zarafshân) which waters the territory round Bokhâra is called Kuan (V. de St. Martin, p. 282.　We observe that Hiuen Tsiang went to Kashania, and there we leave him; the accounts now given are bearsay.　Reinaud's *Abulfeda*, int. pp. ccxx–ccxxiv.; *Jour. R. Geog. Soc.*, vol. xlii. p. 502 n.; Darmesteter's *Zend-Avesta*, vol. ii. p. 67 n.

[111] Middle repose country.—*Ch. Ed.*

[112] Pu-ho is probably Bokhâra; the distance of course is too great, unless we consider the reference to be to the limits of the country.　The symbols used by Hwui-lih are the same as in the *Si-yu-ki*; Julien has misled V. St. Martin by writing "*Pou-kho.*"　Conf. *Jour. R. Geog. Soc.*, vol. xxxviii. p. 432; Baber's *Mem.*, p. 38; Moorcroft and Trebeck's *Travels*; Wolff's *Mission*; &c.

[113] Western repose country.—*Ch. Ed.*

FA-TI [BETIK].[114]

This country is 400 li or so in circuit. In point of customs and produce it resembles Sa-mo-kien. From this going south-west 500 li or so, we come to the country Ho-li-sih-mi-kia.

HO-LI-SIH-MI-KIA [KHWÂRAZM].

This country lies parallel with [115] the banks of the river Po-tsu (Oxus). From east to west it is 20 or 30 li, from north to south 500 li or so. In point of customs and produce it resembles the country of Fa-ti; the language, however, is a little different.

From the country of Sa-mo-kien [116] going south-west 300 li or so, we come to Ki-shwang-na.[117]

[114] Fa-ti is no doubt Bêtik. The distance from Pu-ho in the text differs from that given by Hwui-lih; the latter gives 100 li, which is doubtless correct. The whole distance from Samarkand west to the Oxus would thus be 1000 li, which corresponds to 200 miles, the actual measurement. The importance of Bêtik is derived from its being the most usual place of passage over the river by those going from Bokhâra to Khorasân.

[115] Ho-li-sih-mi-ka corresponds with Khwârazm. It is the Khorasmia of Strabo, lib. xi. c. 8 (p. 513), Pliny, vi. 16. Pharasmanes, king of the Khorasmii, came to Alexander with 1500 horsemen and said that his kingdom was "next to the nation of the Kolkhi and the Amazon women."—Arrian, *Anab.*, lib. iv. 15; conf. Herodotus, lib. iii. 93, 117; Ptolemy, *Geog.*, lib. vi. c. 12, 4; Q. Curt., vii. 4, viii. 1; Dionys. Per., 746; Steph. Byz. *sub voc.*; Baber, *Mem.*, p. xxxi. The bearing *south-west* in the text is *west* in Hwui-lih. The distance 500 li is the same in both. M. Viv. de St. Martin suggests north-west as the bearing, and adds

that Hwui-lih makes the distance 100 li (*Mémoire*, p. 283, n. 1). This is a mistake. For notices respecting the power of the Khwârizmian empire and the proceedings of Chenghiz Khân in destroying it;—vid. R. K. Douglas, *Life of Jenghiz Khan*, pp. xv. seq. It is true that Hiuen Tsiang says that Khwârazm runs parallel to both banks of the Oxus. But as Hwui-lih says it is bounded on the east by the Oxus, I think the symbol *liang* (two) is a mistake for *si* (west), in which case the text would make the country parallel to the west bank of the Oxus.

[116] The pilgrim now takes us back to the *country* of Samarkand; he reckons 300 li in a south-west direction to Kesh. The reckoning, I think, is from Kashania, where we left him; this was probably the western limit of the kingdom of Samarkand. Kesh or Shahr-sabz (39° 2′ N., 66° 53′ E.) lies due south-west from this point about 70 miles. Baber's *Memoirs*, pp. 36 and 54; *Jour. R. Geog. Soc.*, vol. xl p. 460; D'Herbelot, *Bib. Or.*, p. 238; and see note 83 *supra*.

[117] Country of historians.—*Ch. Ed.*

KI-SHWANG-NA [KESH].[118]

This kingdom is about 1400 or 1500 li in circuit; in customs and produce it resembles the kingdom of Sa-mo-kien.

From this place going south-west 200 li or so, we enter the mountains; the mountain road is steep and precipitous, and the passage along the defiles dangerous and difficult. There are no people or villages, and little water or vegetation. Going along the mountains 300 li or so south-east, we enter the Iron Gates.[119] The pass so called is bordered on the right and left by mountains. These mountains are of prodigious height. The road is narrow, which adds to the difficulty and danger. On both sides there is a rocky wall of an iron colour. Here there are set up double wooden doors, strengthened with iron and furnished with many bells hung up. Because of the protection afforded to the pass by these doors, when closed, the name of *iron gates* is given.

Passing through the Iron Gates we arrive at the country

---

[118] Hwui-lih also gives Ki-shwang-na as the name of this country (conf. V. St. Martin, *Mémoire*, p. 283, n. 3.

[119] The iron gates, Kohlûgha or Kalugah (Mong. "a barrier"), a mountain pass about 90 miles south-south-east from Samarkand, 50 miles south-south-east from Kesh, and 8 miles west of Derbent, in lat. 38° 11′ N., long. 66° 54′ E.

The distance and bearing from Kesh given in the text is south-west 200 li + south-east 300 li, which would give about the right distance in a straight line. These Iron Gates are marked on the Chinese maps; they are called *tich men to*, *i.e.*, the iron-gate-island (or eminence) from which the Muh-ho (Amu) flows. There has been some confusion between this place and the iron gates at Derbend on the Caspian, called by the Turks *Demír Kápi*; compare Yule's *Marco Polo* (book i. cap. iv.), vol. i. pp. 52 and notes, pp. 55–58; and vol. ii. pp. 494, 495, 537. M. V. de St. Martin (*Mémoire*, p. 284) says that the pilgrim "indicates the beginning of the mountains at 200 li to the south-east of Ki-shwang-na, and the defile properly so called at 300 li farther on, in the same direction." But this is not so; the first bearing is *south-west*, then through the mountains in a south-east direction. For a notice of the Irongate pass, in connection with Chenghiz Khân, see Douglas, *u. s.*, p. 66. Conf. Baber's *Mem.*, pp. xxxvi. 132; Gaubil, *Hist. de Gentchiscan*, p. 257; P. de la Croix, *Hist. de Timurbec*, tom. i. pp. 33, 62, &c.; Édrisi, tom. i. p. 484; Wood's *Oxus*, Yule's int., p. lxi.; Markham's *Clavijo*, p. 122; Bretschneider, *Chin. Med. Trav.*, p. 41 and n.; *Med. Geog.*, p. 61.

of the Tu-ho-lo.[120] This country, from north to south, is about 1000 li or so in extent, from east to west 3000 li or so. On the east it is bounded by the T'sung-ling mountains, on the west it touches on Po-li-sse (Persia), on the south are the great Snowy Mountains, on the north the Iron Gates.[121] The great river Oxus flows through the midst of this country in a westerly direction. For many centuries past the royal race has been extinct. The several chieftains have by force contended for their possessions, and each held their own independently, only relying upon the natural divisions of the country. Thus they have constituted twenty-seven states,[122] divided by natural boundaries, yet as a whole dependent on the Tuh-

[120] Formerly written by mistake To-fo-lo.

[121] The country here described as Tu-ho-lo is the Tukhára of Sanskrit, and the Tokháristán of the Arabian geographers. It corresponds with the Ta-hia of Sze-ma-t'sien. Ta-hia is generally identified with Baktria, but the limits of Baktria are not defined, except that it is separated from Sogdhiana by the Oxus. No doubt this land of Tukhára was that inhabited by the Tokhari, who were neighbours to the Dahæ, both of them mountain tribes (see the question discussed *Jour. R. As. Soc.*, N.S., vol. vi. pp. 95, 96). Mr. Kingsmill has given the substance of Sze-ma-tsien's account of Ta-hia and the surrounding tribes (*Jour. R. As. Soc.*, N.S., vol. xiv. pp. 77 ff). It is to be observed, however, that Hiuen Tsiang, when speaking of the Turks, *i.e.*, the Yueh-chi and Ye-tha, who had overrun this part of Central Asia, uses different symbols from those employed here. In the first case the people are called Tuh-kiueh; in this case the country is called Tu-ho-lo. The land of the Tokhári (Tokháristán) need not be connected with the people called Tuh-kiueh—the Hiung-nû or Kara-nirûs—although it was afterwards overrun by them. See n. 62 *supra.*

For notices of the Tokhári (v.l. Takhari) consult Strabo, *Geog.*, lib. xi. cap. 8. 2 (p. 511); Pliny, lib. vi. c. 17, 20; Amm. Marcell., xxiii. 6, 57; Ptol., *Geog.*, lib. vi. c. 11, 6; Justin, xlii. 2; Lassen, *Ind. Alt.* (2d ed.), vol. i. pp. 1019, 1023; Ritter, *Asien*, vol. v. p. 701, vii. p. 697; *Jour. R. As. Soc.*, vol. xix. p. 151; Rawlinson's *Herodotus*, vol. iv. pp. 45, 46; Bretschneider, *Med. Geog.*, p. 170. Tushâra (snowy, frigid) and Tushkâra are used as equivalents of Tukhâra; Wilson, *Vishnu Pur.* (Hall), vol. ii. p. 186, vol. iv. p. 203; *Mahábhárata*, ii. 1850, iii. 1991, 12,350, vi. 3652; *Harivamsa*, v. 311, xiv. 784, cxiii. 6441; *Brihat Samhitâ*, xiv. 22, xvi. 6; *Jour. R. Geog. Soc.*, vol. xlii. p. 498. *Tu-ho-lo* might phonetically represent Tûr, and so indicate the origin of Turân, the region to which Wilford assigned the Tukhâras.

[122] So also the Greeks when they took possession of Baktria divided it into satrapies, two of which, Aspionia and Turiva, the Parthians wrested from Eukratides.—Strabo, lib. xi. c. 11,2 (p. 517). The numerous coins belonging to the Greek period in Baktria probably relate to these satrapies, and not to an undivided Baktrian kingdom. See *Ariana Antiqua*, p. 160.

kiueh tribes (*Turks*). The climate of this country is warm and damp, and consequently epidemics prevail.

At the end of winter and the beginning of spring rain falls without intermission; therefore from the south of this country, and to the north of Lamghân (Lân-po), diseases from moisture (*moist-heat*) are common. Hence the priests retire to their rest (*rain-rest*) on the sixteenth day of the twelfth month, and give up their retirement on the fifteenth day of the third month. This is in consequence of the quantity of rain, and they arrange their instructions accordingly. With regard to the character of the people, it is mean and cowardly;[123] their appearance is low and rustic. Their knowledge of good faith and rectitude extends so far as relates to their dealings one with another. Their language differs somewhat from that of other countries. The number of radical letters in their language is twenty-five; by combining these they express all objects (*things*) around them. Their writing is across the page, and they read from left to right. Their literary records have increased gradually, and exceed those of the people of Su-li. Most of the people use fine cotton for their dress; some use wool. In commercial transactions they use gold and silver alike. The coins are different in pattern from those of other countries.

Following the course of the Oxus as it flows down from the north, there is the country of Ta-mi.

TA-MI [TERMED].

This country[124] is 600 li or so from east to west, and 400 li or so from north to south. The capital of the country

---

[123] So Sze-ma-t'sien describes the people of Ta-hia : "There was no supreme ruler; each city and town elected its own chief. Its soldiers were weak and cowards in battle, fit only for traders." (Kingsmill, *loc. cit.*)

[124] Termed or Terniz, on the north bank of the Amu-daria. Conf. Ba-

ber's *Memoirs*, int., p. xxxv. ; Bret schneider, *Med. Geog.*, pp. 57, 167 ; Deguignes, *Histoire des Huns*, tom. ii. p. 328 ; Yule, *Cathay*, p. ccxxxv ; Édrisi, tome i. p. 273 ; *Jour. Asiat.*, ser. vi. tome v. p. 270 ; *Jour. R. Geog. Soc.*, vol. xxxvi. p. 263 ; vol. xlii. p. 510.

is about 20 li in circuit, extended from east to west, and narrow from north to south. There are about ten *saṅghárámas* with about one thousand monks. The *stúpas* and the images of the honoured Buddha are noted for various spiritual manifestations. Going east we arrive at Ch'i-ngoh-yen-na.[125]

CH'I-NGOH-YEN-NA [CHAGHÂNIÂN].[126]

This country extends about 400 li from east to west, and about 500 li from north to south. The capital is about 10 li in circuit. There are some five *saṅghárámas*, which contain a few monks. Going east we reach Hwŭh-lo-mo.

HWŬH-LO-MO [127] [GARMA].

This country is some 100 li in extent from east to west,

<hr>

[125] Before entering on this excursus, it will be better to explain Hiuen Tsiang's actual route. From a comparison of the text with the narrative of Hwui-lih, it will be seen that, after leaving the Iron gates, and entering Tukhâra, he proceeded across the Oxus to the country called Hwo. This almost certainly is represented by Kunduz, on the eastern bank of the Surkh-âb. Here he met with the eldest son of the Khân of the Turks. This prince had married the sister of the king of Kao-chang, from whom Hiuen Tsiang had letters of recommendation. After some delay the pilgrim proceeded, in company with some priests from Balkh, to that city (Po-ho). Here he remained examining the sacred relics of his religion for some days. From this he departs southwards along the Balkh river to Dara-gaz, and there entering the mountains, he proceeds still southwards to Bâmiyân. So that of all the countries named betwixt the Oxus and the Hindu Kush, Hiuen Tsiang only himself visited Hwo (Kunduz), Po-ho (Balkh), Kie-chi (Gaz), and Fan-yen-na (Bâmiyân). This is gathered not only from the records found in Hwui-lih, but also from the use of the symbol *hing*. The excursus begins from Termed, at which point he probably crossed the Oxus, and proceeds, as the text says, along the northern flow of the river.

[126] Chaghâniân, or Saghâniân, probably corresponds with Hissâr, on the Karateghîn (or northern) branch of the Oxus, as the text says; the town is in lat. 38° 29' N., long. 69° 17' E. It included the valley of the Surkhan and Upper Kafirnahan. *Jour. R. As. Soc.*, N.S., vol. vi. p. 96; Baber's *Mem.*, p. xxxv. ; Ouseley, *Or. Geog.*, p. 277 ; Édrisi, tom. i. p. 480 ; Wood's *Oxus.*, Yule's int., p. lxii ; *Ocean Highways*, 1876, p. 328.

[127] From the eastern direction given we should expect the river to bend eastwards ; we find it does so. There can be little question, therefore, that Colonel Yule is right in restoring Hwŭh-lo-mo to Garma, the capital of Karateghîn district, on the Surkh-âb or Vakhsb. *Jour. R. As. Soc.*, N.S., vol. vi. p. 96 ; *Jour. R. Geog. Soc.*, vol. xli. pp. 338 ff ; Wood's *Oxus*, p. lxx. ; V. de St. Martin conjecturally identified it with Shadumân Hissâr.

and 300 li from north to south. The capital is about 10 li in circuit. The king is a Turk of the Hi-su tribe. There are two convents and about one hundred monks. Going east [128] we arrive at the Su-man country.

SU-MAN [SUMÂN AND KULÂB].

This country extends 400 li or so from east to west, and 100 li from north to south. The capital of the country is 16 or 17 li in circuit; its king is a Hi-su Turk. There are two convents and a few monks. On the south-west this country borders on the Oxus, and extends to the Kio-ho-yen-na country.

KIO-HO-YEN-NA [KUBÂDIÂN].

From east to west it is 200 li or so in extent; from north to south 300 li or so. The capital is 10 li or so in circuit. There are three convents and about one hundred monks. Still eastward is the country of Hu-sha.

HU-SHA [129] [WAKHSH].

This country is about 300 li from east to west, and 500 li or so from north to south. The capital is 16 or 17 li in circuit. Going eastwards we arrive at Kho-to-lo.

KHO-TO-LO [130] [KHOTL].

This kingdom is 1000 li or so from east to west, and

<hr>

[128] This expression "going east" need not imply that the country indicated lies to the eastward of the last named, but that it is eastward of the line of advance, which would in this case be the northern branch of the Oxus. Hence this country of Sumân, which has been identified with the Shumân of the Arab geographers (Édrisi, tom. ii. p. 203; Abulfeda, *Chor. et Marar.*, p. 38; Ouseley, *Or. Geog.*, p. 277), is said to have the Oxus on the south-west, extending to Kubâdiân (Kio-ho-yen-na), which lies between the Kafirnahan and Wagesh rivers,—the town of Kubâdiân being in lat. 37° 21′ N., long. 68° 9′ E., 57 miles N.N.E. of Khulm. *Jour. R. Geog. Soc.*, vol. xlii. pp. 456, 509 n.

[129] Hu-sha is no doubt Wakhsh, which lies to the north of Shumân and Khotlân. Conf. *Jour. R. Geog. Soc.*, vol. xl. p. 143.

[130] Kho-to-lo is represented by Khotl or Khotlân, the Kutl of

the same from north to south. The capital is 20 li or so in circuit. On the east it borders on the T'sung-ling mountains, and extends to the country of Kiu-mi-to.

KIU-MI-TO [KUMIDHA,[131] OR DARWÂZ AND ROSHÂN].

This country extends 2000 li from east to west, and about 200 li from north to south. It is in the midst of the great T'sung-ling mountains. The capital of the country is about 20 li in circuit. On the south-west it borders on the river Oxus;[132] on the south it touches the country of Shi-ki-ni.[133]

Passing the Oxus on the south,[134] we come to the kingdom of Ta-mo-sih-teh-ti,[135] the kingdom of Po-to-

Édrisi, and is described in the text as stretching eastward to the T'sung-ling mountains (Pamir), and bordered on the south by the valley of the Kômêdai, or plain of Kurgan-tubê and lower valley of the Vakhsh. It would thus correspond with the country to the north-east of Kulâb. Conf. Deguignes, *II. des Huns*, tom. v. p. 28 ; Bretschneider, *Med. Geog.*, p. 170 n. ; Ouseley, *Orient. Geog.*, pp. 230, 276.

[131] Kiu-mi-to would correctly be restored to Kumidha, which naturally represents the country of the Kômêdai of Ptolemy (*Geog.*, lib. vi. c. 12, 3, c. 13, 2, 3; lib. vii. c. 1, 42), through which the ancient caravans travelled eastward for silk. It corresponds with Darwâz (the gate), or the valley of Râsht. See *Jour. R. As. Soc.*, N.S., vol. vi. pp. 97, 98 ; *Jour. Asiat.*, ser. vi. tom. v. p. 270 ; Édrisi, tom. i. p. 483 ; *Jour. As. S. Beng.*, vol. xvii. pt. ii. p. 15 ; Wood's *Oxus*, pp. xxxix, lxxv, 248, 249 ; *Jour. R. Geog. Soc.*, vol. xli. p. 339 ; *Proc. R. G. S.*, vol. i. (1879) p. 65.

[132] The chief town of Darwâz—still called Khum or Kala-i-khum—is on the Ab-i-Panj or south branch of the Amu, which runs just within the south-west limit of the district. *Proc. R. Geog. Soc.*, vol. iv. (1882), pp. 412 ff. ; *Jour. R. Geog. Soc.*, vol. xlii. pp. 458, 471, 498. Roshân lies to the south-east of Darwâz and between it and Shignân, and on the northern branch of the river which joins the Panja near Bartang.

[133] Shi-ki-ni has been identified with Shignân or Shakhnân by Cunningham and Yule.—*J. R. As. Soc.*, N.S., vol. vi. pp. 97, 113 ; *J. R. Geog. Soc.*, vol. xlii. p. 508 n. ; *J. As. S. Beng.*, vol. xvii. pt. ii. p. 56 ; Wood's *Oxus*, pp. 248, 249. Edrisi has Saknia, tom. i. p. 483.

[134] That is, to the south of the Amu or Panja. The pilgrim having described the districts first in a northerly direction, then east of the main stream, now leaving the valley of the Shignân, which runs along the northern side of the Panja, he recounts the names of districts to the south of that river.

[135] Ta-mo-sih-teh-ti was restored doubtfully to Tamasthiti by Julien. It is the Termistât of the Arab geographers, one stage from the famous stone bridge on the Waksh-âb or Surkh-âb, and one of the chief towns of Khutl.—*Jour. R. Geog. Soc.*, vol. xlii. p. 508 n. See also Wood's *Oxus*, pp. lxxi, 260;

chang-na,[136] the kingdom of In-po-kin,[137] the kingdom of
Kiu-lang-na,[138] the kingdom of Hi-mo-to-lo,[139] the kingdom of Po-li-ho,[140] the kingdom of Khi-li-seh-mo,[141] the
kingdom of Ho-lo-hu,[142] the kingdom of O-li-ni,[143] the
kingdom of Mung-kin.[144]

Going from the kingdom of Hwo (Kunduz) south-east,

Istakhri, pp. 125, 126, and Gardi-
ner's 'Memoir' in *Jour. As. Soc.
Bengal*, vol. xxii. pp. 289, 291.

Julien has made a mistake (*Mém.*
t. ii. p. 201) in giving the width of
the valley at 400 or 500 li ; it should
be 4 or 5 li, according to the India
Office Library copy. It would
thus be a valley some 300 miles
long, and about a mile wide. On
Captain Trotter's map the long
valley of Wakhân extends through
more than two degrees of longitude,
viz., from 72° to 74° 30′ E. long. ;
but following the winding of the
river it might probably approach the
length assigned by Hiuen Tsiang.
See also Yule, *u. s.* pp. 111-113.

[136] Po-to-chang-na. This represents Badakshân, celebrated for its
ruby mines. For an interesting account of this country, its inhabitants,
and their character, see Wood's *Oxus*,
pp. 191 seq.; conf. *Jour. R. Geog. Soc.*,
vol. xxxvi. pp. 252, 260, 265, 278 ;
vol. xxxvii. pp. 8, 10 ; vol. xl. pp.
345, 393 ; vol. xlii. pp. 440 ff.; vol.
xlvi. pp. 278, 279.

[137] In-po-kin, probably Yamgân,
the old name of the valley of the
Kokchâ, from Jerm upwards.—Yule.

[138] Kiu-lang-na represents Kurân,
a name applied to the upper part of
the Kokchâ valley, about Lajward
(Wood). Celebrated for mines of
lapis-lazuli.—See Yule, *u. s.*

[139] Hi-mo-to-lo. This certainly
would correspond with Himatala,
the Chinese explanation being
" under the Snowy Mountains "
(*hima + tala*).—Julien, *Mem.*, tom. i.
p. 178. Colonel Yule has identified
it with Darâim, or, as it is otherwise given, Darah-i-aim. (See his
remarks, *Jour. R. As. Soc.*, N.S., vol.
vi. p. 108 ; Wood's *Oxus*, p. lxxvii.

[140] Po-li-ho must be in the neighbourhood of the Varsakh river, a
tributary of the Kokchâ. Wood, in
his map, has a district called Faro-
khar or Farkhar, which may represent Po-li-ho or Parika.

[141] Khi - li - seh - mo is no doubt
Khrishma or Kishm, north of Farkhar, and thirty-two miles east of
Tâlikân. Yule's *Marco Polo*, vol. i.
p. 163.

[142] Ho-lo-hu represents Râgh, an
important fief in the north of Badakshân between the Kokchâ and the
Oxus (Yule).

[143] O-li-ni. This, as Colonel Yule
says, "is assuredly a district on both
sides of the Oxus," of which the
chief place formerly bore the name of
Ahreng ; the Hazrat Imâm of Wood's
map, 26 miles north of Kunduz.
Yule, *u. s.* p. 106 ; P. de la Croix,
H. de Timurbec, t. i. pp. 172, 175 ;
Institutes of Timur, p. 95.

[144] Mung-kin. Julien has by mis-
take given the circuit of this district
as 4000 li (*Mém.*, tom. ii. p. 194),
instead of 400 li. This has been
observed by Colonel Yule (p. 105,
u. s.) It probably is represented by
the district from Tâlikân and
Khânâbâd, and the valley of the
Furkhan, in the east of Kunduz or
Kataghân. This Tâlikân is the
Thâikân of the Arab geographers.
Marco Polo visited it. Ouseley,
Orient. Geog., pp. 223, 224, 230, 231 ;
Baber's *Mem.*, pp. 38, 130 ; Yule's
Marco Polo, vol. i. p. 160. Conf.
Burnes, *Trav. in Bokhara*, vol. iii.,
p. 8 ; Wood's *Oxus*, pp. lxxxi, 156 ;
Bretschneider, *Med. Geog.*, p. 195.
There is a district called Munjân, in
the south of Badakshân, between the
sources of the Kokchâ and Gogar-
dasht.

we come to the kingdom of Chen-seh-to,[145] the kingdom of 'An-ta-la-po [146] (Andarâb), remarks concerning which may be found in the return records.

Going south-west from the country of Hwo, we arrive at the kingdom of Fo-kia-lang (Baghlân).

FO-KIA-LANG [BAGHLÂN].

This country[147] is 50 li or so from east to west, and 200 li or so from north to south; the capital is about 10 li in circuit. Going south, we come to the country of Hi-lu-sih-min-kien (Rúi-samangân).

HI-LU-SIH-MIN-KIEN [RÚI-SAMANGÁN].[148]

This country is about 1000 li in circuit, the capital about 14 or 15 li. On the north-west it borders on the kingdom of Ho-lin (Khulm).

HO-LIN [KHULM].

This country is 800 li or so in circuit, the capital is 5 or 6 li in circumference; there are about ten convents and 500 monks. Going west, we come to the country of Po-ho (Balkh).

PO-HO [BALKH].

This country is about 800 li from east to west, and 400 li from north to south; on the north it borders on the Oxus. The capital is about 20 li in circuit. It is

[145] Chen-seh-to, for *Kwo-sch-to*, *i.e.*, Khousta or Khost, located by Yule between Tâlikân and Indarâb. A district now known as Khost is in Afghanistan, south of the Kuram valley. *Jour. R. Geog. Soc.*, vol. xxxii. p. 311.

[146] An-ta-la-po, *i.e.*, Andarâb or Indarâb. Lat. 35° 40′ N.; long. 69° 27′ E.

[147] In the valley of the southern Surkh-âb or Kunduz river, about 34 miles south from Kunduz. Ouseley, *Orient. Geog.*, p. 223; *Jour. R As. Soc.*, N.S., vol. vi. p. 101.

[148] In the upper valley of the Khulm river, including the towns of Rûi, Kuram, and Haibak, formerly called Samangân, and about 42 miles west from Baghlân. Moorcroft, *Travels*, vol. ii. p. 402; Sprenger, *Post u. Reise Routen*, p. 37; Burnes, *Travels* (1st ed.), vol. i. pp. 201–205.

called generally the little Râjagṛiha.[149]   This city, though well (*strongly*) fortified, is thinly populated.   The products of the soil are extremely varied, and the flowers, both on the land and water, would be difficult to enumerate.   There are about 100 convents and 3000 monks, who all study the religious teaching of the Little Vehicle.

Outside the city, towards the south-west,[150] there is a convent called Navasaṅghârâma, which was built by a former king of this country.   The Masters (*of Buddhism*), who dwell to the north of the great Snowy Mountains, and are authors of *Śâstras*, occupy this convent only, and continue their estimable labours in it.   There is a figure of Buddha here, which is lustrous with (*reflects the glory of*) noted gems, and the hall in which it stands is also adorned with precious substances of rare value.   This is the reason why it has often been robbed by chieftains of neighbouring countries, covetous of gain.

This convent also contains (*possesses*)[151] a statue of Pi-

[149] So I think it ought to be translated.   It is called the "Little Râjagṛiha" in consequence of the numerous Buddhist sites in its neighbourhood, vying in that respect with the Magadha capital. This is plainly intimated in the *Life* of Hiuen Tsiang (Julien's trans., p. 64), where the Khân says that "it is called the Little Râjagṛiha: its sacred relics are exceedingly numerous;" the latter being the explanation of the former.   On Balkh, see Burnes, *Travels* (1st ed.), vol. i. pp. 237–240; Ferrier, *Caravan Journ.*, pp. 206, 207; B. de Meynard, *Les Prairies d'Or*, t. iv. p. 48; *Dict. Géog.-Hist. de Perse*, p. 571; *Jour. R. Geog. Soc.*, vol. xlii. p. 510; De Herbelot, *Bibl. Orient.*, p. 167; Hyde, *Hist. Rel. vet. Pers.*, p. 494; Yule's *Marco Polo*, vol. i. p. 158; *Cathay*, p. 179; Bretschneider, *Mal. Geog.*, p. 196; *Chin. Mal. Trav.*, pp. 47, 117.

[150] Julien gives *south-east* by mistake.

[151] This passage seems to require the use of a past tense, "this convent formerly (*su*) had;" and so Julien renders it.   But it appears to me improbable, if the statue of Vaiśravaṇa was in existence when the foray was made, "in recent times," that it should have been lost or destroyed so soon afterwards.   Moreover, the symbol *su* has sometimes the sense of "a present condition" (as, for example, in the *Chung Yung*, xiv. 1, 2).   Considering the sentence which follows, where the *interior* of the Saṅghârâma is spoken of, I should prefer to think that *su* is a mistake for *ts'ien*; they both have the meaning of "before" or "formerly," but *ts'ien* also has the sense of "in front of."   In this case the passage would run: "In front of the Saṅghârâma there is a figure of Vaiśravaṇa Dêva."   This Dêva was the protector of the convent, not so much that he was Kubêra, the god of wealth, as that he was the guardian of the north.

sha-men (Vaiśravaṇa) Dêva, by whose spiritual influence, in unexpected ways, there is protection afforded to the precincts of the convent. Lately the son of the Khân Yeh-hu (*or* She-hu), belonging to the Turks, becoming rebellious, Yeh-hu Khân broke up his camping ground, and marched at the head of his horde to make a foray against this convent, desiring to obtain the jewels and precious things with which it was enriched.[152] Having encamped his army in the open ground, not far from the convent, in the night he had a dream. He saw Vaiśravaṇa Dêva, who addressed him thus: "What power do you possess that you dare (*to intend*) to overthrow this convent?" and then hurling his lance, he transfixed him with it. The Khân, affrighted, awoke, and his heart penetrated with sorrow, he told his dream to his followers, and then, to atone somewhat for his fault, he hastened to the convent to ask permission to confess his crime to the priests; but before he received an answer he died.

Within the convent, in the southern hall of Buddha, there is the washing-basin which Buddha used. It contains about a peck,[153] and is of various colours, which dazzle the eyes. It is difficult to name the gold and stone of which it is made.[154] Again, there is a tooth of Buddha about an inch long, and about eight or nine tenths of an inch in breadth. Its colour is yellowish white; it is pure and shining. Again, there is the sweeping brush of Buddha, made of the

---

This was perhaps the most northern Buddhist establishment in existence; at any rate, it was built for the convenience of northern priests.

[152] This sentence may otherwise be rendered: "Lately the son of the Turk Yeh-hu-khân, whose name was Sse-yeh-hu-khân, breaking up his camping ground," &c. Yeh-hu is the Khân that Hiuen Tsiang met on the rich hunting grounds of the Chu'i river (*Vie de Hiouen Thsang,* p. 55). If the name of his son was Sse-yeh-hu, then doubtless it is he who purposed to sack the Sangh-ârâma. But if *sse* has the sense of "rebelling," then it would be Yeh-hu-khân himself who is referred to. I am inclined to think it must have been the son, whose name was *Sse;* but the repetition of the name Yeh-hu-khân is perplexing. The symbols *po-lo* correspond with the Turkish work *bulak,* camping ground or cantonment.

[153] *Teou,* a dry measure of ten pints.

[154] This may mean—the golden-like stone of which it is made has a difficult name, or the metal (gold) and stone are difficult to name.

plant " Ka-she " (*kâśâ*). It is about two feet long and about seven inches round. Its handle is ornamented with various gems. These three relics are presented with offerings on each of the six fast-days by the assembly of lay and cleric believers. Those who have the greatest faith in worship see the objects emitting a radiance of glory.

To the north of the convent is a *stûpa*, in height about 200 feet, which is covered with a plaster hard as [155] the diamond, and ornamented with a variety of precious substances. It encloses a sacred relic (*she-li*), and at times this also reflects a divine splendour.

To the south-west of the convent there is a *Vihâra*. Many years have elapsed since its foundation was laid. It is the resort (*of people*) from distant quarters. There are also a large number of men of conspicuous talent. As it would be difficult for the several possessors of the four different degrees (*fruits*) of holiness to explain accurately their condition of saintship, therefore the Arhats (*Lo-han*), when about to die, exhibit their spiritual capabilities (*miraculous powers*), and those who witness such an exhibition found *stûpas* in honour of the deceased saints. These are closely crowded together here, to the number of several hundreds. Besides these there are some thousand others, who, although they had reached the fruit of holiness (*i.e.*, *Arhatship*), yet having exhibited no spiritual changes at the end of life, have no memorial erected to them.

At present the number of priests is about 100; so irregular are they morning and night in their duties, that it is hard to tell saints from sinners.[156]

To the north-west of the capital about 50 li or so we arrive at the town of Ti-wei; 40 li to the north of this

---

[155] It may be "hard as the diamond," or "shining like the diamond."

[156] There is evidently a false reading here. I think the character *fi*, which, in connection with the following character, *hai*, means "remiss and idle," is for *mi*, which would qualify *hai* in the sense of "absence of idleness." The passage would then read : "Morning and night there is an absence of idleness, but it is difficult to conjecture who are saints and who not."

town is the town of Po-li. In each of these towns there is a *stûpa* about three chang (30 *feet*) in height. In old days, when Buddha first attained enlightenment after advancing to the tree of knowledge,[157] he went to the garden of deer;[158] at this time two householders[159] meeting him, and beholding the brilliant appearance of his person, offered him from their store of provisions for their journey some cakes and honey. The lord of the world, for their sakes, preached concerning the happiness of men and Dêvas, and delivered to them, his very first disciples,[160] the five rules of moral conduct and the ten good qualities (*shen*, virtuous rules).[161] When they had heard the sermon, they humbly asked for some object to worship (*offer gifts*). On this Tathâgata delivered to them some of his hair and nail-cuttings. Taking these, the merchants were about to return to their own country,[162] when they asked of Buddha the right way of venerating these relics. Tathâgata forthwith spreading out his *Sanghâti* on the ground as a square napkin, next laid down his *Uttarâsanga* and then his *Sankakshikâ;* again over these he placed as a cover his begging-pot, on which he erected his mendicant's staff.[163] Thus he placed them in order, making thereby

---

[157] This passage might perhaps also be rendered "after gazing with delight on the Bôdhi tree." The symbol *tsu* has such a meaning, and it would be in strict agreement with the legend.

[158] That is, the garden at Banâras.

[159] Two merchant-lords (*chang-chè*).

[160] "The very first to hear the five," &c.

[161] That is, the five *S'îlas* and the ten *S'îlas.* See Childers, *Pali Dict.*, sub *silam.* The story of the two merchants alluded to in the text is one well known in the Buddhist legend. It will be found in Spence Hardy's *Manual of Buddhism* (2d ed.) pp. 186, 187, and note; also in the *Fo-sho-hing-tsan-king*, p. 167; Bigandet, *Legend of Gaudama*, vol. i. p. 108; Beal, *Rom. Legend*, p. 236. The incident is also found amongst the Amarâvâtî sculptures (*Tree and Serp. Worship*, pl. lviii. fig. 1, middle disc).

[162] Their own country was Suvarṇabhûmi or Burma.

[163] This translation differs from that of M. Julien. I take the construction thus: *I săng kia chi*, "taking his sanghâti;" *fany thee po*, "as a square napkin" (*i.e.*, folding it into this shape); *hia*, "he placed it underneath." The rest of the sentence, then, will follow as I have translated it. The monument erected as a shrine for the relics given on this occasion is said to be the far-famed Shwè-dagun at Râangun.— *As. Researches*, vol. xvi., quoted by Spence Hardy, *M. B.*, p. 187 n.

(*the figure of*) a *stûpa*. The two men taking the order, each went to his own town, and then, according to the model which the holy one had prescribed, they prepared to build a monument, and thus was the very first *Stûpa* of the Buddhist religion erected.

Some 70 li to the west of this town is a *Stûpa* about two chang (20 *feet*) in height. This was erected in the time of Kâśyapa Buddha. Leaving the capital and going south-west, entering the declivities of the Snowy Mountains, there is the country of Jui-mo-to [Jumadh?].

Jui-mo-to [Jumadha ?].[164]

This country is 50 or 60 li from east to west, and 100 li or so from north to south. The capital is about 10 li in circuit. Towards the south-west is the country of Hu-shi-kien (Jûzgân).

Hu-shi-kien [Jûzgâna].

This country is about 500 li from east to west, and about 1000 li from north to south. The capital is 20 li in circuit. It has many mountains and river-courses. It produces excellent (*shen*) horses. To the north-west is Ta-la-kien.

Ta-la-kien [Tâlikân].[165]

This country is 500 li or so from east to west, and 50 or 60 li from north to south. The capital is 10 li about in circuit. On the west it touches the boundaries of Persia. Going[166] 100 li or so south from the kingdom of Po-ho (Balkh), we arrive at Kie-chi.

---

[164] A position near Sir-i-pul seems indicated.—Yule, *u. s.*, p. 101.

[165] On the borders of Khorasân, in the valley of the Murghâb.— Ouseley, *Orient. Geog.*, pp. 175, 220; Édrisi, tom. i. pp. 468, 478; *Jour. As.*, ser. vi., tom. xiii. pp. 175–179. There is a Tâlikân also in Badak-shân. See n. 145 *ante*.

[166] Here the true itinerary is re-sumed. Hiuen Tsiang now leaves Balkh, and travels south about twenty miles to Gaz or Darah-Gaz. "This valley will be found in Mac-artney's map to Elphinstone, in the map to Ferrier's Travels, &c., about one march south of Balkh, about half-way between that town and

KIE-CHI [GACHI OR GAZ].

This country from east to west is 500 li or so, from west to south 300 li. The capital is 4 or 5 li in circuit. The soil is stony, the country a succession of hills. There are but few flowers or fruits, but plenty of beans and corn. The climate is wintry; the manner of the people hard and forbidding. There are some ten convents or so, and about 200 [167] priests. They all belong to the school of the Sarvâstivâdas, which is a branch of the Little Vehicle.

On the south-east we enter the great Snowy Mountains. These mountains are high and the valleys deep; the precipices and hollows (*crevasses*) are very dangerous. The wind and snow keep on without intermission; the ice remains through the full summer; the snow-drifts fall into the valleys and block the roads. The mountain spirits and demons (*demon sprites*) send, in their rage, all sorts of calamities; robbers crossing the path of travellers kill them.[168] Going with difficulty 600 li or so, we leave the country of Tukhâra, and arrive at the kingdom of Fan-yen-na (Bâmiyân).

FAN-YEN-NA [BÁMIYÁN].[169]

This kingdom is about 2000 li from east to west, and 300 li from north to south. It is situated in the midst

Dehas. Ibn Haukal also states that the hill-country south of Balkh is called Ghaz (Ouseley, *Or. Geog.*, pp. 243, 244, 270). Darah-Gaz is mentioned in Timur's *Institutes* (p. 59), and it was the scene of a rout of Humayûn's little army by the Uzbeks in 1549.—Erskine's *Baber and Humayun*, vol. ii. pp. 373, 376; Yule, *Jour. R. As. Soc.*, N.S., vol. vi. p. 102; *Jour. As. Soc. Bengal*, vol. xxii. p. 164.

[167] My text gives 200 as the number of the priests; but the error is in the printing: it ought to be 300.

[168] This phrase, *wei wu*, may refer to the former statement, "that the robbers kill the travellers;" in which case *wei wu* would mean, "as a profession or business;" referring perhaps to the existence of a dacoit system.

[169] The country of Bâmiyân has been described by Burnes and other travellers. Wood, in his journey to the source of the Oxus, passed through it. It lies immediately to the north of the Hajiyak Pass. Wood's *Oxus* (2d ed.), pp. 130, 131; *Proc. R. Geog. Soc.*, vol. i. (1879), pp. 244 ff.; Baber's *Memoirs*, p. 139.

of the Snowy Mountains. The people inhabit towns either in the mountains or the valleys, according to circumstances.[170] The capital leans on a steep hill, bordering on a valley 6 or 7 li in length.[171] On the north it is backed by high precipices. It (*the country*) produces spring-wheat[172] and few flowers or fruits. It is suitable for cattle, and affords pasture for many sheep and horses. The climate is wintry, and the manners of the people hard and uncultivated. The clothes are chiefly made of skin and wool, which are the most suitable for the country. The literature, customary rules, and money used in commerce are the same as those of the Tukhâra country. Their language is a little different, but in point of personal appearance they closely resemble each other. These people are remarkable, among all their neighbours, for a love of religion (*a heart of pure faith*); from the highest form of worship to the three jewels,[173] down to the worship of the hundred (*i.e., different*) spirits, there is not the least absence (*decrease*) of earnestness and the utmost devotion of heart. The merchants, in arranging their prices as they come and go, fall in with the signs afforded by the spirits. If good, they act accordingly; if evil, they seek to propitiate the powers.[174] There are ten convents and about 1000 priests. They belong to the Little Vehicle, and the school of the Lôkôttaravâdins (Shwo-ch'uh-shi-pu).

To the north-east of the royal city there is a mountain, on the declivity of which is placed a stone figure of Buddha,

---

Grote (*Hist. Greece*, vol. xii. p. 271 n.) supposes that Alexander crossed into Baktria by Bâmiyân : see Arrian, *Anab.*, lib. iii. c. 29, 1 ; Strabo, *Geog.*, lib. xv. c. 2, 11 ; Wilson, *Ariana Ant.*, pp. 179 f. ; also note 175 *inf.*

[170] Or, "according to the resources or strength of the place."

[171] Such it appears is the meaning. The town rests on, or is supported by, a precipitous cliff, and borders on a valley 6 or 7 li in length.

[172] The *suh-mai* is " late wheat ;" wheat sown in the spring.

[173] Buddha, Dharma, and Saṅgha.

[174] This sentence might be rendered better thus : " The merchants conjecture in coming and going whether the gods and spirits (or the heavenly spirits) afford propitious omens ; if the indications are calamitous, they offer up their prayers (seek religious merit)."

erect, in height 140 or 150 feet.[175]   Its golden hues sparkle on every side, and its precious ornaments dazzle the eyes by their brightness.

To the east of this spot there is a convent, which was built by a former king of the country.   To the east of the convent there is a standing figure of Sâkya Buddha, made of metallic stone (*tcou-shih* [176]), in height 100 feet.   It has been cast in different parts and joined together, and thus placed in a completed form as it stands.

To the east of the city 12 or 13 li there is a convent, in which there is a figure of Buddha lying in a sleeping position, as when he attained *Nirvâṇa*   The figure is in length about 1000 feet or so.[177]   The king of this (*country*),

---

[175] These rock-hewn figures of Buddha in Bâmiyân have been objects of curiosity down to the present day.   They were seen during the campaign in Afghanistan in 1843, and doubtless remain to the present day.   The most recent notice of them is in General Kaye's paper. *Proc. R. Geog. Soc.*, vol. i. (1879), pp. 248, 249.   He says: "On the opposite side of the valley from the great (standing) image, about a mile to the west, a stony gully leads into the hills.   A short way up this there is a nearly insulated rock, on the flat summit of which there is in relief a recumbent figure, bearing a rude resemblance to a huge lizard," which figure the people now call Azhdahâ, or the dragon slain by a Muhammadan pîr (see also *ib.*, p. 338).   Hyde, quoting Masâlik Maniâlik and the *Farhang-i-Jahângiri* of Ibn Fakred-dîn Angju, says the two larger statues are 50 cubits high, one called *Surkh-but* (red image) and the other *Khink-but* (grey image), and at some distance is a smaller one "in formæ vetulæ," called *Nesr*.   The *Aîn-i-Akbarî* says the larger of the two is 80 ells (cubits?) and the lesser 50 in height; Burnes's estimate is 120 and 70 feet. Wilford gives a tolerably minute account of Bâmiyân and these figures.

Masson mentions five statues.   See Ritter, *Die Stupa's oder die Architektonischen Denkmale an der Indo-Baktr. Königstr. u. d. Colosse von Bamiyan*, pp. 24 f.; Hyde, *Hist. Relig. vet. Pers.*, p. 132; Burnes, *Travels*, vol. i. pp. 182–188, and *J. A. S. Ben.*, vol. ii. pp. 561 f.; Masson, *ibid.*, vol. v. pp. 707 f.; Wood's *Oxus*, pp. lxvii, 125 f.; *Asiat. Res.*, vol. vi. pp. 462–472, 495, 523–528; Bretschneider, *Med. Geog.*, pp. 58, 193; Gladwin, *Ayeen Akbery*, vol. ii. p. 208, vol. iii. pp. 168, 169.

[176] This *tcou-shih* is described by Medhurst (*sub voc.*) as "a kind of stone resembling metal.   The Chinese call it the finest kind of native copper.   It is found in the Po-sze country (Persia) and resembles gold.   On the application of fire it assumes a red colour, and does not turn black.   When mercury falls to the ground this substance will attract it."   But from the statement that each part of this figure was *cast* separately, it is plain that it was made of metal, probably brass or bronze.   Julien translates it by *laiton*, brass.

[177] If this sleeping figure of Buddha was lying within the building, it is unreasonable to suppose it could be 1000 feet in length.   The sleeping figures of Buddha at Moulmein, I

every time he assembles the great congregation of the Wu-che (*Môksha*),[178] having sacrificed all his possessions, from his wife and children down to his country's treasures, gives in addition his own body; then his ministers and the lower order of officers prevail on the priests to barter back these possessions; and in these matters most of their time is taken up.[179]

To the south-west of the convent of the sleeping figure (*of Buddha*), going 200 li or so, passing the great Snowy Mountains on the east, there is a little watercourse (*or valley*), which is moist with (*the overflowings of*) standing springs, bright as mirrors; the herbage here is green and bright.[180] There is a *sanghârâma* here with a tooth of Buddha, also the tooth of a Pratyêka [181] Buddha, who lived at the beginning of the *Kalpa*, which is in length about five inches, and in breadth somewhat less than four inches. Again, there is the tooth of a golden-wheel king,[182] in length three inches, and in surface (*breadth*) two inches. There is also the iron begging-dish of Śaṇakavâsa,[183] a great Arhat, which is capable of holding eight or nine *shing* (*pints*). These three sacred objects, be-

am told by a friend who visited the caves there and measured the figures, were 60 yards in length. The figures of Buddha entering *Nirvâṇa* in the Sinhalese temples are often very large. One in Cave xxvi. at Ajaṇṭâ is fully 23 feet in length. See Fergusson and Burgess, *Cave Temples*, p. 344; and note 175 *supra*. The text of Hiuen Tsiang is probably corrupt in this passage.

[178] The *Môksha Mahâparishad;* a meeting, as it seems, held every five years for the benefit of the priests (Buddhist community). On these occasions there were recitations of the law, and offerings were made to the priesthood. These assemblies were generally made on some favourite mountain. It was also called *Pañchavarshikâ parishad.* See *Abstract of Four Lectures*, p. 170; and note 66 *supra.*

[179] In such matters as these there is most concern shown.

[180] *Ts'ung*, a light green.

[181] A Pratyêka Buddha is one who has attained enlightenment, that is, become a Buddha, but for himself alone.

[182] That is, a monarch of the four *drîpas* or *suvarṇachakravartin.*

[183] Śaṇakavâsa, or Sâṇavâsika, according to some Northern accounts, was the fourth patriarch or president of the Buddhist community (*Fo-sho-hing-tsan-king*, xiv.) Other authorities speak of him as the third patriarch. See Eitel, *Handbook*, sub voc.; Rémusat, *Mél. Asiat.*, tom. i. p. 118; Neumann, *Zeitschr. f. d. Kunde d. Morg.*, vol. iii. p. 124; Edkins, *Chin. Buddhism*, pp. 66–69; Lassen, *Ind. Alterthums.* (2d edit.), vol. ii. p. 1201. He lived 100 years after Buddha.

queathed by the holy personages referred to, are all contained in a yellow-golden sealed case. Again, there is here the *Sanghâti* robe, in nine pieces [184] of Śanakavâsa; the colour is a deep red (*rose-red*); it is made of the bark (*peel*) of the *She-no-kia* plant.[185] Śanakavâsa was the disciple of Ânanda.[186] In a former existence he had given the priests garments made of the *Sanaka* plant (*fibre*), on the conclusion of the rainy season.[187] By the force of this meritorious action during 500 successive births he wore only this (*kind of*) garment, and at his last birth he was born with it. As his body increased so his robe grew larger, until the time when he was converted by Ânanda and left his home (*i.e.*, became an ascetic). Then his robe changed into a religious garment; [188] and when he was fully ordained it again changed into a *Sanghâti*, composed of nine pieces. When he was about to arrive at *Nirvâna* he entered into the condition of *Samâdhi*, bordering on complete extinction, and by the force of his vow in attaining wisdom (*he arrived at the knowledge*)[189] that this *kashâya* garment would last till the bequeathed law (*testament*) of Śâkya (*was established*), and after the destruction of this law then his garment also would perish. At the present time it is a little fading, for faith also is small at this time!

Going eastward from this, we enter the defiles of the Snowy Mountains, cross over the black ridge (Siâh Kôh), and arrive at the country of Kia-pi-shi.

---

[184] *I.e.*, composed of nine parts sewn together.

[185] The *Sanaka* plant, a kind of hemp called the Bengal *san*.

[186] The ordinary succession of the patriarchs is, after Buddha, (1) Kâśyapa, (2) Ânanda, (3) Madhyântika, (4) Sanakavâsa. The last named is sometimes identified with Yaśa, the son of Kana, who was one of the chief leaders in the second council 100 years after Buddha. He may be the same as Sonaka in the Southern records, who died, according to Rhys Davids (*Numismata Orientalia*, pp. 46, 47), in A.B. 124; conf. Bühler, *Ind. Ant.*, vol. vii. p. 150.

[187] "At the conclusion of the retirement during the rainy season." It was customary for the priests to retire into a fixed residence during the three months of the rainy season. When the retirement broke up (*kiai ngan ku jih*) robes and other presents were given to the priests.

[188] *I.e.*, a vestment worn by the religious.

[189] Or "he secured the privilege, by the earnestness of his vow, that his robe," &c.

KIA-PI-SHI [KAPIŚA].

This country [190] is 4000 li or so in circuit. On the north it abuts on the Snowy Mountains, and on three sides it borders on the "black ridge" (*the Hindu Kush*). The capital of the country is 10 li or so in circuit. It produces cereals of all sorts, and many kinds of fruit-trees. The *shen* horses are bred here, and there is also the scent (*scented root*) called *Yu-kin*.[191] Here also are found objects of merchandise from all parts. The climate is cold and windy. The people are cruel and fierce; their language is coarse and rude; their marriage rites a mere intermingling of the sexes. Their literature is like that of the Tukhâra country, but the customs, common language, and rules of behaviour are somewhat different. For clothing they use hair garments (*wool*); their garments are trimmed with fur. In commerce they use gold and silver coins, and also little copper coins, which in appearance and stamp [192] differ .from those of other countries. The king is a Kshattriya by caste. He is of a shrewd

[190] Kapiśa is the Καπισα (or Κά-πισα) of Ptolemy (*Geog.*, lib. vi. c. 18, 4), and the Capissa of Pliny (*H. N.*, lib. vi. c. 23, 25), the capital of a district called Capissene. It is perhaps also the Caphusa of Solinus (*Polyh.*, c. 54). See Lassen's discussion, *Ind. Alterth.*, vol. iii. pp. 135, 591, 879–889. Ptolemy placed it 155 miles N. 15° E. from Καβούρα or Kabul, the Kâpûl or Kâvul of the *Bundahiś*; but this distance is far too great. Julien supposes the district to have occupied the Panjshir and Tagaô valleys in the north border of Kohistân, and that the capital may have been either in the valley of the Nijraô or of the Tagaô. Conf. Baber's *Mem.*, pp. 144 f.; Masson, *Narrative of Jour.*, vol. iii. p 168; Wilson, *Ariana Ant.*, p. 117; Pânini has Kâpiśî (iv. 2, 99).

[191] *Curcuma* (Jul.) The *Curcuma* belongs to the natural order of *Zingiberaceæ*; the different species are stemless plants with tuberous roots. The scented species referred to in the text is probably the *Curcuma zedoaria*, or broad-leaved turmeric. The tubers are aromatic, and when ground the powder is used not only as a stimulating condiment in curry powders, &c., but as a perfume. In Sanskrit it is called *haridrâ*, with forty-six synonyms.

[192] The original, *kwei keu mu yang*, has, I suspect, the meaning of "stamp and inscription;" literally it would mean the pattern or fashion (*mu yang*) of the compass and square (*kwei keu*), or the circular and square part are different, &c. But the expression may also simply mean, "the size and form." It possibly refers to the copper coins of Kanishka or Kanêrki.

character (*nature*),[193] and being brave and determined, he has brought into subjection the neighbouring countries, some ten of which he rules. He cherishes his people[194] with affection, and reverences much the three precious objects of worship. Every year[195] he makes a silver figure of Buddha eighteen feet high, and at the same time he convokes an assembly called the *Môksha Mahâparishad* when he gives alms to the poor and wretched, and relieves the bereaved (*widows and bereaved*).

There are about 100 convents in this country and some 6000 priests. They mostly study the rules of the Great Vehicle. The *stûpas* and *sanghârâmas* are of an imposing height, and are built on high level spots, from which they may be seen on every side, shining in their grandeur (*purity*).[196] There are some ten temples of the Dêvas, and 1000 or so of heretics (*different ways of religion*); there are naked ascetics, and others who cover themselves with ashes, and some who make chaplets of bones, which they wear as crowns on their heads.[197]

To the east of the capital[198] 3 or 4 li, at the foot of a

---

[193] This passage may also be rendered: "He is distinguished for wisdom and tact; he is by nature brave and determined," &c. Hwui-lih uses the expression *ming lioh*, instead of *chi lioh*; evidently alluding to his tact or shrewdness, by which he had brought the neighbouring countries into his power.

[194] "The hundred families."

[195] The expression *sui* certainly means "a year" or "yearly;" but it may also have the sense of "periodically." This would suit the context perhaps better, as the "great assemblies" were usually convoked "every five years."

[196] It seems that the passage requires some such rendering as this. The symbol *ch'hang* indicates "a high level spot, from which there is a good prospect" (Medhurst). Mr. Simpson's account of the *stûpas* in the Jellalâbâd valley would favour this translation (*Buddhist Architec-ture*, a paper read by W. Simpson before the Royal Institute of British Architects, 12th January 1880). We may gather from the connection of *stûpa* and *sanghârâma* in the text, that Hiuen Tsiang alludes to the *stûpa* with its *vihâra*.

[197] The three sects here enumerated are known as (1) the Nirgranthas or Digambara Jainas; (2) Pâsupatas; and (3) Kapâladhârinas.

[198] There is some difficulty in fixing the name and site of the capital of Kapisa. General Cunningham identifies it with Opiân (*Anc. Geog. of India*, p. 19). His opinion is based on a statement I have not been able to verify, viz., that on leaving Bâmiyân, Hiuen Tsiang travelled 600 li in an easterly direction over "snowy mountains and black hills" to the capital of Kia-pi-shi. I can find no distance given either in the *Si-yu-ki* or by Hwui-lih. From Bâmiyân south-

mountain in the north, is a great *sanghârâma* with 300 or so priests in it. These belong to the Little Vehicle and adopt its teaching.[199]

According to tradition, Kanishka Râja of Gandhâra[200] in old days having subdued all the neighbouring provinces and brought into obedience people of distant countries, he governed by his army a wide territory, even to the east of the T'sung-ling mountains. Then the

east to the "humid valley" is 200 li. After this the account simply says : "Going in an easterly direction, &c., we come to Kia-pi-shi." Nor can I find any corroboration of the statement that "on leaving the capital of Kapisene, Hiuen Tsiang was accompanied by the king as far as the town of Kiu-lu-sa-pang, a distance of one yôjana to the north-east" (*op. cit.*, p. 20). Hwui-lih indeed states (i. 266) that the king of Kapiśa accompanied the pilgrim 6 li from the *frontiers* of his kingdom; but that gives us no clue to the name or site of the capital. V. St. Martin makes Opiân the capital of Fo-li-shi-sa-t'ang-na (*Mém.*, tom. ii. p. 190). Hiuen Tsiang does not give the name of the chief city, but he places it 600 li to the west of Lau-po (Lamghân), which again is 100 li to the north-west of Na-kie-lo-ho (Nagarahâra). Supposing the site of Nagarahâra to be at the point of junction of the Kâbul river with the Surkhar or Surkh-rud, we should have to place the capital of Kapiśa on the declivity of the Hindu Kush, not far from the little town of Ghorband, or perhaps near Kushân, 10 miles west of Opian.

[199] I find in Julien's translation that this *sanghârâma* was called Jin-kia-lan (the humane sanghârâma, or, of "the man"). It is wanting in my text. India Office, No. 1503.

[200] Kanishka-râja, of Gandhâra. He is often called in Chinese Buddhist books "the Chandan Kanika" (see *Fo-sho-hing-t'san-king*, pages xxviii., xxix.) This may simply

mean Kanishka of Gandhâra, the use of *Chandana* for *gandha* being common. The mountains of Gândhâra are often explained as the "perfume mountains," as though from *gandha*. But in an old Buddhist map in my possession the Gândhâra mountains are called the earth-holding (*ti chi*), as though *gan* were from an old root, γᾶν or γῆν, and *dhri*, to hold. Kanishka was king of the Yueï-chi, and the rise of his dynasty is placed by Chinese authors in the first century B.C. On his coins he is styled in the corrupt Greek legends Κανηρκι Κορανο, and in the Baktrian-Pali legends and Manikyâla inscription he is called Kanishka the Kushâna, or "of the Gushana family," connecting him with the tribe called by the Chinese Kweï-shwang. Korano and Kushâna are only different forms of the same word. Prinsep, *Essays*, vol. i. pp. 145 f. ; Lassen, *Ind. Alt.*, vol. ii. pp. 806 f. ; *J. As. S. Ben.*, vol. xxxii. pp. 144 f. ; *Arch. Sur. W. Ind. Rep.*, vol. ii. p. 50 ; *Num. Chron.*, N.S., vol. xiv. pp. 161 f. The date of Kanishka is yet undetermined. According to Lassen (*Ind. Alt.*, vol. ii. [2d ed.] pp. 766, 768), he lived between A.D. 10 and A.D. 40. The Northern Buddhists place him (as we shall see farther on) 400 years after the *Nirvâna*. But as Hiuen Tsiang places Aśôka only 100 years after Buddha, the error appears to be in the date of the *Nirvâna*; and thus Kanishka was really about 300 years after Aśôka. Recent writers argue that Kanishka lived in the latter part of the first century, and tribes who occupy the territory to the west of the river,[201] fearing the power of his arms, sent hostages to him. Kanishka-râja having received the hostages,[202] treated them with singular attention, and ordered for them separate establishments for the cold and hot weather; during the cold they resided in India and its different parts, in the summer they came back to Kapiśa, in the autumn and spring they remained in the kingdom of Gandhâra; and so he founded *sanghâramas* for the hostages according to the three seasons. This convent (*of which we are now speaking*) is the one they occupied during the summer, and it was built for that purpose.[203]

that the Śaka era (A.D. 78) originated with his reign. See Bühler, *Ind. Ant.*, vol. vi. pp. 149 ff.; vol. vii. pp. 141 ff.; Oldenberg, *ib.*, vol. x. pp. 213 ff.; Fergusson, *Jour. R. As. Soc.*, N.S., vol. xii. pp. 261 ff.; Max Müller, *India*, p. 293. R. Davids has come to the conclusion that the *Nirvâna* is within a few years of 412 B.C. (*Numismata Oriental.*, part vi. p. 56). If this could be established, it would accord pretty well with the Northern legend referred to, and the date of Kanishka's power might have been, as Lassen supposes, between 10 A.D. and 40 A.D

[201] The district to the west of the river, *i.e.*, the Yellow River, were the people of the Tangut empire. (For an explanation of the word Tangut, and other particulars, see Yule, *Marco Polo*, vol. i. p. 209; Bretschneider, *Med. Geog.*, p. 123). In my copy there is no mention made of "dependent princes" (Julien *in loc.*); the expression is "*fan wei*," which I take to be equivalent to "the associated tribes." The word *fan* is used for the Tibetans. This would explain Yule's remark (*op. cit.*, p. 209) that "the word Tanggod (Tangut) is properly a Mongol plural designating certain tribes of Tibetan blood."

[202] In Hwui-lih's account (*Vie de Hiouen Thsang*, p. 72), we are told

there was only one hostage, and he was a son of the Emperor of China. There is a curious story found among the sermons of Aśvaghôsha—who was contemporary with Kanishka—of a son of the Emperor of China coming to India to seek a cure for his blindness. He dwelt in a monastery in which there was a great preacher. On a certain occasion he preached so eloquently that the entire congregation was moved to tears. Some of these tears were applied to the eyes of the blind prince, and he recovered (Sermon 54). There was plainly an intercourse kept up between China, or the eastern frontiers of China, and North India from an early period.

[203] The name of this convent is given by Hwui-lih (K. ii. fol. 10 a) as Sha-lo-kia, which is restored by Julien (t. ii. p. 503) doubtfully to Sharaka. Dr. Eitel (*Handbook* sub voc.) has followed him in this restoration. It seems to be referred to by I-Tsing in his account of the travels of Hwui-lun (*Jour. R. As. Soc.*, N.S., vol. xlii. p. 570). I am of opinion that Sha-lo-kia ought to be restored to Serika, and that it was so called because it was built for the Chinese hostages or hostage. This name for China (Serika) indeed is not known in Chinese literature; but it is plain that this establish-

Hence the pictures of these hostages on the walls; their features, and clothing, and ornaments are like the people of Eastern Hia (China).[204]   Afterwards, when they were permitted to return to their own country, they were remembered in their old abode,[205] and notwithstanding the intervening mountains and rivers, they were without cessation reverenced with offerings, so that down to the present time the congregation of priests on each rainy season [206] (*frequent this spot*); and on the breaking up of the fast they convene an assembly and pray for the happiness of the hostages,—a pious custom still existing.

To the south of the eastern door of the hall of Buddha

ment was not only very rich, but also provided with celebrated mural paintings. I have already called attention (*Abstract*, &c., p. 136 n.), to the way in which artists from Baktria were employed to paint the Buddhist vihâras at an early date, but more particularly, as it would seem, during the time of Kanishka; for Aśvaghôsha, who relates the story referred to, was a follower of Kanishka. Nothing would be more natural than that an artist or artists from Baktria should speak of this vihâra as the Serika vihâra; the common term for China being Σηρική (Ptol., vi. 16, 1, 3, 4, 6, &c.; Pliny, *H. N.*, lib. vi. c. 20, 5). This conjecture is confirmed by the translation of the term Sha-lo-kia given by Hiuen Tsiang. It is not given indeed in my copy, but in the original used by M. Julien the convent is called "the Sanghârâma of men" (*jin-kia-lan*). This is restored by Julien doubtfully to Narasaṅgh-ârâma (p. 42). But this (*nara*) is an epithet of the king of China, according to Arabian travellers (vid. *supra*, p. 14, n. 41). It seems, therefore, probable that this Sanghârâma was originally called after the king's son by the Baktrian term, *Serika*.

[204] The Eastern Hia people, *i.e.*, the Chinese, in distinction from the Western Hia, *i.e.*, the Tanguts.

Bretschneider, *Notes, Med. Geog.*, &c., p. 35, n. 81.

[205] So I understand the passage. It is not that the hostages remembered their old abode, but that the memory of the hostages remained with the priests of the Sha-lo-kia convent. Hence, after the summer rest was over, the priests used to hold a special assembly in order to invoke a blessing on their memory. M. Julien has translated it so in the *Life* of Hiouen Thsang, p. 72, but in this passage he has inverted the sense.

[206] The rainy season (*varsha*), as is well known, was observed by the Buddhists as a period of retreat, not in the sense of fasting, or, as it has been translated, Lent, but for the purpose of shelter, and also, as stated in the *Vinaya*, to avoid trampling down the young herbage. After the three months' rest, of which there were two kinds,—viz., either the first three months, *i.e.*, beginning at the appointed time, and continuing for three consecutive months, or else the second three months, that is, when through inability to begin at the appointed time the retreat was entered on a month later, and therefore lasted a month later,—the retreat was broken up, and presents, &c., were made to the congregation.

belonging to this *sanghârâma* there is a figure of the Great Spirit King;[207] beneath his right foot they have hollowed the earth for concealing treasures therein. This is the treasury place of the hostages, therefore we find this inscription, " When the *sanghârâma* decays let men take (*of the treasure*) and repair it." Not long ago there was a petty (*frontier*) king of a covetous mind and of a wicked aud cruel disposition; hearing of the quantity of jewels and precious substances concealed in this convent, he drove away the priests and began digging for them. The King of the Spirits had on his head the figure of a parrot, which now began to flap its wings and to utter screams. The earth shook and quaked, the king and his army were thrown down prostrate on the ground; after a while, arising from the earth, he confessed his fault and returned.

Above a mountain pass[208] to the north of this convent there are several stone chambers; it was in these the hostages practised religious meditation. In these recesses many and various gems (*precious things*) are concealed: on the side there is an inscription that the Yakshas (*Yo-cha*) guard and defend the places (*precincts*). If any one wishes to enter and rob the treasures, the Yakshas by spiritual

---

[207] This great spirit-râja is the same as Vaiśravana, "the celebrated" (περικλυτος). He is called Mahâkâla, "the great black one;" in Japan he is still called Dai Gakf, "the great black," and is generally figured as an old man of dwarfish size, with a sack on his back. I have often myself examined the figure on the hearths of the kitchens at Hakodate. He is in one sense the same as Kuvêra. For further remarks on this point see *Academy,* July 3, 1880; *Indian Antiquary,* vol. ix. p. 203.

[208] The convent was three or four li to the east of the capital, and at the foot of a northern mountain, which mountain formed one side of a pass. In General Cunningham's map referred to, there is such a northern mountain detached from the Paghman range, and a pass between it and the main line of hills. Just beyond this pass we find Chârikar, close to Opiân. If we may rely on these coincidences, the capital of Kapiśa would be to the west of this pass about a mile, whilst Chârikar would derive its name from the Sha-lo-kia monastery. The text, it must be noticed, does not require the mountain pass to be distinct from the northern mountain, at the base of which the convent was built, but it means that the chambers were excavated on the northern scarp of the pass. The context, moreover, requires this. For some interesting notices respecting the Buddhist caves of Afghanistân, see *Jour. Roy. As. Soc.,* N.S., vol. xiv. pp. 319 ff.

transformation appear in different forms, sometimes as lions, sometimes as snakes, and as savage beasts and poisonous reptiles; under various appearances they exhibit their rage. So no one dares to attempt to take the treasures.

At 2 or 3 li to the west of the stone chambers, above a great mountain pass,[209] there is a figure of Kwan-tsz'-tsai Bôdhisattva;[210] those who with sincere faith desire (*vow or pray*) to see him, to them the Bôdhisattva appears coming forth from the image, his body of marvellous beauty, and he gives rest and reassurance to the travellers.

Thirty li or so to the south-east of the capital we arrive at the convent of Râhula (Ho-lo-hu-lo); by its side is a *stûpa* about 100 feet in height. On sacred days (*fast days*) this building reflects a brilliant light. Above the cupola,[211] from between the interstices of the stone, there exudes a black scented oil, whilst in the quiet night may be heard the sounds of music. According to tradition, this *stûpa* was formerly built by Râhula, a great minister of this country. Having completed this work of merit (*religious work*), he saw in a night-dream a man who said to him, " This *stûpa* you have built has no sacred relic (*she-li*) in it as yet; to-morrow, when they come to offer, you must make your request to the king " (*for the offering brought*).

---

[209] The meaning is, above a high mountain-side, *i.e.*, as it seems, above a high peak, which would form the beginning of the pass on the western side.

[210] Kwan-tsz'-tsai or Avalôkitêś-vara, "the god that looks down." He is best known in Nepâl as Pad-mapâni; in Tibet he is called sPyan-ras-gzigs-dvang-phyug (pron. Chen-resi-vanchug); in China, as Kwan-yin; and in Japan as Kuan-nŏn. In Sanskrit he is also known as Karu-nârnava, Abhayamdada (" the re-mover of fear"), Abhyutgatarâja (" the great august king "), &c. See Burnouf, *Int. à l'Hist. d. Budd. Ind.*, 2d ed.), pp. 92, 101, 197–202, 557–559; *Lotus*, pp. 261 ff., 301, 352, 428; *Trans. Roy. As. Soc.*, vol. ii. pp. 233, 239, 247, 253; *Jour. Roy. As. Soc.*, N.S., vol. ii. pp. 136 ff., 411 ff.; Vassilief, *Le Bouddh.*, pp. 125, 175, 178, 186, 197; *Ind. Antiquary*, vol. viii. pp. 249–253; Burgess, *Cave Temples*, pp. 357, &c.; *Arch. Sur. Reports, W. India*, vol. iii. pp. 75, 76; vol. v. pp. 11, 14. He is gene-rally described as "the god of mercy," because he hears the cries of men. Probably a relic or revival of the old worship of hill-gods. Hence his figure placed on this mountain-top.

[211] Above "the covering shaped liked a pâtra," *i.e.*, the cupola or dome.

On the morrow, entering the royal court, he pressed his claim (*or* he advanced and requested), and said: " Your unworthy subject ventures to make a request." The king replied: " And what does my lord require ? " Answering, he said, " That your majesty would be pleased to favour me by conferring on me the first[212] offering made this day." The king replied: " I consent."

Râhula on this went forth and stood at the palace gate. Looking at all who came towards the spot, suddenly he beheld a man holding in his hand a relic casket (*pitcher*). The great minister said, " What is your will ? what have you to offer ? " He replied, " Some relics of Buddha." The minister answered, " I will protect them for you. I will first go and tell the king." Râhula, fearing lest the king on account of the great value of the relics should repent him of his former promise, went quickly to the *sanghârâma* and mounted the *stûpa ;* by the power of his great faith, the stone cupola opened itself, and then he placed the relics therein. This being done, he was quickly coming out when he caught the hem of his garment in the stone.[213] The king sent to pursue him, but by the time the messengers arrived at the *stûpa*, the stones had closed over him ; and this is the reason why a black oily substance exudes from the crevices of the building.

To the south[214] of the city 40 li or so, we come to the town of Si-pi-to-fa-la-sse (Śvêtavâras).[215] In the case

---

[212] So it appears to me the passage should be translated, "the first offering." Julien renders it as if there were only a single offering.

[213] That is, he caught his garment in the stone of the inner portion of the *stûpa* before he could escape to the exterior. The relic casket, as is well known, is placed in a chamber in the upper-middle part of the cupola or dome.

[214] This bearing is given in my text ; it seems to be wanting in Julien's.

[215] Julien restores this name to Sphîtavaras doubtfully. V. de St. Martin (*Mémoire*, &c., p. 300) suggests Śvêtavâras. As this seems to be more in agreement with the Japanese equivalents in my text, I have adopted it. The situation or name of this city is unknown. General Cunningham suggests Saptavarsha or Sattavasa, and connects with this name, " the Thatagush of the inscriptions of Darius, who are the Sattagudai of Herodotus" (*Anc. Geog.*, p. 26). If we suppose the Chehêl Dukhtarân peak to be the same as the mountain called O-lu-no

of earthquakes, and even when the tops of the mountains fall, there is no commotion around this city.

Thirty li or so to the south of the town of Si-po-to-fa-la-sse we come to a mountain called 'O-lu-no (Aruṇa).[216] The crags and precipices of this mountain are of a vast height, its caverns and valleys are dark and deep. Each year the peak increases in height several hundred feet, until it approaches the height of Mount Tsu-na-hi-lo (Śunagir) [217] in the kingdom of Tsu-ku-cha (Tsaukûṭa);[213] then when it thus faces it, suddenly it falls down again. I have heard this story in neighbouring countries. When first the heavenly spirit Śuna came from far to this mountain desiring to rest, the spirit of the mountain, affrighted, shook the surrounding valleys. The heavenly spirit said, " Because you have no wish to entertain me, therefore this tumult and confusion; if you had but entertained me for a little while, I should have conferred on you great riches and treasure; but now I go to Tsu-ku-cha to the mountain Tsu-na-hi-lo, and I will visit it every year. On these occasions, when the king and his ministers offer me their tribute, then you shall stand face to face with me." Therefore Mount 'O-lu-no having increased to the height (*aforesaid*), suddenly falls down again at the top.

About 200 li to the north-west of the royal city we come to a great snowy mountain, on the summit of which

---

(about to be noticed), then measuring north about six miles, we should come to Beg-âm ; from this, eight miles north—according to our text —would take us up the Panjshir river, and not to the capital. There is no bearing given in the French translation, and it is possible that the symbol for south in our text has been interpolated. From Hiuen Tsiang's remark "that the city of Śvêtavâras could not be destroyed," we may perhaps identify it with the Tetragonis of Pliny, *Hist. Nat.*, lib. vi. c. 25.

[216] 'O-lu-no may be restored to

Aruṇa, "the red." The symbol *na*, however, is especially referred to in a note as being equal in sound to n(oo) + (k)o, *i.e.*, no.

[217] The symbols *Tsu-na-hi-lo* would give Śunahir. The Japanese phonetic equivalent for *hi* is given as *ki* or *gi*, which (if correct) gives us Śunagir. Julien suggests Kshunahila.

[218] The kingdom of Tsaukûṭa appears, from the return journey, to be the same as Sewistân. The high mountain of Tukatu may perhaps represent the *Tsu-na-hi-lo* of the text. Lassen, *Ind. Alt.*, vol. iii. p. 884.

is a lake. Here whoever asks for rain or prays for fine weather, according to his request so he receives.

Tradition says in old time there was an Arhat (*Lo-han*) belonging to Gandhâra (Kien-t'o-lo) who constantly received the religious offerings of the Nâga king of this lake. On the arrival of the time for the mid-day meal, by his spiritual power he rose with the mat on which he sat into the air, and went (*to the place where the Nâga dwelt*). His attendant, a Śrâmaṇêra (*novice*), secretly catching hold of the under part of the mat, when the time came for the Arhat to go, was transported in a moment with him (*to the palace of the Nâga*). On arriving at the palace, the Nâga saw the Śrâmaṇêra. The Nâga-râja asking them to partake of his hospitality, he provided the Arhat with "immortal food," but gave to the Śrâmaṇêra food used by men. The Arhat having finished his meal, began then to preach for the good of the Nâga, whilst he desired the Śrâmaṇera, as was his custom, to wash out his alms-bowl. Now the bowl happened to have in it some fragments of (*the heavenly*) food. Startled at the fragrance of this food,[219] forthwith there arose in him an evil determination (*vow*). Irritated with his master, and hating the Nâga, he uttered the prayer (*vow*) that the force of all his religious merit might now be brought into operation with a view to deprive the Nâga of life, and, "May I," he said, "myself become a Nâga-king."

No sooner had the Śrâmaṇêra made this vow than the Nâga perceived his head to be in pain.

The Arhat having finished his preaching concerning the duty of repentance, the Nâga-râja confessed his sins, condemning himself. But the Śrâmaṇêra still cherishing hatred in his heart, confessed not. And now having returned to the *saṅghârâma*, in very truth the prayer he had put up in consequence of the power of his religious merit was accomplished, and that very night he died and

---

[219] That is, startled to find from the fragrance that this food was different from that which he had received.

became a Nâga-râja. Then filled with rage, he entered the lake and killed the other Nâga king, and took possession of his palace; moreover, he attached to himself the whole fraternity of his class (*i.e., all the Nâgas*) to enable him to carry out his original purpose. Then fiercely raising the winds and tempests, he rooted up the trees and aimed at the destruction of the convent.

At this time Kanishka-râja, surprised at the ravages, inquired of the Arhat as to the cause, on which he told the whole circumstance. The king therefore, for the sake of the Nâga,[220] founded a *sanghârâma* at the foot of the Snowy Mountains, and raised a *stûpa* about 100 feet in height. The Nâga, cherishing his former hatred, raised the wind and rain. The king persevering in his purpose of charity, the Nâga redoubled his fury (*angry poison*), and became exceedingly fierce. Six times he destroyed the *sanghârâma* and the *stûpa*, and on the seventh occasion Kanishka, confused by his failure, determined to fill the Nâga's lake and overthrow his palace. He came therefore with his soldiers to the foot of the Snowy Mountains.

Then the Nâga-râja, being terrified and shaken with apprehension, changed himself into an aged Brâhman, and bowing down before the king's elephant, he remonstrated with the king, and said, "Mahârâja, because of your accumulated merit in former births, you have now been born a king of men, and you have no wish which is not gratified. Why then to-day are you seeking a quarrel with a Nâga? Nâgas are only brutish creatures. Nevertheless amongst lower creatures[221] the Nâga possesses great power, which cannot be resisted. He rides on the clouds, drives the winds, passes through space, and glides over the waters; no human power can conquer him.[222] Why then is the king's heart so angry? You have now raised the army

---

[220] That is (as it seems), for the sake of the Nâga who was dead.

[221] Among the lower creatures belonging to an evil class; referring to the evil ways or modes of birth (*jâti*). The three evil ways are birth as a beast, as a prêta, or a demon.

[222] Or, "it is no human power which restrains him."

of your country to fight with a single dragon ; if you conquer, your renown will not spread very far ; [223] but if you
are conquered, then you will suffer the humiliation of defeat. Let me advise the king to withdraw his troops."

The king Kanishka hesitating to comply, the dragon
returned to his lake. His voice, like the thunderclap, shook
the earth, and the fierce winds tore up the trees, whilst
stones and sand pelted down like rain ; the sombre clouds
obscured the air, so that the army and the horses were filled
with terror. The king then paid his adoration to the Three
Precious ones, and sought their help, saying, " My abound-
ing merit during former births has brought about my state
as king of men. By my power I have restrained the strong
and conquered the world (*Jambudvípa*). But now (*as it
appears*), by the onslaught of a dragon-beast overcome, this,
verily, is proof of my poor merit ! Let the full power of
all my merit now appear !"

Then from both his shoulders there arose a great flame
and smoke. [224] The dragon fled, the winds hushed, the
mists were melted, and the clouds were scattered. Then
the king commanded each man of his army to take a stone
and thus to fill up the dragon lake.

Again the dragon king changed himself into a Brâhman,
and asked the king once more, " I am the Nâga king of
yonder lake. Affrighted by your power, I tender my
submission. Would that the king in pity might forgive
my former faults ! The king indeed loves to defend and
cherish all animated beings, why then alone against
me is he incensed ? If the king kill me, then we both
shall fall into an 'evil way'—the king, for killing ; I, for
cherishing an angry mind. Deeds and their consequences

<hr>

[223] Or, " an acknowledged - afar renown ;" or it may be, as in Julien's translation, " the renown of one who conquers the distant ;" this, how-ever, appears strained.

[224] A great smoke - brightness. The flames on the shoulders are ob-servable on some of the Kanerki coins. We may compare with these flames the two ravens that sit on the shoulders of Oðinn, and also "the echo of heathen thought" which makes the dove sit on Christ's shoulder at his baptism (Grimm's *Teutonic Mythology*, by Stallybrass, vol. I. p. 148).

will be plainly manifested when the good and evil are brought to light."

The king then agreed with the Nâga that if hereafter he should again be rebellious there should be no forgiveness. The Nâga said, " Because of my evil deeds I have received a dragon form. The nature of Nûgas is fierce and wicked, so that they are unable to control themselves ; if by chance an angry heart rises in me, it will be from forgetfulness of our present compact. The king may now build the *sanghârâma* once more; I will not venture to destroy it again. Each day let the king send a man to observe the mountain top; if it is black with clouds, then let him sound the *ghaṇṭâ* (drum *or* cymbal) loudly; when I hear the sound of it, my evil purpose will subside."

Forthwith the king renewed his work in raising the *sanghârâma* and *stûpa*. People look out for the clouds and mists on the mountain top down to the present day. Tradition says that in this *stûpa* there is a considerable quantity (a pint, or *shing*) of relics [225] of Tathâgata, consisting of his bones and flesh, and that wonderful miracles are wrought thereby, which it would be difficult to name separately. At one time, from within the *stûpa* there arose suddenly a smoke, which was quickly followed by a fierce flame of fire. On this occasion the people said the *stûpa* was consumed. They gazed for a long time till the fire was expended and the smoke disappeared, when they beheld a *Sarîra* like a white pearl gem,[226] which moved with a circular motion round the surmounting pole of the *stûpa*; it then separated itself and ascended up on high to the region of the clouds, and after scintillating there awhile, again descended with a circular motion.[227]

---

[225] The words rendered "relics," &c., are in the original "bone and flesh *sarîras*;" that is, "bone and flesh remains," or body-relics.

[226] The symbol for "gem" is of uncertain meaning. There is a precious gem from the Lu country called *yu-fan.* It is the latter of these two words that occurs in the text, connected with *chu,* a pearl. I have therefore translated *chu-fan* by pearl-gem.

[227] This account probably refers to some electrical phenomenon. The surmounting pole of the *stûpa* was provided with metal rings or discs,

To the north-west of the capital there is a large river[228] on the southern bank of which, in a convent of an old king, there is a milk-tooth of Śâkya Bôdhisattva; it is about an inch in length.

To the south-east of this convent there is another, which is also called the convent of the old king; in this is a piece of the skull-bone of Tathâgata; the surface of it is about an inch in breadth, its colour a yellowish white; the little hair orifices are plainly seen. There is, moreover, a hair-top[229] of Tathâgata of a dark auburn colour; the hair turns to the right; drawing it out, it is about a foot long; when folded up it is only about half an inch. These three objects are reverenced with offerings by the king and the great ministers on each of the six fast (*holy*) days.

To the south-west of the convent of the skull-bone is the convent of the wife of the old king, in which there is a gilded *stûpa* (*copper gilt*), about 100 feet in height. Tradition says in this *stûpa* is about a pint of the relics of Buddha. On the fifteenth day of each month, in the evening, it reflects a circular halo of glory which lights up the dew-dish.[230] Thus it shines till the morning, when it gradually disappears and enters the *stûpa*.

To the south-west of the town is Mount Pi-lo-sa-lo (Pilusâra);[231] the mountain spirit takes the form of an elephant, hence the name. In old days, when Tathâgata was alive, the spirit, called Pîlusâra (*siang-kien, i.e.,* elephant-fixed), asked the Lord of the World and 1200 Arhats (*to partake of his hospitality*). On the mountain crag is a great solid rock; here it was Tathâgata received the offerings of the spirit. Afterwards Aśôka-râja erected

and was capped generally with a metal "pitcher" (so called). This would naturally act as a lightning conductor.

[228] This great river may be the affluent of the Kâbul river flowing through the Ghôrband valley. It flows about east and west after leav-ing the valley; the southern bank, therefore, would be that nearest the site of the capital.

[229] That is, a hair from the top-knot hair.

[230] *I.e.*, the circular dish at the top of the surmounting pole.

[231] Elephant-firm.

on this same rock a *stûpa* about 100 feet in height. It is now called the *stûpa* of the Elephant-strength (Pîlusâra). They say that in this also is about a pint measure of the relics of Tathâgata.

To the north of the Pîlusâra Stûpa is a mountain cavern, below which is a Nâga fountain. It was here that Tathâgata, having received from the spirit some food (*rice*) with the Arhats, cleansed his mouth and rubbed his teeth with a piece of willow branch.[232] This he planted in the ground, and it forthwith took root, and is now a bushy grove. Afterwards men built here a *sanghârama*, and called it the convent of the Pi-to-kia (*the willow twig*).

Going eastward from this 600 li or so, across a continuation of mountains and valleys, the peaks being of a stupendous height, and skirting the "black ridge,"[233] we enter North India, and crossing the frontier, come to the country of Lan-po (Lamghân).

[232] The wood commonly used in India is that of the *Khadira* tree, the *Acacia Catechu.* After being used as a tooth-cleaner it is generally split in two, and one part used to scrape the tongue. Hence probably the name *Pi-to-kiu* given in the text, which seems to be a form of the Sanskrit *vidala*, leafless; or, as Julien suggests, of *Vaitraka*, a reed, a twig.

[233] That is, the Siâh Kôh, or the range which separates Lamghân from the upper valley of the Kâo and that of the Pîcha.

END OF BOOK I.

BOOK II.

Relates to Three Countries, viz., (1) Lan-po, (2) Na-kie lo-ho and (3) Kien-t'o-lo.

1. *Names of India.*

On examination, we find that the names of India (T'ien-chu) are various and perplexing as to their authority. It was anciently called Shin-tu, also Hien-tau; but now, according to the right pronunciation, it is called In-tu. The people of In-tu call their country by different names according to their district. Each country has diverse customs. Aiming at a general name which is the best sounding, we will call the country In-tu.[1] In Chinese this name signifies the Moon. The moon has many names, of which this is one. For as it is said that all living things ceaselessly revolve in the wheel (*of trans-migration*) through the long night of ignorance, without a guiding star, their case is like (*the world*), the sun gone down; as then the torch affords its connecting light, though there be the shining of the stars, how different from the bright (*cool*) moon; just so the bright con-nected light of holy men and sages, guiding the world as the shining of the moon, have made this country eminent, and so it is called In-tu.

The families of India are divided into castes, the Brâh-maṇs particularly (*are noted*) on account of their purity and nobility. Tradition has so hallowed the name of this tribe that there is no question as to difference of place, but the people generally speak of India as the country of the Brâhmaṇs (Po-lo-men).

---

[1] See *Jour. Asiat.*, sér. iv. tom. x. p. 91.

2. *Extent of India, Climate, &c.*

The countries embraced under this term of India are generally spoken of as the five Indies. In circuit this country is about 90,000 li; on three sides it is bordered by the great sea; on the north it is backed by the Snowy Mountains. The north part is broad, the southern part is narrow. Its shape is like the half-moon. The entire land is divided into seventy countries or so. The seasons are particularly hot; the land is well watered[2] and humid. The north is a continuation of mountains and hills, the ground being dry and salt. On the east there are valleys and plains, which being well watered and cultivated, are fruitful and productive. The southern district is wooded and herbaceous; the western parts are stony and barren. Such is the general account of this country.

3. *Measures of Length.*

To give a brief account of matters. In point of measurements, there is first of all the *yôjana (yu-shcn-na)*; this from the time of the holy kings of old has been regarded as a day's march for an army. The old accounts say it is equal to 40 *li;* according to the common reckoning in India it is 30 *li*, but in the sacred books (*of Buddha*) the *yôjana* is only 16 *li*.

In the subdivision of distances, a *yôjana* is equal to eight *krôsas (kcu-lu-she)*; a *krôsa* is the distance that the lowing of a cow can be heard; a *krôsa* is divided into 500 bows (*dhanus*); a bow is divided into four cubits (*hastas*); a cubit is divided into 24 fingers (*angulis*); a finger is divided into seven barleycorns (*yavas*); and so on to a louse (*yûka*), a nit (*likshâ*), a dust grain, a cow's hair, a sheep's hair, a hare's down, copper-water,[3] and so on for seven divisions,

---

[2] Has many fountains.

[3] An enumeration corresponding to that in the text will be found in the *Lalita Vistara* (Foucaux, p. 142) and in the *Romantic Legend of Bud-* dha (p. 87). The expression copper-water may refer to the size of the small hole made in the *tamrî* or copper cup for the admission of water.

till we come to a small grain of dust; this is divided sevenfold till we come to an excessively small grain of dust (*anu*); this cannot be divided further without arriving at nothingness, and so it is called the infinitely small (*paramânu*).

4. *Astronomy, the Calendar, &c.*

Although the revolution of the *Yin* and *Yang* principles and the successive mansions of the sun and moon be called by names different from ours, yet the seasons are the same; the names of the months are derived from the position (*of the moon in respect*) of the asterisms.

The shortest portion of time is called a *t'sa-na* (kshana); 120 *kshanas* make a *ta-t'sa-na* (takshana); 60 of these make a *la-fo* (lava); 30 of these make a *mau-hu-li-to* (muhûrta); five of these make "a period of time" (*kâla*); six of these make a day and night (*ahôrâtra*),[4] but commonly the day and night are divided into eight *kalâs*.[5]

The period from the new moon till full moon is called the white division (*Śukla-paksha*) of the month; the period from the full moon till the disappearance (*of the light*) is called the dark portion (*Kṛishṇa-paksha*). The dark portion comprises fourteen or fifteen days, because the month is sometimes long and sometimes short. The preceding dark portion and the following light portion together form a month; six months form a "march" (*hing, s. ayana*). The sun when it moves within (*the equator*) is said to be on its northward march;[6] when it moves without (*the equator*) it is on its southern march.[7] These two periods form a year (*vatsara*).

The year, again, is divided into six seasons. From the 16th day of the 1st month till the 15th day of the 3d month is the season of gradual heat; from the 16th day of

---

[4] Three in the day, three in the night.—*Ch. Ed.*

[5] Four for the day and four for the night; each of these *kalâs* is again divided into four parts or periods (*she*).—*Ch. Ed.*

[6] *Uttarâyana.*

[7] *Dakshiṇâyana.*

the 3d month till the 15th day of the 5th month is called the season of full heat; from the 16th day of the 5th month till the 15th day of the 7th month is called the rainy season; from the 16th day of the 7th month till the 15th day of the 9th month is called the season of growth (*vegetation*); from the 16th day of the 9th month to the 15th day of the 11th month is called the season of gradual cold; from the 16th day of the 11th month to the 15th day of the 1st month is called the season of great (*full*) cold.[8]

According to the holy doctrine of Tathâgata, the year is divided into three seasons. From the 16th day of the 1st month till the 15th day of the 5th month is called the hot season; from the 16th day of the 5th month till the 15th day of the 9th month is called the wet season; from the 16th day of the 9th month to the 15th day of the 1st month is called the cold season. Again, there are four seasons, called spring, summer, autumn, winter. The three spring months are called *Chi-ta-lo* (Chaitra) month, *Feï-she-kie* (Vaisâka) month, *She-se-ch'a* (Jyêshṭha); these correspond with the time from the 16th day of the 1st mouth to the 15th of the 4th month. The three summer months are called *'An-sha-cha* (Âshâḍha) month, *Chi-lo-fa-na* (Srâvaṇa) month, *Po-ta-lo-pa-to* (Bhâdrapada) month; these correspond to the time between the 16th day of the 4th month to the 15th day of the 7th month. The three autumn months are called, *'An-shi-fo-ku[9]-che* (Âsvayuja) month, *Kia-li-ta-ka* (Kârttika) month, *Wi-[10]kia-chi-lo* (Mârgaśîrsha) month; these correspond to the time between the 16th day of the 7th month to the 15th day of the 10th month. The three months of winter are called *P'o-sha* (Pushya) month, *Ma-ku* (Mâgha) month, and *P'o-li-kiu-na* (Phâlguna) month; these cor-

---

[8] These six seasons (*ṛîtavas*) are respectively (1) *Vasanta*, including the months of Chaitra and Vaiśâkha; (2) *Gṛîshma*—Jyêshṭha and Âshâḍha; (3) *Varshâs*—Srâvaṇa and Bhâdrapada; (4) *Saradâ*—Âśvina and Kârttika; (5) *Hemanta*—Mârgaśîrsha and Pushya; and (6) *Siśira*—Mâgha and Phâlguna. In the south they are reckoned as beginning a month later.

[9] The symbol *ku* is for *yu*.—Julien *in loc.*

[10] The symbol *wi* is for *mo*.—Jul.

respond with the time between the 16th day of the 10th month to the 15th day of the 1st month in China. In old times in India the priestly fraternity, relying on the holy teaching of Buddha, had a double [11] resting-time (*during the rains*), viz., either the former three months or the latter three months; these periods were either from the 16th day of the 5th month to the 15th day of the 8th month, or from the 16th day of the 6th month to the 15th day of the 9th month.

Translators of the *Sûtras* (*king*) and the *Vinaya* (*liu*) belonging to former generations employed the terms *Tso-hia* and *Tso-la-hia* [12] to signify the rest during the rainy season; but this was because the ignorant (*common*) people of the frontier countries did not understand the right sounds of the language of the middle country (*India*), or that they translated before they comprehended the local phrases: this was the cause of error. And for the same reason occur the mistakes about the time of Tathâgata's conception, birth, departure from his home, enlightenment, and *Nirvâna*, which we shall notice in the subsequent records.

5. *Towns and Buildings.*

The towns and villages have inner gates; [13] the walls are wide and high; the streets and lanes are tortuous, and the roads winding. The thoroughfares are dirty and

---

[11] I have preferred not to alter the text, and so translate the passage literally. The "double period" of rest during the rainy season was an early ordinance, found in the *Vinaya*. It was so arranged that those who were prevented from arriving at the appointed time might begin their "rest" a month later. If, however, we suppose the symbol *liang* to be a mistake for *yu*, then the passage will run thus: "The priestly fraternity retired into fixed dwellings during the rainy season." See Burnouf, *Introd.*, p. 254.

[12] I cannot but think that *hia* and *la* in these phrases are intended to be phonetic equivalents for *Varsha*, and that the author is pointing out the error of those who adopted such inadequate sounds. M. Julien's explanation, however, may be the correct one (vid. Julien *in loc.*, n. 1).

[13] Such is the meaning generally assigned to the symbols *leu yen*. I do not understand the translation given by Julien; the texts perhaps are different.

the stalls arranged on both sides of the road with appropriate signs. Butchers, fishers, dancers, executioners, and scavengers, and so on, have their abodes without the city. In coming and going these persons are bound to keep on the left side of the road till they arrive at their homes. Their houses are surrounded by low walls, and form the suburbs. The earth being soft and muddy, the walls of the towns are mostly built of brick or tiles. The towers on the walls are constructed of wood or bamboo; the houses have balconies and belvederes, which are made of wood, with a coating of lime or mortar, and covered with tiles. The different buildings have the same form as those in China: rushes, or dry branches, or tiles, or boards are used for covering them. The walls are covered with lime and mud, mixed with cow's dung for purity. At different seasons they scatter flowers about. Such are some of their different customs.

The *sanghârâmas* are constructed with extraordinary skill. A three-storied tower[14] is erected at each of the four angles. The beams and the projecting heads are carved with great skill in different shapes. The doors, windows, and the low walls are painted profusely; the monks' cells are ornamental on the inside and plain on the outside.[15] In the very middle[16] of the building is the hall, high and wide. There are various storeyed chambers and turrets of different height and shape, without any fixed rule. The doors open towards the east; the royal throne also faces the east.

---

[14] The phrase *chung koh* means "a storeyed room or pavilion;" so at least I understand it. M. Julien translates as though it meant a double-storeyed room, or a pavilion with *two* storeys. The passage literally translated is : "Angle towers rise on the four sides ; there are (*or* they are) storeyed buildings of three stages."

[15] I take *li shu* to mean "the monks" or "the religious," the dark-clad.

[16] The phrase *ngau shih* may mean "the sleeping apartments," as Julien translates ; but I hesitate to give it this meaning, because the monks slept in their cells, and not in a dormitory. The hall I take to be the hall for religious worship. The account here given corresponds very closely with the description of the

6. *Seats, Clothing, &c.*

When they sit *or rest* they all use mats ;[17] the royal family and the great personages and assistant officers use mats variously ornamented, but in size they are the same. The throne of the reigning sovereign is large and high, and much adorned with precious gems: it is called the Lion-throne (*simhâsana*). It is covered with extremely fine drapery ; the footstool is adorned with gems. The nobility use beautifully painted and enriched seats, according to their taste.

7. *Dress, Habits, &c.*

Their clothing is not cut or fashioned ; they mostly affect fresh-white garments ; they esteem little those of mixed colour or ornamented. The men wind their garments round their middle, then gather them under the armpits, and let them fall down across the body, hanging to the right. The robes of the women fall down to the ground ; they completely cover their shoulders. They wear a little knot of hair on their crowns, and let the rest of their hair fall loose. Some of the men cut off their moustaches, and have other odd customs. On their heads the people wear caps (*crowns*), with flower-wreaths and jewelled necklets. Their garments are made of *Kiau-she-ye* (kauśêya) and of cotton. *Kiau-she-ye* is the product of the wild silkworm. They have garments also of *Ts'o-mo* (kshauma), which is a sort of hemp; garments also made of *Kien-po-lo* (kambala) which is woven from fine goat-hair; garments also made from *Ho-la-li* (karûla)[18] This stuff is made from the fine hair of a wild animal: it is seldom this can be woven, and therefore the stuff is very valuable, and it is regarded as fine clothing.

In North India, where the air is cold, they wear short

Vihâras in Nepâl at the present day.

[17] The expression here used may mean "matted beds" or "seats." It is commonly used to denote the *nishadyâ* (Pâli, *nisîdanam*) or mats used by Buddhists.

[18] The Japanese equivalents are *Ka-ra-tsi.*

and close-fitting garments, like the Hu people. The dress
and ornaments worn by non-believers are varied and
mixed. Some wear peacocks' feathers; some wear as
ornaments necklaces made of skull bones (the *Kapâladhârinas*); some have no clothing, but go naked (*Nirgranthas*); some wear leaf or bark garments; some pull
out their hair and cut off their moustaches; others have
bushy whiskers and their hair braided on the top of their
heads. The costume is not uniform, and the colour, whether
red or white, not constant.

The Shamans (Śramaṇas) have only three kinds [19] of
robes, viz., the *Sang-kio-ki*, the *Ni-fo-si-na*. The cut of the
three robes is not the same, but depends on the school.
Some have wide or narrow borders, others have small or
large flaps. The *Sang-kio-ki* covers the left shoulder and
conceals the two armpits. It is worn open on the left and
closed on the right. It is cut longer than the waist. The
Ni-fo-se-na has neither girdle nor tassels. When putting
it on, it is plaited in folds and worn round the loins with
a cord fastening. The schools differ as to the colour of
this garment: both yellow and red are used.

The Kshattriyas and the Brâhmaṇs are cleanly and
wholesome in their dress, and they live in a homely and
frugal way. The king of the country and the great ministers wear garments and ornaments different in their character. They use flowers for decorating their hair, with
gem-decked caps; they ornament themselves with bracelets and necklaces.

There are rich merchants who deal exclusively [20] in
gold trinkets, and so on. They mostly go bare-footed; few
wear sandals. They stain their teeth red or black; they
bind up their hair and pierce their ears; they ornament [21]
their noses, and have large eyes. Such is their appearance.

[19] There are only two names
given in the text. The first, viz., the
Seng-kia-chi—Saṅghâti is omitted.
The other two are the *Saṅkakshikâ*
and the *Nirâsana*.

[20] It may also mean that the great
merchants use only bracelets.

[21] This may also mean "they
have handsome noses."

8. *Cleanliness, Ablutions, &c.*

They are very particular in their personal cleanliness, and allow no remissness in this particular. All wash themselves before eating; they never use that which has been left over (*from a former meal*); they do not pass the dishes. Wooden and stone vessels, when used, must be destroyed; vessels of gold, silver, copper, or iron after each meal must be rubbed and polished. After eating they cleanse their teeth with a willow stick, and wash their hands and mouth.

Until these ablutions are finished they do not touch one another. Every time they perform the functions of nature they wash their bodies and use perfumes of sandal-wood or turmeric.

When the king washes[22] they strike the drums and sing hymns to the sound of musical instruments. Before offering their religious services and petitions, they wash and bathe themselves.

9. *Writing, Language, Books, the Vêdas, Study.*

The letters of their alphabet were arranged by Brahmâ-dêva, and their forms have been handed down from the first till now. They are forty-seven in number, and are combined so as to form words according to the object, and according to circumstances (*of time or place*): there are other forms (*inflexions*) used. This alphabet has spread in different directions and formed diverse branches, according to circumstances; therefore there have been slight modifications in the sounds of the words (*spoken language*); but in its great features there has been no change. Middle India preserves the original character of the language in its integrity. Here the pronunciation is soft and agreeable, and like the language of the Dêvas. The pronunciation of the words is clear and pure, and fit as a

---

[22] Julien translates "when the king is going out;" but in my copy it is as in the text.

model for all men. The people of the frontiers have contracted several erroneous modes of pronunciation; for according to the licentious habits of the people, so also will be the corrupt nature of their language.

With respect to the records of events, each province has its own official for preserving them in writing. The record of these events in their full character is called *Ni-lo-pi-ch'a* (Nîlapiṭa, *blue deposit*). In these records are mentioned good and evil events, with calamities and fortunate occurrences.

To educate and encourage the young, they are first taught (*led*) to study the book of twelve chapters (*Siddhavastu*).[23]

After arriving at the age of seven years and upwards, the young are instructed in the five *Vidyâs*, *Śâstras* of great importance.[24] The first is called the elucidation of sounds (*Śabdavidyâ*.) This treatise explains and illustrates the agreement (*concordance*) of words, and it provides an index for derivatives.

The second *vidyâ* is called *Kiau-ming* (*Śilpasthânavidyâ*); it treats of the arts, mechanics, explains the principles of the *Yin* and *Yang* and the calendar.

The third is called the medicinal treatise (*Chikitsâvidyâ*); it embraces formulæ for protection, secret charms (*the use of*) medicinal stones, acupuncture, and mugwort.

The fourth *vidyâ* is called the *Hêtuvidyâ* (*science of causes*); its name is derived from the character of the work, which relates to the determination of the true and false, and reduces to their last terms the definition of right and wrong.

The fifth *vidyâ* is called the science of "the interior"

<hr>

[23] This work in twelve chapters is that called *Siddhavastu* (*Sih-ti-chang*) in the *Fan-i-ming-i-tsi* (book xiv. 17 a). It is called *Sih-ti-lo-su-to* by I-tsing (*Nan hâe*, iv. 8 a) by mistake for *Sih-ti-po-su-to*, *i.e.*, *Siddhavastu*. For some remarks on this subject see Max Müller's letter to the *Academy*, Sept. 25, 1880; also *Indian Antiq.*, vol. ix, p. 307.

[24] Or, it may be translated "the great *Śâstra*, or *Śâstras* of the five *Vidyâs*," in Chinese, *Ming*. See below, Book iii. note 102.

(*Adhyâtmavidyâ*); it relates to the five vehicles,[25] their causes and consequences, and the subtle influences of these.

The Brâhmans study the four *Vêda Sâstras.* The first is called *Shau* (*longevity*); it relates to the preservation of life and the regulation of the natural condition. The second is called *Sse* (*sacrifice*); it relates to the (*rules of*) sacrifice and prayer. The third is called *Ping* (*peace or regulation*); it relates to decorum, casting of lots, military affairs, and army regulations. The fourth is called *Shu* (*secret mysteries*); it relates to various branches of science, incantations, medicine.[26]

The teachers (*of these works*) must themselves have closely studied the deep and secret principles they contain, and penetrated to their remotest meaning. They then explain their general sense, and guide their pupils in understanding the words which are difficult. They urge them on and skilfully conduct them. They add lustre to their poor knowledge, and stimulate the desponding. If they find that their pupils are satisfied with their acquirements, and so wish to escape to attend to their worldly duties, then they use means to keep them in their power. When they have finished their education, and have attained· thirty years of age, then their character is formed and their knowledge ripe. When they have secured an occupation they first of all thank their master for his attention. There are some, deeply versed in antiquity, who devote themselves to elegant studies, and live apart from the world, and retain the simplicity of their character. These rise above mundane presents, and are as insensible to renown as to the contempt of the world. Their name having spread afar, the rulers appreciate them highly, but

---

[25] The five Vehicles, *i.e.*, the five degrees of religious advance among the Buddhists : (1) The vehicle of Buddha, (2) of the Bôdhisattvas, (3) of the Pratyéka Buddha, (4) of the ordained disciple, (5) of the lay disciple.

[26] The four *Vêdas*, in the order they are here spoken of, are the *Ayur Vêda*, the *Yajur Vêda*, the *Sâma Vêda*, the *Atharva Vêda*.

'are unable to draw them to the court. The chief of the country honours them on account of their (*mental*) gifts, and the people exalt their fame and render them universal homage. This is the reason of their devoting themselves to their studies with ardour and resolution, without any sense of fatigue. They search for wisdom, relying on their own resources. Although they are possessed of large wealth, yet they will wander here and there to seek their subsistence. There are others who, whilst attaching value to letters, will yet without shame consume their fortunes in wandering about for pleasure, neglecting their duties. They squander their substance in costly food and clothing. Having no virtuous principle, and no desire to study, they are brought to disgrace, and their infamy is widely circulated.

So, according to the class they belong to, all gain knowledge of the doctrine of Tathâgata; but, as the time is distant since the holy one lived, his doctrine is presented in a changed form, and so it is understood, rightly or not, according to the intelligence of those who inquire into it.

10. *Buddhist Schools, Books, Discussions, Discipline.*

The different schools are constantly at variance, and their contending utterances rise like the angry waves of the sea. The different sects have their separate masters, and in various directions aim at one end.

There are Eighteen schools, each claiming pre-eminence. The partisans of the Great and Little Vehicle are content to dwell apart. There are some who give themselves up to quiet contemplation, and devote themselves, whether walking or standing still or sitting down, to the acquirement of wisdom and insight; others, on the contrary, differ from these in raising noisy contentions about their faith. According to their fraternity, they are governed by distinctive rules and regulations, which we need not name.

The *Vinaya* (*liu*), discourses (*lun*), *sûtras* (*king*), are equally Buddhist books. He who can entirely explain one class of these books is exempted from the control of the *karmadâna.* If he can explain two classes, he receives in addition the equipments of an upper seat (*room*); he who can explain three classes has allotted to him different servants to attend to and obey him; he who can explain four classes has "pure men" (*upâsakas)* allotted to him as attendants; he who can explain five classes of books is then allowed an elephant carriage; he who can explain six classes of books is allowed a surrounding escort. When a man's renown has reached to a high distinction, then at different times he convokes an assembly for discussion. He judges of the superior or inferior talent of those who take part in it; he distinguishes their good or bad points; he praises the clever and reproves the faulty; if one of the assembly distinguishes himself by refined language, subtle investigation, deep penetration, and severe logic, then he is mounted on an elephant covered with precious ornaments, and conducted by a numerous suite to the gates of the convent.

If, on the contrary, one of the members breaks down in his argument, or uses poor and inelegant phrases, or if he violates a rule in logic and adapts his words accordingly, they proceed to disfigure his face with red and white, and cover his body with dirt and dust, and then carry him off to some deserted spot or leave him in a ditch. Thus they distinguish between the meritorious and the worthless, between the wise and the foolish.

The pursuit of pleasure belongs to a worldly life, to follow knowledge to a religious life; to return to a worldly life from one of religion is considered blameworthy. If one breaks the rules of discipline, the transgressor is publicly reproved: for a slight fault a reprimand is given or a temporary banishment (*enforced silence*); for a grave fault expulsion is enforced. Those who are thus expelled for life go out to seek some dwelling-place, or, finding no place of refuge, wander about the roads; sometimes they go back to their old occupation (*resume lay life*).

11. *Castes—Marriage.*

With respect to the division of families, there are four classifications. The first is called the Brâhman (*Po-lo-men*), men of pure conduct. They guard themselves in religion, live purely, and observe the most correct principles. The second is called Kshattriya (*T'sa-ti-li*), the royal caste. For ages they have been the governing class: they apply themselves to virtue (*humanity*) and kindness. The third is called Vaiśyas (*fei-she-li*), the merchant class: they engage in commercial exchange, and they follow profit at home and abroad. The fourth is called Śûdra (*Shu-t'o-lo*), the agricultural class: they labour in ploughing and tillage. In these four classes purity or impurity of caste assigns to every one his place. When they marry they rise or fall in position according to their new relationship. They do not allow promiscuous marriages between relations. A woman once married can never take another husband. Besides these there are other classes of many kinds that intermarry according to their several callings. It would be difficult to speak of these in detail.

12. *Royal Family, Troops, Weapons.*

The succession of kings is confined to the Kshattriya (*T'sa-li*) caste, who by usurpation and bloodshed have from time to time raised themselves to power. Although a distinct caste, they are regarded as honourable (*or* lords).

The chief soldiers of the country are selected from the bravest of the people, and as the sons follow the profession of their fathers, they soon acquire a knowledge of the art of war. These dwell in garrison around the palace (*during peace*), but when on an expedition they march in front as an advanced guard. There are four divisions of the army, viz.—(1) the infantry, (2) the cavalry, (3) the chariots, (4) the elephants.[27] The elephants are covered with strong armour, and their tusks are provided with

---

[27] *I.e.,* the *pattakâya, aśvakâya, rathakâya,* and *hastikâya* divisions.

sharp spurs.　A leader in a car gives the command, whilst
two attendants on the right and left drive his chariot,
which is drawn by four horses abreast.　The general of
the soldiers remains in his chariot; he is surrounded by a
file of guards, who keep close to his chariot wheels.

The cavalry spread themselves in front to resist an
attack, and in case of defeat they carry orders hither and
thither.　The infantry by their quick movements contribute to the defence.　These men are chosen for their courage and strength.　They carry a long spear and a great
shield; sometimes they hold a sword or sabre, and advance to the front with impetuosity.　All their weapons
of war are sharp and pointed.　Some of them are these—
spears, shields, bows, arrows, swords, sabres, battle-axes,
lances, halberds, long javelins, and various kinds of slings.[28]
All these they have used for ages.

13. *Manners, Administration of Law, Ordeals.*

With respect to the ordinary people, although they are
naturally light-minded, yet they are upright and honourable.
In money matters they are without craft, and in admini-
stering justice they are considerate.　They dread the retri-
bution of another state of existence, and make light of the
things of the present world.　They are not deceitful or
treacherous in their conduct, and are faithful to their
oaths and promises.　In their rules of government there is
remarkable rectitude, whilst in their behaviour there is
much gentleness and sweetness.　With respect to criminals or rebels, these are few in number, and only occasion-
ally troublesome.　When the laws are broken or the power
of the ruler violated, then the matter is clearly sifted and
the offenders imprisoned.　There is no infliction of corporal punishment; they are simply left to live or die, and are
not counted among men.　When the rules of propriety or

[28] Compare the weapons in the hands of soldiers represented in the Ajaṇṭâ frescoes.—Burgess, *Notes on* *the Buddhist Rock-Temples of Ajaṇṭâ,* &c., pp. 11, 20, 51, 67, 68, 72, 73, &c.

justice are violated, or when a man fails in fidelity or
filial piety, then they cut his nose or his ears off, or his
hands and feet, or expel him from the country or drive
him out into the desert wilds. For other faults, except
these, a small payment of money will redeem the punishment. In the investigation of criminal cases there is no
use of rod or staff to obtain proofs (*of guilt*). In questioning an accused person, if he replies with frankness the
punishment is proportioned accordingly; but if the accused obstinately denies his fault, or in despite of it
attempts to excuse himself, then in searching out the
truth to the bottom, when it is necessary to pass sentence,
there are four kinds of ordeal used—(1) by water, (2) by
force, (3) by weighing, (4) by poison.

When the ordeal is by water, then the accused is placed
in a sack connected with a stone vessel and thrown into
deep water. They then judge of his innocence (*truth*) or
guilt in this way—if the man sinks and the stone floats
he is guilty; but if the man floats and the stone sinks
then he is pronounced innocent.

Secondly, by fire. They heat a plate of iron and make
the accused sit on it, and again place his feet on it, and
apply it to the palms of his hands; moreover, he is made
to pass his tongue over it; if no scars result, he is
innocent; if there are scars, his guilt is proved. In case of
weak and timid persons who cannot endure such ordeal,
they take a flower-bud and cast it towards the fire; if it
opens, he is innocent; if the flower is burnt, he is guilty.

Ordeal by weight is this: A man and a stone are placed
in a balance evenly, then they judge according to lightness
or weight. If the accused is innocent, then the man
weighs down the stone, which rises in the balance; if he
is guilty, the man rises and the stone falls.

Ordeal by poison is this: They take a ram and make
an incision in its right thigh, then mixing all sorts of
poison with a portion of the food of the accused man,
they place it in the incision made in the thigh (*of the ani-*

mal); if the man is guilty, then the poison takes effect and the creature dies; if he is innocent, then the poison has no effect, and he survives.

By these four methods of trial the way of crime is stopped.

14. *Forms of Politeness.*

There are nine methods of showing outward respect— (1) by selecting words of a soothing character in making requests; (2) by bowing the head to show respect; (3) by raising the hands and bowing; (4) by joining the hands and bowing low; (5) by bending the knee; (6) by a prostration;[29] (7) by a prostration on hands and knees; (8) by touching the ground with the five circles; (9) by stretching the five parts of the body on the ground.

Of these nine methods the most respectful is to make one prostration on the ground and then to kneel and laud the virtues of the one addressed. When at a distance it is usual to bow low;[30] when near, then it is customary to kiss the feet and rub the ankles (*of the person addressed*).

Whenever orders are received at the hands of a superior, the person lifts the skirts of his robes and makes a prostration. The superior or honourable person who is thus reverenced must speak gently (*to the inferior*), either touching his head or patting his back, and addressing him with good words of direction or advice to show his affection.

When a Śramaṇa, or one who has entered on the religious life, has been thus respectfully addressed, he simply replies by expressing a good wish (*vow*).

Not only do they prostrate themselves to show reverence, but they also turn round towards the thing reverenced in many ways, sometimes with one turn, sometimes with three: if from some long-cherished feeling there is a call for marked reverence, then according to the desire of the person.

---

[29] To kneel on all-fours.—Wells Williams.
[30] *K'i sang*, to bow to the ground.—W. W.

15. *Medicines, Funeral Customs, &c.*

Every one who falls sick fasts for seven days. During this interval many recover, but if the sickness lasts they take medicine. The character of these medicines is different, and their names also. The doctors differ in their modes of examination and treatment.

When a person dies, those who attend the funeral raise lamentable cries and weep together. They rend their garments and loosen their hair; they strike their heads and beat their breasts. There are no regulations as to dress for mourning, nor any fixed time for observing it.

There are three methods of paying the last tribute to the dead: (1) by cremation—wood being made into a pyre, the body is burnt; (2) by water—the body is thrown into deep flowing water and abandoned; (3) by desertion—the body is cast into some forest-wild, to be devoured by beasts.

When the king dies, his successor is first appointed, that he may preside at the funeral rites and fix the different points of precedence. Whilst living they give (*their rulers*) titles according to their character (*virtue*); when dead there are no posthumous titles.

In a house where there has been a death there is no eating allowed; but after the funeral they resume their usual (*habits*). There are no anniversaries (*of the death*) observed. Those who have attended a death they consider unclean; they all bathe outside the town and then enter their houses.

The old and infirm who come near to death, and those entangled in a severe sickness, who fear to linger to the end of their days, and through disgust wish to escape the troubles of life, or those who desire release from the trifling affairs of the world and its concerns (*the concerns of life*), these, after receiving a farewell meal at the hands of their relatives or friends, they place, amid the sounds of music, on a boat which they propel into the midst of the Ganges, where such persons drown themselves. They think thus to secure a birth among the Dêvas. Rarely one of these may be seen not yet dead on the borders (*of the river*).

The priests are not allowed to lament or cry for the dead; when a father or mother of a priest dies they recite their prayers, recounting (*pledging*) their obligations to them; reflecting on the past, they carefully attend to them now dead. They expect by this to increase the mysterious character of their religious merit.

16. *Civil Administration, Revenues, &c.*

As the administration of the government is founded on benign principles, the executive is simple. The families are not entered on registers, and the people are not subject to forced labour (*conscription*). The private demesnes of the crown are divided into four principal parts; the first is for carrying out the affairs of state and providing sacrificial offerings; the second is for providing subsidies for the ministers and chief officers of state; the third is for rewarding men of distinguished ability; and the fourth is for charity to religious bodies, whereby the field of merit is cultivated (*planted*). In this way the taxes on the people are light, and the personal service required of them is moderate. Each one keeps his own worldly goods in peace, and all till the ground for their subsistence. These who cultivate the royal estates pay a sixth part of the produce as tribute. The merchants who engage in commerce come and go in carrying out their transactions. The river-passages and the road-barriers are open on payment of a small toll. When the public works require it, labour is exacted but paid for. The payment is in strict proportion to the work done.

The military guard the frontiers, or go out to punish the refractory. They also mount guard at night round the palace. The soldiers are levied according to the requirements of the service; they are promised certain payments and are publicly enrolled. The governors, ministers, magistrates, and officials have each a portion of land consigned to them for their personal support.

17. *Plants and Trees, Agriculture, Food, Drink, Cookery.*

The climate and the quality of the soil being different according to situation, the produce of the land is various in its character. The flowers and plants, the fruits and trees are of different kinds, and have distinct names. There is, for instance, the Amala fruit (*Ngán-mo-lo*), the Âmla fruit (*Ngán-mi-lo*), the Madhuka fruit (*Mo-tu-kia*), the Bhadra fruit (*po-ta-lo*), the Kapittha fruit (*kie-pi-ta*), the Amalû fruit (*'O-mo-lo*), the Tinduka fruit (*Chin-tu-kia*), the Udumbara fruit (*Wu-tan-po-lo*), the Môcha fruit (*Mau-che*), the Nârikêla fruit (*Na-li-ki-lo*), the Panasa fruit (*Pan-na-so*). It would be difficult to enumerate all the kinds of fruit; we have briefly named those most esteemed by the people. As for the date (*Tsau*), the chestnut (*Lih*), the loquat (*P'i*), and the persimmon (*Thi*), they are not known. The pear (*Li*), the wild plum (*Nai*), the peach (*T'au*), the apricot (*Hang* or *Mui*), the grape (*Po-tau*), &c., these all have been brought from the country of Kaśmîr, and are found growing on every side. Pomegranates and sweet oranges are grown everywhere.

In cultivating the land, those whose duty it is sow and reap, plough and harrow (*weed*), and plant according to the season; and after their labour they rest awhile. Among the products of the ground, rice and corn are most plentiful. With respect to edible herbs and plants, we may name ginger and mustard, melons and pumpkins, the *Heun-to* (*Kaṇḍu?*) plant, and others. Onions and garlic are little grown; and few persons eat them; if any one uses them for food, they are expelled beyond the walls of the town. The most usual food is milk, butter, cream, soft sugar, sugar-candy, the oil of the mustard-seed, and all sorts of cakes made of corn are used as food. Fish, mutton, gazelle, and deer they eat generally fresh, sometimes salted; they are forbidden to eat the flesh of the ox, the ass, the elephant, the horse, the pig, the dog, the fox, the wolf, the lion, the monkey, and all the hairy kind. Those who eat them are despised and scorned, and are universally reprobated; they live outside the walls, and are seldom seen among men.

With respect to the different kinds of wine and liquors, there are various sorts. The juice of the grape and sugarcane, these are used by the Kshattriyas as drink; the Vaiśyas use strong fermented drinks;[31] the Śramaṇs and Brâhmaṇs drink a sort of syrup made from the grape or sugarcane, but not of the nature of fermented wine.[32]

The mixed classes and base-born differ in no way (*as to food or drink*) from the rest, except in respect of the vessels they use, which are very different both as to value and material. There is no lack of suitable things for household use. Although they have saucepans and stewpans, yet they do not know the steamer used for cooking rice. They have many vessels made of dried clay; they seldom use red copper vessels: they eat from one vessel, mixing all sorts of condiments together, which they take up with their fingers. They have no spoons or cups, and in short no sort of chopstick. When sick, however, they use copper drinking cups.

18. *Commercial Transactions.*

Gold and silver, *tcou-shih* (native copper), white jade, fire pearls,[33] are the natural products of the country; there are besides these abundance of rare gems and various kinds of precious stones of different names, which are collected from the islands of the sea. These they exchange for other goods; and in fact they always barter in their com-

---

[31] *Shun lo*, high-flavoured spirits.

[32] Called, therefore, "not-wine-body," *i.e.*, non-alcoholic.

[33] If *fo* is a mistake for *kiang*, as it probably is, the substance would be "amber."

mercial transactions, for they have no gold or silver coins, pearl shells, or little pearls.[34]

The boundaries of India and the neighbouring countries are herein fully described ; the differences of climate and soil are briefly alluded to. Details referring to these points are grouped together, and are stated succinctly; and in referring to the different countries, the various customs and modes of administration are fully detailed.

LAN-PO [LAMGHÂN].

The kingdom of Lan-po[35] is about 1000 li in circuit, and on the north is backed by the Snowy Mountains; on three sides it is surrounded by the Black-ridge Mountains. The capital of the country is about 10 li in circuit. As for some centuries the royal family has been extinct, the chiefs have disputed for power among themselves, without the acknowledged superiority of any one in particular. Lately it has become tributary to Kapiśa. The country is adapted for the production of rice, and there are many forests of sugar-cane. The trees, though they produce many fruits, yet few are ripened. The climate is backward; the hoar-frosts are plenty, but not much snow. In common there is abundance and contentment. The men (*people*) are given to music. Naturally they are untrustworthy and thievish; their disposition is exacting one over the other, and they never give another the preference over themselves. In respect of stature they are little, but they are active and impetuous. Their garments are made of white linen for the most part, and what they

[34] This translation differs from Julien's. The text is probably corrupt.

[35] Lan-po corresponds with the present Lamghân, a small country lying along the northern bank of the Kâbul river, bounded on the west and east by the Alingar and Kunar rivers.—Cunningham. The Sanskrit name of the district is Lampaka, and the Lampâkas are said to be also called Murandas (*Mahâbh.*, vii. 4847; Reinaud, *Mém. s. l'Inde,* p. 353; and Lassen, *Ind. Alt.,* vol. ii. p. 877, vol. iii. p. 136 f.). Ptolemy (lib. vii. c. 1, 42) places a tribe called Λαμάται, Λαμβάται, or Λαμπάγαι in this district. The modern name is vulgarly pronounced Laghmân. See Baber's *Memoirs,* pp. 133, 136, 140 ff. ; Cunningham, *Anc. Geog. Ind.,* p. 43.

wear is well appointed.   There are about ten *sanghá-rámas*, with few followers (*priests*).   The greater portion study the Great Vehicle.   There are several scores of diffe-rent Dêva temples.   There are few heretics.   Going south-east from this country 100 li or so, we cross a great mountain (*ridge*), pass a wide river, and so come to Na-kie-lo-ho [the frontiers of North India].

NA-KIE-LO-HO [NAGARAHÂRA].

The country of Nagarahâra (Na-kie-lo-ho) is about 600 li from east to west, and 250 or 260 li from north to south.   It is surrounded on four sides by overhanging precipices and natural barriers.   The capital is 20 li or so in circuit.[36]   It has no chief ruler ; the commandant and his subordinates come from Kapiśa.   The country is rich in cereals, and produces a great quantity of flowers and fruits.   The climate is moist and warm. Their manners are simple and honest, their disposition ardent and courageous.   They think lightly of wealth and love learning.   They cultivate the religion of Buddha, and few believe in other doctrines.   The *sanghârâmas* are many, but yet the priests are few ; the *stúpas* are deso-late and ruined.   There are five Dêva temples, with about one hundred worshippers.[37]

---

[36] The situation of the town of Nagarahâra (the old capital of the Jalálâbâd district) has been satisfac-torily determined by Mr. W. Simp-son (*J. R. A. S.*, N.S., vol. xiii. p. 183). He places the site of the town in the angle formed by the junction of the Surkhar aud Kâbul rivers, on their right banks.   Both the direction and the distance from Lamghân (about twenty miles south - east) would place us on this spot.   The mountains crossed by the pilgrim were the Siâh Kôh, and the river would be probably the Kâbul river at Darunta.   The Sanskrit name— Nagarahâra—occurs in an inscription which was discovered by Major Kittoe in the ruined mound of Gho-srâwâ in the district of Bihâr (*J. A. S. B.*, vol. xvii. pt. i. pp. 492, 494, 498 f.) The district corresponds with the Νάγαρα Διονυσόπολις of Ptolemy (lib. vii. c. 1, 43).   It is called the city of Dípankara by Hwui-lih (Jul. *Vie*, p. 78), just as he calls Hiḍḍa the city of "the skull-bone" (*l. c.*) Conf. Lassen, *I. A.*, vol. iii. p. 137.

[37] Worshippers or "men of diffe-rent religious faith."   The usual term for "non-believer" in Chinese is *wai-tau*, an "outside - religion man."   This term corresponds with the Pâli *bâhiro*, used in the same way.   The Buddhists are now spoken of by the Muhammadans as *Kaffir log*, "infidel people" (Simpson, *u. s.*, p. 186.

Three li to the east of the city there is a *stûpa* in height about 300 feet, which was built by Aśôka Râja. It is wonderfully constructed[38] of stone beautifully adorned and carved. Śâkya, when a Bôdhisattva, here met Dîpankara[39] Buddha (*Jen-tang-fo*), and spreading out his deerskin doublet, and unbinding his hair and covering with it the muddy road, received a predictive assurance. Though the passed kalpa brought the overthrow of the world, the trace of this event was not destroyed; on religious (*fast*) days the sky rains down all sorts of flowers, which excite a religious frame of mind in the people, who also offer up religious offerings.

To the west of this place is a *Kia-lan* (*sanghârâma*) with a few priests. To the south is a small *stûpa:* this was the place where, in old time, Bôdhisattva covered the mud (*with his hair*). Aśôka-râja built (*this stûpa*) away from the road.[40]

Within the city is the ruined foundation of a great *stûpa.* Tradition says that it once contained a tooth of Buddha, and that it was high and of great magnificence. Now it has no tooth, but only the ancient foundations remain.

By its side is a *stûpa* 30 feet or so in height; the old stories of the place know nothing of the origin of this fabric; they say only that it fell from heaven and placed itself here. Being no work of man's art, it is clearly a spiritual prodigy.

---

[38] The Chinese expression seems to refer to the successive layers of checkered stones peculiar to these topes. See W. Simpson's and also Mr. Swinnerton's account.—*Ind. Antiq.*, vol. viii. pp. 198 & 227 f.

[39] The incident referred to in the text, viz., the interview between Dipankara Buddha and the Bôdhisattva Sumedha, is a popular one in Buddhist sculpture and mythology. There is a representation of it among fragments in the Lahor Museum ; another representation is among the sculptures of the Kanheri caves (*Archæol. Sur. W. Ind, Rep.,*

vol. iv. p. 66). The legend I translated from the Chinese (*J. R. A. Soc.*, N.S., vol. vi. pp. 377 ff). Fa-hien also refers to it (*Buddhist Pilgrims,* p. 43). See also some remarks on this legend, *Ind. Antiq.*, vol. xi. p. 146 ; and conf. Rhys David's *Buddh. Birth-Stories*, pp. 3 f.

[40] This is a difficult passage, and is probably corrupt. The phrase "*ts'ui-pi,*" towards the end, may mean "in an out-of-the-way place." The reference is to the spot where predictive assurance was given to Sumêdha that he should become a Buddha.

To the south-west of the city about 10 li is a *stúpa*. Here Tathâgata, when living in the world, alighted, having left Mid-India and passed through the air for the sake of converting men. The people, moved by reverence, erected this building. Not far to the east is a *stúpa* ; it was here Bôdhisattva met Dîpankara Buddha and bought the flowers.[41]

About 20 li to the south-west of the city we come to a small stone ridge, where there is a *sanghârâma* with a high hall and a storied tower made of piled-up stone. It is now silent and deserted, with no priests. In the middle is a *stúpa* 200 feet or so in height, built by Aśôka-râja.

To the south-west of this *sanghârâma* a deep torrent rushes from a high point of the hill and scatters its waters in leaping cascades. The mountain sides are like walls ; on the eastern side of one is a great cavern, deep and profound, the abode of the Nâga Gôpâla. The gate (*or* entrance) leading to it is narrow ; the cavern is dark ; the precipitous rock causes the water to find its way in various rivulets into this cavern. In old days there was a shadow of Buddha to be seen here, bright as the true form, with all its characteristic marks.[42] In later days men have not seen it so much. What does appear is only a feeble likeness. But whoever prays with fervent faith, he is mysteriously endowed, and he sees it clearly before him, though not for long.

In old times, when Tathâgata was in the world, this dragon was a shepherd who provided the king with milk and cream. Having on one occasion failed to do so, and having received a reprimand, he proceeded in an angry temper to the *stúpa* of " the predictive assurance," and

---

[41] He bought the flowers of a girl, who consented to sell them only on condition that she should ever hereafter be born as his wife. See the account in the "Legend of Dipankara Buddha" (*J. R. A. S.*, N.S., vol. vi. pp. 377 ff.) The incident of the flowers remaining over the head as a "baldachin," is represented in the Labor sculpture referred to above, note 39. See Fergusson, *Tree and Serp. Worship*, pl. L.

[42] See note 5 p. 1, and p. 145, note 76.

there made an offering of flowers, with the prayer that he might become a destructive dragon for the purpose of afflicting the country and destroying the king. Then ascending the rocky side of the hill, he threw himself down and was killed. Forthwith he became a great dragon and occupied this cavern, and then he purposed to go forth and accomplish his original wicked purpose. When this intention had risen within him, Tathâgata, having examined what was his object, was moved with pity for the country and the people about to be destroyed by the dragon. By his spiritual power he came from Mid-India to where the dragon was. The dragon seeing Tathâgata, his murderous purpose was stayed, and he accepted the precept against killing, and vowed to defend the true law; he requested Tathâgata to occupy this cavern evermore, that his holy disciples might ever receive his (*the dragon's*) religious offerings.[43]

Tathâgata replied, "When I am about to die; I will leave you my shadow, and I will send five Arhats to receive from you continual offerings. When the true law is destroyed,[44] this service of yours shall still go on; if an evil heart rises in you, you must look at my shadow, and because of its power of love and virtue your evil purpose will be stopped. The Buddhas who will appear throughout this *Bhadra-kalpa*[45] will all, from a motive of pity, intrust to you their shadows as a bequest." Outside the gate of the Cavern of the Shadow there are two square stones; on one is the impression of the foot of Tathâgata, with a wheel-circle (*lun-siang*) beautifully clear, which shines with a brilliant light from time to time.

On either side of the Cavern of the Shadow there are

---

[43] This is evidently the meaning of the passage : the request was, *not* that the dragon might dwell in the cavern, but that Tathâgata would live there with his disciples. Fa-hian refers to this cave.

[44] The "true law" was to last 500 years; the "law of images" 1000 years.

[45] This period is that in which we now are, during which 1000 Buddhas are to appear.

several stone chambers; in these the holy disciples of Tathâgata reposed in meditation.

At the north-west corner of the cave of the shadow is a *stûpa* where Buddha walked up and down. Beside this is a *stûpa* which contains some of the hair and the nail-parings of Tathâgata.

Not far from this is a *stûpa* where Tathâgata, making manifest the secret principles of his true doctrine, declared the *Skandha-dhâtu-âyatanas* (*Yun-kiaï-king*).[46]

At the west of the Cave of the Shadow is a vast rock, on which Tathâgata in old time spread out his *kashâya*[47] robe after washing it; the marks of the tissue still exist.

To the south-east of the city 30 li or so is the town of Hi-lo (Hiḍḍa);[48] it is about 4 or 5 li in circuit; it is high in situation and strong by natural declivities. It has flowers and woods, and lakes whose waters are bright as a mirror. The people of this city are simple, honest, and upright. There is here a two-storied tower; the beams are painted and the columns coloured red.

[46] The symbol "*chu*" (*âyatana*) in this passage must be connected with the previous "*yun kiaï.*" The *yun kiaï chu* are the eighteen *dhâtus*, for which see Childers' *Pâli Dict.* (*sub voc.*) Vide also the *Surangama Sûtra* (*Catena of Buddhist Scrip.*, p. 297 n. 2). There is no word in my text for *king*, given by Julien.

[47] *Kashâya* refers to the colour of the Buddhist upper robe, which was of brick-red or yellow colour (*kashaya*).

[48] The city of Hi-lo or Hiḍḍa (concerning which restoration, see V. de St. Martin's *Mém.*, *u. s.*, p. 304), about six miles south-east of Nagarahâra, is described by Fa-hian (cap. xiii.) The *Vihâra* of the skull-bone is there said to be placed within a square enclosure, and it is added, "though the heavens should quake and the earth open, this place would remain unmoved." Compare with this the remark of Hiuen Tsiang respecting Svêtavâras (*sup.* p. 61) and its name of Τετραγωνις. It is curious, too, that this place (the neighbourhood of Hiḍḍa) is called Bêgrâm, and so also is Svêtavâras (*i.e.*, Karsana or Tetragônis). Both Bêgrâm and Nagara appear to mean "the city." This town or Nagarahâra may be the Nyssa or Nysa of Arrian (lib. v. cap. i.) and Curtius (lib. viii. cap. x. 7), in which case there would be no need to derive Dionysopolis—the Nagara of Ptolemy—from Udyânapura, although, as General Cunningham remarks (*Anc. Geog. of Ind.*, p. 46), the name Ajûna, given to Nagarahâra (according to Masson) might well be corrupted from Ujjâna or Udyâna. Compare with the text the account found in Hwui-lih (*Vie*, p. 76). Conf. *Nouv. Jour. Asiatique*, tom. vii. pp. 338 f.; Masson, *Var. Jour.*, vol. iii. pp. 254 ff.; Wilson, *Ariana Ant.*, pp. 43, 105 f.

In the second storey is a little *stûpa*, made of the seven precious substances; it contains the skull-bone of Tathâgata; it is 1 foot 2 inches round; the hair orifices are distinct; its colour is a whitish-yellow. It is enclosed in a precious receptacle, which is placed in the middle of the *stûpa*. Those who wish to make lucky or unlucky presages (*marks*) make a paste of scented earth, and impress it on the skull-bone; then, according to their merit, is the impression made.

Again there is another little *stûpa*, made of the seven precious substances, which encloses the skull-bone of Tathâgata. Its shape is like a lotus leaf;[49] its colour is the same as that of the other, and it is also contained in a precious casket, sealed up and fastened.

Again, there is another little *stûpa*, made of the seven precious substances, in which is deposited the eye-ball of Tathâgata, large as an *Âmra* fruit and bright and clear throughout; this also is deposited in a precious casket sealed up and fastened. The *Sanghâtî* robe of Tathâgata, which is made of fine cotton stuff of a yellow-red colour,[50] is also enclosed in a precious box. Since many months and years have passed, it is a little damaged. The staff[51] of Tathâgata, of which the rings are white iron (*tin ?*) and the stick of sandalwood, is contained in a precious case (*a case made of a precious substance*). Lately, a king, hearing of these various articles that they formerly belonged to Tathâgata as his own private property, took them away by force to his own country and placed them in his palace. After a short time,[52] going to look at them, they were gone;

---

[49] The *ho hwa* is the water-lily, but it is also a general name for mallows (Medhurst, *s. v.*) This bone is that of the *ushnisha* or top of the skull.

[50] Such seems to be the meaning. Julien has taken it as though *kia-sha* referred to another garment, but it seems merely to denote the robe called *Sanghâtî.*

[51] The religious staff, *khakkharam* or *hikkala*, was so called from the noise it made when shaken. Conf. *hikk;* Ch. *sck ; Sck cheung*, an abbot's crosier or staff (Wells Williams). It is described in the *Sha-men-yih-yung* (fol. 14 a). See p. 47, *ante.*

[52] Scarcely had an hour elapsed.

and after further inquiries he found they had returned to their original place. These five sacred objects (*relics*) often work miracles.

The king of Kapiśa has commanded five pure-conduct men (*Brâhmans*) to offer continually scents and flowers to these objects. These pure persons, observing the crowds who came to worship incessantly, wishing to devote themselves to quiet meditation, have established a scale of fixed charges, with a view to secure order, by means of that wealth which is so much esteemed by men. Their plan, in brief, is this:—All who wish to see the skull-bone of Tathâgata have to pay one gold piece; those who wish to take an impression pay five pieces. The other objects [53] in their several order, have a fixed price; and yet, though the charges are heavy, the worshippers are numerous.

To the north-west of the double-storied pavilion is a *stûpa*, not very high or large, but yet one which possesses many spiritual (*miraculous*) qualities. If men only touch it with a finger, it shakes and trembles to the foundation, and the bells and the jingles moving together give out a pleasant sound.

Going south-east from this, crossing mountains and valleys for 500 li or so, we arrive at the kingdom of Kien-t'o-lo (Gandhâra).

KIEN-T'O-LO—GANDHÂRA.

The kingdom of Gandhâra is about 1000 li from east to west, and about 800 li from north to south. On the east it borders on the river Sin (Sindh). The capital of the country is called Po-lu-sha-pu-lo; [54] it is about 40 li

---

[53] The phrase *tsze chu*, which is of frequent occurrence in Buddhist composition, seems to mean "moreover" or "besides this."

[54] The country of Gandhâra is that of the lower Kâbul valley, lying along the Kâbul river between the Khoaspes (Kunar) and the Indus. It is the country of the Gandaræ of Ptolemy (*Geog.*, lib. vi. c. 1, 7). The capital was Purushapura now Peshâwer. The Gandarii are mentioned by Hekataios (*Fr.* 178, 179) and Herodotos (lib. iii. c. 91, lib. vii. c.

in circuit. The royal family is extinct, and the kingdom is governed by deputies from Kapiśa. The towns and villages are deserted, and there are but few inhabitants. At one corner of the royal residence [55] there are about 1000 families The country is rich in cereals, and produces a variety of flowers and fruits; it abounds also in sugar-cane, from the juice of which they prepare "the solid sugar." The climate is warm and moist, and in general without ice or snow. The disposition of the people is timid and soft: they love literature; most of them belong to heretical schools; a few believe in the true law. From old time till now this border-land of India has produced many authors of *śâstras*; for example, Nârâyaṇadêva,[56] Asaṅga Bôdhisattva, Vasubandhu Bôdhisattva, Dharmatrâta, Manôrhita, Pârśva the noble, and so on. There are about 1000 *saṅghârâmas*, which are deserted aud in ruins. They are filled with wild shrubs,[57] and solitary to the last degree. The *stûpas* are mostly decayed. The heretical temples, to the number of about 100, are occupied pell-mell by heretics.

Inside the royal city, towards the north-east,[58] is an old foundation (*or* a ruinous foundation). Formerly this was the precious tower of the *pâtra* of Buddha. After the *Nirvâṇa* of Buddha, his *pâtra* coming to this country, was

66), and the district of Gandaritis by Strabo (*Geog.*, lib. xv. c. 1, 26). See Wilson, *Ariana Ant.*, pp. 125, 131; *J. R. As. Soc.*, vol. v. p. 117; Lassen, *Ind. Alt.*, vol. i. pp. 502 f., vol. ii. pp. 150, 854; *Pentapot*, pp. 15 f., 105; *Asiat. Res.*, vol. xv. pp. 103, 106 f.; *Vishṇu-pur.*, vol. ii. pp. 169, 174, vol. iii. p. 319, vol. iv. p. 118; *Mahâbh.*, viii. 2055 f.; Troyer's *Râja-Taraṅgiṇî*, tom. ii. pp. 316-321; Elliot, *Hist. Ind.*, vol. i. p. 48 n.; Bunbury, *Hist. Anc. Geog.*, vol. i. pp. 142, 238; Reinaud, *Mém. sur l'Inde*, pp. 106 f. Pâṇini (iv. 2, 133) mentions the Gândhâra in the group Kachchhâdi.

[55] The *Kung shing* is the fortified or walled portion of the town, in which the royal palace stood.

[56] There is a symbol *puh* before this name, which, as Julien has remarked, is inserted by mistake. The Chinese equivalents for the names of these writers are as follows: Na-lo-yen-tin (Nârâyanadêva), Wu-ch'o-p'u-sa (Asaṅgha Bôdhisattva), Shi-shin-p'u-sa (Vasubandhu Bôdhisattva), Fa-kiu (Dharmatrâta), Ju-i (Manôrhita), Hie-tsun (Arya Pârśvika). All these, the text says, were born in Gandhâra.

[57] M. Julien has pointed out the error in the text and supplied this meaning.

[58] Julien has *north-west*.

worshipped during many centuries. In traversing different countries it has come now to Persia.[59]

Outside the city, about 8 or 9 li to the south-east, there
is a pipala tree about 100 feet or so in height. Its branches
are thick and the shade beneath sombre and deep. The
four past Buddhas have sat beneath this tree, and at the
present time there are four sitting figures of the Buddhas
to be seen here. During the Bhadrakalpa, the 996 other
Buddhas will all sit here. Secret spiritual influences
guard the precincts of the tree and exert a protecting
virtue in its continuance. Śâkya Tathâgata sat beneath
this tree with his face to the south and addressed Ânanda
thus :—" Four hundred years after my departure from the
world, there will be a king who shall rule it called Kanishka (*Kia-ni-se-kia*); not far to the south of this spot
he will raise a *stûpa* which will contain many various
relics of my bones and flesh."

To the south of the Pippala tree is a *stûpa* built by King
Kanishka; this king ascended the throne four hundred
years after the *Nirvâna*,[60] and governed the whole of Jambudvîpa. He had no faith either in wrong or right (*crime
or religious merit*), and he lightly esteemed the law of
Buddha. One day when traversing a swampy grove
(*bushy swamp*) he saw a white hare, which he followed as
far as this spot, when suddenly it disappeared. He then
saw a young shepherd-boy, who was building in the
wood hard by a little *stûpa* about three feet high. The
king said, " What are you doing?" The shepherd-boy
answered and said, " Formerly Śâkya Buddha, by his
divine wisdom, delivered this prophecy: ' There shall be a
king in this victorious (*superior*) land who shall erect a
stûpa, which shall contain a great portion of my bodily
relics.' The sacred merits of the great king (*Kanishka*)

<hr>

[59] For the wanderings of the
Pâtra of Buddha (called in Chinese
"the measure vessel," compare *gra-
duale* and *grail*), see Fa-hian, pp.
36 f., 161 f.; Köppen, *Die Rel. des
Buddha*, vol. i. p. 526; *J. R. A. S.*,
vol. xi. p. 127; also consult Yule's
Marco Polo, vol. ii. pp. 301, 310 f.

[60] See *ante*, p. 56, note 200, and
inf. p 151, note 97.

in former births (*suh*), with his increasing fame, have made the present occasion a proper one for the fulfilment of the old prophecy relating to the divine merit and the religious superiority of the person concerned. And now I am engaged for the purpose of directing you to these former predictions."[61] Having said these words he disappeared.

The king hearing this explanation, was overjoyed. Flattering himself that he was referred to in the prophecy of the great saint, he believed with all his heart and paid reverence to the law of Buddha. Surrounding the site of the little *stûpa* he built a stone *stûpa*, wishing to surpass it in height, to prove the power of his religious merit. But in proportion as his *stûpa* increased the other always exceeded it by three feet, and so he went on till his reached 400 feet, and the circumference of the base was a li and a half. The storeys having reached to five, each 150 feet in height, then he succeeded in covering the other. The king, overjoyed, raised on the top of this *stûpa* twenty-five circlets of gilded copper on a staff, and he placed in the middle of the *stûpa* a peck of the *Sarîras* of Tathâgata, and offered to them religious offerings. Scarcely had he finished his work when he saw the little *stûpa* take its place at the south-east of the great foundation, and project from its side about half-way up.[62] The king was disturbed

[61] Or, to arouse you to a sense of your destiny (your previous forecast).

[62] Julien translates this differently —"he saw the little *stûpa* raise itself by the side of the other and exceed it by one-half." The passage is undoubtedly a difficult one, and rendered more so by a faulty text. To understand it, we must observe that the building was a tower of five storeys, each 150 feet in height. The small *stûpa* or tower was enclosed in the middle of the lower basement. Suddenly, when the large tower was finished, the smaller one changed its position, and came to the south-east angle of the great foundation—*i.e.*, of the lowest division or storey—and pierced through the wall of the larger building about half way up. Kanishka, ill at ease in the presence of this portent, ordered the greater building to be destroyed down to the second stage. On this being done the little tower again went back to the middle of the space enclosed by the basement of the larger one, and there overtopped it as before. So I understand the passage; and if this be so, the only alteration required in the text is in the last clause, where instead of *siu*, "little," I would substitute *ta*, "great," "it came out of, *i.e.*, towered above, the great *stûpa*."

at this, and ordered the *stûpa* to be destroyed. When they had got down to the bottom of the second storey, through which the other projected, immediately that one removed to its former place, and once more it surpassed in height the other. The king retiring said, " It is easy to commit errors in human affairs,[63] but when there is divine influence at work it is difficult to counteract it. When a matter is directed by spiritual power, what can human resentment effect ? " Having confessed his fault, therefore, he retired.

These two *stûpas* are still visible. In aggravated[64] sickness, if a cure is sought, people burn incense and offer flowers, and with a sincere faith pay their devotions. In many cases a remedy is found.

On the southern side of the steps, on the eastern face of the great *stûpa*, there are engraved (*or* carved) two *stûpas*,[65] one three feet high, the other five feet. They are the same shape and proportion as the great *stûpa*. Again, there are two full-sized figures of Buddha, one four feet, the other six feet in height. They resemble him as he sat cross-legged beneath the *Bôdhi* tree. When the full rays of the sun shine on them they appear of a brilliant gold colour, and as the light decreases the hues of the stone seem to assume a reddish-blue colour. The old people say, " Several centuries ago, in a fissure of the stone foundation, there were some gold-coloured ants, the greatest about the size of the finger, the longest about a barleycorn in size. Those of the same species consorted together; by gnawing the stone steps they have left lines and marks as if engraved on the surface, and by the gold sand which they left (*as deposits*) they have caused the figures of Buddha to assume their present appearance."

---

[63] Or, human affairs are change-able and deceptive.

[64] The sense of *ying* in this passage is doubtful; it may mean "complicated" or "threatening (sickness)," or it may refer to complaints peculiar to children.

[65] The expression *lo c'ho* would seem to mean that the *stûpas* were engraved, not *built*. The particular named as to steps leading up to the *stûpa* is significant, as illustrating the architectural appearance and character of these buildings.

On the southern side of the stone steps of the great *stûpa* [66] there is a painted figure of Buddha about sixteen feet high. From the middle upward there are two bodies, below the middle, only one. The old tradition says: In the beginning, there was a poor man who hired himself out to get a living; having obtained a gold coin, he vowed to make a figure of Buddha. Coming to the *stûpa*, he spoke to a painter and said, " I wish now to get a figure of Tathâgata painted, with its beautiful points of excellence; [67] but I only have one gold coin; this is little enough to repay an artist. I am sorry to be so hampered by poverty in carrying out my cherished aim."

Then the painter, observing his simple truth, said nothing about the price, but promised to set to work to furnish the picture.

Again there was a man, similarly circumstanced, with one gold coin, who also sought to have a picture of Buddha painted. The painter having received thus a gold piece from each, procured some excellent colours (*blue and vermilion*) and painted a picture. Then both men came the same day to pay reverence to the picture they had had done, and the artist pointed each to the same figure, telling them, "This is the figure of Buddha which you ordered to be done." The two men looking at one another in perplexity, the mind of the artist understanding their doubts, said, " What are you thinking about so long ? If you are thinking about the money, I have not defrauded you of any part. To show that it is so there must be some spiritual indication on the part of the picture."

[66] This is the literal translation ; it may mean "on the southern side of the steps," as though there were steps only on the eastern side of the *stûpa ;* or it may, by license, mean " on the steps of the *stûpa*, its southern face," as though the steps referred to were on the southern face. But the literal translation is preferable, in which case we may assume that a flight of steps on the eastern side led up to the platform on which the tower (*stûpa*) was built, and that the figures referred to were engraved between the pilasters of the terrace on the north and south sides of the steps.

[67] Or, " a beautifully-marked figure of Tathâgata." The marks (*siang* or *lakshana*) of Buddha are well known.—See Burnouf, *Lotus,* p. 616, and *ante,* p. 1, note 5.

Scarcely had he finished when the picture, by some spiritual power, divided itself (*from the middle upwards*), and both parts emitted a glory alike. The two men with joy believed and exulted.

To the south-west of the great *stûpa* 100 paces or so, there is a figure of Buddha in white stone about eighteen feet high. It is a standing figure, and looks to the north. It has many spiritual powers, and diffuses a brilliant light. Sometimes there are people who see the image come out of an evening and go round[68] the great *stûpa*. Lately a band of robbers wished to go in and steal. The image immediately came forth and went before the robbers. Affrighted, they ran away; the image then returned to its own place, and remained fixed as before. The robbers, affected by what they had seen, began a new life, and went about through towns and villages telling what had happened.

To the left and right of the great *stûpa* are a hundred little *stûpas* standing closely together,[69] executed with consummate art. Exquisite perfumes and different musical sounds at times are perceived, the work of Ṛishis, saints, and eminent sages; these also at times are seen walking round the *stûpas*.

According to the prediction of Tathâgata, after this *stûpa* has been seven times burnt down and seven times rebuilt, then the religion of Buddha will disappear. The record of old worthies says this building has already been destroyed and restored three times. When (*I*) first arrived in this country it had just been destroyed by a fire calamity. Steps are being taken for its restoration, but they are not yet complete.

To the west of the great *stûpa* there is an old *sanghârâma* which was built by King Kanishka. Its double towers, connected terraces, storeyed piles, and deep chambers

---

[68] That is, circumambulate it, or perform the *pradakshina.*

[69] The expression means, as M.

Julien explains, arranged in order like the scales of a fish, that is, with regularity.

bear testimony to the eminence of the great priests who have here formed their illustrious religious characters (*gained distinction*). Although now somewhat decayed, it yet gives evidence of its wonderful construction. The priests living in it are few; they study the Little Vehicle. From the time it was built many authors of *Śâstras* have lived herein and gained the supreme fruit (*of Arhatship*). Their pure fame is wide-spread, and their exemplary religious character still survives.

In the third tower (*double-storeyed tower*) is the chamber of the honourable Pârśvika (Pi-lo-shi-po), but it has long been in ruins; but they have placed here a commemorative tablet to him. He was at first a master of the Brâhmaṇs (*or* a Brâhmaṇ doctor), but when eighty years of age he left his home and assumed the soiled robes (*of a Buddhist disciple*). The boys of the town ridiculed him, saying, "Foolish old man! you have no wisdom, surely! Don't you know that they who become disciples of Buddha have two tasks to perform, viz., to give themselves to meditation and to recite the Scriptures? And now you are old and infirm, what progress can you make as a disciple?[70] Doubtless you know how to eat (*and that is all*)!" Then Pârśvika, hearing such railing speeches, gave up the world[71] and made this vow, "Until I thoroughly penetrate[72] the wisdom of the three *Piṭakas* and get rid of the evil desire of the three worlds, till I obtain the six miraculous powers[73] and reach the eight deliverances (*vimokshas*), I will not lie down to rest (*my side shall not touch the sleeping mat*)." From that day forth the day was not enough for him to walk in meditation or to sit upright in deep thought. In the daytime he studied incessantly the doctrine of the

[70] *Lit.*, in the pure streams of the high calling (*traces*).

[71] Withdrew from "time and men." It may be, withdrew for a time from men.

[72] Whilst I do not understand, &c.

[73] The six miraculous or spiritual powers are the *abhijñâs*, so called; for which see Eitel's *Handbook*, s. v., or Childers, *Pali Dict.*, s. v. *abhiññâ*. Five are enumerated in the *Lotus*, cap. v. see pp. 291, 345, 372, 379, 820; *Introd.*, p. 263. For the *vimôkshas* see *Lotus*, pp. 347. 824; Childers, *Pali Dict.*, s. v. *vimokho*. See note 88, p 149, *inf.*

sublime principles (*of Buddhism*), and at night he sat silently meditating in unbroken thought. After three years he obtained insight into the three piṭakas, and shook off all worldly desires,[74] and obtained the threefold knowledge.[75] Then people called him the honourable Pârśvika[76] and paid him reverence.

To the east of Pârśvika's chamber is an old building in which Vasubandhu[77] Bôdhisattva prepared the *'O-pi-ta-mo-ku-shc-lun* (*Abhidharmakôsha Śâstra*);[78] men, out of respect to him, have placed here a commemorative tablet to this effect.

To the south of Vasubandhu's house, about fifty paces or so, is a second storied-pavilion in which Manorhita,[79] a master of *Śâstras*, composed the *Vibhâshâ Śâstra*. This learned doctor flourished in the midst of the thousand

[74] Desire of the three worlds.

[75] The *trividyâ*, the threefold knowledge, viz., of the impermanence of all things (*anitya*), of sorrow (*dukha*), and of unreality (*anâtmâ*).

[76] Pârśvika, Chin. Hie-ts'un, so named from *pârśva* (Chin. *hie*), "the side," from his vow, here related, not to lie on his side. He is reckoned the ninth or tenth Buddhist patriarch (according as Vasumitra, the seventh, is excluded or not); Edkins, *Chin. Buddh.*, p. 74; Lassen, *I. A.*, vol. ii. p. 1202; Vassilief, pp. 48, 75 f. 203 f. 211; *Ind. Ant.*, vol. iv. p. 141.

[77] Vasubandhu (Fo-siu-fan-tho) translated Thien-sin and Shi-sin, according to northern accounts, the twenty-first patriarch of the Buddhist church, and younger brother of Asaṅga. But this succession of patriarchs is more than doubtful, for Budhidharma, who is represented as the twenty-eighth patriarch, arrived in China A.D. 520; but according to Max Müller, Vasubandhu flourished in India in the second half of the sixth century (*India*, p. 306). If this date can be established, many of the statements of dates found in the Chinese Bud-

dhist books will have to be discredited (*inf.* p. 119, n. 1). Lassen, *I. A.*, vol. ii. p. 1205; Edkins, *Ch. Buddh.*, pp. 169, 278; Vassilief, pp. 214 ff., or *Ind. Ant.*, vol. iv. pp. 142 f.

[78] This is a work frequently named in these records. It was written by Vasubandhu to refute the errors of the Vaibhâshikas, and was translated into Chinese by Paramârtha, A.D. 557-589. For an account of its origin see the Life of Buddha by Wong Pûh, § 195, in *J. R. A. S.*, vol. xx. p. 211; Edkins, *Ch. Buddh.*, p. 120; Vassilief, pp. 77 f. 108, 130, 220.

[79] Manôrhita, otherwise written Manorata, Manôrhata, or Manôratha (Jul., *Vie*, p. 405), also Manura. This is explained by the Chinese Ju-i, an expression used for the *Kalpavṛiksha* or "wishing tree," denoting power to produce whatever was wished; literally, "conformable (*hita*) to thought (*mana*, mind)." He is probably the same as Maṇirata (Vassilief, *Bouddhisme*, p. 219). He is reckoned the twenty-second patriarch.—Lassen, *I. A.*, vol. ii. p. 1206; Edkins, *Ch. Buddh.*, pp. 82-84; M. Müller, *India*, pp. 289, 302; and note 77 *ante*.

years [80] after the *Nirvâṇa* of Buddha. In his youth he was devoted to study and had distinguished talent. His fame was wide spread with the religious, and laymen sought to do him hearty reverence. At that time Vikramâditya,[81] king of the country of Śrâvastî, was of wide renown. He ordered his ministers to distribute daily throughout India[82] five lakhs of gold coin; he largely (*everywhere*) supplied the wants of the poor, the orphan, and the bereaved. His treasurer, fearing that the resources of the kingdom would be exhausted, represented the case to the king, and said, "Mahârâja! your fame has reached to the very lowest of your subjects, and extends to the brute creation. You bid me add (*to your expenditure*) five lakhs of gold to succour the poor throughout the world. Your treasury will thus be emptied, and then fresh imposts will have to be laid (on

---

[80] This expression, "in the midst of, or during, the thousand years," has a particular reference to the period of 1000 years which succeeded the period of 500 years after Buddha's death. The 500 years is called the period of the "true law," the 1000 years "the period of images," *i.e.*, image-worship; after that came the period of "no law." The phrase "during the 1000 years," therefore, in these records, means that the person referred to lived during the middle portion of the second period, that is, about a thousand years after Buddha. There is a useful note in Wong Pûh's life of Buddha (§ 204, *J. R. A. S.*, vol. xx. p. 215) relating to this point, from which it appears that the accepted date of the *Nirvâṇa* in China at this time was 850 B.C. The period of 1000 years, therefore, would extend from 350 B.C. to 650 A.D. Wong Pûh uses the expression *ke-shi* "the latter age," for "the thousand years." Manôrhita is placed under Vikramâditya Harsha of Ujjain, and therefore lived about the middle of the 6th century A.D., according to M. Müller, *India*, p. 290.

[81] This is supposed to be the same as Vikramâditya or Harsha of Ujjayinî, according to Dr. J. Fergusson and Prof. M. Müller, the founder of the usual Samvat era, 56 B.C. The Chinese equivalent for his name is *chaou jih*, or "leaping above the sun," or "the upspringing light," "the dawn." As to the mode in which this era of Vikramâditya might have been contrived, see Fergusson (*J. R. A. S.*, N. S., vol. xii. p. 273). The starting-point from which these writers suppose it came into use is 544 A.D. The expression Vikramâditya of Śrâvastî, is the same as Vikramâditya of Ayôdhya (Oudh), where we are told (Vassilief, p. 219) he held his court. The *town* of Śrâvastî was in ruins even in Fahian's time (cap. xx.)

[82] "Throughout all the Indies." This passage may also be translated thus: "An envoy (*shi shan*) coming to India, he daily," &c. Julien refers it to one of his own envoys, but in any case the passage is obscure. Judging from the context, I think the meaning is, "he ordered his minister, in the next sentence called "his treasurer," to give throughout India on one day five lakhs for the poor."

the land cultivators), until the resources of the land be also exhausted; then the voice of complaint will be heard and hostility be provoked. Your majesty, indeed, will get credit for charity, but your minister[83] will lose the respect of all." The king answered, "But of my own surplus I (*wish to*) relieve the poor. I would on no account, for my own advantage, thoughtlessly burthen (*grind down*) the country." Accordingly he added five lakhs for the good of the poor. Some time after this the king was engaged chasing a boar. Having lost the track, he gave a man a lakh for putting him on the scent again. Now Manôrhita, the doctor of *Sâstras*, once engaged a man to shave his head, and gave him offhand a lakh of gold for so doing.[84] This munificent act was recorded in the annals by the chief historian. The king reading of it, was filled with shame, and his proud heart continually fretted about it,[85] and so he desired to bring some fault against Manôrhita and punish him. So he summoned an assembly of different religious persons whose talents were most noted,[86] to the number of one hundred, and issued the following decree: "I wish to put a check to the various opinions (*wanderings*) and to settle the true limits (*of inquiry*); the opinions of different religious sects are so various that the mind knows not what to believe. Exert your utmost ability, therefore, to-day in following out my directions." On meeting for discussion he made a second decree: "The doctors of law belonging to the heretics [87] are distinguished

[83] Such is plainly the meaning; the treasurer is speaking of himself. The antithesis requires it, "*kun shang, shan hia.*" M. Julien translates it as referring to all the subjects.

[84] M. Julien translates as follows: "Un jour le maître des *Çastras* Jou-i (Manôrhita) ayant envoyé un homme pour couper les cheveux au roi;" but in my text there is no word for "king," and the whole context seems to require another rendering. I translate the passage as referring to Manôrhita himself, who, although a writer of *S'âstras*, was also a prince (vid. Eitel, *s.v.*)

[85] *I.e.*, that Manôrhita should have equalled him in munificence, and that he should be held up as an example.

[86] "Whose virtuous deeds (*good qualities*) were high and profound." I find nothing about Brâhmaṇs in the text.

[87] Or it may be, "the unbelievers and the doctors of *śâstras* are both eminent," &c.

for their ability. The Shamans and the followers of the law (*of Buddha*) ought to look well to the principles of their sect; if they prevail, then they will bring reverence to the law of Buddha; but if they fail, then they shall be exterminated."[88] On this, Manôrhita questioned the heretics and silenced[89] ninety-nine of them. And now a man was placed (*sat on the mat to dispute with him*) of no ability whatever,[90] and for the sake of a trifling discussion (Manôrhita) proposed the subject of fire and smoke. On this the king and the heretics cried out, saying, " Manôr-hita, the doctor of *Śástras*, has lost the sense of right connection (*mistaken the order or sense of the phrase*); he should have named smoke first and fire afterwards: this order of things is constant." Manôrhita wishing to explain the difficulty, was not allowed a hearing; on which, ashamed to see himself thus treated by the people, he bit out his tongue and wrote a warning to his disciple Vasubandhu, saying, "In the multitude of partisans there is no justice; among persons deceived there is no discernment." Having written this, he died.

A little afterwards Vikramâditya-râja lost his kingdom and was succeeded by a monarch who widely patronised those distinguished for literary merit.[91] Vasubandhu, wishing to wash out the former disgrace, came to the king and said, " Mahârâja, by your sacred qualities you rule the empire and govern with wisdom. My old master, Manôr-hita, was deeply versed in the mysterious doctrine. The former king, from an old resentment, deprived him of his high renown. I now wish to avenge the injury done to my master." The king, knowing that Manôrhita was a man of superior intelligence, approved of the noble project of Vasubandhu; he summoned the heretics who had discussed with Manôrhita. Vasubandhu having exhibited

---

[88] It ought probably to be rendered thus: "If they prevail, then I will reverence the law of Buddha; if they are defeated, I will utterly exterminate the priests."

[89] Made to retire.

[90] Or, who looked at him with a dispirited (*downcast*) air.

[91] This would appear to be Śílá-ditya of Ujjain, spoken of by Hiuen Tsiang (Book xi.) as having lived about sixty years before his own time.

afresh the former conclusions of his master, the heretics were abashed and retired.

To the north-east of the *sanghârâma* of Kanishka-râja about 50 li, we cross a great river and arrive at the town of Pushkalâvatî (Po-shi-kie-lo-fa-ti).[92] It is about 14 or 15 li in circuit; the population is large; the inner gates are connected by a hollow (*tunnel?*).[93]

Outside the western gate is a Deva temple. The image of the god is imposing and works constant miracles.

To the east of the city is a *stûpa* built by Asôka-râja. This is the place where the four former Buddhas delivered the law (*preached*). Among former saints and sages many have come (*descended spiritually*) from Mid-India to this place to instruct all creatures (*things*). For example, Vasumitra,[94] doctor of *Sâstras*, who composed the *Chung-sse-fen-o-pi-ta-mo* (*Abhidharmaprakaraṇa-pâda*) *Sâstra* in this place.

To the north of the town 4 or 5 li is an old *sanghârâma*, of which the halls are deserted and cold. There are very few priests in it, and all of them follow the teaching of

---

[92] Or Pushkarâvatî, the old capital of Gandhâra, said to have been founded by Pushkara or Pushkala, the son of Bharata and nephew of Râma (Wilson, *Vishṇu-pur.*, vol. iii. p. 319). The district is called Πευκελαωτις and Πευκελαιῆτις by Arrian (*Anab.*, lib. iv. c. 22, s. 9; *Ind.*, c. 4, s. 11), and the capital Πευκελαιῆτις or Πευκέλα (*Ind.*, c. 1, s. 8), while Strabo calls the city Πευκελαῖτις (lib. xv. c. 21 s. 27). Pliny has Peucolais (lib. vi. c. 21, s. 62) and the people Peucolaitæ (c. 23, s. 78). Dionysius Perigetis has Πευκαλᾶις (v. 1143), and the author of the *Periplus Mar. Æryth.* (s. 47) and Ptolemy Προκλαῖς (lib. vii. c. 1, s. 44; v. l. Ποκλαῖς). Alexander the Great besieged and took it from Astes (Hasti) and appointed San-gæus (Sañjaya) as his successor. It was probably at Hashtanagara, 18 miles north of Pêshâwar, on the Svât (Suastos), near its junction with the Kâbul (Kôphên or Kôphês),

the great river which the traveller here crossed. See Baber's *Mem.*, pp. 136, 141, 251 ; Cunningham, *Anc. Geog.*, pp. 49 f. ; St. Martin, *Géog. de l'Inde*, p. 37 ; Bunbury, *Hist. Anc. Geog.*, vol. i. p. 498 ; Wilson, *Ariana Ant.*, pp. 185 f. ; *Ind. Ant.*, vol. v. pp. 85 f., 330 ; Lassen, *I. A.*, vol. i. p. 501, vol. iii. p. 139 ; Reinaud, *Mém. s. l'Inde*, p. 65.

[93] The phrase *leu yen* means the inner gates of a town or village (Medhurst, *s. v. Yen*), and *tung lin* means "deeply connected," or "are deep and connected." Julien translates it, "the houses rise in thick lines." The readings must be different.

[94] Vasumitra, in Chinese *Shi Yu*, friend of the world.—*Ch. Ed.* He was one of the chief of the 500 great Arhats who formed the council convoked by Kanishka. Vassilief, pp. 49 f., 58 f., 78, 107, 113, 222 f. ; Edkins, *Ch. Buddh.*, pp. 72 f., 283 ; Burnouf, *Int.*, pp. 399, 505 f.

the Little Vehicle. Dharmatrâta, master of *Śâstras*, here composed the *Ts'a-o-pi-ta-ma-lun* (*Samyuktâbhidharma Śâstra*).[95]

By the side of the *sanghârâma* is a *stûpa* several hundred feet high, which was built by Aśôka-râja. It is made of carved wood and veined stone, the work of various artists. Śâkya Buddha, in old time when king of this country, prepared himself as a Bôdhisattva (*for becoming a Buddha*). He gave up all he had at the request of those who asked, and spared not to sacrifice his own body as a bequeathed gift (*a testamentary gift*). Having been born in this country a thousand times as king, he gave during each of those thousands births in this excellent country, his eyes as an offering.

Going not far east from this, there are two stone *stûpas*, each about 100 feet in height. The right-hand one was built by Brahmâ Dêva, that on the left by Śakra (*king of Dêvas*). They were both adorned with jewels and gems. After Buddha's death these jewels changed themselves into ordinary stones. Although the buildings are in a ruinous condition, still they are of a considerable height and grandeur.

Going north-west about 50 li from these *stûpas*, there is another *stûpa*. Here Śâkya Tathâgata converted the Mother of the demons[96] and caused her to refrain from

[95] According to the *Ch'uh-yau king* (*Udânavarga*), Dharmatrâta was uncle of Vasumitra. (See Beal, *Texts from the Buddhist Canon* (*Dharmapada*), p. 8 ; Rockhill's *Udânavarga*, p. xi.) There was another Dharmatrâta, according to Târânâtha (Rockhill, p. xi.), who was one of the leaders of the Vaibhâshika school, and also another Vasumitra, who commented on the *Abhidharma Kôsha* written by Vasubandhu, who lived probably in the fifth century A.D. But as the Chinese versions of the *Dharmapada* were made before Vasubandhu's time, and the second Vasumitra lived after Vasubandhu, for he commented on his work, it is highly probable that the Dharmatrâta alluded to in the text was the compiler of the Northern versions of the "Verses of the Law" (*Dharmapada*) known both in China and Tibet. Dharmatrâta, according to a note in the text, was erroneously called Dharmatara.

[96] The mother of the demons was, according to I-tsing (K. i. §9), called Hâritî (Ko-li-ti), and was venerated by the Buddhists. "She had made a vow in a former birth to devour the children of Râjagṛiha, and was accordingly born as a Yaksha, and became the mother of 500 children.

hurting men. It is for this reason the common folk of this country offer sacrifices to obtain children from her.

Going north 50 li or so from this, there is another *stúpa*. It was here Sâmaka Bôdhisattva[97] (*Shang-mu-kia*), walking piously, nourished as a boy his blind father and mother. One day when gathering fruits for them, he encountered the king as he was hunting, who wounded him by mistake with a poisoned arrow. By means of the spiritual power of his great faith he was restored to health through some medicaments which Indra (*Tien-ti*), moved by his holy conduct, applied to the wound.

To the south-east of this place[98] about 200 li, we arrive at the town Po-lu-sha.[99] On the north of this town is

To nourish these she each day took a child (boy or girl) of Râja-grlha. People having told Buddha of it, he hid one of the Yaksha's children called "the loved one." The mother, having searched everywhere, at last found it by Buddha's side. On this the Lord addressed her as follows: "Do you so tenderly love your child? but you possess 500 such. How much more would persons with only one or two love theirs?" On this she was converted and became a Upâsikâ, or lay disciple. She then inquired how she was to feed her 500 children. On this Buddha said, "The Bhikshus who live in their monasteries shall every day offer you food out of their portion for nourishment." Therefore in the convents of the western world, either within the porch of the gates or by the side of the kitchen, they paint on the wall a figure of the mother holding a child, and below sometimes five, sometimes three others in the foreground. Every day they place before this image a dish of food for her portion of nourishment. She is the most powerful among the followers (*retinue*) of the four heavenly kings (Dêva-râjas). The sick and those without children offer her food to obtain their wishes. In China she is called *Kwei-tseu-mu.*—Julien, *Mémoires*, tom. i. p. 120 n. My translation of I-tsing, however, differs from Julien's. The Chalukyas and other royal families of the Dekhan claim to be descendants of Hâritî (*Hârittputra*). The above account from I-tsing relates to the figure of Hâritî in the Varâha temple at Tâmralipti. Possibly this temple may have been a Châlukya foundation, for the Varâha (boar) was one of their principal insignia.

[97] This refers to Sâma, the son of Dukhula, in the *Sâmajâtaka*. He is called in Fa-hian *Shen* (for *Shen-ma*), and this equivalent is also given in the text. See *Trans. Int. Cong. Orient.* (1874), p. 135. The *Jâtaka* is represented among the Sânchi sculptures (*Tree and Scrp. Worship*, pl. xxxvi, fig. 1). For an account of it see Spence Hardy's *Eastern Monachism*, p. 275; conf. *Man. Budh.*, p. 460. The story is also a Brahmanical one, occurring in the *Râmâyaṇa.—Ind. Ant.*, vol. i. pp. 37–39.

[98] That is, south-east from the *stûpa* of Sâmaka Bôdhisattva. I have not repeated the name of the place in this and other passages.

[99] Following the route described in the text, we are taken first 4 or 5 li to the north of Pushkalâvatî, next a little way to the east, then 50

a *stûpa;* here it was S u d â n a [100] the prince, having given in charity to some Brâhmaṇs the great elephant of his father the king, was blamed and banished. In leaving his friends, having gone out of the gate of the wall, it was here he paid adieu. Beside this is a *saṅghârâma* [101] with about fifty priests or so, who all study the Little Vehicle. Formerly Îśvara, master of *śâstras*, in this place composed the *O-pi-ta-mo-ming-ching-lun.* [102]

Outside the eastern gate of the town of Po-lu-sha is a *saṅghârâma* with about fifty priests, who all study the Great Vehicle. Here is a *stûpa* built by Aśôka-râja. In old times Sudâna the prince, having been banished from his home, dwelt in Mount D a n t a l ô k a. [103] Here a Brahmaṇ begged his son and daughter, and he sold them to him.

To the north-east of Po-lu-sha city about 20 li or so we come to Mount Dantalôka. Above a ridge of that mountain is a *stûpa* built by Aśôka-râja; it was here the prince

li to the north-west, then 50 li to the north. It is from this point we are to reckon 200 li to the south-west to Po-lu-sha. M. V. de St. Martin (*Mémoire,* p. 309) substitutes 250 li for 200, and he then reckons from Pushkalâvatî. General Cunningham falls into the same mistake (*Anc. Geog.,* p. 52), and identifies Po-lu-sha with Palo-dheri, or the village of Pali, situated on a *dheri* or mound of ruins (*op. cit.,* p. 52). This would agree with Hiuen Tsiang's distance and bearing, that is, from the *stûpa* of Sâmaka, which was some 90 to 100 li to the north-north-east of Pushkalâvatî.

[100] That is, Visvântara, Visvaṅtara, or Vêssantara, the prince. His history is a popular one among Buddhists. See Spence Hardy's *Man. of Budhism.,* p. 118; Fergusson, *Tree and Serp. Worship,* pl. xxxii.; Beal's *Fah-hian,* p. 194 n. 2; Burnouf, *Lotus,* p. 411; conf. *Kathâsarit.,* 113, 9; *Aitar. Brâhm.,* vii. 27, 34. The particulars given in the text and in Fa-hian led to the identification of pl. xxxii. in *Tree and Serp. Worship*

with this history. The same *Jâtaka* is also found amongst the Amarâvatî sculptures, *op. cit.,* pl. lxv. fig. 1. With respect to the name Sudâna, the Chinese explanation (*good teeth*) is erroneous, as M. Julien has pointed out (p. 122 n.) Sudânta is the name of a Pratyêkabuddha mentioned in the *Trikâṇḍaśêsha,* i. 1, 13.

[101] So I translate the passage. M. Julien understands the number fifty to refer to the *saṅghârâmas.* But it would be an unusual circumstance to find fifty or more convents near one spot, nor does the text necessarily require it.

[102] Restored doubtfully by Julien to *Abhidharmaprakâśa-sâdhana Sâstra.* It was perhaps the *Samyuktabhidharmahṛidaya Sâstra,* which Îśvara is said to have translated in 426 A.D. Îśvara's name is given in Chinese as *Tsü-tsai,* "master," "lord," "self-existent."

[103] *Tan-ta-lo-kia,* which might also be restored to Dandarika. The Japanese equivalent given in the text for *lo* is *ra.* General Cunningham identifies this mountain with the *Montes Dædali* of Justin (*op. cit.,* p. 52.)

Sudâna dwelt in solitude. By the side of this place, and close by, is a *stûpa.* It was here the prince gave his son and daughter to the Brahman, who, on his part, beat them till the blood flowed out on the ground. At the present time the shrubs and trees are all of a deep red colour. Between the crags (*of the mountain*) there is a stone chamber, where the prince and his wife dwelt and practised meditation. In the midst of the valley the trees droop down their branches like curtains. Here it was the prince in old time wandered forth and rested.

By the side of this wood, and not far from it, is a rocky cell in which an old Rĭshi dwelt.

Going north-west from the stone cell about 100 li or so, we cross a small hill and come to a large mountain. To the south of the mountain is a *sanghârama,* with a few priests as occupants, who study the Great Vehicle. By the side of it is a *stûpa* built by Asôka-râja. This is the place which in old time was occupied by Ekaśrĭnga Rĭshi.[104] This Rĭshi being deceived by a pleasure-woman, lost his spiritual faculties. The woman, mounting his shoulders, returned to the city.

To the north-east of the city of Po-lu-sha 50 li or so, we come to a high mountain, on which is a figure of the wife of Îśvara Dêva carved out of green (*bluish*) stone. This is Bhîmâ Dêvî.[105] All the people of the better class, and the lower orders too, declare that this figure was self-wrought. It has the reputation of working numerous miracles, and therefore is venerated (*worshipped*) by all, so that from every part of India men come to pay their vows and seek prosperity thereby. Both poor and rich assemble here from every part, near and distant. Those who wish to see the form of the divine spirit, being filled

---

[104] This story of Ekaśrĭnga seems to be connected with the episode of Srĭnga in the *Râmâyana.* It is constantly referred to in Buddhist books. See Eitel's *Handbook, s. v.; Catena of Buddh. Scrip.,* p. 260; *Romantic Legend,* p. 124; and compare the notice in Yule's *Marco Polo,* vol. ii. p. 233; *Ind. Ant.,* vol. i. p. 244, vol. ii. pp. 69, 140 f.

[105] Bhîmâ is a form of Durgâ, probably = Si-wang-mu of the Chinese.

with faith and free from doubt, after fasting seven days
are privileged to behold it, and obtain for the most part
their prayers.[106]   Below the mountain is the temple of
Mahêśvara Dêva; the heretics who cover themselves with
ashes[107] come here to offer sacrifice.

Going south-east from the temple of Bhîmâ 150 li, we
come to U-to-kia-han-ch'a.[108]   This town is about 20
li in circuit; on the south it borders on the river Sindh
(Sin-to).   The inhabitants are rich and prosperous.   Here
is amassed a supply of valuable merchandise, and mixed
goods from all quarters.

To the north-west of U-to-kia-han-c'ha 20 li or so
we come to the town of P'o-lo-tu-lo.[109]   This is the
place where the Ṛishi Pâṇini, who composed the *Ching-
ming-lun*[110] was born.

Referring to the most ancient times, letters were very
numerous; but when, in the process of ages, the world
was destroyed and remained as a void, the Dêvas of long
life[111] descended spiritually to guide the people.   Such
was the origin of the ancient[112] letters and composition.

---

[106] The same thing is said about Kwan - yin (Avalôkitêśvara).   For some account of the worship of Durgâ or Pârvatî, and of Kwan - yin or Avalôkitêśvara, as mountain deities, see *J. R. A. S.*, N.S., vol. xv. p. 333.

[107] That is, the Pâśupatas.   Compare what Hiuen Tsiang says in reference to Kwan-yin or Avalô-kitêśvara, viz., when he reveals himself on Mount Potaraka, he sometimes takes the form of Îśvara and sometimes that of a Pâśupata (book x. fol. 30). See also p. 60, n. 210 *ante*.

[108] Restored by Julien to Uḍakhânda; identified by V. St. Martin with Ohind.   Its south side rests on the Indus.   The distance is 150 li from the temple of Bhîmâ.   If we actually project 150 li (30 miles) north-west from Ohind, it would bring us near Jamâlgarhi.   About 50 li or 8 miles E.S.E. from it is Takht-i-Bhaï, standing on an iso-lated hill 650 feet above the plain.   The vast quantities of ruins found in this place indicate that it was once a centre of religious worship.   Is this the site of Po-lu-sha ?   Kapurdagarhi is 20 miles north-west from Ohind, and Takht-i-Bhaï 13 miles E.N.E. from Kapurdagarhi.   See p. 135.

[109] The symbol *p'o* is for *so* (Jul.)   The town is Salâtura, the birthplace of Pâṇini, who is known by the name of Śâlâturîya (Panini, iv. 3, 94).   Cunningham identifies it with the village of Lahor, which he says is four miles *north-west* of Ohind.— *Geog.*, p. 57.   Conf. Weber, *Hist. Sansk. Lit.*, p. 218, n.

[110] The *Vyâkaraṇam.*

[111] Or, the Dêvas who possessed long life.

[112] I understand the symbol *ku* in this passage to mean "old" or "ancient."

From this time and after it the source (*of language*)
spread and passed its (*former*) bounds. Brahmâ Dêva
and Śakra (*Devendra*) established rules (*forms* or *ex-
amples*) according to the requirements. Ṛishis belonging
to different schools each drew up forms of letters. Men
in their successive generations put into use what had been
delivered to them; but nevertheless students without
ability (*religious ability*) were unable to make use (*of
these characters*). And now men's lives were reduced to
the length of a hundred years, when the Ṛishi Pâṇini
was born; he was from his birth extensively informed
about things (*men and things*). The times being dull
and careless, he wished to reform the vague and false
rules (*of writing and speaking*)—to fix the rules and correct improprieties. As he wandered about asking for right
ways,[113] he encountered Îśvara Dêva, and recounted to him
the plan of his undertaking. Îśvara Dêva said, " Wonderful! I will assist you in this." The Ṛishi, having received
instruction, retired. He then laboured incessantly and put
forth all his power of mind. He collected a multitude
of words, and made a book on letters which contained
a thousand *ślôkas;* each *ślôka* was of thirty-two syllables.
It contained everything known from the first till then, without exception, respecting letters and words. He then
closed it and sent it to the king (*supreme ruler*), who
exceedingly prized it, and issued an edict that throughout
the kingdom it should be used and taught to others ; and
he added that whoever should learn it from beginning to
end should receive as his reward a thousand pieces of gold.
And so from that time masters have received it and
handed it down in its completeness for the good of the
world. Hence the Brâhmaṇs of this town are well
grounded in their literary work, and are of high renown
for their talents, well informed as to things (*men and
things*), and of a vigorous understanding (*memory*).

In the town of So-lo-tu-lo is a *stûpa.* This is the

<hr>

[113] Or, asking for wisdom or knowledge.

spot where an Arhat converted a disciple of Pânini. Tathâgata had left the world some five hundred years, when there was a great Arhat who came to the country of Kaśmîr, and went about converting men. Coming to this place, he saw a Brahmachârin occupied in chastising a boy whom he was instructing in letters. Then the Árhat spake to the Brâhmaṇ thus: "Why do you cause pain to this child?" The Brâhmaṇ replied, "I am teaching him the *Shing-ming* (*Śabdavidyâ*), but he makes no proper progress." The Arhat smiled significantly,[114] on which the Brâhmaṇ said, "Shamans are of a pitiful and loving disposition, and well disposed to men and creatures generally; why did you smile, honoured sir? Pray let me know!"

The Arhat replied, "Light words are not becoming,[115] and I fear to cause in you incredulous thoughts and unbelief. No doubt you have heard of the Ṛishi Pânini, who compiled the *Śabdavidyâ Śâstra*, which he has left for the instruction of the world." The Brâhmaṇ replied, "The children of this town, who are his disciples, revere his eminent qualities, and a statue erected to his memory still exists." The Arhat continued: "This little boy whom you are instructing was that very (*Pâṇini*) Ṛishi. As he devoted his vigorous mind to investigate worldly literature, he only produced heretical treatises without any power of true reason in them. His spirit and his wisdom were dispersed, and he has run through the cycles of continued birth from then till now. Thanks to some remnant of true virtue, he has been now born as your attached child; but the literature of the world and these treatises on letters are only cause of use-

---

[114] The symbol *yew*, according to Medhurst, means "to put forth vital energy;" *yew ne*, therefore, I take to denote "significance" or "meaning." The smile of Buddha or an Arhat was supposed to indicate prophetic insight or vision. The same meaning is attached to "a smile" in many of our own mediæval legends (vid. *Romantic History of Buddha*, p. 12 n.) Julien's "*se derida*" hardly meets the idea of the original.

[115] "Light words," in the sense of trifling or unmeaning words, or words spoken lightly.

less efforts to him, and are as nothing compared to the holy teaching of Tathâgata, which, by its mysterious influences, procures both happiness and wisdom. On the shores of the southern sea there was an old decayed tree, in the hollows of which five hundred bats had taken up their abodes. Once some merchants took their seats beneath this tree, and as a cold wind was blowing, these men, cold and hungry, gathered together a heap of fuel and lit a fire at the tree-foot. The flames catching hold of the tree, by degrees it was burnt down. At this time amongst the merchant troop there was one who, after the turn of the night, began to recite a portion of the *Abhidharma Piṭaka.* The bats, notwithstanding the flames, because of the beauty of the sound of the law patiently endured the pain, and did not come forth After this they died, and, according to their works, they all received·birth as men. They became ascetics, practised wisdom, and by the power of the sounds of the law they had heard they grew in wisdom and became Arhats as the result of merit acquired in the world. Lately the king, Kanishka, with the honourable Pârśvika, summoning a council of five hundred saints and sages in the country of Kaśmîr, they drew up the *Vibâshâ Śâstra.* These were the five hundred bats who formerly dwelt in that decayed tree. I myself, though of poor ability, am one of the number. It is thus men differ in their superior or inferior abilities. Some rise, others live in obscurity. But now, O virtuous one! permit your pupil (*attached child*) to leave his home. Becoming a disciple of Buddha, the merits we secure are not to be told."

The Arhat having spoken thus, proved his spiritual capabilities by instantly disappearing. The Brâhmaṇ was deeply affected by what he saw, and moved to believe. He noised abroad through the town and neighbourhood what had happened, and permitted the child to become a disciple of Buddha and acquire wisdom. Moreover, he himself changed his belief, and mightily reverenced the three precious ones. The people of the village, following his example, became disciples, and till now they have remained earnest in their profession.

From U-to-kia-han-ch'a, going north, we pass over some mountains, cross a river, and travelling 600 li or so, we arrive at the kingdom of U-chang-na (Udyâna).

END OF BOOK II.

BOOK III.

Relates to eight countries, viz., (1) U-chang-na, (2) Po-lu-lo, (3) Ta-ch'a-shi-lo, (4) Sang-ho-pu-lo, (5) Wu-la-shi, (6) Kia-shi-mi-lo, (7) Pun-nu-tso, (8) Ko-lo-chi-pu-lo.

1. U-CHANG-NA (UDYÂNA).

THE country of U-chang-na[1] is about 5000 li in circuit; the mountains and valleys are continously connected, and the valleys and marshes alternate with a succession of high plateaux. Though various kinds of grain are sown, yet the crops are not rich. The grape is abundant, the

---

[1] Udyâna (Prâkṛit, Ujjâna), the *U-chang* of Fa-hian (cap. viii.), is so called because of its garden-like appearance. "Udyâna lay to the north of Peshâwar on the Swât river, but from the extent assigned to it by Hiuen Tsiang the name probably covered the whole hill-region south of the Hindu Kush and the Dard country from Chitral to the Indus."—Yule, *Marco Polo*, vol. i. p. 173; compare also Cunningham's remarks, *Geog. Anc. Ind.*, p. 81; Lassen, *I. A.*, vol. i. p. 505, vol. iii. p. 138; and *Bactrian Coins*, (Eng. trans.) p. 96. It is described by Sung-yun as bordering on the T'sung-ling mountains to the north, and on India to the south. This writer gives a glowing description of the fertility and beauty of the valley and its neighbourhood (Beal's *Buddhist Pilgrims*, p. 189). It was a flourishing centre of Buddhist worship. Fa-hian (cap. viii.) says "the law of Buddha is universally hon-

oured." He tells us, moreover, that there were five hundred *sanghârâmas* in the country, all belonging to the Little Vehicle; but in Hiuen Tsiang's time all the convents were desolate and ruined. We may therefore fix the persecution of Mahirakula (or Mihirakula), who was a contemporary of Balâditya, between the time of Fa-hian and Hiuen Tsiang (A.D. 400 and 630 A.D.) Balâditya and Mahirakula, indeed, are placed "*several centuries* before the time of Hiuen Tsiang" (*infra*); but we can scarcely suppose that Fa-hian would have described the country as he does if the persecution had happened before his time. The common statement is that Siṁha was the last patriarch of the North, and that he was killed by Mahirakula (see *Hong Pu*, § 179, in *J. R. As. Soc.*, vol. xx. p. 204). He is generally stated to be the 23d patriarch, and Bodhidharma, who was the 28th, certainly lived in A.D. 520, when he arrived in

sugar-cane scarce.   The earth produces gold and iron, and
is favourable to the cultivation of the scented (*shrub*)
called Yo-kin (*turmeric*).   The forests are thick and shady,
the fruits and flowers abundant.   The cold and heat are
agreeably tempered, the wind and rain come in their season.   The people are soft and effeminate, and in disposition are somewhat sly and crafty.   They love learning
yet have no application.   They practise the art of using
charms (*religious sentences as charms*).[2]   Their clothing
is white cotton, and they wear little else.   Their language,
though different in some points, yet greatly resembles that
of India.   Their written characters and their rules of eti-
quette are also of a mixed character as before.   They
greatly reverence the law of Buddha and are believers
in the Great Vehicle.[3]

On both sides of the river Su-po-fa-su-tu,[4] there are
some 1400 old *sanghârâmas*.   They are now generally
waste and desolate; formerly there were some 18,000
priests in them, but gradually they have become less, till
now there are very few.   They study the Great Vehicle;
they practise the duty of quiet meditation, and have pleasure in reciting texts relating to this subject, but have no
great understanding as to them.   The (*priests who*) practise
the rules of morality lead a pure life and purposely prohibit

China from South India.   If we
allow an interval of 100 years between the 23d patriarch (Simha) and
the 28th (Bôdhidharma), we should
thus have the date of Mahirakula
cir. 420 A.D., that is, just after Fa-
hian's time.   But in this case Vasubandhu, who was the 20th patriarch, must have flourished in the
fourth century and not in the
sixth, as Max Müller proposes (*India*, p. 290); *ante*, p. 105, n. 77.
Mahirakula is, however, placed by
Cunningham in A.D. 164–179, and
Ârya Simha's death is usually placed
in the middle of the third century A.D.
Remusat, *Mél. Asiat.*, tome i. p. 124.

[2] The employment of magical sentences is with them an art and a
study, or a work of art.   This country
of Udyâna was the birthplace of
Padma Sambhava, a great master of
enchantments.   Yule, *Marco Polo*,
vol. i. p. 173.

[3] Fa-hian says that in his days
the people of this country were all
followers of the Little Vehicle.
Probably the re-introduction of
Buddhist doctrine after the persecution had been effected by teachers
of the Mahâyâna school.

[4] That is, the Subhavastu, the
Swât river of the present day.   It is
named by Arrian the Σόαστος, and
he says that it flows into the Κωφην
at Peukalaitis.   See note 24 *infra*.

the use of charms.[5] The schools[6] of the *Vinaya* tradi-
tionally known amongst them are the Sarvâstivâdins,
the Dharmaguptas, the Mahîsâsakas, the Kâśyapîyas,[7]
and the Mahâsanghikas : these five.[8]

There are about ten temples of Dêvas, and a mixed
number of unbelievers who dwell in them. There are four
or five strong towns. The kings mostly reign at Mungali
(Mung-kie-li)[9] as their capital. This town is about 16 or
17 li in circuit and thickly populated. Four or five li
to the east of Mungali is a great *stûpa*, where very many
spiritual portents are seen. This is the spot where Buddha, when he lived in old time,[10] was the Rĭshi who practised patience (Kshânti-rĭshi), and for the sake of Kali-
râja endured the dismemberment of his body.

To the north-east of the town of Mungali about 250 or
260 li, we enter a great mountain[11] and arrive at the foun-

---

[5] This translation differs from Julien's, but I understand Hiuen Tsiang to be alluding to the Hĭnayânists. "Those who follow the rules" (viz., of the *Vinaya*).

[6] The rules of the *Vinaya* are handed down and followed; they have (*or*, there are) five schools." The purport of the text is apparently to show that there was a traditional knowledge of the old teaching to which Fa-hian refers. The new school, given to magic, had been introduced after the persecution ; the old teaching was opposed to this, and the followers of that teaching resisted its use.

[7] Called in the text *Yin-kwong-pu*, "the drink-brightness school." See Eitel's *Handbook*, s. v. *Mahâ-kâśyapa*.

[8] These five schools belong to the Little Vehicle—(1) The Dharma-gupta (Fa-mih-pu), (2) Mahîsâsaka (Fa-ti-pu), (3) Kâśyapîya (Yin-kwong-pu), (4) Sarvâstivâda (Shwo-yih-tsai-yeou-pu), (5) Mahâsanghika (Ta-chong-pu).

[9] Mungali or Mangala, probably the Mangora of Wilford's surveyor, Mogal Beg, and the Manglavor of General Court's map (Cunningham, *Anc. Geog. of India*, p. 82). According to V. de St. Martin (*Mém.*, p. 314), it should be Mangalâvor (Mangala-pura). It was on the left bank of the Swât river. See *J. A. S. Ben.*, vol. viii. pp. 311 f. ; Lassen, *I. A.*, vol. i. p. 138.

[10] *I.e.*, as a Bôdhisattva. The history of the Bôdhisattva when he was born at Kshântirĭshi is frequently met with in Chinese Buddhist books. The account will be found in Wong Pŭh, § 76 (*J. R. A. S.*, vol. xx. p. 165). The name Kie-li (Kali) is interpreted in the original by "fight-quarrel." The lacuna which occurs in the text was probably the history of this Jin-jo-sien (Kshântirĭshi), who suffered his hands to be cut off by Kali-râja, and not only was not angry, but promised the king that he should be born as Kondinya and become one of his (Buddha's) first disciples (Burnouf, *Introd.*, p. 198).

[11] "Enter a great mountain," *i.e.*, a mountainous range. There is no mention made of "traversing a valley," as in Julien.

tain of the Nâga Apalâla; this is the source of the river Su-po-fa-su-tu. This river flows to the south-west.[12] Both in summer and spring it freezes, and from morning till night snow-drifts are flying in clouds, the fine reflected colours of which are seen on every side.

This Nâga, in the time of Kâśyapa Buddha, was born as a man and was called King-ki (Gaṅgi). He was able, by the subtle influences of the charms he used, to restrain and withstand the power of the wicked dragons, so that they could not (*afflict the country*) with violent storms of rain. Thanks to him, the people were thus able to gather in an abundance of grain. Each family then agreed to offer him, in token of their gratitude, a peck of grain as a yearly tribute. After a lapse of some years there were some who omitted to bring their offerings, on which Gaṅgi in wrath prayed that he might become a poisonous dragon and afflict them with storms of rain and wind to the destruction of their crops. At the end of his life he became the dragon of this country; the flowings of the fountain emitted a white stream which destroyed all the products of the earth.

At this time, Śâkya Tathâgata, of his great pity guiding the world, was moved with compassion for the people of this country, who were so singularly afflicted with this calamity. Descending therefore spiritually,[13] he came to this place, desiring to convert the violent dragon. Taking the mace of the Vajrapâṇi[14] spirit, he beat against the mountain side. The dragon king, terrified, came forth and paid him reverence. Hearing the preaching of the law by Buddha, his heart became pure and his faith was awakened. Tathâgata forthwith for-

---

[12] It may also be translated, "it branches off and flows to the south-west." The river is the Śubhavastu. See below, note 24, p. 126.

[13] The expression *kiáng shin*, to descend spiritually, is of frequent occurrence in Chinese Buddhist books; it corresponds to the Sanskrit *ava-* *tára* or *aratárin*, to make an appearance.

[14] This may be otherwise translated, "he who holds the diamond spirit club, knocking," &c. The reference is to the thunderbolt of Indra. See Eitel's *Handbook*, s. voc. *Vadjrapâṇi*.

bad him to injure the crops of the husbandmen. Where-upon the dragon said, "All my sustenance comes from the fields of men; but now, grateful for the sacred instructions I have received, I fear it will be difficult to support myself in this way; yet pray let me have one gathering in every twelve years." Tathâgata compassion-ately permitted this. Therefore every twelfth year there is a calamity from the overflowing of the White River.

To the south-west of the fountain of the dragon Apalâla ('O-po-lo-lo), about 30 li on the north side of the river, there is a foot trace of Buddha on a great rock. According to the religious merit of persons, this impression appears long or short. This is the trace left by Buddha after having subdued the dragon. Afterwards men built up a stone residence (*over the impression*). Men come here from a distance to offer incense and flowers.

Following the stream downwards 30 li or so, we come to the stone where Tathâgata washed his robe. The tissues of the kashâya stuff are yet visible as if engraved on the rock.

To the south of the town of Mungali 400 li or so we come to Mount Hila (Hi-lo). The water flowing through the valley here turns to the west, and then flowing again eastward remounts (*towards its source*). Various fruits and flowers skirt the banks of the stream and face the sides of the mountains. There are high crags and deep caverns, and placid streams winding through the valleys: sometimes are heard the sounds of people's voices, sometimes the reverberation of musical notes. There are, moreover, square stones here like long narrow bedsteads,[15] perfected as if by the hand of men; they stretch in continuous lines from the mountain side down the valley. It was here Tathâgata dwelling in old days,

[15] The expression *t'ah yuen* may refer to the soft cushion of a bed, or it may have a technical meaning. Has the story arisen from the use of *prastara* for "bed" and "stone" alike?

by listening to half a *Gâtha* of the law was content to kill himself.[16]

Going south about 200 li from the town of Mungali, by the side of a great mountain, we come to the Mahâvana [17] *sanghârâma.*   It was here Tathâgata in old days practised the life of a Bôdhisattva under the name of Sarvadata-râja.[18]   Fleeing from his enemy, he resigned his country and arrived secretly in this place.   Meeting with a poor Brâhman who asked alms from him, and having nothing to give in consequence of his losing his country, he ordered him to bind him as a prisoner and take him to the king, his enemy, in order that he might receive a reward, which would be in the place of charity to him.

Going north-west from the Mahâvana *sanghârâma* down the mountain 30 or 40 li, we arrive at the Mo-su *sanghârâma.*[19]   Here there is a *stûpa* about 100 feet or so in height.

By the side of it is a great square stone on which is the impress of Buddha's foot.   This is the spot where Buddha in old time planted his foot, (*which*) scattered a kôṭi of rays of light which lit up the Mahâvana *sanghârâma,* and then for the sake of Dêvas and men he recited the history of his former births (*Jâtakas*).   Underneath this *stûpa* (or at the foot of it) is a stone of a yellow-white colour, which is always damp with an unctuous (*fatty*) moisture ; this is where Buddha, when he was in old time practising the life of a Bôdhisattva, having heard the words of the true law, breaking a bone of his own body, wrote (*with the marrow*) the substance of a book containing the words he had heard.

---

[16] A *gâtha* is a verse of thirty-two syllables.— *Ch. Ed.* This story of Bôdhisattva sacrificing his life for the sake of a half-gâtha will be found in the *Mahâparinirvâṇa Sûtra* of the Northern School, K. xiv. fol. 11. I have translated it in *Trübner's Record.* See also *Ind. Antiq.,* vol. iv. p. 90 ; Upham, *Doctrines and Literature of Buddhism,* vol. iii. p. 306.

[17] In Chinese *Tu-lin,* " great forest."—*Ch. Ed.*

[18] The Chinese equivalents are *Sa-po-ta-ta,* which are explained by, *tsi-shi,* "he who gives all."

[19] For Mo-su-lo, Masûra.—Julien. Mo-su is explained in text to mean "lentils" (*musura*).

Going west 60 or 70 li from the Mo-su *sanghârâma*
is a *stûpa* which was built by Aśôka-râja. It was here
Tathâgata in old time, practising the life of a Bôdhisattva,
was called Śivika (*or* Sibika) Râja.[20]   Seeking the fruit
of Buddhaship, he cut his body to pieces in this place to
redeem a dove from the power of a hawk.

Going north-west from the place where he redeemed
the dove, 200 li or so, we enter the valley of Shan-ni-
lo-shi, where is the convent of Sa-pao-sha-ti.[21]   Here
is a *stûpa* in height 80 feet or so.   In old time, when
Buddha was Lord Śakra, famine and disease were preva-
lent everywhere in this country.   Medicine was of no
use, and the roads were filled with dead.   Lord Śakra was
moved with pity and meditated how he might rescue and
save the people.   Then changing his form, he appeared as
a great serpent, and extended his dead body all along the
void of the great valley, and called from the void to those
on every side (*to look*).   Those who heard were filled with
joy, and running together hastened to the spot, and the
more they cut the body of the serpent the more they
revived, and were delivered both from famine and disease.

By the side of this *stûpa* and not far off is the great
stûpa of Sûma.   Here in old time when Tathâgata was
Lord Śakra, filled with concern for the world, afflicted

[20] For the *Siri Jâtaka* see my
Abstract of Four Lectures, pp. 33 seq.
This story is a favourite one, and
forms an episode in the *Mahâbhârata*, iii. 13275–13300; the same story
of the hawk and pigeon is told of
Uśînara in iii. 10560–10596. See
also *Tree and Serpent Worship*, pl.
lx. and lxxxiii. fig. 1, pp. 194, 225.
The figures of the dove and hawk,
which are sometimes seen in other
Buddhist sculptures, *e.g.*, Cunningham, *Bharhut Stûpa*, pl. xlv. 7, probably allude to this *jâtaka*. Conf.
Jour. Ceylon Br. R. As. Soc., vol. ii.
(1853), pp. 5, 6 ; S. Hardy's *Eastern
Monachism*, pp. 277–279 ; Burgess,
Notes on Ajantâ Rock Temples, p. 76 ;
Cave-Temples of India, pp. 291, 315.

[21] The valley of Shan-ni-lo-shi
may be restored to Sanirâja, "the
giving king." There is a note in
the original which explains Shi-pi-
kia (Śivika) by the word "to give;"
but Śivika is generally interpreted
in Chinese Buddhist books by "silver-white," alluding perhaps to the
"birch tree," with its silver-white
bark, which is one of the meanings
of *hiri*. The explanation "to give"
ought to be referred to *sani*, in the
compound Sanirâja. The name of
the convent, Sa-pao-sha-ti, is explained in the text by *she-yo—serpent
medicine*, and is restored by Julien
to Sarpâushadi.

with every kind of disease and pestilence, with his perfect knowledge of the case, he changed himself into the serpent Sûma;[22] none of those who tasted his flesh failed to recover from their disease.

To the north of the valley Shan-ni-lo-shi, by the side of a steep rock, is a *stûpa*. Of those who, being sick, have come there to seek (*restoration*), most have recovered.

In old time Tathâgata was the king of peacocks;[23] on one occasion he came to this place with his followers. Being afflicted with tormenting thirst, they sought for water on every side without success. The king of the peacocks with his beak struck the rock, and forthwith there flowed out an abundant stream which now forms a lake. Those who are afflicted on tasting or washing in the water are healed. On the rock are still seen the traces of the peacock's feet.

To the south-west of the town of Mungali 60 or 70 li there is a great river,[24] on the east of which is a *stûpa* 60 feet or so in height; it was built by Shang-kiun (Uttarasêna). Formerly when Tathâgata was about to die, he addressed the great congregation and said: "After my *Nirvâṇa*, Uttarasêna - râja, of the country Udyâna (U-chang-na), will obtain a share of the relics of my body. When the kings were about to divide the relics equally, Uttarasêna-râja arrived after (*the others*); coming from a frontier country, he was treated with little regard by the others.[25] At this time the Dêvas published afresh the

---

[22] The serpent Sûma (*Su-mo-shc*), translated by Julien, "serpent of water;" but I take Sûma to be a proper name. The serpent Sûma is probably another form of the Ahi, or cloud-snake of the *Véda* (compare Tiele, *Outlines of the History of Anc. Nations*, p. 174). The Dêva of Adam's Peak, who has so much to do with the serpents converted by Buddha, is called Sumana.

[23] Mayûra-râja.

[24] The Śubhavastu or Suvâstu (*Rig-Véda*, viii. 19, 37; *Mahâbhâr.*, vi. 333), the Σόαστος of Arrian (*Ind.*, iv. 11), the Σουδστος of Ptolemy (lib. vii. c. 1, 42), and the modern Swât river, at the source of which the dragon Apalâla lived. Conf. Fah-hian, ch. viii.; *Vie de Hiouen Thsang*, p. 86; Reinaud, *Mém. sur l'Inde*, p. 277; Saint-Martin, *Géographie du Veda*, p. 44; *Mém Analitique s. la Carte*, &c., pp. 63, 64; Burnouf, *Introd.*, p. 336, n. 2; Lassen, *Ind. Alt.*, vol. ii. (2d ed.), p. 140; *J. A. S. Beng.*, vol. ix. p. 480; Wilson, *Ariana Ant.*, pp. 183, 190, 194; and *ante*, notes 4 and 12, pp. 120, 122.

[25] This may be also construed, "he was treated lightly on account of his rustic (frontier) appearance."

words of Tathâgata as he was about to die.   Then obtaining a portion of relics, the king came back to his country,
and, to show his great respect, erected this *stûpa.*   By the
side of it, on the bank of the great river, there is a large
rock shaped like an elephant.   Formerly Uttarasêna-râja
brought back to his own land the relics of Buddha on a
great white elephant.   Arrived at this spot, the elephant
suddenly fell down and died, and was changed immediately into stone.   By the side of this the *stûpa* is built.

Going west of the town of Mungali 50 li or so, and
crossing the great river, we come to a *stûpa* called Lu-hi-
ta-kia (Rôhitaka) ; it is about 50 feet high, and was built
by Asôka-râja.   In former days, when Tathâgata was practising the life of a Bôdhisattva, he was the king of a great
country, and was called Ts'z'-li (*power of love*).[26]   In this
place he pierced his body, and with his blood fed the five
Yakshas.

To the north-east of the town of Mungali 30 li or so is
the Ho-pu-to-shi *stûpa,*[27] about 40 feet in height.   In
former days Tathâgata here expounded the law for the
sake of men and Dêvas, to instruct (*enlighten*) and guide
them.   After Tathâgata had gone, from the earth suddenly
arose (*this stûpa*) ; the people highly reverenced it, and
offered flowers and incense without end.

To the west of the stone *stûpa,* after crossing the great
river and going 30 or 40 li, we arrive at *Vihâra,* in which
is a figure of Avalôkitêśvara Bôdhisattva.[28]   Its spiritual

[26] *Ts'z' li,* restored by Julien to Maitribala ; for this *Jâtaka* see R. Mitra's *Nepalese Buddhist Litera-ture,* p. 50.

[27] *Ho-pu-to* is for *adbhuta,* mira-culous or unique (Ch. *k'i-te*).   Julien suggests Adbhutâśma, the name of this *stûpa* of miraculous stone (*k'i-te-shi*), but it may be simply "a mi-raculous stone stûpa."   The expres-sion "stone stûpa" is a common one, and indeed occurs in the following section.

[28] Avalôkitêśvara, in Chinese the phonetic symbols are '*O-fo-lu-che-to-i-shi-fa-lo.*   There is a note in the text explaining the meaning of this name to be "the looking (*kwan*) or beholding god" (*Iśvara,* Ch. *tsz' tsai,* "self-existent").   The note adds that the old forms of translation, viz., *K'wong-shai-yin,* "luminous voice," *K'wan-shai-yin,* "beholding or regarding voice," *K'wan-shai-tsz'-tsai,* "beholding the world god," are all erroneous.   But there is good reason for believing that the form *K'wan-shai-yin,* "be-

influences exhibit themselves in a mysterious way, and its miraculous powers (*evidences*) are manifested in an illustrious manner. The votaries of the law come together from every side, and offer it continual sacrifices (*presents*).

Going north-west 140 or 150 li from the statue of Kwan-tsz'-tsai Bôdhisattva, we come to the mountain of Lan-po-lu. The crest of this mountain has a dragon lake about 30 li or so in circuit. The clear waves roll in their majesty, the water pure as a bright mirror. In old days Pi-lu-tse-kia (Virûḍhaka-râja) having led his army to attack the Śâkyas, four of the tribe resisted the advance.[29] These were driven away by their clansmen, and each fled in a different direction. One of the Śâkyas, having left the capital of the country, and being worn out by travel, sat down to rest in the middle of the road.

There appeared now a wild goose, who, in his flight (*progress*), alighted before him; and because of his docile ways, he at last mounted on his back. The goose then flying away, took him to the side of this lake. By this mode of conveyance the Śâkya fugitive visited different kingdoms in various directions. Once having mistaken his way, he went to sleep by the side of the lake under

holding or attending to the voice of men," arose from a confusion of the "looking-down god" with a quality attributed to a similar deity of "hearing prayers" (Al Makah). (See *J. R. As. S., N.S.,* vol. xv. p. 333 f.) It is singular, if the expression *Kwan-yin* is erroneous, that Hiuen Tsiang, or rather Hwui-lih, uses it so constantly in his biography (see *Vie,* pp. 88, 141, 146, 163, 172, and in the context); *ante,* p. 60, n. 210.

[29] For an account of this incident see below, Book vi. There is a corresponding account in the *Mahâranso,* p. 55. "While Buddha yet lived, driven by the misfortunes produced by the war of Prince Viḍuḍhabho, certain members of the Śâkya line retreating to Himavanto discovered a delightful and beautiful location, well watered and situated in the midst of a forest of lofty bo and other trees, &c." The account then goes on to speak of the *peafowls* (*mayuros*), and from that to trace the origin of the Môriyan dynasty, to which Chandragupta belonged. The tale of the peacock bringing water from the rock, the serpent to which the dying people were to look, and the Môriyan line of kings, might perhaps justify some reference to the name of the people inhabiting this district, viz., the Yûzafzaïs, Yûzaf being the Oriental form of the name of Joseph (V. de St. Martin, *Mémoire,* p. 313, n. 3). Conf. Max Müller, *Hist. Anc. Sans. Lit.,* p. 285; *Fo-sho-hing-tsan-king,* p. 336. The account of the Nâga maiden and the exiled wanderer (holy youth) which follows is also suggestive.

the shadow of a tree.   At this time a young Nâga maiden
was walking beside the lake, and suddenly espied the
Śâkya youth.   Fearing that she might not be able otherwise to accomplish her wish,[30] she transformed herself
into a human shape and began to caress him.   The
youth, because of this, awoke affrighted from his sleep,
and addressing her said, "I am but a poor wanderer worn
out with fatigue; why then do you show me such tenderness?"   In the course of matters the youth, becoming
deeply moved, prayed her to consent to his wishes.   She
said, "My father and mother require to be asked and
obeyed in this matter.   You have favoured me with your
affection, but they have not yet consented."   The Śâkya
youth replied, "The mountains and valleys (*surround us*)
with their mysterious shades; where then is your home?"
She said, "I am a Nâga maiden belonging to this pool.
I have heard with awe of your holy tribe having suffered
such things, and of your being driven away from home to
wander here and there in consequence.   I have fortunately
been able, as I wandered, to administer somewhat to your
comfort, and you have desired me to yield to your wishes
in other respects, but I have received no commands to
that effect from my parents.   Unhappily, too, this Nâga
body is the curse following my evil deeds."[31]

The Śâkya youth answered, "One word uttered from the
ground of the heart and agreed to (*by us both*) and this
matter is ended."[32]   She said, "I respectfully obey your

[30] That is, to approach near and inquire or look upon him (*tang*). The word rendered "caress" in this passage means to smooth, or pat the head.

[31] This passage may be rendered literally thus: "How much rather, alas! since on account of accumulated misery I have received this Nâga (*serpent*) body." The expression *tsih ho*, "misery accumulated from evil deeds," corresponds with the phrase *tsih fuh*, "much happiness derived from good works." (See Wells Williams, *Tonic Dict.*, sub *tsik*, to gather or hoard up.) There is a passage following the above omitted in the text: "A man and beast are different in their ways (*of birth*); such a union has not been heard of."

[32] This may otherwise be translated: "One word permitted by you, my cherished desire is then accomplished." I take *suh sin* to be equal to *suh yuen*, a cherished desire; but the expression may also refer to the power of accumulated merit to effect

orders; let that follow whatever it be." [33]   Then the Sâkya youth said, "By the power of my accumulated merit let this Nâga woman be turned into human shape."   The woman was immediately so converted.   On seeing herself thus restored to human shape she was overjoyed, and gratefully addressed the Sâkya youth thus: "By my evil deeds (*through the accumulation of evil deeds*), I have been compelled to migrate through evil forms of birth, till now happily, by the power of your religious merit, the body which I have possessed through many kalpas has been changed in a moment.   My gratitude is boundless, nor could it be expressed if I wore my body to dust (*with frequent prostrations*).   Let me but acquaint my father and mother; I will then follow you and obey you in all things."[34]

The Nâga maiden then returning to the lake addressed her father and mother, saying, "Just now, as I was wandering abroad, I lighted upon a Sâkya youth, who by the power of his religious merit succeeded in changing me into human form.   Having formed an affection for me, he desires to marry me.   I lay before you the matter in its truth."

The Nâga-râja was rejoiced to see his daughter restored to human form, and from a true affection to the holy tribe he gave consent to his daughter's request.   Then proceeding from the lake, he expressed his deep gratitude to the Sâkya youth, and said, "You have not despised creatures of other kinds, and have condescended to those beneath you.   I pray you come to my abode, and there receive my humble services." [35]

---

an object, the *sachcha kiriyá* (*satya-krityá*) of the Southern School of Buddhism. See Childers, *Páli Dict.,* sub voc. ; also *Abstract of Four Lectures,* p. 40.

[33] Julien translates this passage: "I am prepared to follow you." The meaning may also be, "only let that follow which you desire;" or, "only let that be accomplished which is the consequence of the past," *i.e.*, your past deeds.

[34] The literal translation of this passage is : "Desiring to make returns for this goodness, grinding my body to dust, I should not yet thank you enough. My heart desires to follow you in your travels ; one thing restrains me, the propriety of things; let me," &c. Instead of "obey you," the word *li* may refer to ceremonial or marriage rites.

[35] Literally, "sweepings and bathings."

The Śâkya youth having accepted the Nâga-râja's invitation, went forthwith to his abode. On this all the family of the Nâga received the youth with extreme reverence, and desired to delight his mind by an excess of feasting and pleasure; but the youth, seeing the dragon forms of his entertainers, was filled with affright and disgust, and he desired to go. The Nâga-râja detaining him said, "Of your kindness depart not. Occupy a neighbouring abode; I will manage to make you master of this land and to obtain a lasting fame. All the people shall be your servants, and your dynasty shall endure for successive ages."

The Śâkya youth expressed his gratitude, and said, "I can hardly expect your words to be fulfilled." Then the Nâga-râja took a precious sword and placed it in a casket covered with white camlet, very fine and beautiful, and then he said to the Śâkya youth, "Now of your kindness go to the king and offer him this white camlet as a tribute. The king will be sure to accept it as the offering of a remote (*distant*) person; then, as he takes it, draw forth the sword and kill him. Thus you will seize his kingdom. Is it not excellent?"

The Śâkya youth receiving the Nâga's directions, went forthwith to make his offering to the king of U-chang-na (Udyâna). When the king was about to take the piece of white camlet, then the youth took hold of his sleeve, and pierced him with the sword. The attendant ministers and the guards raised a great outcry and ran about in confusion. The Śâkya youth, waving the sword, cried out, "This sword that I hold was given me by a holy Nâga wherewith to punish the contumelious and subdue the arrogant." Being affrighted at the divine warrior, they submitted, and gave him the kingdom. On this he corrected abuses and established order; he advanced the good and relieved the unfortunate; and then with a great cortége he advanced towards the Nâga palace to acquaint him with the completion of his undertaking;

and then taking his wife he went back to the capital. Now the former demerits of the Nâga girl were not yet effaced, and their consequences still remained. Every time he went to rest by her side, from her head came forth the ninefold crest of the Nâga. The Śâkya prince, filled with affright and disgust, hitting on no other plan, waited till she slept, and then cut off (*the dragon's crest*) with his sword. The Nâga girl, alarmed, awoke and said, "This will bring no good hereafter to your posterity; it will not be ineffectual in slightly afflicting me during my life, and your children and grandchildren will all suffer from pains in the head." And so the royal line of this country are ever afflicted with this malady, and although they are not all so continually, yet every succession brings a worse affliction. After the death of the Śâkya youth his son succeeded under the name of Uttarasêna (U-ta-lo-si-na).

Just after Uttarasêna had come to power his mother lost her sight. Tathâgata, when he was going back from the subjugation of the Nâga Apalûla, descended from space and alighted in this palace. Uttarasêna was out hunting, and Tathâgata preached a short sermon to his mother. Having heard the sermon from the mouth of the holy one, she forthwith recovered her sight. Tathâgata then asked her, "Where is your son ? he is of my family." She said, "He went out hunting for a while this morning, but he will soon be back." When Tathâgata with his attendants were bent on going, the king's mother said, " Of my great fortune I have borne a child belonging to the holy family ; and Tathâgata of his great compassion has again come down to visit my house as connected with him. My son will soon return ; oh, pray remain for a short time !" The Lord of the World said, "This son of yours belongs to my family ; he need only hear the truth to believe it and understand it. If he were not my relative I would remain to instruct his heart, but now I go. On his return, tell him that Tathâgata has gone from this to Kuśinagara (Keu-shi), where between the *Sâla* trees he is about to die, and let your son come for a share of the relics to honour them."

Then Tathâgata with all his attendants took flight through the air and went. Afterwards Uttarasêna-râja, whilst engaged in the chase, saw, a long way off, his palace lighted up as if with a fire. Being in doubt about it, he quitted the chase and returned. On seeing his mother with her sight restored he was transported with joy, and addressed her, saying, " What fortunate circumstance has occurred to you during my short absence that you should have got your sight again as of old time ? " The mother said, " After you had gone out Tathâgata came here, and after hearing him preach I recovered my sight. Buddha has gone from here to Kuśinagara ; he is going to die between the *Sâla* trees. He commands you to go quickly to the spot to get some of his relics."

The king having heard these words, uttered cries of lamentation, and fell prostrate on the ground motionless. Coming to himself, he collected his cortége and went to the twin-trees, where Buddha had already died. Then the kings of the other countries treated him scornfully, and were unwilling to give him a share of the much-prized relics they were taking to their own countries. On this a great assembly of Dêvas acquainted them with Buddha's wishes, on which the kings divided the relics equally, beginning with him.

Going north-west from the town of Mung-kia-li, crossing a mountain and passing through a valley, we reascend the Sin-tu river.[30] The roads are craggy and steep; the mountains and the valleys are dark and gloomy. Sometimes we have to cross by ropes, sometimes by iron chains stretched (*across the gorges*). There are foot-bridges (*or covered ways*) suspended in the air, and flying bridges across the chasms, with wooden steps let into the ground for climbing the steep embankments. Going thus 1000 li or

---

[30] That is, we strike on the Indus river, and ascend it against its course.

so, we reach the river valley of Ta-li-lo,[37] where stood once the capital of U-chang-na. This country produces much gold and scented turmeric. By the side of a great *sanghârâma* in this valley of Ta-li-lo is a figure of Maitrêya [38] Bôdhisattva, carved out of wood. It is golden coloured, and very dazzling in appearance, and possesses a secret spiritual power (*of miracle*). It is about 100 feet high, and is the work of the Arhat Madhyântika.[39] This saint by his spiritual power caused a sculptor to ascend into the Tushita (Tu-si-to) heaven, that he might see for himself the marks and signs (*on the person of Maitrêya*); this he did three times, till his task was finished. From the time of the execution of this image the streams of the law (*religious teaching*) began to flow eastward.

Going east from this, after climbing precipices and crossing valleys, we go up the course of the Sin-tu river; and then, by the help of flying bridges and footways made

[37] Ta-li-lo, or Dâril or Dârail, a valley on the right or western bank of the Indus (long. 73° 44' E.), watered by a river Daril, containing half-a-dozen towns, and occupied by Dârdus or Dards, from whom it received its name (Cunningham, *Anc. Geog. of India*, p. 82). It is perhaps the same as the To-li of Fa-hian. Conf. Cunningham in *J. A. S. Ben.*, vol. xvii. pt. ii. p. 19; and *Ladak*, pp. 2, 46 f. Julien has Talila.

[38] Maitrêya is the "Buddha to come." He is supposed now to be dwelling as a Bôdhisattva in the fourth Dêvalôka heaven called Tushita (Hardy, *Man. Budh.*, p. 25; Burnouf, *Introd.*, pp. 96, 606). This heaven is the place of desire for Buddhists like Hiuen Tsiang, who constantly prayed on his death-bed for the happiness of being born there. The short Chinese inscription lately found at Buddha Gayâ is occupied chiefly with aspirations after this heaven (*J. R. A. S.*, N.S., vol. xiii. pp. 552 f.; *Ind. Ant.*, vol. x. p. 193). It is a belief opposed to the "paradise of the west" (*Su-*

khâratî), which probably is of foreign origin.

[39] Madhyântika, according to the Northern School of Buddhism, was a disciple of Ânanda (*Fo-sho-hing-tsan-king*, xi.), converted shortly before the death of the latter. In Tibetan he is called *Ni-mahi-gung*. See *Asiat. Res.*, vol. xx. p. 92. By some he is reckoned as one of the first five patriarchs, and placed between Ânanda and Sânavâsa, but others do not reckon him among them. At Banâras the people were annoyed at the number of Bhikshus, and Madhyântika, taking ten thousand of them, flew through the air to Mount Usira, in Kasmîr, which he converted to Buddhism. See Vassilief, pp. 35, 39, 45, 225; Köppen, vol. i. pp. 145, 189 f. The *Mahâwaǹso* (p. 71) speaks of a Majjhima who, after the third Buddhist synod, was sent to Kasmîr and the Himavanta country to spread the Buddhist faith. (See also Oldenberg, *Dîpavaṁsa*, viii. 10.) Fa-hian (chap. vii.) says this image was carved about 300 years after the *Nirvâṇa*.

of wood across the chasms and precipices, after going 500 li or so, we arrive at the country of Po-lu-lo (Bolor).

PO-LU-LO (BOLOR.)

The country of Po-lu-lo[40] is about 4000 li in circuit; it stands in the midst of the great Snowy Mountains. It is long from east to west, and narrow from north to south. It produces wheat and pulse, gold and silver. Thanks to the quantity of gold, the country is rich in supplies. The climate is continually cold. The people are rough and rude in character; there is little humanity or justice with them; and as for politeness, such a thing has not been heard of. They are coarse and despicable in appearance, and wear clothes made of wool. Their letters are nearly like those of India, their language somewhat different. There are about a hundred *sanghárámas* in the country, with something like a thousand priests, who show no great zeal for learning, and are careless in their moral conduct. Leaving this country and returning to U-to-kia-han-cha (Uḍakhâṇḍa),[41]

---

[40] According to Cunningham, Bolor is the modern Balti, Baltistân, or Little Tibet (*Anc. Geog. of India*, p. 84). Marco Polo also mentions a country called Bolor, but he places it E.N.E. from the Pamir plateau (Yule's *Marco Polo*, vol. i. p. 187). Bolor may have included both Balti and the mountains adjoining the southern margin of Pamir. Indeed the Chinese included Chitral to the northern boundary of Swât under this term (Yule). Sung Yun refers to this country (*Buddhist Pilgrims*, p. 187). For other references see Yule (*op. cit.*, p. 188). Although Hwui-lih says nothing about this visit to Bolor, yet the use of the symbol *king* shows that Hiuen Tsiang personally visited the country. Marco Polo says of the people, "they are indeed an evil race." He also calls them "savage idolaters" (*op. cit.*, chap. xxxii.) Ptolemy (*Geog.*, lib. vi. c. 13, 3) places the Βυλται

[41] There seems little doubt that this should be identified with Ohind or Wahand on the right bank of the Indus, about 16 miles above Atak at the foot of the Imaus mountains, in Little Tibet or Baltistân. This district was noted for its gold in very early times (conf. Herodotos, lib. iii. cc. 102, 105; Strabo, lib. ii. c. 1, 9; lib. xv. c. 1, 37; Arrian, *Anab. Alex.*, lib. v. c. 4; *Indika*, c. 5; and *Ind. Ant.*, vol. iv. pp. 225 ff. Albirûnî calls it Wayhand, the capital of Kandahâr (Gandhâra). V. St. Martin, *Mem., u. s.*, p. 310; Lassen, *Ind. Alt.*, vol. ii. p. 474 n.; Reinaud, *Fragm. Arab. et Pers.*, p. 114; *Mém. sur l'Inde*, pp. 196, 276; Court, *J. A. S. Ben.*, vol. v. p. 395; Cuningham, *ib.*, vol. xvii. p. 130, and *Anc. Geog.*, pp. 55 f.; Benfey, *Indien*, p. 115; Elliot, *Hist. Ind.*, vol. i. pp. 48, 63, 445; vol. ii. pp. 28, 33, 150, 426, 438 f.; and *ante*, p. 114, n. 108.

we cross at the south the river Sin-tu. The river is about 3 or 4 li in width, and flows south-west. Its waters are pure and clear as a mirror as they roll along with impetuous flow. Poisonous Nâgas and hurtful beasts occupy the caverns and clefts along its sides. If a man tries to cross the river carrying with him valuable goods or gems or rare kinds of flowers or fruits, or especially relics of Buddha, the boat is frequently engulphed by the waves.[42] After crossing the river we arrive at the kingdom of Ta-ch'a-shi-lo (Takshaśilâ).

TA-CH'A-SHI-LO (TAKSHAŚILÂ).

The kingdom of Ta-ch'a-shi-lo[43] is about 2000 li in circuit, and the capital is about 10 li in circuit. The royal family being extinct, the nobles contend for power by force. Formerly this country was in subjection to Kapiśa, but latterly it has become tributary to Kia-shi-

[42] So we find on his return journey Hiuen Tsiang lost his books and flowers, and was nearly drowned in crossing the river about this spot (see Hwui-lih, K. v.; Vie, p. 263).

[43] On the return journey, Hiuen Tsiang makes the distance from Takshaśilâ to the Indus three days' journey N.W. (Hwui-lih, Vie, p. 263). Fa-hien makes it seven days' journey from Gandhâra (cap. xi.); Sung-yun also places it three days to the east of the Indus (Beal's *Bud. Pilgrims*, p. 200). General Cunningham places the site of the city near Shah-dheri, one mile to the north-east of Kâla-ka-sarai, where he found the ruins of a fortified city, and was able to trace the remains of no less than fifty-five *stûpas*—of which two were as large as the great Mânikyâla tope—twenty-eight monasteries, and nine temples (*Anc. Geog. of India*, p. 105). The classical writers notice the size and wealth of the city of Τάξιλα (Arrian, *Anab. Alex.*, lib. v. c. 8; Strabo, *Geog.*, lib. xv. c. 1. 17, and 28; Pliny, *Hist. Nat.*, lib. vi. c. 17, 62, and c. 23; Ptolemy, *Geog.*, lib. vii. 1, 45; Dionysius Perieg., 1141). Apollonius and Damis are said also to have visited Taxila about A.D. 45. Philostratus describes the carvings and pictures of a temple near the town, representing scenes from the conflict of Porus with Alexander (cap. 20, p. 71, ed. Olearii, 1709). For further remarks on the ruins and antiquities see Cunningham, *op. cit.*, pp. 104 f. M. V. de St. Martin, relying on the measurements given by Pliny derived from the records of Alexander's expedition, places Taxila at Hassan-Abdal, eight miles north-west of Shah-dheri (vid. *Mémoire*, p. 319); conf. Wilson, *Ariana Ant.*, p. 196; *J. R. A. S.*, vol. v. p. 118; Burnouf, *Introd.*, pp. 322 f., 332, 361; *Lotus*, pp. 689 f.; Bunbury, *Hist. Anc. Geog.*, vol. i. pp. 443, 499. It is frequently mentioned in Sanskrit literature, *e.g.*, *Mahâbh.*, i. 682, 834; *Râmâyaṇa*, iv. 53, śl. 23; *Bṛih. Saṁh.*, x. 8, and xiv. 26; Pâṇini, iv. 2, 82 and 3, 93.,

mi-lo (Kaśmîr). The land is renowed for its fertility, and
produces rich harvests. It is very full of streams and fountains.   Flowers and fruits are abundant. The climate is
agreeably temperate.   The people are lively and courageous, and they honour the three gems. Although there
are many *sanghârâmas*, they have become ruinous and
deserted, and there are very few priests ; those that there
are study the Great Vehicle.

North-west of the capital about 70 li is the tank of the
Nâga-râja Êlâpatra (I-lo-po-to-lo) ;[44] it is about 100 paces
round, the waters are pure and sweet ; lotus flowers of
various colours, which reflect different tints in their common beauty (*garnish the surface*) ; this Nâga was a Bhikshu
who anciently, in the time of Kâśyapa Buddha, destroyed
au Êlâpatra tree.   Hence, at the present time, when the
people of that country ask for rain or fine weather, they
must go with the Shamans to the side of the tank, and
then cracking their fingers (*or*, in a moment), after praying
for the desired object, they obtain it.

Going 30 li or so to the south-east of the Nâga tank,
we enter a gorge between two mountains, where there is a
stûpa built by Aśôka-râja.   It is about 100 feet in height.
This is where Śâkya Tathâgata delivered a prediction, that
when Maitrêya, Lord of the World, appeared hereafter,
there should also appear of themselves four great gem
treasures, and that in this excellent land there should be
one.   According to tradition, we find that whenever there
is an earthquake, and the mountains on every side are
shaken, all round this sacred spot (*treasure*) to the distance of 100 paces there is perfect stillness.   If men are

<hr>

[44] The story of the Naga-râja Êlâpatra is a favourite one in Chinese
Buddhist books.   See *Romantic Hist.
of Buddha*, p. 276 ff. (*Stûpa of Bharhut*, p. 27).   Cunningham identifies
the tank of Êlâpatra with the fountain of Hasan Abdal called Bâbâ-
Wali.   In the legend referred to
above we are told that the Nâga
stretched his body from Takshaśilâ
to Banâras (compare the sculpture).
In this case we should be led to
Hasan Abdal as the site of Takshaśilâ.   This Nâga is mentioned in
Brahmanical literature also as the
son of Kaśyapa and Kadrâ. *Mahâbhârata*, i. 1551 ; *Harivaṃśa*, 228,
12821 ; *Vishnu-purâṇa* (Hall's ed.),
vol. ii. pp. 74, 285, 287, and vol. v.
p. 251.

so foolish as to attempt to dig into the place (*or* ground surrounding it), the earth shakes again, and the men are thrown down headlong.

By the side of the *stûpa* is a *sanghârâma* in ruins, and which has been for a long time deserted and without priests.

To the north of the city 12 or 13 li is a *stûpa* built by Aśôka-râja. On feast-days (*religious commemoration days*) it glows with light, and divine flowers fall around it, and heavenly music is heard. According to tradition, we find in late times there was a woman whose body was grievously afflicted with leprosy. Coming to the *stûpa* secretly, she offered worship in excess and confessed her faults. Then seeing that the vestibule (*the open court in front of the stûpa*) was full of dung and dirt, she removed it, and set to work to sweep and water it and to scatter flowers and perfumes; and having gathered some blue lotus flowers, she covered the ground with them. On this her evil leprosy left her, and her form became lovely, and her beauty doubled, whilst from her person there came the famed scent of the blue lotus, and this also is the reason of the fragrance of this excellent place. This is the spot where Tathâgata formerly dwelt when he was practising the discipline of a Bôdhisattva; he was then the king of a great country and was called Chen-ta-lo-po-la-po (Chandraprabha) ; he cut off his head, earnestly seeking the acquirement of *Bôdhi:* and this he did during a thousand successive births, (*for the same object and in the same place*).[45]

By the side of the *stûpa* of the "sacrificed head" is a *sanghârâma*, of which the surrounding courts are deserted and overgrown ; there are (*nevertheless*) a few priests. It

---

[45] This legend was the origin of the name Taksha-śirâ, "the severed head," given to the place, as noticed by Fa-hian and Sung-yun. The legend will be found in Râjèndralâl Mitra's *Nepalese Buddhist Litera-*ture, pp. 310, viii. "The man" for whose sake he gave his head, as stated by Sung-yun (*Buddhist Pilgrims,* p. 200) and by Fa-hian (cap. xi.) was the wicked Brâhman Rudrâksha.

was here in old days the master of *śâstras* Kumâralabdha,[46] belonging to the school of *Sûtras* (Sâutrântikas),[47] composed several treatises.

Outside the city to the south-east, on the shady[48] side of a mountain,[49] there is a *stûpa*, in height 100 feet or so; this is the place where they put out the eyes of Ku-lang-na (for *Ku-na-lang-na*, Kunâla), who had been unjustly accused by his step-mother; it was built by Aśôka-râja.

When the blind pray to it (*or* before it) with fervent faith, many of them recover their sight. This prince (Kunâla) was the son of the rightful queen. His person was graceful and his disposition loving and humane. When the queen-royal was dead, her successor (*the step-queen*) was dissolute and unprincipled. Following her wild and foolish preference, she made proposals to the prince; he, when she solicited him, reproached her with tears, and departed, refusing to be guilty of such a crime. The step-mother, seeing that he rejected her, was filled with wrath and hatred; waiting for an interval when she was with the king, she addressed him[50] thus: "To whom should your majesty intrust the government of Ta-ch'a-shi-lo but to your own son? The prince is renowned for his humanity and obedience; because of his attachment to the good his fame is in every mouth." The king listening to her seducing words,[51] agreed willingly with the vile plot, and forthwith gave orders to his eldest son in these

---

[46] In Chinese *Tong-shau*, youth-receiving; the phonetic symbols are *Ku-mo-lo-lo to*.

[47] The Sautrântika school of Buddhism was, according to Vassilief (*Buddhisme*, p. 233), founded by Dharmottara or Utaradharma; it was one of the two principal branches of the Hînayâna, or Little Vehicle, of Buddhism; the other branch being the Vaibhâshika school. On their tenets see Colebrooke, *Misc. Essays*, vol. I. pp. 391 f.; Köppen, *Die Relig. d. Buddha*, vol. i. pp. 151 f.; Burnouf, *Introd.*, pp. 109, 397 f.; Lassen, *Ind. Alt.*, vol. ii. p. 460; Vassilief, pp. 34, 38, 48, 63 f., 114 f., 268, 273–286, 321.

[48] That is, on the northern side.

[49] Or, a south mountain; but probably *nan* is redundant.

[50] The text requires some such expression as "winningly" or "when on easy terms with the king" she addressed him thus.

[51] The text implies that he was gratified to accede to the terms of this plot of the adulteress, or this adulterous (*kien*) plot.

words : "I have received my royal inheritance in succession, and I desire to hand it down to those who follow me; my only fear is lest I should lose aught of it and so dishonour my ancestors.   I now confide to you the government of Ta-ch'a-shi-lo.[52]   The affairs of a country are of serious importance; the feelings of men are contradictory; undertake nothing rashly, so as to endanger your authority; verify the orders sent you; my seal is the impression of my teeth; here in my mouth is my seal.   There can be no mistake."

On this the prince, receiving his orders, went to establish order.   And so months passed on, yet the step-mother's hatred did but increase.   Accordingly she wrote a dispatch and sealed it with red wax, and then, waiting till the king was asleep, she stamped it secretly with his tooth impression, and sent it off by a messenger with all dispatch as a letter of accusation.   His ministers having read the letter,[53] were confused, and looked at one another with dismay.

The prince then asked them what moved them so. They said, " The Mahârâja has sent a dispatch accusing the prince, and ordering both his eyes to be put out, and that he be taken with his wife to the mountains,[54] and there left to die.   Although this order has come, we dare not obey it; but we will ask afresh for directions, and keep you bound till the reply comes."[55]

The prince said, "My father, if he has ordered my death, must be obeyed; and the seal of his teeth is a sure sign of the truth of the order.   There can be no error." Then he ordered a Chaṇḍâla to pluck out his eyes; and

---

[52] About fifty years after Alexander's campaign the people of Takhaśilâ rebelled against Bindusâra, king of Magadha, who sent his eldest son, Susima, to besiege the place. On his failure the siege was intrusted to Aśôka, his younger son, to whom the people at once submitted.   Here Aśôka dwelt as viceroy of the Panjâb during his father's lifetime, and here on the occasion of another revolt he placed his son Kuṇâla, the hero of the legend in the text. Conf. Burnouf, *Introd.*, pp. 163, 357. 360 ; *J. A. S. Ben.*, vol. vi. p. 714.

[53] Having perused the letter on their knees.

[54] To the mountain valleys.

[55] Awaiting the sentence or punishment.

having thus lost his sight, he wandered forth to beg for his daily support. As he travelled on far away, he came to his father's capital town. His wife said to him,[56] "There is the royal city." "Alas!" he said, "what pain I endure from hunger and cold. I was a prince; I am a beggar. Oh, that I could make myself known and get redress for the false charge formerly brought against me!"[57] On this he contrived to enter the king's inner bureau, and in the after part of the night he began to weep, and with a plaintive voice, accompanied with the sound of a lute,[58] he saug a mournful song.

The king, who was in an upper chamber,[59] hearing these wonderful strains full of sadness and suffering, was surprised, and inquired. "From the notes of the lute and the sound of the voice I take this to be my son; but why has he come here?"

He immediately said to his court attendant, "Who is that singing so?"

Forthwith he brought the blind man into his presence and placed him before the king. The king, seeing the prince, overwhelmed with grief, exclaimed, "Who has thus injured you? Who has caused this misery, that my beloved son should be deprived of sight? Not one of all his people can he see. Alas! what an end to come to![60] O heavens! O heavens! what a misfortune is this!"[61]

The prince, yielding to his tears, thanked (his father) and replied, "In truth,[62] for want of filial piety have I thus been

---

[56] Kunâla's wife was called Chin-kin-man, pure-gold-garland (Kâñchanamâlâ). The stepmother's name was Tishyarakshitâ, and his mother's Padmavatî (Lien-hwa). His name is also spelt Kuṇâla.

[57] This may be otherwise rendered: "Would that I could obtain a hearing, so as to vindicate myself completely from the former accusation." Julien translates it: "I will expose anew my past faults."

[58] A rind.

[59] A high tower or pavilion.

[60] Or it may simply mean, "how was this brought about?"

[61] Julien translates it, "how virtue has degenerated." The symbol *tih*, however, need not be rendered "virtue;" it refers to the reversal of fortune or condition.

[62] The sense of the passage seems to require the force of *ching* to be, "Do you not know?" or "You are aware that my punishment is due to a charge of filial disobedience."

punished by Heaven.   In such a year and such a month and such a day suddenly there came a loving order (*or an order from my mother*).   Having no means of excusing myself, I dared not shrink from the punishment."   The king's heart, knowing that the second wife had committed this crime, without any further inquiry caused her to be put to death.[63]

At this time in the *saṅghârâma* of the *Bôdhi* tree [64] there was a great Arhat called Ghôsha (Kiu-sha).   He had the fourfold power of " explanation without any difficulties." [65]   He was completely versed in the *Trividyâs.*[66] The king taking to him his blind son, told him all the matter, and prayed that he would of his mercy restore him to sight.   Then that Arhat, having received the king's request, forthwith addressed to the people this order: " To-morrow I desire to declare the mysterious principle (*of the law*); let each person come here with a vessel in his hands to hear the law and receive in it his tears." Accordingly, they came together from every side (*far and near*), both men and women, in crowds.   At this time the Arhat preached on the twelve *Nidânas*,[67] and there was not one of those who heard the sermon but was moved to tears.   The tears were collected in the vessels, and then, when his sermon was finished, he collected all these tears in one golden vessel, and then, with a strong affirmation, he said, " What I have said is gathered from the most mysterious of Buddha's doctrines ; if this is not true, if there be error in what I have said, then let things remain as they are; but if it is otherwise, I desire that this blind

---

[63] This story is also given by Burnouf, *Introd.*, pp. 362 f.

[64] The *saṅghârâma* of the *Bôdhi* tree was the convent built on the site of the Buddha Gayâ temple.

[65] For this fourfold power of unimpeded explanation consult Childers' *Pâli Dict. s. v. patisambhidâ,* also Eitel, *Handbook s. v. pratisaṁvid.* Julien has an instructive note on this point. Conf. Burnouf, *Lotus,* p. 839.

[66] For the *trividyâs* consult Eitel, *sub voc.* ; Burnouf, *Lotus,* p. 372 ; Julien, *Mém. s. l. Cont. Occid.,* tome i. p. 160; and *ante,* p. 105, n. 75.

[67] See Burnouf, *Introd. au Buddh.,* pp. 52, 432, 574, 577 f. ; *Lotus,* p. 380; Hardy, *East. Mon.,* pp. 6, 193, 301.

man may recover his sight after washing his eyes with these tears." [68]

After finishing this speech he washed his eyes with the water, and lo! his sight was restored.

The king then accused the ministers (*who had executed the order*) and their associates. Some he degraded, others he banished, others he removed, others he put to death. The common people (*who had participated in the crime*) he banished to the north-east side of the Snowy Mountains, to the middle of the sandy desert.

Going south-east from this kingdom, and crossing the mountains and valleys about 700 li, we come to the kingdom of Săng-ho-pu-lo (Simhapura).

SANG-HO-PU-LO [SIMHAPURA].

The kingdom of Săng-ho-pu-lo [69] is about 3500 or 3600 li in circuit. On the west it borders on the river Sin-tu. The capital is about 14 or 15 li in circuit; it borders on the mountains. The crags and precipices which surround it cause it to be naturally strong. The ground is not highly cultivated, but the produce is abundant. The climate is cold, the people are fierce and value highly the quality of courage; moreover, they are much given to deceit. The country has no king or rulers, but is in dependence on Kaśmîr. Not far to the south of the capital is a *stûpa* built by Aśôka-râja. The decorations

[68] There is a similar story told by Aśvaghôsha; the Ghôsha of the text, however, must not be confused with him.

[69] The distance from Takshaśilâ to Simhapura being 700 li, or about 140 miles, we should expect to find it near Taki or Narasinha (Cunningham, *Anc. Geog.*, map vi.). But the capital is described as being surrounded by mountain crags, which will not apply to the plain country of Taki. For the same reason the town of Sangohi, which M. V. de St. Martin refers to, cannot be the place in question. General Cunningham identifies it with Khetâs or Ketaksh, the holy tanks of which are still visited by crowds of pilgrims from all parts of India (*Anc. Geog.*, p. 124). If this be so, the distance may probably include the *double* journey. The expression used by Hwui-lih (*kan*) seems to imply this. According to the subsequent account, Hiuen Tsiang went to Simhapura as an excursion, and returned to Takshaśilâ. He probably went with Jain pilgrims who were visiting this *tirtha*, or holy place.

are much injured: spiritual wonders are continually connected with it.   By its side is a *sanghârâma*, which is deserted and without priests.

To the south-east of the city 40 or 50 li is a stone *stûpa* which was built by Aśôka-râja; it is 200 feet or so in height.   There are ten tanks, which are secretly connected together, and on the right and left (*of the walks joining them*) are covered stones (*balustrades*) in different shapes and of strange character.   The water of the tanks is clear, and the ripples are sometimes noisy and tumultuous.   Dragons and various fishes [70] live in the clefts and caverns bordering on the tanks or hide themselves [71] in the waters.   Lotus flowers of the four colours cover the surface of the limpid water. A hundred kind of fruits surround them, and glisten with different shades.   The trees are reflected deep down in the water, and altogether it is a lovely spot for wandering forth.

By the side there is a *sanghârâma*, which for a long time has been without priests.   By the side of the *stûpa*, and not far off, is the spot where the original teacher of the white-robed heretics [72] arrived at the knowledge of the principles he sought, and first preached the law.   There is an inscription placed there to that effect.   By the side of this spot is a temple of the Dêvas. The persons who frequent it subject themselves to austerities; day and night they use constant diligence without relaxation.   The laws of their founder are mostly filched

<hr>

[70] The text has dragon-fishes, or dragons (serpents) and fishes, the tribes of the water.

[71] Or disport themselves in the stream.

[72] This refers to the Śvêtâmbaras, a sect of the Jains; Colebrooke (*Essays*, vol. i. p. 381) says that "this is a less strict order, and of more modern date and inferior note compared with the Digambaras" (noticed below, note 74).   The Jainas were very influential about the time of Pulikêśî (*Ind. Antiq.*, vol. ii. p. 194); Lassen, *Ind. Alt.*, vol. iv. pp. 97 f., 756 f.   Whether the Jains preceded or succeeded the Buddhists, it is curious to have this testimony of Hiuen Tsiang that their original teacher arrived at enlightenment and first preached the law in this place, viz., Siṁhapura, and that there was an inscription placed here to that effect. Conf. *Ind. Ant.*, vol. ii. pp. 14 f., 134 f., 193 f., 258 f.

from the principles of the books of Buddha. These men are of different classes, and select their rules and frame their precepts accordingly.[72]   The great ones are called Bhikshus; the younger are called Śrâmaṇêras.   In their ceremonies and modes of life they greatly resemble the priests (*of Buddha*), only they have a little twist of hair on their heads, and they go naked.[74]   Moreover, what clothes they chance to wear are white.   Such are the slight differences which distinguish them from others. The figure of their sacred master [75] they stealthily class with that of Tathâgata; it differs only in point of clothing ; [76] the points of beauty are absolutely the same.

From this place going back to the northern frontiers of Ta-ch'a-shi-lo, crossing the Sin-tu [77] river and going south-east 200 li or so, we pass the great stone gates where formerly Mahâsattva, as a prince,[78] sacrificed his body to feed

[73] Julien translates this passage thus : "On these laws (viz., of Buddha) he depended in framing his precepts and rules."   This may perhaps be correct, but the plain translation of the passage is : "According to (*their*) classes, they frame (or possibly, "he framed") their laws, and arrange their regulations and precepts."

[74] The Digambaras, or "sky-clad," are another division of the Jainas, and are identical with the Nirgranthas.   Hiuen Tsiang appears to confuse these with the "white-clad."   For an account of the Digambara Jainas, see *Ind. Antiq.*, vol. vii. p. 2S ; and vol. viii. p. 30, for the argument as to the relative antiquity of the Buddhist and Jaina sects ; also conf. vol. i. p. 310 ; Fergusson and Burgess, *Cave Temples of India*, pp. 485 ff. ; Vassilief, pp. 52, 70, 275.

[75] The text has *tin-see*, heavenly master; but if *tin* be a mistake for *ta*, it would be their *great* master, viz., Mahâvîra.

[76] That is, the statues are alike, except that the Jaina ones are naked.   This only applies to those of the Digambara Jainas.   For

these statues, see Fergusson and Burgess, *Cave Temples*, pp. 485–590 and pl. xcv. ; Burgess, *Arch. Sur. West. India Reports*, vol. v. pp. 43–50, 51, 58.   From this interesting allusion to the Jainas it is evident that Hiuen Tsiang regarded them as dishonest separatists from Buddhism.   The "points of beauty" referred to in the text are the thirty-two superior signs (*siang*), and the eighty inferior (*ho*), for which see references in note 5, p. 1, *ante*.

[77] It may be either that Hiuen Tsiang went back to Ohind, and so crossed and recrossed the Indus, or that he calls the Suhân (Sukhôma, Σώαϝοϛ) river by this name.   The distance from Hasan Abdal to Mânikyâla (the body-offering spot) is just 40 miles (200 li), according to Cunningham's map (No. vi., *Anc. Geog. of India*).

[78] The incident of feeding the tigress is narrated in Hardy's *Manual of Budhism*, pp. 93, 94 ; but there it is said that the Bôdhisattva was a Brâhmaṇ ; here he is called a prince.   The rock or gate where he practised asceticism was called Munda or Eraka (*op. cit. ibid*).

a hungry Wu-t'u (*Ôtu*, a cat).[79]   To the south of this
place 40 or 50 paces there is a stone *stûpa*.   This is
the place where Mahâsattva, pitying the dying condition
of the beast,[80] after arriving at the spot, pierced his body
with a bamboo splinter, so as to nourish the beast with
his blood.   On this the animal, taking the blood, revived.
On this account all the earth and the plants at this place
are dyed with a blood colour,[81] and when men dig the
earth they find things like prickly spikes.   Without
asking whether we believe the tale or not, it is a piteous
one.

To the north of the body-sacrifice place there is a stone
stûpa about 200 feet high, which was built by King
Aśôka.   It is adorned with sculptures and tastefully constructed (*built*).   From time to time spiritual indications [82]
are apparent.   There are a hundred or so small *stûpas*,
provided with stone niches for movable images (*or
stone movable niches*) around this distinguished spot.[83]
Whatever sick there are who can circumambulate it are
mostly restored to health.

To the east of the *stûpa* there is a *sanghârâma*,
with about 100 priests given to the study of the Great
Vehicle.

Going east from this 50 li or so, we come to an iso-
lated mountain, where there is a *sanghârâma* with about
200 priests in it.   They all study the Great Vehicle.

[79] The compound *wu-t'u*, which is
translated by Julien "a tiger" without explanation, is probably the Sanskrit *ôtu*, a cat.

[80] "Pitying the exhausted condition of the hungry beast" The
original implies that the beast had
no strength and was dying from
hunger.   There is no reference to
the tiger-cubs, nor is the number
seven mentioned either here or by
Fa-hian.   For a full account of the
legend and the ruins about Mani-
kvâla, see Cunningham, *op. cit.*,
p. 153 ff., and conf. *Ind. Ant.*, vol.
xi. pp. 347 f., &c.

[81] This *stûpa* has been identified
by General Cunningham with
that marked No. 5 on his plan of
Manîkyâla (*Arch. Survey*, vol. ii. pl.
lxii. p. 153).   The clay is even now
of a red colour.

[82] "It is resplendent with divine
brightness or glory."

[83] Julien translates it "this
funereal monument." but the symbol *yung* means "lustrous," referring, no doubt, to the glory which
surrounded the *stûpa*.

Fruits and flowers abound here, with fountains and
tanks clear as a mirror.   By the side of this convent
is a *stúpa* about 300 feet in height.   Here Tathâgata
dwelt in old time, and restrained a wicked Yaksha from
eating flesh.

Going from this kingdom about 500 li or so along the
mountains in a south-easterly direction, we come to the
country of Wu-la-shi (Urasa).

WU-LA-SHI [URAŚA].

The kingdom of Wu-la-shi (Uraśa) [84] is about 2000 li
in circuit; the mountains and valleys form a continuous chain.   The fields fit for cultivation are contracted
as to space.   The capital is 7 or 8 li in circuit; there is no
king, but the country is dependent on Kaśmîr.   The
soil is fit for sowing and reaping, but there are few flowers
or fruits.   The air is soft and agreeable; there is very
little ice or snow.   The people have no refinement; the
men are hard and rough in their disposition, and are much
given to deceit.   They do not believe in the religion of
Buddha.

To the south-west of the capital 4 or 5 li is a *stúpa*
about 200 feet or so in height, which was built by
Aśôka-râja.   By its side is a *sanghârâma*, in which there
are but a few disciples, who study the Great Vehicle. [85]

Going south-east from this, crossing over mountains and
treading along precipices, passing over chain bridges,
after 1000 li or so, we come to the country of Kia-shi-
mi-lo [86] (Kaśmîr).

---

[84] Uraśâ appears as the name of
a city in the *Mahâbhârata* under
the form Uragâ (ii. 1027 ; and *Rag-
huv.* vi. 59), probably by a slip (see
Lassen, *I. A.*, vol. ii. p. 155, n. 1); in
the *Râjataranginî* (v. 216) it is Uraśâ,
the capital of Uraśa—mentioned in
Pâṇini (iv. 1, 154 and 178, and
Uraśâ in iv. 2, 82, and iv. 3, 93).
Ptolemy (lib. vii. c. 1, 45) calls
the country Ἄρσα or Οὔαρσα, and
its towns Ἰθάγουρος and Τάξιλα
(v. l. Ταξίαλα), placing it between
the upper waters of the Bidaspes
and Indus, that is, in the Hazâra
country.   Conf. Cunningham, *Anc.
Geog. Ind.*, p. 103 ; *J. A. S. Beng.*,
vol. xvii. pt. ii. pp. 21, 283 ; Lassen,
I. A., vol. ii. p. 175.

[85] Julien has "Little Vehicle."

[86] Formerly written Ki-pin by
mistake.—*Ch. Ed.*

KIA-SHI-MI-LO [KAŚMÎR].

The kingdom of Kaśmîr [87] is about 7000 li in circuit, and on all sides it is enclosed by mountains. These mountains are very high. Although the mountains have passes through them, these are narrow and contracted. The neighbouring states that have attacked it have never succeeded in subduing it. The capital of the country on the west side is bordered by a great river. It (*the capital*) is from north to south 12 or 13 li, and from east to west 4 or 5 li. The soil is fit for producing cereals, and abounds with fruits and flowers. Here also are dragon-horses and the fragrant turmeric, the *fŏ-chü*,[88] and medicinal plants.

The climate is cold and stern. There is much snow but little wind. The people wear leather doublets and clothes of white linen. They are light and frivolous, and of a weak, pusillanimous disposition. As the country is protected by a dragon, it has always assumed superiority among neighbouring people. The people are handsome in appearance, but they are given to cunning. They love learning and are well instructed. There are both heretics and believers among them. There are about 100 *saṅghârâmas* and 5000 priests. There are four *stûpas* built by Aśôka-râja. Each of these has about

---

[87] Kaśmîr in early times appears to have been a kingdom of considerable extent. The old name is said to have been Kâśyapapura, which has been connected with the Κασπάπυρος of Hekataios (*Frag.* 179, and Steph. Byzant.), πόλις Γανδαρικὴ Σκυθῶν ἀκτὴ, said to have been in or near Πακτυϊκή and called Κασπάτυρος by Herodotos (lib. iii. c. 102, lib. iv. c. 44), from which Skylax started on his voyage down the Indus. Ptolemy has Κασπειρία and its capital Κάσπειρα (lib. vii. c. 1, 42, 47, 49; lib. viii. c. 26, 7), possibly for Κάσμειρα. The name Kaśmîr is the one used in the *Mahâbhârata*, Pâṇini, &c. The character ascribed to the people by the Chinese pilgrim, is quite in accord with that given to them by modern travellers (see Vigne, *Travels in Kashmir*, vol. ii. p. 142 f.) For further information see Lassen, *Ind. Alt.*, vol. i. pp. 50-53; and conf. Wilson, *Ariana Ant.*, pp. 136 f.; *Asiat. Res.*, vol. xv. p. 117; Köppen, *Die Relig. d. Buddha*, vol. ii. pp. 12 f. 78; Remusat, *Nouv. Mél. Asiat.*, tome i. p. 179; Vassilief, p. 40; *J. A. S. Ben.*, vol. vii. p. 165, vol. xxv. pp. 91-123; Yule's *Marco Polo*, vol. i. pp. 177 f.; Cunningham, *Anc. Geog. Ind.*, pp. 90 ff.; Troyer's *Râjataraṅgiṇî*, tome ii. pp. 293 ff.; Humboldt's *Cent. Asien*, vol. i. p. 92. The "great river" is the Vitastâ.

[88] Lentilles de verre.—Jul.

a pint measure of relics of Tathâgata. The history of the country says: This country was once a dragon lake. In old times the Lord Buddha was returning to the middle kingdom (*India*) after subduing a wicked spirit in U-chang-na (Udyâna), and when in mid-air, just over this country, he addressed Ânanda thus: "After my *Nirvâna*, the Arhat Madhyântika will found a kingdom in this land, civilise (*pacify*) the people, and by his own effort spread abroad the law of Buddha."

In the fiftieth year after the *Nirvâna*, the disciple of Ânanda, Madhyântika (Mo-t'ien-ti-kia) the Arhat— having obtained the six spiritual faculties [89] and been gifted with the eight *Vimôkshas* [90]—heard of the prediction of Buddha. His heart was overjoyed, and he repaired to this country. He was sitting tranquilly in a wood on the top of a high mountain crag, and exhibited great spiritual changes. The dragon beholding it was filled with a deep faith, and requested to know what he desired. The Arhat said, "I request you to give me a spot in the middle of the lake just big enough for my knees." [91]

On this the dragon withdrew the water so far, and gave him the spot. Then by his spiritual power the Arhat increased the size of his body, whilst the dragon king kept back the waters with all his might. So the lake became dry, and the waters exhausted. On this the Nâga, taking his flight, asked for a place. [92]

The Arhat (*then said*), "To the north-west of this is a pool about 100 li in circuit; in this little lake you and your posterity may continue to dwell." The Nâga said, " The lake and the land being mutually transferred, let me then be allowed to make my religious offerings to you." Madhyântika said, "Not long hence I shall enter on the *Nirvâna* without remnants (*anupadhisêsha*); although I should wish to allow your request, how can I do it ?"

[89] *Shadabhijñâ.* See *ante*, note 73, p. 104.

[90] See references in note 73, p. 104.

[91] *I.e.*, to sit.

[92] This is an abrupt combination ; it means asked for a place "to live in."

The Nâga then pressed his request in this way: "May 500 Arhats then ever receive my offerings till the end of the law?[93]   After which (*I ask to be allowed*) to return to this country to dwell (*in it*) as a lake." Madhyântika granted his request.

Then the Arhat, having obtained this land by the exercise of his great spiritual power, founded 500 *saṅghârâmas* He then set himself to procure by purchase from surrounding countries a number of poor people who might act as servitors to the priests.   Madhyântika having died, these poor people constituted themselves rulers over the neighbouring countries.   The people of surrounding countries despising these low-born men, would not associate with them, and called them Kritîyas[94] (Ki-li-to).   The fountains now have begun to bubble up (*in token of the end of the law having come*).

In the hundredth year after the *Nirvâṇa* of Tathâgata, Aśôka, king of Magadha, extended his power over the world, and was honoured even by the most distant people. He deeply reverenced the three gems, and had a loving regard for all living things.[95]   At this time there were 500 Arhats and 500 schismatical priests, whom the king honoured and patronised without any difference.   Among the latter was a priest called Mahâdêva, a man of deep learning and rare ability; in his retirement he sought a true renown; far thinking, he wrote treatises the principles of which were opposed to the holy doctrine.   All who heard of him resorted to his company and adopted his views.   Aśôka-râja, not knowing either holy or common

---

[93] *I.e.*, till religion be done with.

[94] In Chinese *Maï-te*, "bought people" (Sans. *kṛîta*).   In the *Vishṇu Purâṇa* it is said that "unregenerate *tribes*, barbarians and other Śûdras, will rule over the banks of the Indus and the regions of the Dârvikâ, of the Chandrabhâgâ and of Kaśmîra" (Wilson, in Hall's ed., vol. iv. p. 223), and the *Bhâgavata* has a similar statement, calling the "unregenerate" "other outcasts not enlightened by the *Vêdas*" (*ib.* p. 224).   See p. 156, n. 119 *infra*.

[95] *Sse-sing*, the four *varṇa* or castes, or the four classes of living beings, according to the Chinese, produced (1) from eggs, (2) embryos (animals and men), (3) moisture, and (4) by transformation

men,[96] and because he was naturally given to patronise those who were seditious, was induced to call together an assembly of priests to the banks of the Ganges, intending to drown them all.

At this time the Arhats having seen the danger threatening their lives, by the exercise of their spiritual power flew away through the air and came to this country and concealed themselves among the mountains and valleys. Aśôka-râja having heard of it, repented, and confessing his fault, begged them to return to their own country; but the Arhats refused to do so with determination. Then Aśôka-râja, for the sake of the Arhats, built 500 *sanghârâmas*, and gave this country as a gift to the priesthood.

In the four-hundredth year[97] after the *Nirvâna* of Tathâgata, Kanishka, king of Gandhâra, having succeeded to the kingdom, his kingly renown reached far, and he brought the most remote within his jurisdiction. During his intervals of duty he frequently consulted the sacred books of Buddha; daily he invited a priest to enter his palace and preach the law, but he found the different views of the schools so contradictory that he was filled with doubt, and he had no way to get rid of his uncertainty. At this time the honoured Pârśva said, " Since Tathâgata left the world many years and months have elapsed. The different schools hold to the treatises of their several masters. Each keeps to his own views, and so the whole body is torn by divisions."

The king having heard this, was deeply affected and gave way to sad regrets. After awhile he spoke to Pârśva and said, " Though of no account personally, yet, thanks to the remnant of merit which has followed me through successive births since the time of the Holy One till now,

---

[96] *I.e.*, the difference between them.

[97] That is, 300 years after Aśôka (B.C. 263-224), or about A.D. 75. Hiuen Tsiang places Aśôka only 100 years after Buddha, while in Aśôka's own inscriptions the Teacher is placed 221 years before the first of Aśôka's reign. The *Avadâna Śataka* supports this, placing the king two hundred years after Buddha. Conf. *Ind. Ant.*, vol. vi. pp. 149 f.; Burnouf, *Introd.*, p. 385; Max Müller's *India, &c.*, p. 306.

I have come to my present state. I will dare to forget my own low degree, and hand down in succession the teaching of the law unimpaired. I will therefore arrange the teaching of the three *piṭakas* of Buddha according to the various schools." The honourable Pârśva replied, " The previous merit of the great king has resulted in his present distinguished position.[98] That he may continue to love the law of Buddha is what I desire above all things.

The king then summoned from far and near a holy assembly (*issued an edict to assemble the holy teachers*).

On this they came together from the four quarters, and, like stars, they hurried together for myriads of li, men the most distinguished for talents and for holiness of life. Being thus assembled, for seven days offerings of the four necessary things were made, after which, as the king desired that there should be an arrangement of the law, and as he feared the clamour of such a mixed assembly (*would prevent consultation*), he said, with affection for the priests, " Let those who have obtained the holy fruit (*as Arhats*) remain, but those who are still bound by worldly influences [99] let them go!" Yet the multitude was too great. He then published another order : "Let those who have arrived at the condition of ' freedom from study' remain, and those who are still in a condition of learners go."[100] Still there were a great multitude who remained. On this the king issued another edict : " Those who are in possession of the three enlightenments and have the six spiritual faculties [101] may remain ; the others can go."[102]   And

<hr>

[98] Literally, "the great king in previous conditions (*suh*) having planted a good root—*or*, the root of virtue — has in consequence at-tained much happiness *or* merit."

[99] The world-influences or bonds refer to the *klêśas*. The five *klêśas* are (1) desire, (2) hate, (3) ignor-ance, (4) vanity, (5) heresy. See Burnouf, *Lotus*, pp. 443 f. Or the reference may be to the five *nîra-ranas*, for which see Childers, *Pali Dict.* sub voc.

[100] In a note on this passage Ju-lien explains that the first class, *Wu-hio*, designates the Arhats ; the second, *Hio-jin*, those studying to become Śramaṇas.

[101] For the *trividyâs* and the *shaḍabhijñas* see *ante*, n. 73 and 75, pp. 104, 105, and note 66, p. 142.

[102] There is a phrase here used, *tsz' chu*, of frequent occurrence in Buddhist books. It means, "with these exceptions,"—*his exceptis*.

yet there was a great multitude who remained. Then he published another edict: "Let those who are acquainted both with the three *Piṭakas* and the five *vidyās*[103] remain; as to others, let them go." Thus there remained 499 men. Then the king desired to go to his own country,[104] as he suffered from the heat and moisture of this country. He also wished to go to the stone grot[105] at Râjagṛiha, where Kâśyapa had held his religious assembly (*convocation*). The honourable Pârśva and others then counselled him, saying, "We cannot go there, because there are many heretical teachers there, and different *śâstras* being brought under consideration, there will be clamour and vain discussion. Without having right leisure for consideration, what benefit will there be in making (*fresh*) treatises?[106] The mind of the assembly is well affected towards this country; the land is guarded on every side by mountains, the Yakshas defend its frontiers, the soil is rich and productive, and it is well provided with food. Here both saints and sages assemble and abide; here the spiritual Ṛishis wander and rest."

The assembly having deliberated, they came to this resolution: "We are willing to fall in with the wishes of the king." On this, with the Arhats, he went from the spot where they had deliberated to another, and there founded a monastery, where they might hold an assembly (*for the purpose of arranging*) the Scriptures and composing the *Vibhâshâ Śâstra.*[107]

---

[103] The five *vidyās* (*Wu-ming*) are (1) *Śabdavidyā*, the treatise on grammar; (2) *Adhyâtmavidyā*, the treatise on inner principles or esoteric doctrines; (3) *Chikitsâvidyā*, the treatise on medicine, magic formulas, and occult science (Eitel); (4) *Hêtuvidyā*, the treatise on causes; (5) *Śilapasthânavidyā*, the treatise on the sciences, astronomy, meteorology, and mechanical arts. See *ante*, p. 78, note 24.

[104] So I translate it. Literally it would be "the king had a desire for his own country;" *i.e.*, for the highlands of Gandhâra.

[105] The phrase may mean a stone, *i.e.*, structural, house; or a stone chamber—a cave. It is generally supposed to have been a cave—the Saptaparṇa cave.

[106] Or, what use in holding discussions?

[107] This passage, which is unusually confused, may be translated also thus: "On this he went with the Arhats from that place, and came (*to a place where*) he founded

At this time the venerable Vasumitra (Shi-Yu) was putting on his robes outside the door (*about to enter*) when the Arhats addressed him and said, " The bonds of sin (the *klêsas*) not loosed, then all discussion is contradictory and useless. You had better go, and not dwell here."

On this Vasumitra answered, " The wise without doubt regard the law in the place of[108] Buddha, appointed for the conversion of the world, and therefore you [109] reasonably desire to compile true (*orthodox*) *sâstras*. As for myself, though not quick, yet in my poor way I have investigated the meaning of words. I have also studied with earnestness the obscure literature of the three *piṭakas* and the recondite meaning of the five *vidyâs;* and I have succeeded in penetrating their teaching,[110] dull as I am."

The Arhats answered, " It is impossible; but if it is as you say, you can stand by a little and presently get the condition of 'past learning.' Then you can enter the assembly; at present your presence is not possible."

Vasumitra answered, " I care for the condition of 'past learning' as little as for a drop of spittle; my mind seeks only the fruit of Buddha;[111] I do not run after little quests [*little sideways*]. I will throw this ball up into the air, and before it comes to earth I shall have got the holy condition [*fruit*] of 'past learning.' "

Then all the Arhats roundly scolded him, saying, " 'Intolerably arrogant' is your right title. The fruit of 'past learning' is the condition praised by all the Buddhas. You are bound to acquire this condition and scatter the doubts of the assembly."

---

a monastery and collected the three *Piṭakas.* Being about to compose the *Pi-p'o-sha-lun* (*Vibhâshâ Sâstra*), then," &c.

[108] That is, taking the place of, or standing in the stead of, Buddha.

[109] The assembly or convocation desires, &c. Or it may be translated thus: " Having collected the general, or right sense, you are now about to compose an orthodox treatise " (*i.e.*, the *Vibhâshâ Sâstra*).

[110] This at least seems to be the sense of the passage, but the force of the phrase *ch'hin in* is doubtful.

[111] That is, I seek only the condition of a Buddha.

Then Vasumitra cast the ball into the air; it was arrested by the Dêvas, who, before it fell, asked him this question: "In consequence of obtaining the fruit of Buddha, you shall succeed Maitrêya in his place (*in the Tushita heaven*); the three worlds shall honour you, and the four kinds of creatures (*all flesh*) shall look up to you with awe. Why then do you seek this little fruit?"

Then the Arhats, having witnessed all this, confessed their fault, and with reverence asked him to become their president. All difficulties that occurred in their discussion were referred to him for settlement. These five hundred sages and saints first composed in ten myriads of verses the *Upadêsa Sâstra* to explain the *Sûtra Piṭaka*.[112] Next they made in ten myriads of verses the *Vinaya Vibhâshâ Sâstra* to explain the *Vinaya Piṭaka;* and afterwards they made in ten myriad of verses the *Abhidharma Vibhâshâ Sâstra* [113] to explain the *Abhidharma Piṭaka.* Altogether they composed thirty myriad of verses in six hundred and sixty myriad of words, which thoroughly explained the three *Piṭakas.* There was no work of antiquity[114] to be compared with (*placed above*) their productions; from the deepest to the smallest question, they examined all,[115] explaining all minute expressions, so that their work has become universally known and is the resource of all students who have followed them.

---

[112] This definition of the *Upadêsa* (*U-po-ti-sho*) *Sâstra*, viz., a treatise to explain the *Sûtra Piṭaka* (*Su-ta-la-t'sang*), confirms the explanation generally given of the whole class of works so named. Burnouf (*Introd. Bud. Ind.*, p. 58) regards the term as equivalent to "instruction" or "explanation of esoteric doctrine." In Nêpâl the word is applied to the Tantra portion of the Buddhist writings. It is also used as an equivalent for *Abhidharma.* The *Upadêsa* class of books is the twelfth in the duodecimal division of the Northern School (Eitel, *Handbook*, s. voc.)

[113] '*O-pi-ta-mo-pi-po-sha-lun.* This work is generally called the *Abhidharma-mahâvibhâshâ Sâstra.* It was translated into Chinese by Hiuen Tsiang. It is said to be a commentary on Kâtyâyanîputra's *Jñânaprasthâna Sâstra*, belonging to the Sarvâstivâda class of books. It is in forty-three chapters (*vargas*), and consists of 438,449 Chinese characters. See Bunyiu Nanjio's *Catalogue*, No. 1263.

[114] Thousand ancient; but is *tsien* an error?

[115] Literally, "branches and leaves were investigated; shallow and deep places fathomed."

Kanishka-râja forthwith ordered these discourses to be engraved on sheets of red copper. He enclosed them in a stone receptacle, and having sealed this, he raised over it a *stûpa* with the Scriptures in the middle. He commanded the Yakshas [116] to defend the approaches to the kingdom, so as not to permit the other sects to get these *śâstras* and take them away, with the view that those dwelling in the country might enjoy the fruit of this labour.[117]

Having finished this pious labour, he returned with his army to his own capital.[118]

Having left this country by the western gate, he turned towards the east and fell on his knees, and again bestowed all this kingdom on the priesthood.

After Kanishka's death the Kritîya race again assumed the government, banished the priests, and overthrew religion.[119]

The king of Himatala,[120] of the country of To-hu-lo (Tukhâra), was by descent of the Śâkya race.[121] In the six-hundredth year after the *Nirvâna* of Buddha, he succeeded to the territory of his ancestor, and his heart was

---

[116] The Yakshas are supernatural beings employed to guard treasure or keep the way to a treasure. Sometimes they are regarded as malevolent beings, but not so necessarily. See General Cunningham, *Stûpa of Bharhut*, p. 20 ff. They are represented in this work as keeping the four gates of the *stûpa*.

[117] "With a view that they who wished to study them should in the country (*chung*) receive instruction." I cannot follow M. Julien's translation. He seems to regard the *stûpa* as a *saṅghârâma* or convent in which instruction was given; and he makes Kanishka give himself to study.

[118] That is, to the capital of Gandhâra.

[119] "The law of Buddha." The Kritîyas or Krityas are defined to be "demons who dig out corpses," or explained as "serfs" (persons bought, *krîta*). They are said to be either Yakshakrityas or Manushakrityas, the former being shaped like Yakshas, the latter like human beings. The Manushakrityas were those domestic slaves whom Madhyântika introduced into Kaśmîr (Eitel, *Handbook*, sub voc.) See also Cunningham, *Anc. Geog. of Ind.*, p. 93; and *ante*, note 94, p. 150.

[120] Himatala, defined in the text as *Sue-shan-hia*, "under the snowy mountains" (see *ante*, p. 42, n. 139).

[121] He was descended from one of the Śâkya youths who were driven from their country for resisting the invasion of Virûdhaka, the account of which will be found in the sixth book. Hiuen Tsiang's date places him about 280 A.D. (note 97, *ante*).

deeply imbued with affection for the law of Buddha.[122]
Hearing that the Kritîyas had overthrown the law of
Buddha, he assembled in his land the most warlike
(*courageous*) of his knights, to the number of three thousand, and under the pretence of being merchants laden
with many articles of merchandise and with valuable
goods, but having secretly concealed on their persons warlike instruments, they entered on this kingdom, and the
king of the country received them as his guests with
special honour.   He [123] then selected five hundred of these,
men of great courage and address, and armed them with
swords and provided them with choice merchandise to
offer to the king.

Then the king of Himatala, flinging off his cap,[124] proceeded towards the throne; the king of the Kritîyas, terrified, was at a loss what to do.   Having cut off the king's
head, (*the king of Himatala*) said to the officers standing
below, " I am the king of Himatala, belonging to Tukhâra.
I was grieved because this low-caste ruler practised such
outrages; therefore I have to-day punished his crimes;
but as for the people, there is no fault to be found with
them."   Having banished the ministers in charge of the
government to other states and pacified this country, he
commanded the priests to return, and built a *sanghârâma*,
and there settled them as in old time.   Then he left the
kingdom by the western gate (*pass*), and when outside he
bowed down with his face to the east, and gave in charity
to the priesthood (*the kingdom*).

As for the Kritîyas, as they had more than once
been put down by the priests and their religion overturned, in lapse of time their enmity had increased so
that they hated the law of Buddha.   After some years

122 "He planted his heart in the
law of Buddha, and the streams of
his affection flowed into the sea of
the law."

123 That is, the king of Himatala.

124 If the symbol in the text is
intended for *ch'hang*, it should be
translated "flinging away his robe,"
that is, the robe (or web of rich
cloth) that concealed the sword.   If
it be *maou*, then it would be "flinging away his cap."

they came again into power. This is the reason why at
the present time this kingdom is not much given to the
faith and the temples of the heretics are their sole
thought.

About 10 li to the south-east of the new city and to
the north of the old city,[125] and on the south of a great
mountain, is a *saṅghârâma* with about 300 priests in
it. In the *stûpa* (*attached to the convent*) is a tooth of
Buddha in length about an inch and a half, of a yellowish-
white colour; on religious days it emits a bright light.
In old days the Kritîya race having destroyed the law of
Buddha, the priests being dispersed, each one selected his
own place of abode. On this occasion one Śramaṇa, wandering throughout the Indies to visit and worship the
relics of Buddha (*traces of the Holy One*) and to exhibit
his sincere faith, after a while came to hear that his
native country was pacified and settled. Forthwith he
set out on his return, and on his way he met with a
herd of elephants rushing athwart his path through the
jungle and raising a trumpeting tumult. The Śramaṇa
having seen them, climbed up a tree to get out of their
way; then the herd of elephants rushed down to drink[126]
at a pool and to cleanse themselves with the water; then
surrounding the tree, they tore its roots, and by force
dragged it to the ground. Having got the Śramaṇa,
they put him on the back of one, and hurried off to
the middle of a great forest, where was a sick elephant
wounded (*swollen with a sore*), and lying on the ground

---

[125] General Cunningham says
Abu Rihân calls the capital Adish-
tan, which is the Sanskrit Adhish-
thâna or "chief town ;" and that is
the present city of Śrînagar, which
was built by Râja Pravarasêna
about the beginning of the sixth
century, and was therefore a comparatively new place at the time of
Hiuen Tsiang's visit. The "old
capital" was about two miles to the
south-east of Takht-i-Sulimân,
and is now called Pândrêthân, a Kaś-
miri corruption of Purânâdhishthâna,
or "the old chief city."—*Anc. Geog.
Ind.,* p. 93. Conf. Troyer's *Râjatar-
angiṇî,* tome i. p. 104, t. iii. pp. 336–
357 ; *Asiat. Res.,* vol. xv. p. 19 ; Lassen, *Ind. Alt.,* vol. ii. p. 912. The
mountain is Hariparvata or Hör-
parvat, now Takht-i-Sulimân.

[126] Not to drink, but to draw in
the water and use it for cooling
themselves.

at rest.   Taking the hand of the priest, it directed it
to the place of the hurt, where a rotten (*broken*) piece
of bamboo had penetrated.   The Śramaṇa thereupon drew
out the splinter and applied some medicinal herbs, and
tore up his garment to bind the foot with it.   Another
elephant taking a gold casket, brought it to the sick
elephant, who having received it gave it forthwith to the
Śramaṇa.   The Śramaṇa opening it, found in the inside
Buddha's tooth.   Then all the elephants surrounding him,
he knew not how to get away.   On the morrow, being a
fast-day, each elephant brought him some fruit for his
mid-day meal.   Having finished eating, they carried the
priest out of the forest a long way (*some hundred li*), and
then they set him down, and, after salutation paid, they
each retired.

The Śramaṇa coming to the western borders of the
country, crossed a rapid river; whilst so doing the boat
was nearly overwhelmed, when the men, consulting together, said, "The calamity that threatens the boat is
owing to the Śramaṇa; he must be carrying some relics
of Buddha, and the dragons have coveted them."

The master of the ship having examined (*his goods*), found
the tooth of Buddha.   Then the Śramaṇa, raising up the
relic, bowed his head, and called to the Nâgas and said, "I
now intrust this to your care; not long hence I will come
again and take it."   Then declining to cross the river,[127]
he returned to the bank and departed.   Turning to the river
he sighed and said, " Not knowing how to restrain these
Nâga creatures has been the cause of my calamity."   Then
going back to India, he studied the rules of restraining
dragons, and after three years he returned towards his
native country, and having come to the river-side he built
and appointed there an altar.   Then the Nâgas brought
the casket of Buddha's tooth and gave it to the Śramaṇa;
the Śramaṇa took it and brought it to this *saṅghârâma*
and henceforth worshipped it.

[127] That is, he did not land on the other side, but went back in the boat.

Fourteen or fifteen li to the south of the *sanghârâma* is
a little *sanghârâma* in which is a standing figure of Avalôkitêśvara Bôdhisattva. If any one vows to fast till he
dies unless he beholds this Bôdhisattva, immediately from
the image it comes forth glorious in appearance.

South-east of the little *sanghârâma* about 30 li or so,
we come to a great mountain, where there is an old (*ruined*)
sanghârâma, of which the shape is imposing and the ma-
sonry strong. But now it is in ruins; there is only left
one angle where there is a small double tower. There
are thirty priests or so, who study the Great Vehicle.
This is where of old Sanghabhadra, a writer of *śâstras*,
composed the *Shun-ching-li-lun* [128] (*Nyâyânusâra Śâstra*);
on the left and the right of the *sanghârâma* are *stûpas*
where are enshrined the relics (*śarîras*) of great Arhats.
The wild beasts and mountain apes gather flowers to offer
as religious oblations. Throughout the year they continue
these offerings without interruption, as if it were a traditional service. Many miraculous circumstances occur in
this mountain. Sometimes a stone barrier is split across;
sometimes on the mountain-top there remain the traces
of a horse; but all things of this sort are only mistaken
traces of the Arhats and Śrâmanêras, who in troops frequent this spot, and with their fingers trace these figures,
as if riding on horses or going to and fro (*on foot*), and
this has led to the difficulty in explaining these marks. [129]

Ten li to the east of the *sanghârâma* of Buddha's tooth,
between the crags of a mountain to the north, [130] is a small

---

[128] The *śâstra* composed by Seng-
kia - po-t'o-lo (Sanghabhadra) was
called in the first instance *K'iu-she-po-
lun*, or "the *śâstra* which destroys the
kôsha like hail" (*karakâ*). This title
was employed to denote the power
of the treatise to overturn the *Abhidharma-kôsha Śâstra* composed by
Vasubandhu. The title was afterwards changed by Vasubandhu himself to *Nyâyânusâra Śâstra* (*Shun-
ching-li-lun*). See Book iv. *infra*.

[129] This passage, which is obscure, seems to mean that the Śrâmanêras who follow the Arhats, or
the Śrâmanêras who are Arhats (for it
appears from one of Aśvaghôsha's
sermons (*Abstract of Four Lectures*,
p. 120) that a Śrâmanêra may arrive
at this condition), amuse themselves
by tracing figures of horses on the
rocks, and therefore such traces
have no meaning beyond this.

[130] That is, as it seems, a range of
mountains called the *Northern
Range*.

sanghârâma. In old days the great master of *sâstras*
called So-kin-ta-lo (Skandhila) composed here the treatise
called *Chung-ssc-fûn-pi-p'o-sha.*[131]

In the little convent is a *stûpa* of stone about 50 feet
high, where are preserved the *sarîras* of the bequeathed
body of an Arhat.

In former times there was an Arhat whose bodily size
was very great, and he eat and drank as an elephant.
People said in raillery, " He knows well enough how to
eat like a glutton, but what does he know of truth or
error ? " The Arhat, when about to pass to *Nirvâṇa*,
addressing the people round him, said, " Not long hence I
shall reach a condition of *anûpadhiścsa (without a remnant)*.[132] I wish to explain how I have attained to the excellent law."[133] The people hearing him again laughed together in ridicule. They all came together in an assembly
to see him put to shame.[134] Then the Arhat spoke thus
to the people : " I will tell you how, for your advantage,
my previous conditions of life and the causes thereof. In
my former birth I received, because of my desert, the body
of an elephant, and I dwelt in Eastern India, in the stable
of a king. At this time this country possessed a Shaman
who went forth to wander through India in search of the
holy doctrine of Buddha, the various *sûtras* and *sâstras*
Then the king gave me to the Shaman. I arrived in this
country carrying on my back the books of Buddha. Not
long after this I died suddenly. The merit I had obtained
by carrying these sacred books eventuated in my being
born as a man, and then again I died as a mortal.[135] But,

---

[131] Restored by Julien to *Vib-
hâshâ-prakaraṇa-pâda Sâstra.* Conf.
Jour. Asiat., ser. iv. tom. xiv.
No. 713; Bunyiu Nanjio's *Catalogue*,
Nos. 1277 and 1292.

[132] *Wou-yu-ni-pan*, that is, a condition of freedom from the *skandhas.*
Childers (*Pâli Dict.*, p. 526). It
means perfect or complete *Nir-
vâ.a.* See below, note 135.

[133] I wish to relate the steps
(*groundwork*) by which this body
(*i.e.*, *I myself*) arrived at this excellent condition, *or law.*

[134] Julien regards this phrase *'tch
shih*) as equivalent to " success or
non-success." It seems, however,
more agreeable to the context to
translate it as here—to see him " get
loss," *i.e.*, disgraced.

[135] I died " with remains ; " that
is, I died, but was destined to be re-

thanks to the merit I possessed, I soon (*was born in the same condition, and*) assumed the coloured clothes of a hermit. I diligently set after the means of putting off (*the shackles of existence*), and gave myself no repose. Thus I obtained the six supernatural powers and cut off my connection with the three worlds. However, when I eat I have preserved my old habits, but every day I moderate my appetite, and only take one-third of what my body requires as nourishment." Although he thus spoke, men were still incredulous. Forthwith he ascended into the air and entered on the *Samâdhi* called *the brilliancy of flame.* From his body proceeded smoke and fire,[136] and thus he entered *Nirvâṇa;* his remains (*bones*) fell to the earth, and they raised a *stûpa* over them.

Going north-west 200 li or so of the royal city, we come to the *sanghârâma* called "Mai-lin."[137] It was here the master of *śâstras* called Pûrṇa[138] composed a commentary on the *Vibhâshâ Śâstra.*

To the west of the city 140 or 150 li there is a great river, on the borders of which, to the north, resting on the southern slope of a mountain, is a *sanghârâma* belonging to the Mahâsaṁghika (Ta-chong-pu) school, with about 100 priests. It was here in old time that Fo-ti-la (Bôdhila),[139] a master of *śâstras*, composed the treatise *Tsih-chin-lun.*[140]

From this going south-west, and crossing some mountains and traversing many precipices, going 700 li or so, we come to the country Puu-nu-tso (Punach).

---

born, not having got rid of the *skandhas,* or "conditions of individual existence." In Note 132 above, we find just the opposite phrase, " *Wou yu,*" *i.e.,* "without remains." Julien has omitted this passage.

[136] This kind of miracle is frequently named in Buddhist books. See *Fo-sho-hing-tsan-king,* v. 1353 ff.

[137] I adopt *mai lin* from Julien. In my text the symbol appears to be *shang,* but there may be a misprint.

Julien doubtfully restores *mai-lin* to Vikritavana.

[138] In Chinese, Yuen-mun.

[139] I have adopted this restoration from Julien. The Chinese symbols might also be restored to Buddhatara.

[140] The *Tsih-chin-lun* is restored by Julien doubtfully to *Tattvasañchaya Śâstra.* This treatise belonged to the Mahâsanghika collection.

PUN-NU-TSO [PUNACH].

This kingdom [141] is about 2000 li in circuit, with many mountains and river-courses, so that the arable land is very contracted. The seed is sown, however, at regular intervals, and there are a quantity of flowers and fruits. There are many sugar-canes, but no grapes. Amalas,[142] Udumbaras, Môchas, &c., flourish, and are grown in large quantities like woods; they are prized on account of their taste. The climate is warm and damp. The people are brave. They wear ordinarily cotton clothing. The disposition of the people is true and upright; they are Buddhists.[143] There are five *sanghârâmas*, mostly deserted. There is no independent ruler, the country being tributary to Kaśmîr. To the north of the chief town is a *sanghârâma* with a few priests. Here there is a *stûpa* which is celebrated for its miracles.

Going south-east from this 400 li or so, we come to the kingdom of Ho-lo-she-pu-lo (Râjapuri).

HO-LO-SHE-PU-LO [RÂJAPURI].

This kindgom [144] is about 4000 li in circuit; the capital town is about 10 li round. It is naturally very strong, with many mountains, hills, and river-courses, which cause the arable land to be contracted. The produce therefore is small. The climate and the fruits of the soil are like those of Pun-nu-tso. The people are quick and hasty; the country has no independent ruler, but is subject to Kaśmîr. There are ten *sanghârâmas*, with a very small number of priests. There is one temple of Dêvas, with an enormous number of unbelievers.

---

[141] Punacha, or Punach, is described by Cunningham (*Anc. Geog.*, 128) as a small state, called Punats by the Kaśmîris, bounded on the west by the Jhelam, on the north by the Pir Pańchâl range, and on the east and south-east by the small state of Râjaurî.

[142] An-mo-lo is *Myrobalan emblica*, and Meu-che, the plantain.

[143] They have faith in the three gems.

[144] Identified by Cunningham with the petty chiefship of Râjaurî or Râjapuri, south of Kaśmîr and south-east of Punach (*op. cit.*, p. 129).

From the country of Lan-po till this, the men are of a coarse appearance, their disposition fierce and passionate, their language vulgar and uncultivated, with scarce any manners or refinement.   They do not properly belong to India, but are frontier people, with barbarous habits.

Going south-east from this, descending the mountains and crossing a river, after 700 li we come to the kingdom of Tsih-kia (Takka).

END OF BOOK III.

BOOK IV.

Relates to fifteen countries, viz., (1) *Tseh-kia;* (2) *Chi-na-po-ti;* (3) *Che-lan-t'o-lo;* (4) *K'iu-lu-to;* (5) *She-to-t'u-lo;* (6) *Po-li-ye-to-lo;* (7) *Mo-t'u-lo;* (8) *Sa-t'a-ni-shi-fa-lo;* (9) *Su-lo-kin-na;* (10) *Mo-ti-pu-lo;* (11) *Po-lo-ki-mo-pu-lo;* (12) *Kiu-pi-shwong-na;* (13) *'O-hi-chi-ta-lo;* (14) *Pi-lo-shan-na;* (15) *Kie-pi-ta.*

1. KINGDOM OF TSEH-KIA (ṬAKKA).

THIS kingdom [1] is about 10,000 li in circuit. On the east it borders on the river Pi-po-che (Vipâśû); [2] on the west it borders on the Sin-tu river. The capital of the country is about 20 li in circuit. The soil is suitable for rice and produces much late-sown corn. It also produces gold,

---

[1] Takkadéśa, the country of the Bâhîkas, is named in the *Râjataraṅgiṇî* (v. 150), and said to be a part of the kingdom of Gurjjara, which Râja Alakhâna was obliged to cede to Kaśmîr between the years 883 A.D. and 901 A.D. (Cunningham, *Geog.*, 149). The Ṭakkas were a powerful tribe living near the Chenâb, and were at one time the undisputed lords of the Panjâb. The kingdom of Tsih-kia is probably, therefore, that of the Ṭakkas. *Asiat. Res.*, vol. xv. pp. 108 f. ; Lassen, *I. A.*, vol. i. p. 973. Julien restores it to Tchéka. It seems that Hiuen Tsiang kept to the south-west from Râjapuri, and crossed the Chenâb after two days' march near the small town of Jammu or Jambu (perhaps the Jayapura of Hwui-lih), and then pressed on the next day to the town of Sâkala, where he arrived the day after. The distance would thus be about 700 li, or 140 miles

(Cunningham's *Anc. Geog.*, map vi., compared with Elphinstone's map (*India*); on this last map the trade route is so marked). In the translation of Hwui-lih, M. Julien has made the distance from Râjapuri to Tchéka to be 200 li (p. 90); it should be 700 li, as in the original. He has also translated *how jih* by to-morrow (lendemain), instead of *the day after the morrow.*

[2] The Vipâśâ or Vipât, the Biyas river, the most eastern of the five rivers of the Panjâb, the Hyphasis (Ὕφασις) of Arrian (*Anab.*, lib. vi. c. 8, *Ind.*, cc. 2, 3, 4 ; Diodoros, lib. xvii. c. 93). Pliny (lib. vii. c. 17, 21) and Curtius (lib. ix. c. 1) call it Hypasis, and Ptolemy (lib. vii. c. i. 26, 27) has Βίβασις, while Strabo has Ὕπανις. It rises in the Himâlaya, and, after a course of about 220 miles, joins the Satlaj south-east of Amṛitsar.

silver, the stone called *teou*,[3] copper and iron.   The climate is very warm, and the land is subject to hurricanes.   The people are quick and violent, their language coarse and uncultivated.   For clothing they wear a very shining white fabric which they call *kiau-che-ye* (*Kauśêya*, silk), and also morning-red cloth (*chau hia*),[4] and other kinds. Few of them believe in Buddha ; many sacrifice to the heavenly spirits (*Dêvas and spirits*).   There are about ten *sanghârâmas* and some hundreds of temples.   There were formerly in this country many houses of charity (*goodness or happiness—Puṇyaśâlâs*) for keeping the poor and the unfortunate.   They provided for them medicine and food, clothing and necessaries; so that travellers were never badly off.

To the south-west of the capital about 14 or 15 li we come to the old town of Śâkala[5] (She-kie-lo).   Although

---

[3] The *teou-shih*, of which such frequent mention is made by Hiuen Tsiang, is said to be a compound of equal parts of copper and calamine (silicate of zinc).   See Julien *in loc.*, n. 2.   Medhurst (*Dict. s. v.*) calls it "native copper."

[4] The *chau-hia* robe.   This may mean either court-red or morning-red ; it may refer to its colour, but more probably to its lightness.   We should have expected a phonetic combination in this name, as in the preceding, viz., *Kauśêya*, but *chau-hia* has no phonetic value, although it might be compared with the Sanskrit *sûksh(ma)*.

[5] Śâkala.   Pâṇini (iv. 2, 75) has Sâṅkala, the Σάγγαλα of Arrian (*Anab. Alex.*, lib. v. c. 22), and probably the same place as Ptolemy (lib. vii. c. i. 46) designates by Σαγαλα ἡ καὶ Εὐθυδημία.   Sâkala occurs in the *Mahâbhârata* (ii. 1196, viii. 2033) as the capital of the Madras. Burnouf, *Introd.*, pp. 559 f.; *Ind. Ant.*, vol. i. pp. 22 f. ; Wilson, *Ariana Ant.*, pp. 196 f. ; *As. Res.*, vol. xv. pp. 107 f.; *J. A. S. Ben.*, vol. vi. pp. 57 f. ; Lassen, *Zeitsch. f. d. K. d. Morg.*, vol. i. p. 353, vol. iii. pp. 154 f., 212; *Ind.*

Alt., vol. i. p. 801.   Śâkala has been identified by General Cunningham with Sâṅglawâla-Tiba, to the west of of the Râvi (*Anc. Geog. of India*, p. 180).   The capital of the country is not named by Hiuen Tsiang.   It appears from Hwui-lih that the pilgrim went straight to Śâkala, and did not visit the capital.   He places it 14 or 15 li to the north-east of Śâkala.   Although the route taken is differently described in "the Life" and in the *Si-yu-ki*, yet in the main it is sufficiently clear.   After leaving Râja-puri the pilgrim travels south-west for two days, and, crossing the Chenâb, he lodged for one night in a temple belonging to the heretics just outside Jayapura.   The second day after leaving this town (direction not given) he arrived at Śâkala. Proceeding a little way to the eastward of a town called Nârasiṃha (the situation of which is not given, but was probably a short distance east of Śâkala), he was robbed by brigands and lodged in a neighbouring village ; starting from which on the next day, he passed the frontiers of the kingdom of Takka, and reached a large town with many thousand

its walls are thrown down, the foundations are still firm
and strong. It is about 20 li in circuit. In the midst
of it they have built a little town of about 6 or 7 li in
circuit; the inhabitants are prosperous and rich. This
was the old capital of the country. Some centuries ago
there was a king called Mo-hi-lo-kiu-lo (Mahirakula),[6]
who established his authority in this town and ruled
over India. He was of quick talent, and naturally brave.
He subdued all the neighbouring provinces without exception.[7] In his intervals of leisure he desired to examine
the law of Buddha, and he commanded that one among
the priests of superior talent[8] should wait on him. Now
it happened that none of the priests dared to attend to
his command. Those who had few desires and were content, did not care about distinction; those of superior
learning and high renown despised the royal bounty
(*glitter*). At this time there was an old servant in the
king's household who had long worn the religious garments. He was of distinguished ability and able to enter
on discussion, · and was very eloquent. The priests put
him forward in answer to the royal appeal. The king
said, "I have a respect for the law of Buddha, and I

inhabitants. This was probably
Lahor, the old Lobâwar (the Râvî
was evidently the boundary *de facto*
of Ṭakka). He remained here one
month, and then proceeding eastward, he arrived at the capital of a
country Chînapati, 500 li from Sâkala. This was probably the large
old town of Patti, 10 miles to the
west of the Biyas river. About 10
miles south-west of this (the *Si-yu-
ki* has 500 *li* by mistake for 50) was
a monastery; this would place us
at the point of the confluence of the
Biyas and Satlaj rivers. The question to be settled is whether at this
point there is a mountain or a hill
round which for a distance of 20 li
monasteries and *stûpas* could be
grouped. General Cunningham
speaks of this neighbourhood as con-
stituting the sandy bed of the Biyas
river (*op. cit.*, p. 201). But, at any
rate, such a situation agrees with
the next measurement of 140 or 150
li to Jâlandhar. We should thus
have a total of 660 li (132 miles)
eastward from Sâkala to Jâlandhara,
which is as nearly as possible correct
as projected on General Cunningham's map (*op. cit.* No. vi.)

[6] For Mahirakula, see *ante*, Book
iii. n. 1. The interpretation of the
name is given by the Chinese editor
as *Ta-tso. i.e.*, "great tribe or family;"
but *mahira* or *mihira* signifies "the
sun;" it should therefore be "the
family of the sun."

[7] The kingdoms of the neighbouring districts all submitted to him.

[8] Or "eminent virtue;" but *tih*
(virtue) refers to general gifts or
endowments.

invited from far any renowned priest (*to come and instruct me*), and now the congregation have put forward this servant to discuss with me.   I always thought that amongst the priests there were men of illustrious ability; after what has happened to-day what further respect can I have for the priesthood?"   He then issued an edict to destroy all the priests through the five Indies, to overthrow the law of Buddha, and leave nothing remaining.

Bâlâditya[9]-râja, king of Magadha, profoundly honoured the law of Buddha and tenderly nourished his people. When he heard of the cruel persecution and atrocities of Mahirakula (Ta-tso), he strictly guarded the frontiers of his kingdom and refused to pay tribute.   Then Mahirakula raised an army to punish his rebellion.   Bâlâditya-râja, knowing his renown, said to his ministers, "I hear that these thieves are coming, and I cannot fight with them (*their troops*); by the permission of my ministers I will conceal my poor person among the bushes of the morass."

Having said this, he departed from his palace and wandered through the mountains and deserts.   Being very much beloved in his kingdom, his followers amounted to

---

[9] Bâlâditya, explained by *yeou jih*, i.e., the young sun or the rising sun. Julien translates it too literally, "le soleil des enfants." Julien has observed and corrected the mistake in the note, where the symbol is *wan* for *yeou*. With respect to the date of Bâlâditya, who was contemporary with Mahirakula who put Siṁha, the twenty-third Buddhist patriarch, to death, we are told that he was a grandson of Buddhagupta (Hwui-lih, p. 150, Julien's trans.), and according to General Cunningham (*Archæolo.. Survey*, vol. ix. p. 21) Buddhagupta was reigning approximately A.D. 349, and his silver coins extend his reign to A.D. 368. His son was Tathâgatagupta, and his successor was Bâlâditya. Allowing fifty years for these reigns, we arrive at 420 A.D. for the end, probably, of Bâlâditya's reign. This, of course, depends on the initial date of the Gupta period; if it is placed, as Dr. Oldenberg (*Ind. Antiq.*, vol. x. p. 321) suggests, A.D. 319, then the reign of Buddhagupta will have to be brought down 125 years later, and he would be reigning 493 A.D.; in this case Bâlâditya would be on the throne too late for the date of Siṁha, who was certainly many years before Buddhadharma (the twenty-eighth patriarch), who reached China A.D. 520. The earlier date harmonises with the Chinese records, which state that a Life of Vasubandhu, the twenty-first patriarch, was written by Kumârajiva A.D. 409, and also that a history of the patriarchs down to Siṁha, whom we place hypothetically about 420 A.D., was translated in China A.D. 472; both these statements are possible if the date proposed be given to Bâlâditya.

many myriads, who fled with him and hid themselves in the islands [10] of the sea.

Mahirakula-râja, committing the army to his younger brother, himself embarked on the sea to go attack Bâlâditya. The king guarding the narrow passes, whilst the light cavalry were out to provoke the enemy to fight, sounded the golden drum, and his soldiers suddenly rose on every side and took Mahirakula alive as captive, and brought him into the presence (*of Bâlâditya*).

The king Mahirakula being overcome with shame at his defeat, covered his face with his robe. Bâlâditya sitting on his throne with his ministers round him, ordered one of them to tell the king to uncover himself as he wished to speak with him.

Mahirakula answered, "The subject and the master have changed places; that enemies should look on one another is useless; and what advantage is there in seeing my face during conversation?"

Having given the order three times with no success, the king then ordered his crimes to be published, and said, "The field of religious merit connected with the three precious objects of reverence is a public [11] blessing; but this you have overturned and destroyed like a wild beast. Your religious merit is over, and unprotected by fortune you are my prisoner. Your crimes admit of no extenuation and you must die."

At this time the mother of Bâlâditya was of wide celebrity on account of her vigorous intellect and her skill in casting horoscopes. Hearing that they were going to kill Mahirakula, she addressed Bâlâditya-râja and said, "I have understood that Mahirakula is of remarkable beauty and vast wisdom. I should like to see him once."

Bâlâditya-râja (Yeou-jih) ordered them to bring in Mahirakula to the presence of his mother in her palace. Then she said, "Alas! Mahirakula, be not ashamed! Worldly

---

[10] It may be translated, "an island of the sea."

[11] Belonging to the world or creatures born in the world.

things are impermanent; success and discomfiture follow one another according to circumstances. I regard myself as your mother and you as my son; remove the covering from your face and speak to me."

Mahirakula said, " A little while ago I was prince of a victorious country, now I am a prisoner condemned to death. I have lost my kingly estate and I am unable to offer my religious services;[12] I am ashamed in the presence of my ancestors and of my people. In very truth I am ashamed before all, whether before heaven or earth. I find no deliverance.[13] Therefore I hide my face with my mantle." The mother of the king said, " Prosperity or the opposite depends on the occasion ; gain and loss come in turn. If you give way to events (*things*), you are lost; but if you rise above circumstances, though you fall, you may rise again. Believe me, the result of deeds depends on the occasion. Lift the covering from your face and speak with me. I may perhaps save your life."

Mahirakula, thanking her, said, " I have inherited a kingdom without having the necessary talent for government, and so I have abused the royal power in inflicting punishment; for this reason I have lost my kingdom. But though I am in chains, yet I desire life if only for a day. Let me then thank you with uncovered face for your offer of safety." Whereupon he removed his mantle and showed his face. The king's mother said, " My son is well-favoured ;[14] he will die after his years are accomplished." Then she said to Bâlâditya, " In agreement with former regulations, it is right to forgive crime and to love to give life. Although Mahirakula has long accumulated sinful actions, yet his remnant of merit is not altogether exhausted. If you kill this man, for twelve

---

[12] The ancestral sacrifices.

[13] Perhaps a better translation would be : " In truth I am ashamed; whether I cast my eyes downward or upward, in heaven or earth I am unable to find deliverance."

[14] This is an obscure sentence ; Julien translates it " have a care for yourself : you must accomplish the term of your life."

years you will see him with his pale face before you. I gather from his air that he will be the king of a small country; let him rule over some small kingdom in the north."

Then Bâlâditya-râja, obeying his dear mother's command, had pity on the prince bereft of his kingdom; gave him in marriage to a young maiden and treated him with exteme courtesy. Then he assembled the troops he had left and added a guard to escort him from the island.

Mahirakula-râja's brother having gone back, established himself in the kingdom. Mahirakula having lost his royal estate, concealed himself in the isles and deserts, and going northwards to Kaśmîr, he sought there an asylum. The king of Kaśmîr received him with honour, and moved with pity for his loss, gave him a small territory and a town to govern. After some years he stirred up the people of the town to rebellion, and killed the king of Kaśmîr and placed himself on the throne. Profiting by this victory and the renown it got him, he went to the west, plotting against the kingdom of Gandhâra. He set some soldiers in ambush and took and killed the king. He exterminated the royal family and the chief minister, overthrew the *stûpas*, destroyed the *sanghârâmas*, altogether one thousand six hundred foundations. Besides those whom his soldiers had killed there were nine hundred thousand whom he was about to destroy without leaving one. At this time all the ministers addressed him and said, "Great king! your prowess has gained a great victory, and our soldiers are no longer engaged in conflict. Now that you have punished the chief, why would you charge the poor people with fault? Let us, insignificant as we are, die in their stead."

The king said, "You believe in the law of Buddha and greatly reverence the mysterious law of merit. Your aim is to arrive at the condition of Buddha, and then you will declare fully, under the form of *Jâtakas*,[15] my evil

<hr>

[15] That is to say, when they had arrived at the condition of omni- science they would in future ages declare how Mahirakula was suffering

deeds, for the good of future generations. Now go back to your estates, and say no more on the subject."

Then he slew three ten myriads of people of the first rank by the side of the Sin-tu river; the same number of the middle rank he drowned in the river, and the same number of the third rank he divided among his soldiers (*as slaves*). Then he took the wealth of the country he had destroyed, assembled his troops, and returned. But before the year was out he died.[16] At the time of his death there was thunder and hail and a thick darkness; the earth shook and a mighty tempest raged. Then the holy saints said in pity, "For having killed countless victims and overthrown the law of Buddha, he has now fallen into the lowest hell,[17] where he shall pass endless ages of revolution." [18]

In the old town of Sâkala (She-ki-lo) is a *sanghârâma* with about 100 priests, who study the Little Vehicle. In old days Vasubandhu (Shi-t'sin) Bodhisattva composed in this place the treatise called *Shing-i-tai* (*Paramârthasatya Sâstra*).

By the side of the convent is a *stûpa* about 200 feet high; on this spot the four former Buddhas preached the law, and here again are the traces of their walking to and fro (*king-hing*).

To the north-west of the *sanghârâma* 5 or 6 li is a *stûpa* about 200 feet high built by Asôka-raja. Here also the four past Buddhas preached.

About 10 li to the north-east of the new capital we come to a *stûpa* of stone about 200 feet in height, built by Asôka. This is where Tathâgata, when he was going

under some form of birth or other, in consequence of his evil deeds. This was one of the methods of Buddha's teaching.

[16] The expression *tsu lo* means "to wither away like a falling leaf."

[17] The lowest hell is the Wu-kan-ti-yuh, the hell without interval (*avîchi*), *i.e.*, without interval of rest, a place of incessant torment. It is the lowest of the places of torment. See *Catena of Buddhist Scriptures*, p. 59.

[18] This may also mean that his torments even then, *i.e.*, after this punishment, would not be finished. The Buddhist idea of the suffering in *Avîchi* was not connected with its eternal duration. See Eitel, *Handbook*, sub voc.

northward on his work of conversion, stopped in the middle of the road.   In the records of India (*In-tu-ki*) it is said, " In this *stúpa* are many relics; on holidays they emit a bright light."

From this [19] going east 500 li or so, we come to Chi-na-po-ti (Chinapati) country.   .

CHI-NA-PO-TI (CHÎNAPATI).[20]

This country is about 2000 li in circuit,   The capital is about 14 or 15 li round.   It produces abundant harvests; [21] the fruit trees are thinly scattered.   The people are contented and peaceful; the resources of the country are abundant.   The climate is hot and humid; the people are timid and listless.   They are given to promiscuous study, and there are amongst them believers and the contrary. There are ten *sanghârâmas* and eight Dêva temples.

Formerly, when Kanishka-râja was on the throne, his fame spread throughout the neighbouring countries, and his military power was recognised by all.   The tributary princes [22] to the west of the (*Yellow*) River, in recognition of his authority, sent hostages to him.   Kanishka-râja having received the hostages, he treated them with marked attention.   During the three seasons of the year

[19] That is, from Sâkala; not from the large city (Lahor) on the frontiers of Takka, as V. de St. Martin states (*Mémoire*, p. 330).

[20] The country of Chinapati appears to have stretched from the Râvî to the Satlaj.   General Cunningham places the capital at Chinô or Chinigari, 11 miles north of Amrîtsar (*Arch. Survey*, vol. xiv. p. 54).   This situation does not agree with the subsequent bearings and distances.   It is, for example, some 60 miles (300 li) north-west from Sultânpur (Tâmasavana) instead of 10 miles (50 li): moreover, Jâlañdhara bears south-east from Chinô instead of north-east, and the distance is nearly 70 miles instead of 28 or 30.   The situation of the large and very old town called Patti or Pati, 10 miles to the west of the Biyas river and 27 to the north-east of Kasûr, appears to suit the measurements and bearings as nearly as possible (*Anc. Geog. Ind.*, p. 200).   It is unfortunate, however, that the distances in General Cunningham's maps in the *Anc. Geog. of Ind.*, and the volume of the *Arch. Survey* do not agree.

[21] Literally, sowing and reaping are rich and productive.

[22] I translate it thus after Julien, as there is some obscurity in the text.   It might, perhaps, be rendered " the united tribes of the Fan people."   The Fan were Tibetans or associated tribes.

he appointed them separate establishments, and afforded them special guards of troops.[23] This country was the residence of the hostages during the winter. This is the reason why it is called Chînapati,[24] after the name of the residence of the hostages.

There existed neither pear nor peach in this kingdom and throughout the Indies until the hostages planted them, and therefore the peach is called *Chînâni*, and the pear is called *Chînarâjaputra*.[25] For this reason the men of this country have a profound respect for the Eastern land. Moreover (*when they saw me*) they pointed with their fingers, and said one to another, "This man is a native of the country of our former ruler.[26]

To the south-east of the capital 500[27] li or so, we come to the convent called Ta-mo-su-fa-na (*dark forest, i.e.,* Tâ-masavana). There are about 300 priests in it, who study the docrine of the Sarvâstivâda school. They (*the congregation*) have a dignified address, and are of conspicuous virtue and pure life. They are deeply versed in the teaching of the Little Vehicle. The 1000 Buddhas of the Bhadrakalpa will explain, in this country, to the assembly of the Dêvas the principles of the excellent law.

Three hundred years after the *Nirvâṇa* of Buddha the

<hr>

[23] Literally, "four soldiers stood on guard," *i.e.*, they had four soldiers outside their quarters to protect them.

[24] Rendered in a note "*Tang fung, i.e.,* "lord of China;" this seems to show that *Pati* is the right restoration of *po-ti* (compare Cunningham, *Arch. Surv. of India*, vol. xiv. p. 54). The fact of the name China being given to this country on account of the hostages confirms the restoration of *Charaka* to *Serika, ante,* Book i. p. 57, n. 203.

[25] Cunningham remarks that there can be no doubt of the introduction of the China peach, as in the north-west of India it is still known by that name (*op. cit.*, p. 54).

[26] That is, of Kanishka and his associates. They belonged to the Gushân tribe of the Yueï-chi, who came originally from the borders of China. See *ante*, p. 56, n. 200.

[27] In the life of Hiuen Tsiang by Hwui-lih, the distance given from the capital of Chînapati to the convent of "the dark forest" is 50 li (Book ii. p. 102, Julien's translation). This is probably the correct distance : the 500 li in the text is an error of the copyist. The convent is fixed by General Cunningham at Sûltanpur or Dalla Sûltanpur. It is one of the largest towns in the Jâlandhara Doab (*op. cit.*, p. 55).

master of *śâstras* called Kâtyâyana composed here the *Fa-chi-lun* (*Abhidharmajñâna-prasthâna Śâstra*).[28]

In the convent of *the dark forest* there is a *stûpa* about 200 feet high, which was erected by Aśôka-râja. By its side are traces of the four past Buddhas, where they sat and walked. There is a succession of little *stûpas* and large stone houses facing one another, of an uncertain number; here, from the beginning of the kalpa till now, saints who have obtained the fruit (*of Arhats*) have reached *Nirvâna*. To cite all would be difficult. Their teeth and bones still remain. The convents gird the mountain[29] for about 20 li in circuit, and the *stûpas* containing relics of Buddha are hundreds and thousands in number; they are crowded together, so that one overshadows the other.

Going north-east from this country, 140 or 150 li, we come to the country of Che-lan-ta-lo (Jâlandhara).

CHE-LAN-T'O-LO (JÂLANDHARA).

This kingdom[30] is about 1000 li from east to west, and about 800 li from north to south. The capital is 12 or 13 li in circuit. The land is favourable for the cultiva-

---

[28] This work was translated into Chinese by Sanghadêva and another in A.D. 383. Another translation was made by Hiuen Tsiang A.D. 657. If the usual date of Buddha's *Nirvâna* be adopted (viz., 400 years before Kanishka), Kâtyâyana would have flourished in the first century or about 20 B.C. See Weber, *Sansk. Liter.*, p. 222. His work was the foundation of the *Abhidharma-mahâvibhâshâ Śâstra*, composed during the council under Kanishka. (See Bunyiu Nanjio, *Catalogue of Buddhist Tripit.*, No. 1263).

[29] There is probably a false reading in the text, either (1) *Shan*, a mountain, is a mistake for *saïg*, which would give us *sang-kia-lan*, "sanghârâma," instead of *kia-lan*, or else (2) *shan* is for *yau*, a very common misprint. In the first case the translation would then be "the teeth and bones still exist around the sanghârâma;" or, if the second reading be adopted, the rendering would be "the teeth and bones still exist all round, *from* (*yau*) the *kia-lan*, for a circuit of 20 li," &c. Perhaps the first correction is preferable. I am satisfied the reading, as it is, is corrupt.

[30] Jâlandhara, a well-known place in the Panjâb (lat. 31° 19' N., long. 75° 28' E.) We may therefore safely reckon from it in testing Hiuen Tsiang's figures. From Sultânpur to Jâlandhara is as nearly as possible 50 miles north-east. Hiuen Tsiang gives 150 or 140 li in the same direction. Assuming the capital of Chinapati to be 50 li north-west of Sultânpur, that distance and bearing would place us on the right bank of the Biyâs river, near the old town of Patti.

tion of cereals, and it produces much rice. The forests are thick and umbrageous, fruits and flowers abundant. The climate is warm and moist, the people brave and impetuous, but their appearance is common and rustic. The houses are rich and well supplied. There are fifty convents, or so; about 2000 priests. They have students both of the Great and Little Vehicle. There are three temples of Dêvas and about 500 heretics, who all belong to the l'âśupatas (*cinder-sprinkled*).

A former king of this land showed great partiality for the heretics, but afterwards, having met with an Arhat and heard the law, he believed and understood it. Therefore the king of Mid-India, out of regard for his sincere faith, appointed him sole inspector of the affairs of religion (*the three gems*) throughout the five Indies. Making light of party distinctions (*this or that*), with no preference or dislike, he examined into the conduct of the priests, and probed their behaviour with wonderful sagacity. The virtuous and the well-reported of, he reverenced and openly rewarded; the disorderly he punished. Wherever there were traces of the holy one (*or*, ones), he built either *stûpas* or *sanghârâmas*, and there was no place within the limits of India he did not visit and inspect.

Going north-east from this, skirting along some high mountain passes and traversing some deep valleys, follow-

Reckoning back to Śâkala, the distance (Cunningham's *Anc. Geog. Ind.*, map vi.) is just 100 miles north of west. Hiuen Tsiang gives 500 li west. From this it seems that the computation of *five* li to the mile is, in this part of India at least, a safe one. For a full account of Jâlandhara and its importance, see Cunningham (*op. cit.*, pp. 137 ff.) It is sometimes stated that the council under Kanishka was held in the Jâlandhara convent, that is, the Tâmasavana Sanghârâma (V. de St. Martin, *Mémoire*, p. 333 n.) The fact that Kâtyâyana lived and wrote in this establishment, and that the great work of the council was to write a commentary on his *śâstra*, would so far be in accord with the statement. Hiuen Tsiang on his return journey was accompanied to Jâlandhara by Udita, the king of North India, who made this his capital (*Vie*, p. 260). Shortly after this a Shaman, Yuan-chiu, from China stopped here four years, studying Sanskrit with the Mung king, perhaps the same Udita (*J. R. A. S.*, N.S., vol. xiii. p. 563). The way through Kapiśa was shortly after this time (664 A.D.) occupied by the Arabs (*op. cit.*, p. 564).

ing a dangerous road, and crossing many ravines, going 700 li or so, we come to the country of K'iu-lu-to (Kulûta).

<h2 style="text-align:center">K'IU-LU-TO (KULÛTA).</h2>

This country[31] is about 3000 li in circuit, and surrounded on every side by mountains. The chief town is about 14 or 15 li round. The land is rich and fertile, and the crops are duly sown and gathered. Flowers and fruits are abundant, and the plants and trees afford a rich vegetation. Being contiguous to the Snowy Mountains, there are found here many medicinal (*roots*) of much value. Gold, silver, and copper are found here—fire-drops (*crystal*) and native copper (*tcou*). The climate is unusually cold, and hail or snow continually falls. The people are coarse and common in appearance, and are much afflicted with goitre and tumours, Their nature is hard and fierce; they greatly regard justice and bravery. There are about twenty *sanghârâmas*, and 1000 priests or so. They mostly study the Great Vehicle; a few practise (*the rules of*) other schools (*nikâyas*). There are fifteen Dêva temples: different sects occupy them without distinction.

Along the precipitous sides of the mountains and hollowed into the rocks are stone chambers which face one another. Here the Arhats dwell or the Rîshis stop.

In the middle of the country is a *stûpa* built by Asôka-râja. Of old the Tathâgata came to this country with his followers to preach the law and to save men. This *stûpa* is a memorial of the traces of his presence.

Going north from this, along a road thick with dangers and precipices, about 1800 or 1900 li, along mountains and valleys, we come to the country of Lo-u-lo (Lahul).[32]

North of this 2000 li or so, travelling by a road dan-

---

[31] Kulûta, the district of Kulu in the upper valley of the Biyâs river. It is also called Kôlûka and Kôlûta, —*Râmây.*, iv. 43, 8; *Brih. Sanh.*, xiv. 22, 29; Wilson, *Hind. Theat.*, vol. ii. p. 165; Saint-Martin, *Etude sur la Géog. Grec.*, pp. 300 f. The present capital is Sultânpur (Cunningham). The old capital was called Nagara or Nagarkôt.

[32] Lahul, the Lho-yal of the Tibetans.

gerous and precipitous, where icy winds and flying snow (*assault the traveller*), we come to the country of Mo-lo-so (called also San-po-ho).[33]

Leaving the country of K'iu-lu-to and going south 700 li or so, passing a great mountain and crossing a wide river, we come to the country of She-to-t'u-lo (Śatadru).

SHE-TO-T'U-LU (ŚATADRU).

This country[34] is about 2000 li from east to west, and borders on a great river. The capital is 17 or 18 li in circuit. Cereals grow in abundance, and there is very much fruit. There is an abundance of gold and silver found here, and precious stones. For clothing the people wear a very bright silk stuff; their garments are elegant and rich. The climate is warm and moist. The manners of the people are soft and agreeable; the men are docile and virtuous. The high and low take their proper place. They all sincerely believe in the law of Buddha and show it great respect. Within and without the royal city there are ten *sanghârâmas*, but the halls are now deserted and cold, and there are but few priests. To the south-east of the city 3 or 4 li is a *stûpa* about 200 feet high, which was built by Aśôka-râja. Beside it are the traces where the four past Buddhas sat or walked.

Going again from this south-west about 800 li, we come to the kingdom of Po-li-ye-to-lo (Pâryâtra).

<hr>

[33] This country is also called San-po-ho (Sampaha?).— *Ch. Ed.* The suggestion of General Cunningham that Mo-lo-so should be read Marpo (Mo-lo-po, St. Martin, *Mém.*, p. 331) is quite admissible. *Mo-lo* is equal to *mar*, and the symbol *so* is often mistaken for *po*. The province of Ladâk is called Mar-po, or the "red district," from the colour of the soil. The distance given by Hiuen Tsiang viz., 4600 li from Jâlandhara, is no doubt much in excess of the straight route to Ladâk, but as he went no further than Kulûta himself, the other distances, viz., 1900 + 2000 li, must have been gathered from hearsay. Doubtless the route would be intricate and winding.

[34] Śatadru—also spelt Śutudrî, Śatudrî, and Śitadrus, "flowing in a hundred branches"—the name of the Satlaj (Gerard's *Koonawur*, p. 28). It is the Hesidrus (or Hesudrus?) of Pliny (*H. N.*, lib. vi. c. 17, 21) and the Ζαρδδρος or Ζαδάδρης of Ptolemy (lib. vii. c. 1, 27, 42). See Lassen, *Ind. Alt.*, vol. i. p. 57. It also appears to have been the name of a kingdom of which Sarhind was probably the chief town, referred to in the text.

PO-LI-YE-TO-LO (PÁRYÁTRA).

This country[35] is about 3000 li in circuit, and the capital about 14 or 15 li. Grain is abundant and late wheat. There is a-strange kind of rice grown here, which ripens after sixty days.[36] There are many oxen and sheep, few flowers and fruits. The climate is warm and fiery, the manners of the people are resolute and fierce.[37] They do not esteem learning, and are given to honour the heretics. The king is of the Vaiśya caste; he is of a brave and impetuous nature, and very warlike.

There are eight *sanghárámas*, mostly ruined, with a very few priests, who study the Little Vehicle. There are ten Dêva temples with about 1000 followers of different sects.

Going east from this 500 li or so, we come to the country of Mo-t'u-lo (Mathurâ).

MO-T'U-LO (MATHURÂ).

The kingdom of Mo-t'u-lo [38] is about 5000 li in circuit. The capital is 20 li round. The soil is rich and fertile, and fit for producing grain (*sowing and reaping*). They give principal care to the cultivation of '*An-mo-lo* (*trees*),

---

[35] Páryátra is said in the next section to be 500 li (100 miles) west of Mathurâ or Muttra. This would favour the restoration of the Chinese *Po-li-ye-to-lo* to Virâta or Bairât. The distance and bearing from Sarhind, however, given in the text, do not agree with this. Bairât is some 220 miles south of Sarhind.

[36] Julien states (p. 206, n. 3) that this is a species of "dry rice" or "mountain rice," called *Tchen-t'ch'ing-tao*, which, according to a Chinese account, ripens in this period of time.

[37] The people of Virâta were always famous for their valour; hence Manu directs that the van of an army should be composed of men of Matsya or Virâta (amongst others). Cunningham, *Anc. Geog. Ind.*, p. 341.

[38] Mathurâ, on the Yamunâ, in the ancient Súrasénaka district, lat. 27° 28' N., long. 77° 41' E. For a description of the Buddhist remains discovered in the neighbourhood of this city, see Cunningham, *Archæol. Surv. of India*, vol. i. pp. 231 ff., and vol. iii. p. 13 ff.; Growse's *Mathurâ* (2d ed.), pp. 95-116; *Ind. Ant.*, vol. vi. pp. 216 f. It is the Μέθορα of Arrian (*Ind.*, c. 8) and Pliny (*H. N.*, lib. vi. c. 19, s. 22), and the Μόδουρα ἡ τῶν θεῶν of Ptolemy (lib. vii. c. 1, 49). Conf. Lassen, *I. A.*, vol. i. p. 158; *Brih. Samh.*, iv. 26, xvi. 17; Pânini, iv. 2, 82; Burnouf, *Intr.*, pp. 130, 336.

which grow in clusters[39] like forests. These trees, though called by one name, are of two kinds; the small species, the fruit of which, when young, is green, and becomes yellow as it ripens; and the great species, the fruit of which is green throughout its growth.

This country produces a fine species of cotton fabric and also yellow gold. The climate is warm to a degree. The manners of the people are soft and complacent. They like to prepare secret stores of religious merit.[40] They esteem virtue and honour learning.

There are about twenty *sanghârâmas* with 2000 priests or so. They study equally the Great and the Little Vehicles. There are five Dêva temples, in which sectaries of all kinds live.

There are three *stûpas* built by Asôka-râja. There are very many traces [41] of the four past Buddhas here. There are also *stûpas* to commemorate the remains of the holy followers of Sâkya Tathâgata, to wit, of Sâriputra (She-li-tseu), of Mudgalaputra (Mo-te-kia-lo-tseu), of Pûrnamaitrâ-yanîputra (Pu-la-na-meï-ta-li-yen-ni-fo-ta-lo), of Upâli (Yeu-po-li), of Ânanda ('O-nan-to), of Râhula (Lo-hu-lo), of Mañjusrî (Man-chu-sse-li), and *stûpas* of other Bôdhi-sattvas. Every year during the three months in which long fasts are observed,[42] and during the six fast-days of each month, the priests resort to these various *stûpas* and pay mutual compliments; they make their religious offerings, and bring many rare and precious objects for presents. According to their school they visit the sacred object (*figure*) of their veneration. Those who study the *Abhidharma* honour Sâriputra; those who practise meditation honour Mudgalaputra; those who recite the *sûtras* honour Pûrnamai-

---

trâyanîputra;[43] those who study the *Vinaya* reverence Upâli. All the Bhikshunîs honour Ânanda, the Srâmanêras[44] honour Râhula; those who study the Great Vehicle reverence the Bôdhisattvas. On these days they honour the *stûpas* with offerings. They spread out (*display*) their jewelled banners; the rich (*precious*) coverings (*parasols*) are crowded together as network; the smoke of incense rises in clouds; and flowers are scattered in every direction like rain; the sun and the moon are concealed as by the clouds which hang over the moist valleys. The king of the country and the great ministers apply themselves to these religious duties with zeal.[45]

To the east of the city about 5 or 6 li we come to a mountain *sanghârâma.*[46] The hill-sides are pierced (*widened*) to make cells (for the priests). We enter it[47]

---

[43] A native of Śûrpâraka, in Western India, for whom see Burnouf, *Introd.*, pp. 426, 503, *Lotus*, p. 2; *Ind. Ant.*, vol. xi. pp. 236, 294; Hardy, *Man. Budh.*, pp. 58, 267 f.; Beal, *Catena*, pp. 287, 344; Edkins, *Chin. Buddh.*, p. 290; *Asiat. Res.*, vol. xx. pp. 61, 427.

[44] Those not yet fully ordained; or, literally, those who have not yet taken on them all the rules, *i.e.*, of the *Pratimôksha.* The Śrâmanêras, or young disciples (novices), are referred to; they are called *anupasampanna*, not fully ordained. See Childers' *Pali Dict.* sub voc.

[45] Literally, "prepare good (*fruit*) by their zeal (*careful attention*).

[46] This passage is obscure and unsatisfactory. In the first place, the bearing from the city must be wrong, as the river Jamnâ washes the eastern side of the city for its whole length. If *west* be substituted for *east*, we are told by General Cunningham (*Arch. Survey of India*, vol. iii. p. 28) that the Chaubâra mounds, about one mile and a half from the town in that direction, have no hollows such as Hiuen Tsiang describes. If *north* be substituted for *east*, the Katrâ mound is not a mile from the town. But in the second place, the Chinese text is obscure. I do not think we can translate *yih shan kia lan*—literally "one-mountain-sanghârâma"—by "a sanghârâma situated on a mountain." There is the same phrase used in connection with the Tâmasavana convent (*supra*, p. 174). I have supposed that *shan* in that passage is a misprint. General Cunningham remarks (*Archæol. Survey*, vol. xiv. p. 56), that Hiuen Tsiang *compares* this monastery to a mountain: if this were so, the text would be intelligible; but I can find no such statement. If the text is not corrupt, the most satisfactory explanation I can offer is that the mounds which seem to abound in the neighbourhood of Mathurâ (and also the high mound at Sultânpur) had been used by the early Buddhist priests as "mountain-convents," that is, the mounds had been excavated, as the sides of mountains were, for dwelling-places. It is possible, also, to make *yi shan* a proper name for *Ekaparvata*; the passage would then read "5 or 6 li to the east of the city is the Ekaparvataka monastery."

[47] The word used in the text (*yin*) favours another rendering, viz., "the valley being the gates."

through a valley, as by gates. This was constructed by the honourable Upagupta.[48] There is in it a *stûpa* containing the nail-parings of the Tathâgata.

To the north of the *saṅghârâma*, in a cavern (*or* between two high banks), is a stone house about 20 feet high and 30 feet wide. It is filled with small wooden tokens (*slips*) four inches long.[49] Here the honourable Upagupta preached; when he converted a man and wife, so that they both arrived at (*confronted*) the fruit of Arhatship, he placed one slip (*in this house*). He made no record of those who attained this condition if they belonged to different families or separate castes (*tribes*).

Twenty-four or five li to the south-east of the stone house there is a great dry marsh, by the side of which is a *stûpa*. In old days the Tathâgata walked to and fro in this place. At this time a monkey holding (*a pot of*) honey offered it to Buddha. Buddha hereupon ordered him to mingle it with water, and to distribute it everywhere among the great assembly.[50] The monkey, filled

<hr>

[48] Upagupta (Yu-po-kiu-to, in Chinese Kiu-hu, and in Japanese Uvakikta), a Śûdra by birth, entered on a monastic life when seventeen years old, became an Arhat three years later, and conquered Mâra in a personal contest. He laboured in Mathurâ as the fourth patriarch. (Eitel, *Handbook.* s. voc.) The personal contest alluded to is related fully as an *Avaddna* by Aśvaghôsha in his sermons. Mâra found Upagupta lost in meditation, and placed a wreath of flowers on his head. On returning to consciousness, and finding himself thus crowned, he entered again into *samâdhi*, to see who had done the deed. Finding it was Mâra, he caused a dead body to fasten itself round Mâra's neck. No power in heaven or earth could disentangle it. Finally Mâra returned to Upagupta, confessed his fault, and prayed him to free him from the corpse. Upagupta consented on condition that he (Mâra) would exhibit himself under the form of Buddha "with all his marks." Mâra does so, and Upagupta, overpowered by the magnificence of the (supposed) Buddha, falls down before him in worship. The tableau then closes amid a terrific storm. Upagupta is spoken of as "a Buddha without marks" (*Alakshaṇako Buddhaḥ*).—Burnouf, *Introd.*, p. 336, n. 4. See also *Fo-sho-hing-tsan king*, p. xii. He is not known to the Southern school of Buddhism. He is made a contemporary of Aśôka by the Northern school, and placed one hundred years after the *Nirvâna*. Conf. Edkins, *Chin. Buddhism*, pp. 67–70; Lassen, *Ind. Alt.*, vol. ii. p. 1201.

[49] Literally, "four-inch wooden tokens fill up its interior." But according to another account (*Wong pûh*, § 177), the tokens or rods were used at the cremation of Upagupta.

[50] Mr. Growse would identify this spot with Damdama mound near Sarai Jamâlpur, "at some distance to the south-east of the *katra*, the tradi-

with joy, fell into a deep hole and was killed. By the power of his religious merit he obtained birth as a man.

To the north of the lake not very far, in the midst of a great wood, are the traces of the four former Buddhas walking to and fro. By the side are *stûpas* erected to commemorate the spots where Sâriputra, Mudgalaputra, and others, to the number of 1250 great Arhats, practised *samâdhi* and left traces thereof. The Tathâgata, when in the world, often traversed this country preaching the law. On the places where he stopped there are monuments (*trees* or *posts*) with titles on them.

Going north-east 500 li or so, we come to the country of Sa-t'a-ni-shi-fa-lo (Sthânêśvara).

SA-T'A-NI-SHI-FA-LO (STHÂNÊŚVARA).

This kingdom [51] is about 7000 li in circuit, the capital 20 li or so. The soil is rich and productive, and abounds with grain (*cereals*). The climate is genial, though hot. The manners of the people are cold and insincere. The families are rich and given to excessive luxury. They are much addicted to the use of magical arts, and greatly honour those of distinguished ability in other ways. Most of the people follow after worldly gain ; a few give themselves to agricultural pursuits. There is a large accumulation here of rare and valuable merchandise from every quarter. There are three *sanghârâmas* in this country, with about 700 priests. They all study (*practise* or *use*)

tional site of ancient Mathurâ."— Growse's *Mathura* (2d ed.), p. 100 ; Cunningham, *Arch. Sur. Rep.*, vol. i. p. 233. The legend of the monkey is often represented in Bauddha sculptures (see *Ind. Ant.*, vol. ix. p. 114). In this translation I follow Julien. The literal rendering is, " Buddha ordered a water-mingling everywhere around the great assembly." The "great assembly" is the *Samghâ* or congregation, generally represented as 1250 in number. Probably the verb *shi* is understood, "*to give* it everywhere," &c.

[51] The pilgrim probably left Mathurâ and travelled back by his former route till he came to Hânsi, where he struck off in a north-west direction for about 100 miles to Thânêsvar or Sthânêśvara. This is one of the oldest and most celebrated places in India, on account of its connection with the Pândus. See Cunningham, *Anc. Geog. of India*, p. 331 ; Lassen, *Ind. Alt.*, vol. i. p. 153, n ; Hall, *Vâsavadattâ*, p. 51.

the Little Vehicle. There are some hundred Dêva temples, and sectaries of various kinds in great number.

On every side of the capital within a precinct of 200 li in circuit is an area called by the men of this place " the land of religious merit." [52] This is what tradition states about it :—In old time there were two kings [53] of the five Indies, between whom the government was divided. They attacked one another's frontiers, and never ceased fighting. At length the two kings came to the agreement that they should select on each side a certain number of soldiers to decide the question by combat, and so give the people rest. But the multitude rejected this plan, and would have none of it. Then the king (*of this country*) reflected that the people are difficult to please (*to deal with*). A miraculous power (*a spirit*) may perhaps move them (*to action*); some project (*out-of-the-way plan*) may perhaps settle (*establish*) them in some right course of action.

At this time there was a Brâhman of great wisdom and high talent. To him the king sent secretly a present of some rolls of silk, and requested him to retire within his after-hall (*private apartment*) and there compose a religious book which he might conceal in a mountain cavern. After some time,[54] when the trees had grown over (*the mouth of the cavern*), the king summoned his ministers before him as he sat on his royal throne, and said: "Ashamed of my little virtue in the high estate I occupy, the ruler of heaven [55] (*or*, of Dêvas) has been pleased to reveal to me in a dream, and to confer upon me a divine book which is now concealed in such-and-such a mountain fastness and in such-and-such a rocky corner."

[52] This is also called the Dharma-kshêtra, or the "holy land;" and Kuru-kshêtra, from the number of holy places connected with the Kau-ravas and Pândavas, and with other heroes of antiquity. For some remarks on the probable extent of this district, see *Anc. Geog. of India*, p. 333, *Arch. Sur. of India*, vol. ii. pp. 212 f., and vol. xiv. p. 100; Thom-son, *Bhagavad. Gîtâ*, c. i. n. 2; Las-sen, *Ind. Alt.*, vol. i. p. 153.

[53] That is, the king of the Kurus and of the Pândus. The struggle be-tween these two families forms the subject of the great Sanskrit epic, the *Mahâbhârata*.

[54] Some years and months after.

[55] This is the general title given to Śakra or Indra, Śakradêvêndra.

On this an edict was issued to search for this book, and it was found underneath the mountain bushes. The high ministers addressed their congratulations (*to the king*) and the people were overjoyed. The king then gave an account of the discovery to those far and near, and caused all to understand the matter; and this is the upshot of his message: "To birth and death there is no limit—no end to the revolutions of life. There is no rescue from the spiritual abyss (*in which we are immersed*). But now by a rare plan I am able to deliver men from this suffering. Around this royal city, for the space of 200 li in circuit, was the land of 'religious merit' for men, apportioned by the kings of old. Years having rolled away in great numbers, the traces have been forgotten or destroyed. Men not regarding spiritual indications (*religion*) have been immersed in the sea of sorrow without power of escape. What then is to be said? Let it be known (*from the divine revelation given*) that all those of you who shall attack the enemy's troops and die in battle, that they shall be born again as men; if they kill many, that, free from guilt,[56] they shall receive heavenly joys. Those obedient grandchildren and pious children who assist (*attend*) their aged parents [57] in walking about this land shall reap happiness (*merit*) without bounds. With little work, a great reward.[58] Who would lose such an opportunity, (*since,*) when once dead, our bodies fall into the dark intricacies of the three evil ways?[59] Therefore let every man stir himself to the utmost to prepare good works."

On this the men hastened to the conflict, and regarded death as deliverance.[60] The king accordingly issued an

---

[56] This differs from Julien's version; the literal translation is "many slain, guiltless, they shall receive the happiness of heaven as their reward (*merit*)." It seems to imply that if they shall be killed after slaying many of the enemy, they shall be born in heaven.

[57] Or, "their relations and the aged." It is an obscure passage, but the allusion is probably to those who attend to the wounded or the bereaved.

[58] There may be a reference to mourning for distant relatives, implying that this also shall be rewarded.

[59] *I.e.*, of hell, of famished demons, and of brutes.

[60] The phrase *ju kwei*, "as re-

edict and summoned his braves. The two countries engaged in conflict, and the dead bodies were heaped together as sticks, and from that time till now the plains are everywhere covered with their bones. As this relates to a very remote period of time, the bones are very large ones.[61] The constant tradition of the country, therefore, has called this "the field of religious merit" (*or* "happiness").

To the north-west of the city 4 or 5 li is a *stûpa* about 300 feet high, which was built by Aśôka-râja. The bricks are all of a yellowish red colour, very bright and shining, within is a peck measure of the relics of Buddha. From the *stûpa* is frequently emitted a brilliant light, and many spiritual prodigies exhibit themselves.

Going south of the city about 100 li, we come to a convent called Ku-hwăn-ch'a (Gôkaṇṭha ?).[62] There are here a succession of towers with overlapping storeys,[63] with intervals between them for walking (*pacing*). The priests are virtuous and well - mannered, possessed of quiet dignity.

Going from this north-east 400 li or so, we come to the country of Su-lo-kin-na (Srughna).

Su-lo-kin-na (Srughna).

This country[64] is about 6000 li in circuit. On the eastern side it borders on the Ganges river, on the north

turned," has a meaning equal to our word "salvation" or "saved." The sentence appears to be interpolated.

[61] There is a Vedic legend about Indra, who slew ninety times nine Vṛitras near this spot. The site of Asthipur, or "bone-town," is still pointed out in the plain to the west of the city.—Cunningham, *Geog.*, p. 336; *Arch. Sur.*, vol. ii. p. 219.

[62] This may also be restored to Gôvinda.

[63] *Lin măng* = connected ridge-poles (?).

[64] Hiuen Tsiang reckons his distance from the capital as usual. The distance indicated from Sthâṇéśvara in a north-east direction would take us to Kâlsi, in the Jaunsâr district, on the east of Sirmur. Cunningham places Srughna at Sugh, a place about fifty miles north-east from the Gôkaṇṭha monastery. Hwui-lih makes the direction *east* instead of north-east. Srughna, north of Hâstinapura, is mentioned by Pâṇini (i. 3, 25; ii. 1, 14 schol.; iv. 3, 25, 86), and by Varâha Mihira, *Brih. Samh.*, xvi. 21). Conf. Hall's *Vâsavadattâ*, int. p. 51. It

it is backed by great mountains. The river Yamunâ
(Chen-mu-na) flows through its frontiers. The capital
is about 20 li in circuit, and is bounded on the east by
the river Yamunâ. It is deserted, although its foundations
are still very strong. As to produce of soil and character
of climate, this country resembles the kingdom of Sa-t'a-
ni-shi-fa-lo (Sthânêśvara). The disposition of the people
is sincere and truthful. They honour and have faith in
heretical teaching, and they greatly esteem the pursuit of
learning, but principally religious wisdom (*or*, the wisdom
that brings happiness).

There are five *saṅghârâmas* with about 1000 priests;
the greater number study the Little Vehicle; a few exercise themselves in other (*exceptional*) schools. They deli-
berate and discuss in appropriate language (*choice words*),
and their clear discourses embody profound truth. Men
of different regions of eminent skill discuss with them to
satisfy their doubts. There are a hundred Dêva temples
with very many sectaries (*unbelievers*).

To the south-west of the capital and west of the river
Yamunâ is a *saṅghârâma*, outside the eastern gate of
which is a *stûpa* built by Aśôka-râja. The Tathâgata,
when in the world in former days, preached the law in
this place to convert men. By its side is another *stûpa*
in which there are relics of the Tathâgata's hair and nails.
Surrounding this on the right and left are *stûpas* enclosing
the hair and nail relics of Sâriputra and of Mu-te-kia-lo
(Maudgalyâyana) and other Arhats, several tens in number.

After Tathâgata had entered *Nirvâṇa* this country was
the seat of heretical teaching. The faithful were per-

appears from Cunningham's account
of the pillar of Firuz Shâh, which
was brought from a place called
Topur or Topera, on the bank of the
Jamnâ, in the district of Salora, not
far from Khizrâbâd, which is at *the
foot of* the mountains, 90 kos from
Dehli, which place Cunningham
identifies with Pantn, not far from
Kâlsi (*Archæol. Surr.*, vol. L p. 166),
that this neighbourhood was famous
in olden days as a Buddhist locality.
I think we should trust Hiuen
Tsiang's 400 li north-east from Sthâ-
nêśvara, and place the capital of
Srughna at or near Kâlsi, which
Cunningham also includes in the
district. Conf. Cunningham, *Arch.
Sur.*, vol. ii. pp. 220 ff.; *Anc.
Geoy.*, p. 345.

verted to false doctrine, and forsook the orthodox views. Now there are five *saṅghârâmas* in places where masters of treatises [65] from different countries, holding controversies with the heretics and Brâhmaṇs, prevailed; they were erected on this account.

On the east of the Yamunâ, going about 800 li, we come to the Ganges river. [66] The source of the river (*or* the river at its source) is 3 or 4 li wide; flowing south-east, it enters the sea, where it is 10 li and more in width. The water of the river is blue, like the ocean, and its waves are wide-rolling as the sea. The scaly monsters, though many, do no harm to men. The taste of the water is sweet and pleasant, and sands of extreme fineness [67] border its course. In the common history of the country this river is called Fo-shwui, the *river of religious merit*, [68] · which can wash away countless [69] sins. Those who are weary of life, if they end their days in it, are borne to heaven and receive happiness. If a man dies and his bones are cast into the river, he cannot fall into an evil way; whilst he is carried by its waters and forgotten by men, his soul is preserved in safety on the other side (in the other world).

At a certain time there was a Bôdhisattva of the island of Siṁhala (Chi-sse-tseu—Ceylon) called Dêva, who profoundly understood the relationship of truth [70] and the nature of all composite things (*fǎ*). [71] Moved with pity at

---

[65] That is, Buddhist doctors or learned writers (writers of *śâstras*).

[66] In Hwui-lih the text seems to require the route to be to the *source* of the Ganges. The distance of 800 li would favour this reading; but it is hard to understand how a river can be three or four li (three-quarters of a mile) wide at its source. See the accounts of Gaṅgadwâra, Gaṅgautri, or Gaṅgôtri, by Rennell, &c.

[67] Hence the comparison so frequently met with in Buddhist books, "as numerous as the sands of the Ganges."

[68] The Mahâbhadrâ.

[69] Heaped-up sin, or although heaped up: I do not think Julien's "quoiqu'on soit chargé de crimes" meets the sense of the original.

[70] Or, all true relationship; the symbol *siang* corresponds with *lakshaṇa*; it might be translated, therefore, "all the marks of truth."

[71] The symbol *fǎ* corresponds with *dharma*, which has a wide meaning, as in the well-known text, *ye dharmâ hêtu-prabhava*, &c.

the ignorance of men, he came to this country to guide and direct the people in the right way.   At this time the men and women were all assembled with the young and old together on the banks of the river, whose waves rolled along with impetuosity.   Then Dêva Bôdhisattva composing his supernatural appearance [72] bent his head and dispersed it (*the rays of his glory?*) again [73]—his appearance different from that of other men.   There was an unbeliever who said, " What does my son in altering thus his appearance ?" [74]

Dêva Bôdhisattva answered: "My father, mother, and relations dwell in the island of Ceylon.   I fear lest they may be suffering from hunger and thirst; I desire to appease them from this distant spot."

The heretic said: "You deceive yourself, my son; [75] have you no reflection to see how foolish such a thing is ? Your country is far off, and separated by mountains and rivers of wide extent from this.   To draw up this water and scatter it in order to quench the thirst of those far off, is like going backwards to seek a thing before you; it is a way never heard of before."   Then Dêva Bôdhisattva said : " If those who are kept for their sins in the dark regions of evil can reap the benefit of the water, why should it not reach those who are merely separated by mountains and rivers ?"

Then the heretics, in presence of the difficulty, confessed themselves wrong, and, giving up their unbelief, received the true law.   Changing their evil ways, they reformed themselves, and vowed to become his disciples. [76]

---

[72] His agreeable splendour, dipping up and drawing in.

[73] This passage is obscure. Julien's translation is as follows : " Dêva Bôdhisattva softened the brightness of his figure and wished to draw some water ; but the moment he bent his head at that point the water receded in streams (*en jaillissant*)."   It may be so ; or it may refer to his miraculous appearance, drawing in and dispersing again the brightness of his figure.   The subse-quent part of the narrative, however, seems to denote that he "drew in " some water, and then scattered or dispersed it.

[74] Literally, "My son ! why this difficult, or wonderful (*occurrence*)?"

[75] Or, " you deceive yourself, sir !" The expression *ngo teru* seems to mean more than "doctor " or " sir."

[76] The history of Dêva Bôdhisattva is somewhat confusing.   We know this much of him, that he was a disciple of Nâgârjuna, and his suc-

After crossing the river and going along the eastern side of it, we come to the country of Ma-ti-pu-lo (Matipura).

MA-TI-PU-LO (MATIPURA).

This country [77] is about 6000 li in circuit; the capital is about 20 li. The soil is favourable for the growth of cereals, and there are many flowers and kinds of fruit. The climate is soft and mild. The people are sincere and truthful. They very much reverence learning, and are deeply versed in the use of charms and magic. The followers of truth and error are equally divided. [78] The king belongs to the caste of the Śûdras (Shu-t'o-lo). He is not a believer in the law of Buddha, but reverences and worships the spirits of heaven. There are about twenty *saṅghârâmas*, with 800 priests. They mostly study the Little Vehicle and belong to the school of Sarvâstivâdas (Shwo-i-tsie-yau). There are some fifty Dêva temples, in which men of different persuasions dwell promiscuously.

Four or five li to the south of the capital we come to a little *saṅghârâma* having about fifty priests in it. In old time the master of *śâstras* called Kiu-na-po-

cessor as fourteenth (or according to others, fifteenth) patriarch. He is called Kanadêva, because, according to Vassilief (p. 219), he gave one of his eyes (*kâṇa*, "one-eyed") to Mahêśvara, but more probably because he bored out (*kâṇa*, "perforated") the eye of Mahêśvara. For this story see *Wong Pâh*, § 188 (*J. R. As. Soc.*, vol. xx. p. 207), where the Chinese *ts'hŏ* answers to *kâṇa*. See Edkins, *Chin. Buddh.*, pp. 77–79; Lassen, *I. A.*, vol. ii. p. 1204. He is also called Âryadêva. According to others he is the same as Chandrakîrtti (*J. As. S. Ben.*, vol. vii. p. 144), but this cannot be the Chandrakîrtti who followed the teaching of Buddhapâlita (Vassilief, p. 207), for Buddhapâlita composed commentaries on the works of Âryadêva

(*ibid.*) It seems probable from the statement in the text that Dêva was a native of Ceylon. B. Nanjio says *not* (*Catalogue*, col. 370); but if not he evidently dwelt there. He was the author of numerous works, for a list of which see B. Nanjio (*loc. cit.*) He probably flourished towards the middle or end of the first century A.D.

[77] Matipura has been identified with Madâwar or Mundore, a large town in Western Rohilkand, near Bijnor (V. de St. Martin, *Mémoire*, p. 344; Cunningham, *Anc. Geog. of India*, p. 349). The people of this town were perhaps the Mathai of Megasthenes (Arrian, *Indica*, c. 4; *Ind. Ant.*, vol. v. p. 332).

[78] That is, the Buddhists and Brâhmaṇs, or other sectaries.

la-po (Guṇaprabha),[79] composed in this convent the treatise called *Pin-chin*,[80] and some hundred others. When young, this master of *śâstras* distinguished himself for his eminent talent, and when he grew up he stood alone in point of learning. He was well versed in knowledge of men (*or* things), was of sound understanding, full of learning, and widely celebrated.[81] Originally he was brought up in the study of the Great Vehicle, but before he had penetrated its deep principles he had occasion to study the *Vibhâshâ Śâstra*, on which he withdrew from his former work and attached himself to the Little Vehicle. He composed several tens of treatises to overthrow the Great Vehicle, and thus became a zealous partisan of the Little Vehicle school. Moreover, he composed several tens of secular books opposing and criticising the writings of former renowned teachers. He widely studied the sacred books of Buddha, but yet, though he studied deeply for a long time, there were yet some ten difficulties which he could not overcome in this school.

At this time there was an Arhat called Dêvasêna,[82] who went once and again to the Tushita (*Tu-shi-to*) heaven. Guṇaprabha begged him to obtain for him an interview with Maitrêya in order to settle his doubts.

---

[79] In Chinese, *Tih kwong,* "the brightness of virtue, or good qualities."

[80] Restored doubtfully by Julien to *Tattva-vibhaṅga Śâstra* (p. 220 n. 2), and by Eitel to *Tattva-satya Śâstra* (*Handbook*, sub voc. Guṇaprabha).

[81] This expression, *to-wan,* may mean "celebrated," or it may refer to Guṇaprabha when a young disciple. It is a phrase applied to Ananda before he arrived at enlightenment (see *Catena of Buddhist Scrip.*, p. 289 and n. 2). It is also generally applied to Vaiśravaṇa, as an explanation of his name "the celebrated" (compare περικλύτος) · and it is very probable that the story found in Buddhist books of Vaiśravaṇa's conversion and his consent to protect the Śrâvakas is simply the result of these names being derived from the same root, *śru.* The Chinese *to-wan,* when referred to a young disciple, is equal to the Sanskrit *śikshaka,* a learner (see Burnouf, *Lotus,* p. 295). Guṇaprabha is said by Vassilief (*Bouddhisme,* p. 78) to have been a disciple of Vasubandhu, and to have lived at Mathurâ in the Agrapura monastery : he was *guru* at the court of the king Śrî Harsha (doubtfully). Perhaps in this quotation Mathurâ has been mistaken for Matipura, in which case the convent referred to in the text would be called Agrapura.

[82] Ti-po-si-na, in Chinese *Tien-kwan,* army of the gods.

Dêvasêna, by his miraculous power, transported him to the heavenly palace. Having seen Maitrêya (Tse-shi) Guṇaprabha bowed low to him, but paid him no worship. On this Dêvasêna said, "Maitrêya Bôdhisattva holds the next place in becoming a Buddha, why are you so self-conceited as not to pay him supreme reverence? If you wish to receive benefit (*building up, edification*) from him, why do you not fall down?"

Guṇaprabha replied: "Reverend sir! this advice is honest, and intended to lead me to right amendment; but I am an ordained Bhikshu, and have left the world as a disciple, whereas this Maitrêya Bôdhisattva is enjoying heavenly beatitude, and is no associate for one who has become an ascetic. I was about to offer him worship, but I feared it would not be right."

Bôdhisattva (Maitrêya) perceived that *pride of self* (*âtmamada*) was bound up in his heart, so that he was not a vessel for instruction; and though he went and returned three times, he got no solution of his doubts. At length he begged Dêvasêna to take him again, and that he was ready to worship. But Dêvasêna, repelled by his pride of self, refused to answer him.

Guṇaprabha, not attaining his wish, was filled with hatred and resentment. He went forthwith into the desert apart, and practised the *samâdhi* called *fa-tung* (*opening intelligence*); but because he had not put away *the pride of self*, he could obtain no fruit.

To the north of the *sanghârâma* of Guṇaprabha about three or four li is a great convent with some 200 disciples in it, who study the Little Vehicle. This is where Sangha-bhadra (Chung-hin), master of *śâstras*, died. He was a native of Kaśmîr, and was possessed of great ability and vast penetration. As a young man he was singularly accomplished, and had mastered throughout the *Vibhâshâ Śâstra* (*Pi-po-sha-lun*) of the Sarvâstivâda school.

At this time Vasubandhu Bôdhisattva was living. He was seeking to explain that which it is beyond the power of words to convey by the mysterious method (*way*) of profound meditation.[83]   With a view to overthrow the propositions of the masters of the Vibhâshika school, he composed the *Abhidharma-kôsha Śâstra.*   The form of his composition is clear and elegant, and his arguments are very subtle and lofty.

Saṅghabhadra having read this work, took his resolution accordingly.   He devoted himself during twelve years to the most profound researches, and composed the *Kin-she-pao-lun* (*Kôshakaraki Śâstra*)[84] in 25,000 ślôkas, containing altogether 800,000 words.   We may say that it is a work of the deepest research and most subtle principles. Addressing his disciples, he said, "Whilst I retire from sight, do you, distinguished disciples,[85] take this my orthodox treatise and go attack Vasubandhu; break down his sharp-pointed arguments, and permit not this old man[86] alone to assume the leading name."

Thereupon three or four of the most distinguished of his disciples took the treatise he had composed, and went in search of Vasubandhu.   At this time he was in the country of Chêka,[87] in the town of Śâkala, his fame being spread far and wide.   And now Saṅghabhadra was coming there; Vasubandhu having heard it, forthwith ordered (*his disciples*) to prepare for removal (*dress for travel*).   His disciples having (*cherishing*) some doubts, the most eminent of them began to remonstrate with him, and said, "The high qualities of our great master transcend those of former men of note, and at the present day your wisdom is far spread and acknowledged by all.   Why, then, on hearing the name of Saṅghabhadra are you so fearful

<hr>

[83] *Yih-sin*, i.e., *samâdhi* or *dhyâna.*

[84] Or *Kôshakarika Śâstra* (?).—Julien. See also *K'ong Pih*, § 199, in *J. R. As. S.*, vol. xx. p. 212.

[85] It will be seen that this translation differs from Julien's, but I think it is in agreement with the text and context.

[86] Saṅghabhadra could not have been the teacher of Vasubandhu, as Professor Max Müller thinks (*India*, pp 303 f., 309, 312).   He is probably the same as Saṅghadâsa, named by Vassilief (*Bouddhisme*, p. 206).

[87] For Chêka, see above, Book iv. p. 165 *ante.*

and timid ?   We, your disciples, are indeed humbled thereat."

Vasubandhu answered, "I am going away not because I fear to meet this man (*doctor*), but because in this country there is no one of penetration enough to recognise the inferiority of Saṅgabhadra.   He would only vilify me as if my old age were a fault.   There would be no holding him to the *śâstra*, or in one word I could overthrow his vagaries.   Let us draw him to Mid-India, and there, in the presence of the eminent and wise, let us examine into the matter, and determine what is true and what is false, and who should be pronounced the victor or the loser." [88] Forthwith he ordered his disciples to pack up their books, and to remove far away.

The master of *śâstras*, Saṅghabhadra, the day after arriving at this convent, suddenly felt his powers of body (*hi*, vital spirits) fail him.   On this he wrote a letter, and excused himself to Vasubandhu thus : "The Tathâgata having died, the different schools of his followers adopted and arranged their distinctive teaching; and each had its own disciples without hindrance.   They favoured those of their own way of thinking; they rejected (*persecuted*) others.   I, who possess but a weak understanding, unhappily inherited this custom from my predecessors, and coming to read your treatise called the *Abhidharma-kôsha*, written to overthrow the great principles of the masters of the Vibhâshika school, abruptly, without measuring my strength, after many years' study have produced this *śâstra* to uphold the teaching of the orthodox school.   My wisdom indeed is little, my intentions great.   My end is now approaching.   If the Bôdhisattva (*Vasubandhu*), in spreading abroad his subtle maxims and disseminating his profound reasonings, will vouchsafe not to overthrow my production, but will let it remain whole and entire for posterity, then I shall not regret my death."

---

[88] It will be seen again that this translation differs materially from that of M. Julien.

Then, selecting from his followers one distinguished for his talents in speaking, he addressed him as follows : " I, who am but a scholar of poor ability, have aspired to surpass one of high natural talent. Wherefore, after my approaching death, do you take this letter which I have written, and my treatise also, and make my excuses to that Bôdhisattva, and assure him of my repentance."

After uttering these words he suddenly stopped, when one said, " He is dead!"

The disciple, taking the letter, went to the place where Vasubandhu was, and having come, he spoke thus : " My master, Sanghabadra, has died; and his last words are contained in this letter, in which he blames himself for his faults, and in excusing himself to you asks you not to destroy his good name so that it dare not face the world."

· Vasubandhu Bôdhisattva, reading the letter and looking through the book, was for a time lost in thought. Then at length he addressed the disciple and said : " Sanghabhadra, the writer of *śâstras*, was a clever and ingenious scholar (*inferior scholar*). His reasoning powers (*li*), indeed, were not deep (*enough*), but his diction is somewhat (*to the point*).[89] If I had any desire to overthrow Sanghabhadra's *śâstra*, I could do so as easily as I place my finger in my hand. As to his dying request made to me, I greatly respect the expression of the difficulty he acknowledges. But besides that, there is great reason why I should observe his last wish, for indeed this *śâstra* may illustrate the doctrines of my school, and accordingly I will only change its name and call it *Shun-ching-li-lun* (*Nyâyânusâra Śâstra*).[90]

The disciple remonstrating said, " Before Sanghabhadra's death the great master (*Vasubandhu*) had removed far away; but now he has obtained the *śâstr*, he proposes

<hr>

[89] Or it may be complimentary, " his phraseology or composition is exceptionally elegant."

[90] In full—'*O-pi-ta-mo-shun-chan-li-lun*. It was translated into Chinese by Hiuen Tsiang himself. See Bunyiu Nanjio's *Catalogue*, No. 1265; Beal's *Tripitaka*, p. 80.

to change the title; how shall we (*the disciples of Sanghabhadra*) be able to suffer such an affront?"

Vasubandhu Bôdhisattva, wishing to remove all doubts, said in reply by verse: "Though the lion-king retires afar off before the pig, nevertheless the wise will know which of the two is best in strength."[91]

Sanghabhadra having died, they burnt his body and collected his bones, and in a *stûpa* attached to the *sanghârâma*, 200 paces or so to the north-west, in a wood of Âmra[92] (*'An-mo-lo*) trees, they are yet visible.

Beside the Âmra wood is a *stûpa* in which are relics of the bequeathed body of the master of *sâstras* Vimalamitra (I'i-mo-lo-mi-to-lo).[93] This master of *sâstras* was a man of Kâsmîr. He became a disciple and attached himself to the Sarvâstivâda school. He had read a multitude of *sûtras* and investigated various *sâstras*; he travelled through the five Indies and made himself acquainted with the mysterious literature of the three *Pitakas*. Having established a name and accomplished his work, being about to retire to his own country, on his way he passed near the *stûpa* of Sanghabhadra, the master of *sâstras*. Putting his hand (*on it*),[94] he sighed and said, "This master was truly distinguished, his views pure and eminent. After having spread abroad the great principles (*of his faith*), he purposed to overthrow those of other schools and lay firmly the fabric of his own. Why then should his fame not be eternal? I, Vimalamitra, foolish as I am, have received at various times the knowledge of the deep principles of his departed wisdom; his distinguished qualities have been cherished through successive generations. Vasubandhu, though dead, yet lives in the tradition of the school. That which I know so perfectly (*ought to be preserved*). I will write, then, such *sâstras* as will cause the learned men of Jambudvîpa to

---

[91] From the *Jâtaka* of the lion and the pig who rolled himself in filth. Fausböll, *Ten Jâtakas*, p. 65.

[92] Mango trees—*Mangifera indica*.

[93] In Chinese, *Wou hau yau*, "spotless friend."

[94] "On his heart."—Julien.

forget the name of the Great Vehicle and destroy the fame of Vasubandhu. This will be an immortal work, and will be the accomplishment of my long-meditated design."

Having finished these words, his mind became confused and wild; his boastful tongue heavily protruded,[95] whilst the hot blood flowed forth. Knowing that his end was approaching, he wrote the following letter to signify his repentance:—"The doctrines of the Great Vehicle in the law of Buddha contain the final principles.[96] Its renown may fade, but its depth of reason is inscrutable. I foolishly dared to attack its distinguished teachers. The reward of my works is plain to all. It is for this I die. Let me address men of wisdom, who may learn from my example to guard well their thoughts, and not give way to the encouragement of doubts." Then the great earth shook again as he gave up life. In the place where he died the earth opened, and there was produced a great ditch. His disciples burnt his body, collected his bones, and raised over them (*a stûpa*).[97]

At this time there was an Arhat who, having witnessed his death, sighed and exclaimed, "What unhappiness! what suffering! To-day this master of *sâstras* yielding to his feelings and maintaining his own views, abusing the Great Vehicle, has fallen into the deepest hell (*Avîchi*)!"

On the north-west frontier of this country, on the eastern shore of the river Ganges, is the town of Mo-yu-lo;[98] it is about 20 li in circuit. The inhabitants are very numerous. The pure streams of the river flow round it on every side; it produces native copper (*tcou shih*), pure crystal, and precious vases. Not far from the town,

[95] The text has "five tongues;" possibly the symbol *wu*, five, is for *wu*, loquacious or bragging.

[96] This may also be rendered, "the masters who teach the doctrines of the Great Vehicle declare the final (*highest*) principles of the law of Buddha."

[97] There is no word for *stûpa* in the original.

[98] That is Mayâpura, or Haridwâra. It is now on the *western* bank of the Ganges. Julien makes it Mayûra.

and standing by the Ganges river, is a great Dêva temple, where very many miracles of divers sorts are wrought. In the midst of it is a tank, of which the borders are made of stone joined skilfully together. Through it the Ganges river is led by an artificial canal. The men of the five Indies call it "the gate of the Gangâ river."[99] This is where religious merit is found and sin effaced. There are always hundreds and thousands of people gathered together here from distant quarters to bathe and wash in its waters. Benevolent kings have founded here "a house of merit" (*Puṇyaśâlâ*). This foundation is endowed with funds for providing choice food and medicines to bestow in charity on widows and bereaved persons, on orphans and the destitute.

Going north from this 300 li or so, we come to P'o-lo-hih-mo-pu-lo country (Brahmapura).

P'O-LO-HIH-MO-PU-LO (BRAHMAPURA).

This kingdom[100] is about 4000 li in circuit, and surrounded on all sides by mountains. The chief town is about 20 li round. It is thickly populated, and the householders are rich. The soil is rich and fertile; the lands are sown and reaped in their seasons. The country produces *teou-shih* (*native copper*) and rock crystal. The climate is rather cold; the people are hardy and uncultivated. Few of the people attend to literature—most of them are engaged in commerce.

The disposition of the men is of a savage kind. There are heretics mixed with believers in Buddha. There are five *sanghârâmas*, which contain a few priests. There are ten Dêva temples, in which persons of different opinions dwell together.

This country is bounded on the north by the great

---

[99] Gangâdwâra. The canal still exists; the present name, Haridwâra, means the gate of Hari or Vishṇu: this is a comparatively modern name (Cunningham, p. 353).

[100] Cunningham identifies Brahmapura with British Garhwâl and Kumâun (*Anc. Geog. of India*, p. 356).

Snowy Mountains, in the midst of which is the country called Su-fa-la-na-kiu-ta-lo (Suvarṇagôtra).[101] From this country comes a superior sort of gold, and hence the name. It is extended from east to west, and contracted from north to south. It is the same as the country of the "eastern women."[102] For ages a woman has been the ruler, and so it is called the *kingdom of the women.* The husband of the reigning woman is called king, but he knows nothing about the affairs of the state. The men manage the wars and sow the land, and that is all. The land produces winter wheat and much cattle, sheep, and horses. The climate is extremely cold (*icy*). The people are hasty and impetuous.

On the eastern side this country is bordered by the Fan kingdom (Tibet), on the west by San-po-ho (Sampaha or Malasa (?)), on the north by Khotan.

Going south-east from Ma-ti-pu-lo 400 li or so, we come to the country of Kiu-pi-shwong-na.

KIU-PI-SHWONG-NA (GÔVIŚANA).

This kingdom [103] is about 2000 li in circuit, and the capital about 14 or 15 li. It is naturally strong, being fenced in with crags and precipices. The population is numerous. We find on every side flowers, and groves, and lakes (*ponds*) succeeding each other in regular order. The climate and the products resemble those of Mo-ti-pu-lo. The manners of the people are pure and honest. They

---

[101] In Chinese *Kin-shi*, "golden people." Below it is said that San-po-ho was limited on the west by Su-fa-la-na-kiu-to-lo (Suvarṇa-gôtra, called also the kingdom of women), which itself touched on the east the country of T'u-fan (Tibet), and on the north the kingdom of Yu-tien (Khotan). Suvarṇagôtra is here placed on the frontier of Brahmapura.

[102] There is a country of the "*western* women " named by Hiuen Tsiang in Book xi. See also Yule's *Marco Polo*, vol. ii. p. 397.

[103] Julien restores this to Gôviśana. Cunningham is satisfied that the old fort near the village of Ujain represents the ancient city of Gôviśana. This village is just one mile to the east of Kâśipur. Hwui-lih does not mention this country, but reckons 400 li from Matipura to Ahikshêtra in a south-easterly direction. This distance and bearing are nearly correct.

are diligent in study and given to good works. There are many believers in false doctrine, who seek present happiness only. There are two *saṅghârâmas* and about 100 priests, who mostly study the Little Vehicle. There are thirty Dêva temples with different sectaries, who congregate together without distinction.

Beside the chief town is an old *saṅghârâma* in which is a *stûpa* built by King Asôka. It is about 200 feet high; here Buddha, when living, preached for a month on the most essential points of religion. By the side is a place where there are traces of the four past Buddhas, who sat and walked here. At the side of this place are two small *stûpas* containing the hair and nail-parings of Tathâgata. They are about 10 feet high.

Going from this south-east about 400 li, we come to the country of 'O-hi-chi-ta-lo (Ahikshêtra).

'O-HI-CHI-TA-LO (AHIKSHÊTRA).

This country [104] is about 3000 li in circuit, and the capital about 17 or 18 li. It is naturally strong, being flanked by mountain crags. It produces wheat, and there are many woods and fountains. The climate is soft and agreeable, and the people sincere and truthful. They love religion, and apply themselves to learning. They are clever and well informed. There are about ten *saṅghârâmas*, and some 1000 priests who study the Little Vehicle of the Ching-liang school. [105]

There are some nine Dêva temples with 300 sectaries. They sacrifice to Îśvara, and belong to the company of "ashes-sprinklers" (Pâśupatas).

Outside the chief town is a Nâga tank, by the side of which is a *stûpa* built by Asôka-râja. It was here the

---

[104] Ahikshêtra, Ahikshatra, or Ahichchhatra, a place named in the *Mahâbhârata*, i. 5515, 6348; *Hari-vaṁśa*, 1114; Pâṇini, iii. 1, 7. It was the capital of North Pâñchâla or Rohilkhaṇḍ. Lassen, *Ind. Alt.*, vol. i. p. 747; Wilson's *Vish.-pur.* (Hall's ed.), vol. ii. p. 161.

[105] In the text *wang* is a mistake for *ching*, but the school is properly the Saṁmatiya school.

Tathâgata, when in the world, preached the law for the sake of a Nâga-râja for seven days.[100]   By the side of it are four little *stúpas;* here are traces where, in days gone by, the four past Buddhas sat and walked.

From this going south 260 or 270 li, and crossing the Ganges river, proceeding then in a south-west direction, we come to Pi-lo-shan-na (Vîrasana) country.

PI-LO-SHAN-NA (VÎRASANA ?)

This country [107] is about 2000 li in circuit.   The capital town about 10 li.   The climate and produce are the same as those of Ahikshêtra.   The habits of the people are violent and headstrong.   They are given to study and the arts.   They are chiefly heretics (*attached in faith to heresy*); there are a few who believe in the law of Buddha.   There are two *sanghârâmas* with about 300 priests, who attach themselves to the study of the Great Vehicle.   There are five Dêva temples occupied by sectaries of different persuasions.

In the middle of the chief city is an old *sanghârâma,* within which is a *stúpa,* which, although in ruins, is still rather more than 100 feet high.   It was built by Aśôka-râja.   Tathâgata, when in the world in old days, preached here for seven days on the *Wen-kiaï-chu-king (Skandha-dhâtu-upasthâna Sûtra ?).*[108]   By the side of it are the

---

[106] The old story connected with this place was that Râja Adi was found by Drôna sleeping under the guardianship of a serpent, hence the name Ahi-chhatra (*serpent canopy*). This story was probably appropriated by the Buddhists. For a full account of this place and its present condition, see Cunningham, *Archæolog. Survey of India,* vol. i. p. 259 ff.

[107] Restored (doubtfully) by Julien to Vîrasana. General Cunningham identifies it (conjecturally) with a great mound of ruins called Atrañji-khêra, four miles to the south of Karsâna. Hiuen Tsiang probably crossed the Ganges near Sahâwar, a few miles from Soron: this appears to answer to the distance of 260 or 270 li—about 50 miles. General Cunningham says 23 to 25 miles, but on his Map x. the distance is 50 miles.

[108] Julien (p. 236, n. 1) renders this literally "one who dwells in the world called *Ouen-kiai;*" but *wen-kiai* represents *skandha-dhâtu,* and *chu* is the Chinese symbol for *upasthâna.*

traces where the four former Buddhas sat and walked in exercise.

Going hence south-east 200 li or so, we come to the country of Kie-pi-tha (Kapitha).[100]

KIE-PI-THA (KAPITHA).

This country[110] is about 2000 li in circuit, and the capital 20 li or so. The climate and produce resemble those of Pi-lo-shan-na. The manners of the people are soft and agreeable. The men are much given to learning. There are four *sanghârâmas* with about 1000 priests, who study the Ching-liang (Saṁmatîya) school of the Little Vehicle. There are ten Dêva temples, where sectaries of all persuasions dwell. They all honour and sacrifice to [111] Mahêsvara (Ta-tseu-t'saï-tien).

To the east of the city 20 li or so is a great *sanghârâma* of beautiful construction, throughout which the artist has exhibited his greatest skill. The sacred image of the holy form (*of Buddha*) is most wonderfully magnificent. There are about 100 priests here, who study the doctrines of the Saṁmatîya (Ching-liang) school. Several myriads of "pure men" (*religious laymen*) live by the side of this convent.

Within the great enclosure of the *sanghârâma* there are three precious ladders, which are arranged side by side from north to south, with their faces for descent to the east. This is where Tathâgata came down on his return from the Trayastriṁśas heaven.[112]   In old days Tathâgata, going up from the "wood of the conqueror" (Shing-lin, Jêtavana),

---

[109] Written formerly Sâng-kia-she Sankâśya.

[110] This corresponds with the present Sankisa, the site of which was discovered by General Cunningham in 1842. It is just 40 miles (200 li) south-east of Atrañji. The name of Kapitha has entirely disappeared, although there is a trace of it in a story referred to in *Arch. Surv. of India*, vol. i. p. 271, n. Dr. Kern thinks that the astronomer Varâha Mihira was probably educated at Kapitha.

[111] I translate *sz'* by "sacrifice," because of the curious analogy with words of the same meaning used in this sense in other languages (compare the Greek ποιέω; Lat. *sacra facere*; Sansk. *kṛi*, &c.) It may mean simply "to worship" or "serve."

[112] This story of Buddha's descent from heaven is a popular one among

ascended to the heavenly mansions, and dwelt in the Saddharma Hall,[113] preaching the law for the sake of his mother. Three months having elapsed, being desirous to descend to earth, Śakra, king of the Dêvas, exercising his spiritual power, erected these precious ladders. The middle one was of yellow gold, the left-hand one of pure crystal, the right-hand one of white silver.

Tathâgata rising from the Saddharma hall, accompanied by a multitude of Dêvas, descended by the middle ladder. Mâha-Brahmâ-râja (Fan), holding a white *châmara*, came down by the white ladder on the right, whilst Śakra (Shi), king of Dêvas (Dêvêndra), holding a precious canopy (*parasol*), descended by the crystal ladder on the left. Meanwhile the company of Dêvas in the air scattered flowers and chanted their praises in his honour. Some centuries ago the ladders still existed in their original position, but now they have sunk into the earth and have disappeared. The neighbouring princes, grieved at not having seen them, built up of bricks and chased stones ornamented with jewels, on the ancient foundations (*three ladders*) resembling the old ones. They are about 70 feet high. Above them they have built a *vihâra* in which is a stone image of Buddha, and on either side of this is a ladder with the figures of Brahmâ and Śakra, just as they appeared when first rising to accompany Buddha in his descent.

On the outside of the *vihâra*, but close by its side, there is a stone column about 70 feet high which was erected by Aśôka-râja (Wu-yeu). It is of a purple colour, and shining as if with moisture. The substance is hard and finely grained. Above it is a lion sitting on his haunches,[114] and

---

Buddhists. It is described by Fa-hian (cap. xvii.), and is represented in the sculptures at Sâñchi, *Tree and Serp. Wor.* pl. xxvii. fig. 3, and Bharhut, *Stûpa of Bharhut*, pl. xvii. See *Jour. R. As. Soc.*, N.S., vol. v. pp. 164 ff. For the Trayastrinśas, see Burnouf, *Introd.* p. 541, and *Lotus*, pp. 219, 249, 279.

[113] That is, the preaching hall used by Śakra and the gods of the "thirty-three heaven" for religious purposes.

[114] *Ts'un ku,* "sitting in a squatting position." This expression is

facing the ladder.   There are carved figures inlaid,[115] of wonderful execution, on the four sides of the pillar and around it.   As men are good or bad these figures appear on the pillar (*or disappear*).

Beside the precious ladder (*temple*), and not far from it, is a *stûpa* where there are traces left of the four past Buddhas, who sat and walked here.

By the side of it is another *stûpa*.   This is where Tathâgata, when in the world, bathed himself.   By the side of this is a *vihâra* on the spot where Tathâgata entered *Samâdhi*.   By the side of the *vihâra* there is a long foundation wall 50 paces in length and 7 feet high; this is the place where Tathâgata took exercise.[116]   On the spots where his feet trod are figures of the lotus flower. On the right and left of the wall are (*two*) little *stûpas*, erected by Śakra and Brahmâ-râja.

In front of the *stûpas* of Śakra and Brahmâ is the place where Utpalavarṇâ (Lin-hwa-sih) the Bhikshuní,[117] wishing to be the first to see Buddha, was changed into a Chakravartin-râja when Tathâgata was returning from the palace of Îśvara Dêva to Jambudvîpa.   At this time Subhûti (Su-pu-ti),[118] quietly seated in his stone cell, thought thus with himself: "Now Buddha is returning down to dwell with men—angels lead and attend him.   And now why should I go to the place?   Have I not heard him declare that all *existing things* are void of reality?   Since this is the nature of all things, I have already seen with

---

rendered by Julien "lying down" (*couchant*), but it appears to mean "sitting on his heels or haunches;" but in either case the position of the animal would differ from that of the *standing* elephant discovered by General Cunningham at Saṇkisa (*Arch. Survey*, vol. i. p. 278).

[115] *Teau low*, vid. Med. *sub loc.*

[116] There was a similar stone path at Nâlanda with lotus flowers carved on it.   (See I-tsing and *Jour. R. As. Soc.*, N.S., vol. xiii. p. 571.)

[117] The restoration to Utpalavarṇâ is confirmed by Fa-hian's account (c. xvii.)   Julien had first Puṇḍarîkavarṇâ, which he afterwards altered to Padmavatî.

[118] Subhûti is the representative of the later idealism of the Buddhist creed.   He is the mouthpiece for arguments put forth in the *Prâjñâ Pâramita* works (the *Vajrachhêdikâ*), to show that *all things* are unreal, the body of the law (*dharmakâya*) being the only reality.

my eyes of wisdom the spiritual (*fǎ*) body of Buddha." [19]

At this time Utpalavarṇâ Bhikshunî, being anxious to be the first to see Buddha, was changed into a Chakravartin monarch, with the seven gems [120] (*ratnâni*) accompanying her, and with the four kinds of troops to escort and defend her. Coming to the place where the lord of the world was, she reassumed her form as a Bhikshunî, on which Tathâgata addressed her and said: " You are not the first to see me! Subhûti (Chen-hien), comprehending the emptiness of all things, he has beheld my spiritual body (*dharmakâya*)." [121]

Within the precinct of the sacred traces miracles are constantly exhibited.

To the south-east of the great *stûpa* is a Nâga tank. He defends the sacred traces with care, and being thus spiritually protected, one cannot regard them lightly. Years may effect their destruction, but no human power can do so. Going north-west from this less that 200 li, we come to the kingdom of Kie-po-kio-she (Kanyâkubja).

[119] This differs somewhat from Julien's version. He gives " je me suis attaché á la nature de toutes les lois ; " but it appears to me that the construction is *chu-fǎ-sing-shi*, " the nature of things (*fǎ—dharma*) being thus (*shi*), therefore I have already seen," &c.

[120] For the Seven Precious Things belonging to a wheel king, see Sénart, *La Legende du Buddha*, c. I.

[121] For an account of the three bodies of all the Buddhas, see *J. R. As. S.*, N.S., vol. xiii. p. 555.

END OF BOOK IV.

BOOK V.

Contains the following countries:—(1) *Kie-jo-kio-she-kwŏ;* (2) *'O-yu-t'o;* (3) *'O-ye-mu-k'ie;* (4) *Po-lo-ye-kia;* (5) *Kiao-shang-mi;* (6) *Pi-su-kia.*

KIE-JO-KIO-SHE-KWŎ (KANYÁKUBJA).

THIS kingdom is about 4000 li in circuit; the capital,[1] on the west, borders on the river Ganges.[2] It is about 20 li in length and 4 or 5 li in breadth. The city has a dry ditch [3] round it, with strong and lofty towers facing one another. The flowers and woods, the lakes and ponds,[4] bright and pure and shining like mirrors, (*are seen on every side*). Valuable merchandise is collected here in great quantities. The people are well off and contented, the houses are rich and well found. Flowers and fruits abound in every place, and the land is sown and reaped in due seasons. The climate is agreeable and soft, the manners

---

[1] The capital, Kanyákubja (Kie-jo-kio-she-kwŏ), now called Kanauj. The distance from Kapitha or Sankisa is given by Hiuen Tsiang as somewhat less than 200 li, and the bearing north-west. There is a mistake here, as the bearing is south-east, and the distance somewhat less than 300 li. Kanauj was for many hundred years the Hindu capital of Northern India, but the existing remains are few and unimportant. Kanauj is mentioned by Ptolemy (lib. vii. c. 2, 22), who calls it Καυόγιζα. The modern town occupies only the north end of the site of the old city, including the whole of what is now called the *Kilah* or citadel (Cunningham, *Anc. Geog. of Ind.*, p. 380). This is probably the part alluded to by Hiuen Tsiang in the context. It is triangular in shape, and each side is covered by a ditch or a dry *nala*, as stated in the text. Fa-hian places Kanauj 7 *yojanas* south-east of Samkisa.

[2] That is, borders or lies near the western bank of the Ganges. Julien translates it, "is near the Ganges."

[3] The reference seems to be to the inner or fortified portion (citadel) of the capital city. Julien translates as if it referred to all the cities. The symbol *hwang* means "a dry ditch."

[4] Or the ponds *only*.

of the people honest and sincere. They are noble and gracious in appearance. For clothing they use ornamented and bright-shining (*fabrics*). They apply themselves much to learning, and in their travels are very much given to discussion [5] (*on religious subjects*). (*The fame of*) their pure language is far spread. The believers in Buddha and the heretics are about equal in number. There are some hundred *sanghârdmas* with 10,000 priests. They study both the Great and Little Vehicle. There are 200 Dêva temples with several thousand followers.

The old capital of Kanyâkubja, where men lived for a long time, was called Kusumapura.[6] The king's name was Brahmadatta.[7] His religious merit and wisdom in former births entailed on him the inheritance of a literary and military character that caused his name to be widely reverenced and feared. The whole of Jambudvîpa resounded with his fame, and the neighbouring provinces were filled with the knowledge of it. He had 1000 sons famed for wisdom and courage, and 100 daughters of singular grace and beauty.

At this time there was a Rîshi living on the border of the Ganges river, who, having entered a condition of ecstasy, by his spiritual power passed several myriad of years in this condition, until his form became like a decayed tree. Now it happened that some wandering birds having assembled in a flock near this spot, one of them let drop on the shoulder (*of the Rîshi*) a Nyagrôdha (*Ni-ku-liu*) fruit, which grew up, and through summer and winter afforded him a welcome protection and shade. After a succession of years he awoke from his ecstasy. He arose and desired to get rid of the tree, but feared to injure the nests of the birds in it. The men of the time,

---

[5] This passage, which is confused, seems to refer to their going about here and there to discuss questions relating to religion. The purity of their discourses, i.e., the clearness of their arguments, is wide-spread or renowned.

[6] Keu-su-mo-pu-lo, in Chinese Hwa-kung, flower palace.

[7] In Chinese *Fan-sheu,* "Brahma-given."

extolling his virtue, called him "The great-tree (Mahâ-vṛīksha) Ṛishi." The Ṛishi gazing once on the river-bank as he wandered forth to behold the woods and trees, saw the daughters of the king following one another and gambolling together. Then the love of the world (*the world of desire—Kâmadhâtu*), which holds and pollutes the mind, was engendered in him. Immediately he went to Kusumapura for the purpose of paying his salutations to the king and asking (*for his daughter*).

The king, hearing of the arrival of the Ṛishi, went himself to meet and salute him, and thus addressed him graciously: "Great Ṛishi! you were reposing in peace—what has disturbed you?"[8] The Ṛishi answered, "After having reposed in the forest many years, on awaking from my trance, in walking to and fro I saw the king's daughters; a polluted and lustful heart was produced in me, and now I have come from far to request (*one of your daughters in marriage*).

The king hearing this, and seeing no way to escape, said to the Ṛishi, "Go back to your place and rest, and let me beg you to await the happy period." The Ṛishi, hearing the mandate, returned to the forest. The king then asked his daughters in succession, but none of them consented to be given in marriage.

The king, fearing the power of the Ṛishi, was much grieved and afflicted thereat. And now the youngest daughter of the king, watching an opportunity when the king was at liberty, with an engaging manner said, "The king, my father, has his thousand sons, and on every side his dependents[9] are reverently obedient. Why, then, are you sad as if you were afraid of something?"

The king replied, "The great-tree-Ṛishi has been pleased to look down on you[10] to seek a marriage with one of you,

---

[8] Or it may be rendered, "What outward matter has been able to excite for a while the composed passions of the great Ṛishi?" It does not seem probable that the king was acquainted with the Ṛishi's inten-tion; he could not, therefore, use the words as if expostulating with him.

[9] His ten thousand kingdoms.

[10] That is, on the daughters gene-rally.

and you have all turned away and not consented to comply with his request. Now this Ṛishi possesses great power, and is able to bring either calamities or good fortune. If he is thwarted he will be exceedingly angry, and in his displeasure destroy my kingdom, and put an end to our religious worship, and bring disgrace on me and my ancestors. As I consider this unhappiness indeed I have much anxiety."

The girl-daughter replied, "Dismiss your heavy grief; ours is the fault. Let me, I pray, in my poor person promote the prosperity of the country."

The king, hearing her words, was overjoyed, and ordered his chariot to accompany her with gifts to her marriage. Having arrived at the hermitage of the Ṛishi, he offered his respectful greetings and said, " Great Ṛishi! since you condescended to fix your mind on external things and to regard the world with complacency, I venture to offer you my young daughter to cherish and provide for you (*water and sweep*)." The Ṛishi, looking at her, was displeased, and said to the king, " You despise my old age, surely, in offering me this ungainly thing."

The king said, "I asked all my daughters in succession, but they were unwilling to comply with your request: this little one alone offered to serve you."

The Ṛishi was extremely angry, and uttered this curse (*evil charm*), saying, "Let the ninety-nine girls (*who refused me*) this moment become hump-backed; being thus deformed, they will find no one to marry them in all the world." The king, having sent a messenger in haste, found that already they had become deformed. From this time the town had this other name of the Kuih-niu-shing (Kanyâkubja), *i.e.*, " city of the humped-backed women." [11]

The reigning king is of the Vaiśya [12] caste. His name

---

[11] The *Purânas* refer this story to the curse of the sage Vayn on the hundred daughters of Kuṣaṇâbha.

[12] Vaiśya is here, perhaps, the name of a Râjput clan (Bais or Vaiss), not the mercantile class or

is Harshavardhana (Ho-li-sha-fa-t'an-na).[13] A commission of officers hold the land. During two generations there have been three kings. (*The king's*) father was called Po-lo-kie-lo-fa-t'an-na (Prabhâkaravardhana);[14] his elder brother's name was Râjyavardhana (Ho-lo-she-fa-t'an-na).[15]

Râjyavardhana came to the throne as the elder brother, and ruled with virtue. At this time the king of Karṇasuvarṇa (Kie-lo-na-su-fa-la-na),[16]—a kingdom of Eastern India—whose name was Śaśâṅgka (She-shang-kia),[17] frequently addressed his ministers in these words: "If a frontier country has a virtuous ruler, this is the unhappiness of the (*mother*) kingdom." On this they asked the king to a conference and murdered him.

The people having lost their ruler, the country became desolate. Then the great minister Po-ni (Bhaṇḍi),[18] whose

caste among the Hindus (Cunningham, *op. cit.*, p. 377). Baiswâra, the country of the Bais Rajputs, extends from the neighbourhood of Lakhnau to Khara-Mânikpur, and thus comprises nearly the whole of Southern Oudh (*ib.*)

[13] In Chinese. Hi-tsang, "increase of joy." This is the celebrated Silâditya Harshavardhana, whose reign (according to Max Müller, *Ind. Ant.*, vol. xii. p. 234) began 610 A.D. and ended about 650 A.D. Others place the beginning of his reign earlier, 606 or 607 A.D. (See Bendall's *Catalogue*, Int., p. xli.) He was the founder of an era (*Śrîharsha*) formerly used in various parts of North India. Bendall, *op. cit.*, Int., p. xl.; Hall's *Vâsavadattâ*, pp. 51 f.; *Jour. Bom. B. R. As. Soc.*, vol. x. pp. 38 ff.; *Ind. Ant.*, vol. vii. pp. 196 ff; Reinaud, *Fragm. Arab. et Pers.*, p. 139.

[14] In Chinese, Tso kwong, to cause brightness. The symbol *p'o* is omitted in the text.

[15] In Chinese, Wang tsang, kingly increase.

[16] In Chinese. Kin 'rh, "gold-ear." The town of Rañjâmati, 12 miles

north of Murshidâbâd, in Bengal, stands on the site of an old city called Kurusona-ka-gadh, supposed to be a Bengâli corruption of the name in the text.—*J. As. S. Beng.*, vol. xxii. pp. 281 f.; *J. R. As. S.*, N.S., vol. vi. p. 248; *Ind. Ant.*, vol. vii. p. 197 n.

[17] In Chinese, Yueh, the moon. This was Śaśâṅgka Narêndragupta, king of Gauḍa or Bengal.

[18] Julien restores Po-ni to Bânî. In Chinese it is equal to Pin-liu, "distinguished." Bâṇa, the well-known author of the *Harshacharita*, informs us that his name was Bhaṇḍi. He is referred to in the preface to Boyd's *Nâgânanda*. I-tsing relates that Silâditya kept all the best writers, especially poets, at his court, and that he (*the king*) used to join in the literary recitals; among the rest that he would assume the part of Jimûtavâhana Bôdhisattva, and transform himself into a Nâga amid the sound of song and instrumental music. *Nan hae*, § 32, k. iv. p. 6. Now Jimûtavâhana (*Shiny yun*, "cloud chariot") is the hero of the *Nâgânanda*. The king Śri Harshadêva, therefore, who is mentioned

power and reputation were high and of much weight, addressing the assembled ministers, said, " The destiny of the nation is to be fixed to-day. The old king's son is dead : the brother of the prince, however, is humane and affectionate, and his disposition, heaven-conferred, is dutiful and obedient. Because he is strongly attached to his family, the people will trust in him. I propose that he assume the royal authority : let each one give his opinion on this matter, whatever he thinks." They were all agreed on this point, and acknowledged his conspicuous qualities.

On this the chief ministers and the magistrates all exhorted him to take authority, saying, " Let the royal prince attend ! The accumulated merit and the conspicuous virtue of the former king were so illustrious as to cause his kingdom to be most happily governed. When he was followed by Râjyavardhana we thought he would end his years (*as king*); but owing to the fault of his ministers, he was led to subject his person to the hand of his enemy, and the kingdom has suffered a great affliction; but it is the fault of your ministers. The opinion of the people, as shown in their songs, proves their real submission to your eminent qualities. Reign, then, with glory over the land ; conquer the enemies of your family ; wash out the insult laid on your kingdom and the deeds of your illustrious father. Great will your merit be in such a case. We pray you reject not our prayer."

The prince replied, " The government of a country is a responsible office and ever attended with difficulties. The duties of a prince require previous consideration. As for myself, I am indeed of small eminence; but as my father

---

as the author both of the *Ratnâvali* and the *Nâgânanda,* is Silâditya of Kanauj ; and I-tsing has left us the notice that this king himself took the part of the hero during the performance of the *Nâgânanda.* The real author, however, Professor Cowell thinks, was Dhâvaka, one of the poets residing at the court of Sri Harsha, whilst Bâṇa composed the *Ratnâvali.* The *Jâtulamâlâ* was also the work of the poets of Sri Harsha's court. *Abstract,* &c., p. 197.

and brother are no more, to reject the heritage of the crown, that can bring no benefit to the people. I must attend to the opinion of the world and forget my own insufficiency. Now, therefore, on the banks of the Ganges there is a statue of Avalôkitêśvara Bôdhisattva which has evidenced many spiritual wonders. I will go to it and ask advice (*request a response*)." Forthwith, coming to the spot where the figure of the Bôdhisattva was, he remained before it fasting and praying. The Bôdhisattva recognising his sincere intention (*heart*), appeared in a bodily form and inquired, "What do you seek that you are so earnest in your supplications?" The prince answered, "I have suffered under a load of affliction. My dear father, indeed, is dead, who was full of kindness; and my brother, humane and gentle as he was, has been odiously murdered. In the presence of these calamities I humble myself as one of little virtue; nevertheless, the people would exalt me to the royal dignity, to fill the high place of my illustrious father. Yet I am, indeed, but ignorant and foolish. In my trouble I ask the holy direction (*of the Bôdhisattva*)."

The Bôdhisattva replied, "In your former existence you lived in this forest as a hermit (*a forest mendicant*),[19] and by your earnest diligence and unremitting attention you inherited a power of religious merit which resulted in your birth as a king's son. The king of the country, Karṇasuvarṇa, has overturned the law of Buddha. Now when you succeed to the royal estate, you should in the same proportion exercise towards it the utmost love and pity.[20] If you give your mind to compassionate the condition of the distressed and to cherish them, then before long you shall rule over the Five Indies. If you would establish your authority, attend to my instruction, and by my

[19] "A forest mendicant" is the translation of Araṇya Bhikshu (*lan-yo-pi-ts'u*). It would appear from the text that the place where this statue of Avalôkitêśvara stood was a wild or desert spot near the Ganges.

[20] So I understand the passage as relating to a corresponding favour to the law of Buddha, in return for the persecution of Śaśāṅgka.

secret power you shall receive additional enlightenment, so that not one of your neighbours shall be able to triumph over you. Ascend not the lion-throne, and call not yourself Mahârâja." [21]

Having received these instructions, he departed and assumed the royal office. He called himself the King's Son (Kumâra); his title was Śîlâditya. And now he commanded his ministers, saying, "The enemies of my brother are unpunished as yet, the neighbouring countries not brought to submission; while this is so my right hand shall never lift food to my mouth. Therefore do you, people and officers, unite with one heart and put out your strength." Accordingly they assembled all the soldiers of the kingdom, summoned the masters of arms (*champions,* or, *teachers of the art of fighting*). They had a body of 5000 elephants, a body of 2000 cavalry, and 50,000 foot-soldiers. He went from east to west subduing all who were not obedient; the elephants were not unharnessed nor the soldiers unbelted (*unhelmeted*). After six years he had subdued the Five Indies. Having thus enlarged his territory, he increased his forces; he had 60,000 war elephants and 100,000 cavalry. After thirty years his arms reposed, and he governed everywhere in peace. He then

[21] This appears to be the advice or direction given oracularly (see *Jour. R. As. Soc.*, N.S., vol. xv. p. 334)—

> fi shing see taou che tso
> fi ching ta wang che ho.

The promise is, that if this advice is followed, then, "by my mysterious energy (*or,* in the darkness), shall be added the benefit (*happiness*) of light, so that in the neighbouring kingdoms there shall be no one strong enough to resist (*your arms*)." Śilâditya did, in fact, conquer the whole of North India, and was only checked in the south by Pulikési (the Pulakésa of Hiuen Tsiang, book xi. *infra*), whose title appears to have been Paramésvara, given him on account of his victory over Śilâditya. (See Cunningham, *Arch. Surv.*, vol. i. p. 281; *Ind. Ant.*, vol. vii. pp. 164, 219, &c.) I may here perhaps observe that I-tsing, the Chinese pilgrim, notices his own visit to a great lord of Eastern India called Jih-yueh-kun, *i.e.*, Chandrâditya râja-bhritya (*kumâ*); this is probably the Chandrâditya, elder brother of Vikramâditya, the grandson of Pulakési Vallabha, the conqueror of Śri Harsha Śilâditya (vid. *Jour. R. As. Soc.*, N.S., vol. I. p. 260; and *Ind. Ant.*, vol. vii. pp. 163, 219; I-tsing, *Nan hae*, k. iv. fol. 6 b, and k. iv. fol. 12 a). I-tsing mentions that Chandrâditya was a poet who had versified the *Vessantara Jâtaka.*

practised to the utmost the rules of temperance,[22] and sought to plant the tree of religious merit to such an extent that he forgot to sleep or to eat. He forbade the slaughter of any living thing or flesh as food throughout the Five Indies on pain of death without pardon. He built on the banks of the river Ganges several thousand *stúpas*, each about 100 feet high; in all the highways of the towns and villages throughout India he erected hospices,[23] provided with food and drink, and stationed there physicians,[24] with medicines for travellers and poor persons round about, to be given without any stint. On all spots where there were holy traces (*of Buddha*) he raised *sanghárámas*.

Once in five years he held the great assembly called *Móksha*. He emptied his treasuries to give all away in charity, only reserving the soldiers' arms, which were unfit to give as alms.[25] Every year he assembled the Śramanas from all countries, and on the third and seventh days he bestowed on them in charity the four kinds of alms (viz., food, drink, medicine, clothing). He decorated the throne of the law (*the pulpit*) and extensively ornamented (*arranged*) the oratories.[26] He ordered the priests to carry on discussions, and himself judged of their several arguments, whether they were weak or powerful. He rewarded the good and punished the wicked, degraded the evil and promoted the men of talent. If any one (*of the priests*) walked according to the moral precepts, and was distinguished in addition for purity in religion (*reason*), he himself conducted such an one to "*the lion-throne*" and received from him the precepts of the law. If any one, though distinguished for purity of life, had no distinction

---

[22] *Temperate restrictions;* but *héen* is difficult in this sense.

[23] Punyaśálás — *Tsing-leu*, pure lodging houses, or *choultries.*

[24] There is an error in the text, as pointed out by Julien, n. 2. The text may mean he placed in these buildings "doctor's medicines," or "physicians and medicines."

[25] The expression in the text is *Tan-she*, which, as Julien has observed, is a hybrid term for giving away in *dána*, or charity.

[26] The expression may refer to mats or seats for discussion or for religious services.

for learning, he was reverenced, but not highly honoured.
If any one disregarded the rules of morality and was no-
torious for his disregard of propriety, him he banished
from the country, and would neither see him nor listen to
him.   If any of the neighbouring princes or their chief
ministers lived religiously, with earnest purpose, and aspired
to a virtuous character without regarding labour, he led
him by the hand to occupy the same seat with himself,
and called him "illustrious friend;" but he disdained to
look upon those of a different character.   If it was necessary to transact state business, he employed couriers who
continually went and returned.   If there was any irregu-
larity in the manners of the people of the cities, he went
amongst them.   Wherever he moved he dwelt in a ready-
made building[27] during his sojourn.   During the excessive rains of the three months of the rainy season he would
not travel thus.   Constantly in his travelling-palace he
would provide choice meats for men of all sorts of religion.[28]   The Buddhist priests would be perhaps a thousand; the Brâhmans, five hundred.   He divided each day
into three portions.   During the first he occupied himself
on matters of government; during the second he practised
himself in religious devotion (*merit*) without interruption, so that the day was not sufficiently long.   When I [29]
first received the invitation of Kumâra-râja, I said I would
go from Magadha to Kâmarûpa.   At this time Silâditya-
râja was visiting different parts of his empire, and found
himself at Kie-mi-[30]-ou-ki-lo, when he gave the following

[27] A hut or dwelling run up for
the purpose.   It seems to refer to a
temporary rest-house, made probably of some light material.   From
the next sentence it seems that he
carried about with him the materials
for constructing such an abode.

[28] It will be seen from this that
Silâditya, although leaning to Buddhism, was a patron of other religious sects.

[29] This refers to the pilgrim himself.   The Kumâra-râja who invited
him was the king of Kâmarûpa,
the western portion of Asam (see
Book x.)   Silâditya was also called
Kumâra.   The invitation referred
to will be found in the last section
of the 4th book of the Life of Hiuen
Tsiang.

[30] Here mi is an error for *chu*.
The restoration will be Kajûghira
or Kajinghara, a small kingdom on
the banks of the Ganges, about 92
miles from Champâ.   (*Vide* V. de
St. Martin, *Memoire*, p. 357.)

order to Kumâra-râja: "I desire you to come at once to the assembly with the strange Śramaṇa you are entertaining at the Nâlanda convent." On this, coming with Kumâra-râja, we attended the assembly. The king, Śîlâditya, after the fatigue of the journey was over, said, "From what country do you come, and what do you seek in your travels?"

He said in reply, "I come from the great Tang country, and I ask permission to seek for the law (*religious books*) of Buddha."

The king said, "Whereabouts is the great Tang country? by what road do you travel? aud is it far from this, or near?"

In reply he said, "My country lies to the north-east from this several myriads of li; it is the kingdom which in India is called Mahâchina."

The king answered, "I have heard that the country of Mahâchina has a king called Ts'in,[31] the son of heaven, when young distinguished for his spiritual abilities, when old then (called) 'divine warrior.'[32] The empire in former generations was in disorder and confusion, everywhere divided and in disunion; soldiers were in conflict, and all the people were afflicted with calamity. Then the king of Ts'in, son of heaven, who had conceived from the first vast purposes, brought into exercise all his pity and love; he brought about a right understanding, and pacified and settled all within the seas. His laws and instruction spread on every side. People from other

---

[31] The context and Hiuen Tsiang's reply indicate the reference to the first emperor (Hwang-ti) *She,* or *Urh she,* of the Ts'in dynasty (221 B.C.) It was he who broke up the feudal dependencies of China and centralised the government. He built the great wall to keep out invaders, settled the country, and established the dynasty of the Ts'in. For his conduct in destroying the books, see Mayer's *Manual,* § 368. The reference (farther on) to the songs sung in honour of this king illustrates the character of Śîlâditya, who was himself a poet.

[32] The first Japanese emperor was called *Zin mu,* divine warrior; the allusion in the text may be to the Ts'in emperor being the first to style himself *Hwang ti;* or it may be simply that he was like a god in the art of war.

countries brought under his influence declared themselves
ready to submit to his rule. The multitude whom he
nourished generously sang in their songs of the prowess
of the king of Ts'in. I have learned long since his praises
sung thus in verse. Are the records (*laudatory hymns*) of
his great (*complete*) qualities well founded? Is this the
king of the great Tang, of which you speak?"

Replying, he said, "China is the country of our former
kings, but the 'great Tang' is the country of our present
ruler. Our king in former times, before he became
hereditary heir to the throne (*before the empire was established*), was called the sovereign of Ts'in, but now he is
called the 'king of heaven' (*emperor*). At the end of the
former dynasty [33] the people had no ruler, civil war raged
on every hand and caused confusion, the people were
destroyed, when the king of Ts'in, by his supernatural gifts,
exercised his love and compassion on every hand; by his
power the wicked were destroyed on every side, the eight
regions [34] found rest, and the ten thousand kingdoms
brought tribute. He cherished creatures of every kind,
submitted with respect to the three precious ones. [35] He
lightened the burdens of the people and mitigated punishment, so that the country abounded in resources and the
people enjoyed complete rest. It would be difficult to
recount all the great changes he accomplished."

Śilâditya-râja replied, "Very excellent indeed! the
people are happy in the hands of such a holy king."

Śilâditya-râja being about to return to the city of Kanyâkubja, convoked a religious assembly. Followed by several
hundreds of thousand people, he took his place on the
southern bank of the river Ganges, whilst Kumâra-râja,

---

[33] This can hardly refer to the
Sui dynasty, which preceded the
"great Tang," as Julien says (p.
256 n.), but to the troubles which
prevailed at the end of the Chow
dynasty, which preceded the Ts'in.

[34] That is, the eight regions of the
empire, or of the world.

[35] It is widely believed in China
that the first Buddhist missionaries
arrived there in the reign of the
Ts'in emperor. For the story of
their imprisonment and deliverance
see *Abstract of Four Lectures*, p. 3.

attended by several tens of thousands, took his place on the northern bank, and thus, divided by the stream of the river, they advanced on land and water. The two kings led the way with their gorgeous staff of soldiers (*of the four kinds*); some also were in boats; some were on elephants, sounding drums and blowing horns, playing on flutes and harps. After ninety days they arrived at the city of Kanyâkubja, (*and rested*) on the western shore of the Ganges river, in the middle of a flowery copse.

Then the kings of the twenty countries who had received instruction from Śilâditya-râja assembled with the Śramaṇas and Brâhmaṇs, the most distinguished of their country, with magistrates and soldiers. The king in advance had constructed on the west side of the river a great *sanghâ-râma*, and on the east of this a precious tower about 100 feet in height; in the middle he had placed a golden statue of Buddha, of the same height as the king himself. On the south of the tower he placed a precious altar, in the place for washing the image of Buddha. From this north-east 14 or 15 li he erected another rest-house. It was now the second month of spring-time; from the first day of the month he had presented exquisite food to the Śramaṇas and Brâhmaṇs till the 21st day; all along, from the temporary palace [36] to the *sanghârâma*, there were highly decorated pavilions, and places where musicians were stationed, who raised the sounds of their various instruments. The king, on leaving the resting-hall (*palace of travel*), made them bring forth on a gorgeously caparisoned great elephant a golden statue of Buddha about three feet high, and raised aloft. On the left went the king, Śilâditya, dressed as Śakra, holding a precious canopy, whilst Kumâra-râja, dressed as Brahmâ-râja, holding a white *châmara*, went on the right. Each of them had as an escort 500 war-elephants clad in armour; in front and behind the statue of Buddha went 100 great elephants,

---

[36] The palace of travel, erected during a travelling excursion.

carrying musicians, who sounded their drums and raised
their music. The king, Śilâditya, as he went, scattered
on every side pearls and various precious substances, with
gold and silver flowers, in honour of the three precious
objects of worship. Having first washed the image in
scented water at the altar, the king then himself bore it
on his shoulder to the western tower, where he offered
to it tens, hundreds, and thousands of silken garments,
decorated with precious gems. At this time there were
but about twenty Śramaṇas following in the procession,
the kings of the various countries forming the escort.
After the feast they assembled the different men of
learning, who discussed in elegant language on the most
abstruse subjects. At evening-tide the king retired in
state to his palace of travel.

Thus every day he carried the golden statue as before,
till at length on the day of separation a great fire suddenly
broke out in the tower, and the pavilion over the gate
of the *saṅghârâma* was also in flames. Then the king
exclaimed, " I have exhausted the wealth of my country
in charity, and following the example of former kings, I
have built this *saṅghârâma*, and I have aimed to distinguish myself by superior deeds, but my poor attempts
(*feeble qualities*) have found no return! In the presence of
such calamities as these, what need I of further life ? "

Then with incense-burning he prayed, and with this vow
(*oath*), " Thanks to my previous merit, I have come to reign
over all India; let the force of my religious conduct
destroy this fire; or if not, let me die ! " Then he rushed
headlong towards the threshold of the gate, when suddenly,
as if by a single blow, the fire was extinguished and the
smoke disappeared.

The kings beholding the strange event, were filled with
redoubled reverence; but he (*the king*), with unaltered
face and unchanged accents, addressed the princes thus:
" The fire has consumed this crowning work of my religious
life. What think you of it ? "

The princes, prostrate at his feet, with tears, replied, " The work which marked the crowning act of your perfected merit, and which we hoped would be handed down to future ages, has in a moment (*a dawn*) been reduced to ashes. How can we bear to think of it? But how much more when the heretics are rejoicing thereat, and interchanging their congratulations!"

The king answered, " By this, at least, we see the truth of what Buddha said; the heretics and others insist on the permanency[37] of things, but our great teacher's doctrine is that all things are impermanent. As for me, my work of charity was finished, according to my purpose; and this destructive calamity (*change*) does but strengthen my knowledge of the truth of Tathâgata's doctrine. This is a great happiness (*good fortune*), and not a subject for lamentation."

On this, in company with the kings, he went to the east, and mounted the great *stûpa*. Having reached the top, he looked around on the scene, and then descending the steps, suddenly a heretic (*or*, a strange man), knife in hand, rushed on the king. The king, startled at the sudden attack, stepped back a few steps up the stairs, and then bending himself down he seized the man, in order to deliver him to the magistrates. The officers were so bewildered with fright that they did not know how to move for the purpose of assisting him.

The kings all demanded that the culprit should be instantly killed, but Śilâditya-râja, without the least show of fear and with unchanged countenance, commanded them not to kill him; and then he himself questioned him thus:

" What harm have I done you, that you have attempted such a deed?"

The culprit replied, " Great king! your virtues shine without partiality; both at home and abroad they bring

---

[37] The heretics hold the view of endurance (*shang*, the opposite of *anitya*).

happiness. As for me, I am foolish and besotted, unequal to any great undertaking; led astray by a single word of the heretics, and flattered by their importunity, I have turned as a traitor against the king."

The king then asked, " And why have the heretics conceived this evil purpose ? "

He answered and said, " Great king! you have assembled the people of different countries, and exhausted your treasury in offerings to the Śramaṇas, and cast a metal image of Buddha; but the heretics who have come from a distance have scarcely been spoken to. Their minds, therefore, have been affected with resentment, and they procured me, wretched man that I am! to undertake this unlucky deed."

The king then straitly questioned the heretics and their followers. There were 500 Brâhmans, all of singular talent, summoned before the king. Jealous of the Śramaṇs, whom the king had reverenced and exceedingly honoured, they had caused the precious tower to catch fire by means of burning arrows, and they hoped that in escaping from the fire the crowd would disperse in confusion, and at such a moment they purposed to assassinate the king. Having been foiled in this, they had bribed this man to lay wait for the king in a narrow passage and kill him.

Then the ministers and the kings demanded the extermination of the heretics. The king punished the chief of them and pardoned the rest. He banished the 500 Brâhmans to the frontiers of India, and then returned to his capital.

To the north-west of the capital there is a *stúpa* built by Aśôka-râja. In this place Tathâgata, when in the world, preached the most excellent doctrines for seven days. By the side of this *stúpa* are traces where the four past Buddhas sat and walked for exercise. There is, moreover, a little *stúpa* containing the relics of Buddha's hair and nails; and also a preaching-place[39] *stúpa*.

[39] That is, erected in a place where Buddha had preached.

On the south and by the side of the Ganges are three *saṅghârâmas*, enclosed within the same walls, but with different gates. They have highly ornamented statues of Buddha. The priests are devout and reverential; they have in their service several thousands of "pure men." [39] In a precious casket in the *vihâra* is a tooth of Buddha about one and a half inches in length, very bright, and of different colours at morning and night. People assemble from far and near; the leading men with the multitude join in one body in worship. Every day hundreds and thousands come together. The guardians of the relic, on account of the uproar and confusion occasioned by the multitude of people, placed on the exhibition a heavy tax, and proclaimed far and wide that those wishing to see the tooth of Buddha must pay one great gold piece. Nevertheless, the followers who come to worship are very numerous, and gladly pay the tax of a gold piece. On every holiday they bring it (*the relic*) out and place it on a high throne, whilst hundreds and thousands of men burn incense and scatter flowers; and although the flowers are heaped up, the tooth-casket is not overwhelmed.

In front of the *saṅghârâma*, on the right and left hand, there are two *vihâras*, each about 100 feet high, the foundation of stone and the walls of brick. In the middle are statues of Buddha highly decorated with jewels, one made of gold and silver, the other of native copper. Before each *vihâra* is a little *saṅghârâma*.

Not far to the south-east of the *saṅghârâma* is a great *vihâra*, of which the foundations are stone and the building of brick, about 200 feet high. There is a standing figure of Buddha in it about 30 feet high. It is of native copper (*bronze?*) and decorated with costly gems. On the four surrounding walls of the *vihâra* are sculptured pic-

---

[39] Julien translates this by "Brâh-mans;" but the expression "pure men" is a common one for lay believers or Upâsakas.

tures. The various incidents in the life of Tathâgata, when he was practising the discipline of a Bôdhisattva are here fully portrayed (*engraved*).

Not far to the south of the stone *vihára* is a temple of the Sun-dêva. Not far to the south of this is a temple of Mahêśvara. The two temples are built of a blue stone of great lustre, and are ornamented with various elegant sculptures. In length and breadth they correspond with the *vihára* of Buddha. Each of these foundations has 1000 attendants to sweep and water it; the sound of drums and of songs accompanied by music, ceases not day nor night.

To the south-east of the great city 6 or 7 li, on the south side of the Ganges, is a *stúpa* about 200 feet in height, built by Aśôka-râja. When in the world, Tathâgata in this place preached for six months on the impermanency of the body (*anâtma*), on sorrow (*dukha*), on unreality (*anitya*), and impurity.[40]

On one side of this is the place where the four past Buddhas sat and walked for exercise. Moreover, there is a little *stúpa* of the hair and nails of Tathâgata. If a sick person with sincere faith walks round this edifice, he obtains immediate recovery and increase of religious merit.

To the south-east of the capital, going about 100 li, we come to the town of Na-po-ti-po-ku-lo (Navadêva-kula).[41] It is situated on the eastern bank of the Ganges, and is about 20 li in circuit. There are here flowery

<hr>

[40] These were the subjects on which he preached—*anâtma, anitya, dukha, aśuddhis.* For some remarks on the last of these, see Spence Hardy, *East. Monach.,* p. 247; and Childers, *Páli Dict.,* sub *Asubho.* Jullen's translation, "sur le vide (l'inutilité) de ses macérations," is outside the mark. Fa-hian alludes to this sermon, cap. xviii. (see Beal's edition, p. 71, n. 1).

[41] For some remarks on this place see V. St. Martin, *Memoire,* p. 350; Cunningham, *Anc. Geog. of India,* p. 382; *Arch. Survey of India,* vol. L. p. 294; and compare Fa-hian, *loc. cit.,* n. 2.

groves, and pure lakes which reflect the shadows of the trees.

To the north-west of this town, on the eastern bank of the Ganges river, is a Dêva temple, the towers and storeyed turrets of which are remarkable for their skilfully carved work. To the east of the city 5 li are three *sanghârâmas* with the same wall but different gates, with about 500 priests, who study the Little Vehicle according to the school of the Sarvâstivâdins.

Two hundred paces in front of the *sanghârâma* is a *stûpa* built by Aśôka-râja. Although the foundations are sunk in the ground, it is yet some 100 feet in height. It was here Tathâgata in old days preached the law for seven days. In this monument is a relic (*śarîra*) which ever emits a brilliant light. Beside it is a place where there are traces of the four former Buddhas, who sat and walked here.

To the north of the *sanghârâma* 3 or 4 li, and bordering on the Ganges river, is a *stûpa* about 200 feet high, built by Aśôka-râja. Here Buddha preached for seven days. At this time there were some 500 demons who came to the place where Buddha was to hear the law; understanding its character, they gave up their demon form and were born in heaven.[42] By the side of the preaching-*stûpa* is a place where there are traces of the four Buddhas who sat and walked there. By the side of this again is a *stûpa* containing the hair and nails of Tathâgata.

From this going south-east 600 li or so, crossing the Ganges and going south, we come to the country of 'O-yu-t'o (Ayôdhyâ).

'O-YU-T'O (AYÔDHYÂ).

This kingdom [43] is 5000 li in circuit, and the capital about

---

[42] This expression, "born in heaven," is one frequently met with in Buddhist books. In the old Chinese inscription found at Buddha Gayâ, the pilgrim Chi-i vowed to exhort 30,000 men to prepare themselves in their conduct for a birth in heaven. *J. R. As. S.*, N.S., vol. xiii. p. 553. And in the *Dhammapada* it is constantly mentioned.

[43] The distance from Kanauj or from Navadêvakula to Ayôdhyâ, on

20 li. It abounds in cereals, and produces a large quantity
of flowers and fruits. The climate is temperate and agreeable, the manners of the people virtuous and amiable;
they love the duties of religion (*merit*), and diligently
devote themselves to learning. There are about 100
sanghârâmas in the country and 3000 priests, who study
both the books of the Great and the Little Vehicle.
There are ten Dêva temples; heretics of different schools
are found in them, but few in number.

In the capital is an old *sanghârâma;* it was in this place
that Vasubandhu [44] Bôdhisattva, during a sojourn of several
decades of years, composed various *śâstras* both of the
Great and Little Vehicle. By the side of it are some
ruined foundation walls; this was the hall in which Vasubandhu Bôdhisattva explained the principles of religion
and preached for the benefit of kings of different countries,
eminent men of the world, Śramaṇs and Brâhmaṇs.

To the north of the city 40 li, by the side of the river
Ganges, is a large *sanghârâma* in which is a *stúpa* about
200 feet high, which was built by Aśôka-râja. It was
here that Tathâgata explained the excellent principles of
the law for the benefit of a congregation of Dêvas during
a period of three months.

By the side is a *stúpa* to commemorate the place where
are traces of the four past Buddhas, who sat and walked
here.

To the west of the *sanghârâma* 4 or 5 li is a *stúpa*
containing relics of Tathâgata's hair and nails. To the
north of this *stúpa* are the ruins of a *sanghârâma;* it was

---

the Ghâghra river is about 130 miles
east - south - east. But there are
various difficulties in the identification
of O-yu-to with Ayôdhya. Even if
the Ghâghra be the Ganges of Hiuen
Tsiang, it is difficult to understand
why he should cross this river and
go south. On the other hand, if we
suppose the pilgrim to follow the
course of the Ganges for 600 li and
then cross it, we should place him
not far from Allahâbâd, which is
impossible. General Cunningham
suggests an alteration of the distance
to 60 li, and identifies O-yu-to with
an old town called Kâkúpur, twenty
miles north - west from Kanhpur
(Cawnpore) (*Anc. Geog.,* p. 385).

[44] Vasubandhu laboured and
taught in Ayôdhya (Vassilief, *Boud-
hisme,* p. 220. Kitel, *Handbook,* sub
voc.)

here that Śrîlabdha[45] (Shi-li-lo-to), a master of *śâstras*
belonging to the Sautrântika school, composed the *Vibhâshâ
Śâstra* of that school.

To the south-west of the city 5 or 6 li, in an extensive
grove of Âmra trees, is an old *sanghârâma*; this is where
Asaṅga[46] Bôdhisattva pursued his studies and directed
the men of the age.[47] Asaṅga Bôdhisattva went up by
night to the palace of Maitrêya Bôdhisattva, and there
received[48] the *Yôgâchârya Śâstra*,[49] the *Mahâyana Sûtrâ-
laṅkâraṭikâ*,[50] the *Madyânta Vibhaṅga Śâstra*,[51] &c., and
afterwards declared these to the great congregation, in
their deep principles.

North-west of the Âmra grove about a hundred paces
is a *stûpa* containing relics of the hair and nails of Tathâgata. By its side are some old foundation walls. This
is where Vasubandhu Bôdhisattva descended from the
Tushita heaven and beheld Asaṅga Bôdhisattva. Asaṅga
Bôdhisattva was a man of Gandhâra.[52] He was born in
the middle of the thousand years following the departure
of Buddha from the world; and possessed of deep spiritual
insight, he soon acquired a knowledge of the doctrine (*of
Buddha*). He became a professed disciple, and attached
himself to the school of the Mahîśâsakas, but afterwards
altered his views and embraced the teaching of the Great
Vehicle. His brother, Vasubandhu Bôdhisattva, belonged
to the school of the Sarvâstivâdins, and had inherited a

---

[45] In Chinese *shing-sheu*, victory-
received.

[46] Asaṅga Bôdhisattva was elder
brother of Vasubandhu. His name
is rendered into Chinese by *Wu-cho*,
without attachment.

[47] I have adopted this translation
from Julien; it is not, however,
entirely satisfactory; *ts'ing-yih* certainly means "to ask for more,"
and in this sense it might refer to
pursuit of study; but I think it
means he requested more information or more light, and it seems from
the sentence following that this was
the case, for he ascended into heaven

and received certain books from
Maitrêya.

[48] Not, as Julien translates, "explained to the great assembly," but
received certain books from Maitrêya,
and afterwards explained them to
the great congregation (*samgha*) in
the Âmra grove.

[49] *Yu-kia-sse-ti-lun.*

[50] *Chwong - yan - ta - shing - hing-
lun.*

[51] *Chung-pin-fen-pi-lun.*

[52] According to the Life of Vasubandhu, translated by Chin-ti, he
was born in Purushapura, in North
India.

wide fame, with a strong intelligence and penetrating wisdom and remarkable acumen. The disciple of Asanga was Buddhasimha, a man whose secret conduct was unfathomable, of high talent and wide renown.

These two or three worthies had often talked together in this way : " We all are engaged in framing our conduct so as to enjoy the presence of Maitrêya after death.[53] Whoever of us first dies and obtains the condition (*of being so born in the heaven of Maitrêya*), let him come and communicate it to us, that we may know his arrival there."

After this Buddhasimha was the first to die. After three years, during which there was no message from him, Vasubandhu Bôdhisattva also died. Then six months having elapsed, and there being no message either from him, all the unbelievers began to mock and ridicule, as if Vasubandhu and Buddhasimha had fallen into an evil way of birth, and so there was no spiritual manifestation.

After this, Asanga Bôdhisattva, during the first division of a certain night, was explaining to his disciples the law of entailing (*or* conferring on others) the power of *samâdhi*, when suddenly the flame of the lamp was eclipsed, and there was a great light in space ; then a Rîshi-dêva, traversing through the sky, came down, and forthwith ascending the stairs of the hall, saluted Asanga. Asanga, addressing him, said, " What has been the delay in your coming ?   What is your present name ? "   In reply he said, " At the time of my death I went to the Tushita heaven, to the inner assembly (*i.e., the immediate presence*) of Maitrêya, and was there born in a lotus flower.[54]   On the flower presently opening, Maitrêya, in laudatory terms,

<hr>

[53] This was the desire of the early Buddhists after death to go to Maitrêya, in the Tushita heaven. It is plainly so in the Gayâ inscription, referred to above. Afterwards the fable of a Western Paradise was introduced into Buddhism, and this took the place of Maitrêya's heaven.

[54] This idea of being born in or on a lotus flower gave rise to the name of " the lotus school," applied to the Tsing-t'u, or " pure land " section of Buddhists. But it is a belief not confined to any one school. The mediæval legend of the flower which opens in Paradise on the death of a pure child is a touching survival of the same thought.

addressed me, saying, ' Welcome! thou vastly learned one! welcome! thou vastly learned one!' I then paid him my respects by moving round his person, and then directly[55] came here to communicate my mode of life." Asanga said, "And where is Buddhasiṁha?" He answered, " As I was going round Maitrêya I saw Buddhasiṁha among the outside crowd, immersed in pleasure and merriment. He exchanged no look with me; how then can you expect him to come to you to communicate his condition?" Asanga answered, " That is settled; but with respect to Maitrêya, what is his appearance and what the law he declares?" He said, " No words can describe the marks and signs (*the personal beauty*) of Maitrêya. With respect to the excellent law which he declares, the principles of it are not different from those (*of our belief*). The exquisite voice of the Bôdhisattva is soft and pure and refined; those who hear it can never tire; those who listen are never satiated."[56]

To the north-west of the ruins of the preaching-hall of Asanga about 40 li, we come to an old *saṅghârâma*, bordering the Ganges on the north. In it is a *stûpa* of brick, about 100 feet high; this is the place where Vasubandhu first conceived a desire to cultivate the teaching of the Great Vehicle.[57] He had come to this place from North India. At this time Asanga Bôdhisattva commanded his followers to go forward to meet him. Having come to the place, they met and had an interview. The disciple of Asanga was reposing outside the open window (*of Vasubandhu*), when in the after part of the night he began to recite the *Daśabhûmi Sûtra*. Vasubandhu having heard it, understood the meaning, and was deeply

---

[55] Of course the idea is that *time* in the Tushita heaven is not measured as on earth. It took six months for this flower to open.

[56] This singular account of the heaven of Maitrêya explains the fervent longing of Hiuen Tsiang on his dying bed. to participate in the happiness of those born there (see *Vie*, p. 345).

[57] Vasubandhu had been brought up in the Little Vehicle school. For the account of his conversion to the principles of the Great Vehicle see *Wong Púh*, § 185, *J. R. As. S.*, vol. xx. p. 206.

grieved that this profound and excellent doctrine had not come to his ears in time past, and he laid the blame on his tongue as the origin of his sin of calumniating (*the Great Vehicle*), "and so," said he, "I will cut it out." Seizing a knife, he was about to do so, when he saw Asanga standing before him, who said, "Indeed the doctrine of the Great Vehicle is very profound; it is praised by all the Buddhas, exalted by all the saints. I would teach it to you, but you yourself now understand it; but now, at the very time of understanding it, what good, in the presence of this holy teaching of the Buddhas, to cut out your tongue? Do it not, but (*rather*) repent; and as in old time you abused the Great Vehicle with your tongue, now with the same member extol it. Change your life and renew yourself; this is the only good thing to do. There can be no benefit from closing your mouth and ceasing to speak." Having said this he disappeared.

Vasubandhu, in obedience to his words, gave up his purpose of cutting out his tongue. On the morrow morning he went to Asanga and accepted the teaching of the Great Vehicle. On this he gave himself up earnestly to think on the subject, and wrote a hundred and more *śâstras* in agreement with the Great Vehicle, which are spread everywhere, and are in great renown.

From this going east 300 li or so on the north of the Ganges, we arrive at 'O-ye-mo-khi (Hayamukha).

'O-YE-MU-KHI [HAYAMUKHA]

This kingdom[58] is 2400 or 2500 li in circuit, and the chief town, which borders on the Ganges, is about 20 li round Its products and climate are the same as those of Ayôdhyâ. The people are of a simple and honest disposition. They diligently apply themselves to learning and cultivate

---

[58] This country has not been satisfactorily identified. Cunningham places the capital at Daundia Khera, about 104 miles north-west of Allahâbâd.

religion.   There are five *sanghârâmas*, with about a thousand priests.   They belong to the Saṁmatîya school of the Little Vehicle.   There are ten Dêva temples, occupied by sectaries of various kinds.

Not far to the south-east of the city, close to the shore of the Ganges, is a *stûpa* built by Aśôka-râja, 200 feet high.   Here Buddha in old time repeated the law for three months.   Beside it are traces where the four past Buddhas walked and sat.

There is also another stone *stûpa*, containing relics of Buddha's hair and nails.

By the side of this *stûpa* is a *sanghârâma* with about 200 disciples in it.   There is here a richly adorned statue of Buddha, as grave and dignified as if really alive.   The towers and balconies are wonderfully carved and constructed, and rise up imposingly (*or*, in great numbers) above the building.   In old days Buddhadâsa (Fo-to-to-so),[59] a master of *Śâstras*, composed in this place the *Mahâvibhâshâ Śâstra* of the school of the Sarvâstivâdins.

Going south-east 700 li, passing to the south of the Ganges, we come to the kingdom of Po-lo-ye-kia (Prayâga).

PO-LO-YE-KIA (PRAYÂGA).

This country[60] is about 5000 li in circuit, and the capital, which lies between two branches of the river, is about 20 li round.   The grain products are very abundant, and fruit-trees grow in great luxuriance.   The climate is warm and agreeable; the people are gentle and compliant in their disposition.   They love learning, and are very much given to heresy.

There are two *sanghârâmas* with a few followers, who belong to the Little Vehicle.

There are several Dêva temples; the number of heretics is very great.

---

[59] Julien has pointed out that the symbol *po* is for *so*. The Chinese rendering is "servant of Buddha."

[60] The modern Prayâga or Allahâbâd, at the junction of the Ganges and Jumnâ rivers.

To the south-west of the capital, in a Champaka (*Chen-po-kia*) grove, is a *stûpa* which was built by Aśôka-râja; although the foundations have sunk down, yet the walls are more than 100 feet high. Here it was in old days Tathâgata discomfited the heretics. By the side of it is a *stûpa* containing hair and nail relics, and also a place where (*the past Buddhas*?) sat and walked.

By the side of this last *stûpa* is an old *sanghârâma;* this is the place where Dêva Bôdhisattva composed the *śâstra* called *Kwang-pih (Śata śâstra vaipulyam)*, refuted the principles of the Little Vehicle and silenced the heretics. At first Dêva came from South India to this *sanghârâma.* There was then in the town a Brâhman of high controversial renown and great dialectic skill. Following to its origin the meaning of names, and relying on the different applications of the same word, he was in the habit of questioning his adversary and silencing him. Knowing the subtle skill of Dêva, he desired to overthrow him and refute him in the use of words. He therefore said :—

"Pray, what is your name ?" Dêva said, "They call me Dêva." The heretic rejoined, "Who is Dêva ?" He answered, "I am." The heretic said, "And 'I,' what is that ?" Dêva answered, "A dog." The heretic said, "And who is a dog ?" Dêva said, "You." The heretic answered, "And 'you,' what is that ?" Dêva said, "Dêva." The heretic said, "And who is Dêva ?" He said, "I." The heretic said, "And who is 'I' ?" Dêva said, "A dog." Again he asked, "And who is a dog ?" Deva said, "You." The heretic said, "And who is 'you' ?" Dêva answered, "Dêva." And so they went on till the heretic understood; from that time he greatly reverenced the brilliant reputation of Dêva.

In the city there is a Dêva temple beautifully ornamented and celebrated for its numerous miracles. According to their records, this place is a noted one (*śrî—fortunate ground*) for all living things to acquire religious merit.

If in this temple a man gives a single farthing, his merit is greater than if he gave a 1000 gold pieces elsewhere. Again, if in this temple a person is able to contemn life so as to put an end to himself, then he is born to eternal happiness in heaven.

Before the hall of the temple there is a great tree [61] with spreading boughs and branches, and casting a deep shadow. There was a body-eating demon here, who, depending on this custom (*viz., of committing suicide*), made his abode here; accordingly on the left and right one sees heaps of bones. Hence, when a person comes to this temple, there is everything to persuade him to despise his life and give it up: he is encouraged thereto both by the promptings of the heretics and also by the seductions of the (*evil*) spirit. From very early days till now this false custom has been practised.

Lately there was a Brâhman whose family name was *Tseu* (*putra*); he was a man of deep penetration and great learning, of lucid wit and high talent. This man coming to the temple, called to all the people and said, "Sirs, ye are of crooked ways and perverse mind, difficult to lead and persuade." Then he engaged in their sacrifices with them, with a view afterwards to convert them. Then he mounted the tree, and looking down on his friends he said, "I am going to die. Formerly I said that their doctrine was false and wicked; now I say it is good and true. The heavenly Ṛishis, with their music in the air, call me. From this fortunate spot will I cast down my poor body." He was about to cast himself down when his friends, having failed by their expostulations to deter him, spread out their garments underneath the place where he was on the tree, and so when he fell he was preserved. When he recovered he said, "I thought I saw in the air the Dêvas calling me to come, but now by the

<hr>

[61] This tree is the well-known *Akshaya Vaṭa*, or "undecaying banyan tree," which is still an object of worship at Allahâbâd (Cunningham).

stratagem of this hateful (*heretical*) spirit (*viz., of the tree*), I have failed to obtain the heavenly joys."

To the east of the capital, between the two confluents of the river, for the space of 10 li or so, the ground is pleasant and upland. The whole is covered with a fine sand. From old time till now, the kings and noble families, whenever they had occasion to distribute their gifts in charity, ever came to this place, and here gave away their goods; hence it is called *the great charity enclosure.* At the present time Sîlâditya-râja, after the example of his ancestors, distributes here in one day the accumulated wealth of five years. Having collected in this space of the *charity enclosure* immense piles of wealth and jewels, on the first day he adorns in a very sumptuous way a statue of Buddha, and then offers to it the most costly jewels. Afterwards he offers his charity to the residentiary priests; afterwards to the priests (*from a distance*) who are present; afterwards to the men of distinguished talent; afterwards to the heretics who live in the place, following the ways of the world; and lastly, to the widows and bereaved, orphans and desolate, poor and mendicants.

Thus, according to this order, having exhausted his treasuries and given food in charity, he next gives away his head diadem and his jewelled necklaces. From the first to the last he shows no regret, and when he has finished he cries with joy, "Well done! now all that I have has entered into incorruptible and imperishable treasuries."

After this the rulers of the different countries offer their jewels and robes to the king, so that his treasury is replenished.

To the east of the *enclosure of charity*, at the confluence of the two rivers, every day there are many hundreds of men who bathe themselves and die. The people of this country consider that whoever wishes to be born in heaven ought to fast to a grain of rice, and then drown himself in the waters. By bathing in this water (*they say*) all the pollution of sin is washed away and destroyed; therefore from various quarters and distant regions people come here together and rest. During seven days they abstain from food, and afterwards end their lives. And even the monkeys and mountain stags assemble here in the neighbourhood of the river, and some of them bathe and depart, others fast and die.

On one occasion when Śilâdatya-râja distributed the alms in charity, there was a monkey who lived apart by the river-side under a tree. He also abstained from food in private, and after some days he died on that account from want.

The heretics who practise asceticism have raised a high column in the middle of the river; when the sun is about to go down they immediately climb up the pillar; then clinging on to the pillar with one hand and one foot, they wonderfully hold themselves out with one foot and one arm; and so they keep themselves stretched out in the air with their eyes fixed on the sun, and their heads turning with it to the right as it sets. When the evening has darkened, then they come down There are many dozens of ascetics who practise this rite. They hope by these means to escape from birth and death, and many continue to practise this ordeal through several decades of years.

Going from this country south-west, we enter into a great forest infested with savage beasts and wild elephants, which congregate in numbers and molest travellers, so that unless in large numbers it is difficult (*dangerous*) to pass this way.

Going 500[62] li or so, we come to the country Kiau-shang-mi (Kauśâmbî).

---

[62] The distance is properly 50 li, as stated by Hwui-lih. The capital, however, is 150 li from Prayâga.

KIAU-SHANG-MI [KAUŚÂMBÍ].

This country [63] is about 6000 li in circuit, and the capital about 30 li. The land is famous for its productiveness; the increase is very wonderful. Rice and sugar-canes are plentiful. The climate is very hot, the manners of the people hard and rough. They cultivate learning and are very earnest in their religious life and in virtue. There are ten *sanghârámas*, which are in ruins and deserted; the priests are about 300; they study the Little Vehicle. There are fifty Dêva temples, and the number of heretics is enormous.

In the city, within an old palace, there is a large *vihâra* about 60 feet high; in it is a figure of Buddha carved out of sandal-wood, above which is a stone canopy. It is the work of the king U-to-yen-na (Udâyana). By its spiritual qualities (*or*, between its spiritual marks) it produces a divine light, which from time to time shines forth. The princes of various countries have used their power to carry off this statue, but although many men have tried, not all the number could move it. They therefore worship copies of it,[64] and they pretend that the likeness is a true one, and this is the original of all such figures.

When Tathâgata first arrived at complete enlightenment, he ascended up to heaven to preach the law for the benefit of his mother, and for three months remained absent. This king (*i.e.*, Udâyana), thinking of him with affection, desired to have an image of his person; therefore he asked Mudgalyâyanaputra, by his spiritual power, to transport an artist to the heavenly mansions to observe the excellent marks of Buddha's body, and carve a sandal-wood

---

[63] This has been identified with Kosâmbi-nagar, an old village on the Jumnâ, about thirty miles from Allahâbâd (Cunningham). Kosâmbi is mentioned in the *Râmayana*. It is the scene of the drama of *Ratna-valí*, composed by Bâna in the court of Srí-Harsha or Síládítya.

[64] A copy of this sandal-wood figure was brought from a temple near Pekin, and is referred to in Beal's *Buddhist Pilgrims*, p. lxxv. A fac-simile of it is stamped on the cover of that work. The story of Udâyana, king of Kosâmbí, is referred to by Kâlidâsa in the *Mêghadûta*.

statue. When Tathâgata returned from the heavenly palace, the carved figure of sandal-wood rose and saluted the Lord of the World. The Lord then graciously addressed it and said, "The work expected from you is to toil in the conversion of heretics,[65] and to lead in the way of religion future ages."

About 100 paces to the east of the *vihâra* are the signs of the walking and sitting of the four former Buddhas. By the side of this, and not far off, is a well used by Tathâgata, and a bathing-house. The well still has water in it, but the house has long been destroyed.

Within the city, at the south-east angle of it, is an old habitation, the ruins of which only exist. This is the house of Ghôshira (*Kun-shi-lo*) the nobleman.[66] In the middle is a *vihâra* of Buddha, and a *stûpa* containing hair and nail relics. There are also ruins of Tathâgata's bathing-house.

Not far to the south-east of the city is an old *sanghârâma*. This was formerly the place where Gôshira the nobleman had a garden. In it is a *stûpa* built by Asôka-râja, about 200 feet high; here Tathâgata for several years preached the law. By the side of this *stûpa* are traces of the four past Buddhas where they sat down and walked. Here again is a *stûpa* containing hair and nail relics of Tathâgata.

To the south-east of the *sanghârâma*, on the top of a double-storeyed tower, is an old brick chamber where Vasubandhu Bôdhisattva dwelt. In this chamber he composed the *Vidyâmâtrasiddhi Sâstra* (*Wei-chi-lun*), intended to refute the principles of the Little Vehicle and confound the heretics.

To the east of the *sanghârâma*, and in the middle of an Âmra grove, is an old foundation wall; this was the place

[65] "To teach and convert with diligence the unbelieving, to open the way for guiding future generations, this is your work." I take the symbol *sie* to refer to unbelievers; Julien makes it an interrogative (*yé*).

[66] Asvaghôsha alludes to the conversion of Ghôshira, *Fo-sho-hing-tsan-king*, v. 1710. See also Fa-hien, c. xxxiv.

where Asanga Bodhisattva composed the *sâstra* called
Hin-yang-shing-kiau.

To the south-west of the city 8 or 9 li is a stone dwelling of a venomous Nâga. Having subdued this dragon,
Tathâgata left here his shadow; but though this is a tradition of the place, there is no vestige of the shadow visible.

By the side of it is a *stûpa* built by Asôka-râja, about
200 feet high. Near this are marks where Tathâgata
walked to and fro, and also a hair and nail *stûpa.* The
disciples who are afflicted with disease, by praying here
mostly are cured.

The law of Sâkya becoming extinct, this will be the
very last country in which it will survive; therefore from
the highest to the lowest all who enter the borders of this
country are deeply affected, even to tears, ere they return.

To the north-east of the Nâga dwelling is a great forest,
after going about 700 li, through which we cross the Ganges,
and going northward we arrive at the town of Kia-shi-po-
lo (Kaśapura).[67] This town is about 10 li in circuit; the
inhabitants are rich and well-to-do (*happy*).

By the side of the city is an old *sanghârâma,* of which
the foundation walls alone exist. This was where Dharmapâla [68] Bôdhisattva refuted the arguments of the heretics.
A former king of this country, being partial to the teaching
of heresy, wished to overthrow the law of Buddha, whilst
he showed the greatest respect to the unbelievers. One
day he summoned from among the heretics a master of
sâstras, extremely learned and of superior talents, who
clearly understood the abstruse doctrines (*of religion*). He
had composed a work of heresy in a thousand *slôkas,* consisting of thirty-two thousand words. In this work he
contradicted and slandered the law of Buddha, and represented his own school as orthodox. Whereupon (*the king*)

---

[67] This place has been identified with the old town of Sultânpur on the Gômatî river. The Hindu name of this town was Kuśabhavanapura, or simply Kuśapura (Cunningham).

[68] In Chinese *U'-fâ*; for some notices of *Dharmapâla* see *Wong Pûh*, § 191; in *J. R. As. Soc.*, vol. xx.; Eitel, *Handbook* sub voc., and B. Nanjio, *Catalogue*, col. 373.

convoked the body of the (*Buddhist*) priests, and ordered them to discuss the question under dispute, adding that if the heretics were victorious he would destroy the law of Buddha, but that if the priests did not suffer defeat he would cut out his tongue as proof of the acknowledgment of his fault.[69] At this time the company of the priests being afraid they would be defeated, assembled for consultation, and said, " The sun of wisdom having set, the bridge of the law[70] is about to fall. The king is partial to the heretics; how can we hope to prevail against them ? Things have arrived at a difficult point; is there any expedient to be found in the circumstances, as a way of escape ? " The assembly remained silent, and no one stood up to suggest any plan.

Dharmapâla Bôdhisattva, although young in years, had acquired a wide renown for penetration and wisdom, and the reputation of his noble character was far spread. He was now in the assembly, and standing up, with encouraging words addressed them thus: " Ignorant though I am, yet I request permission to say a few words. Verily I am ready to answer immediately to the king's summons. If by my lofty argument (*discourse*) I obtain the victory, this will prove spiritual protection ; but if I fail in the subtle part of the argument, this will be attributable to my youth. In either case there will be an escape, so that the law and the priesthood will suffer no loss." They said, " We agree to your proposition," and they voted that he should respond to the king's summons. Forthwith he ascended the pulpit.

Then the heretical teacher began to lay down his captious principles, and to maintain or oppose the sense of the words and arguments used. At last, having fully

---

[69] This refers to the dream of king Ajâtaśatru, for which see *Wong Pûh*, § 178. This section of *Wong Pûh* shows that the great Kâśyapa is supposed by Buddhists still to be within the Cock's-Foot Mountain awaiting the coming of Maitrêya.

[70] It would seem from the context that it was the heretical teacher who asked the king to call the assembly, and that if he was defeated he said he would cut out his own tongue.

explained his own position, he waited for the opposite side to speak.

Dharmapâla Bôdhisattva, accepting his words, said with a smile, " I am conqueror! I will show how he uses false arguments in advocating his heretical doctrines, how his sentences are confused in urging his false teaching."

The opponent, with some emotion, said, " Sir, be not high-minded! If you can expose my words you will be the conqueror, but first take my text fairly and explain its meaning." Then Dharmapâla, with modulated voice, followed the principles of his text (*thesis*), the words and the argument, without a mistake or change of expression.

When the heretic had heard the whole, he was ready to cut out his tongue; but Dharmapâla said, "It is not by cutting out your tongue you show repentance. Change your principles—that is repentance!" Immediately he explained the law for his sake; his heart believed it and his mind embraced the truth. The king gave up his heresy and profoundly respected the law of Buddha (*the orthodox law*).

By the side of this place is a *stûpa* built by Asôka-râja; the walls are broken down, but it is yet 200 feet or so in height. Here Buddha in old days declared the law for six months; by the side of it are traces where he walked. There is also a hair and nail *stûpa*.

Going north from this 170 or 180 li, we come to the kingdom of Pi-so-kia (Visâkhâ).

PI-SO-KIA (VISÂKHÂ).

This kingdom [71] is about 4000 li in circuit, and the capital about 16 li round. The country produces abundance of cereals, and is rich in flowers and fruits. The climate is soft and agreeable. The people are pure and honest. They are very diligent in study, and seek to gain merit (*by doing good*) without relaxation. There are 20 *saṅghârâmas* and about 3000 priests, who study the Little Vehicle according

[71] This country is supposed by Cunningham to be the same as Sâ-keta, the Sa-chi of Fa-hien, which is the same as Ayôdhyâ or Oude.

to the Saṁmatîya school. There are about fifty Dêva temples and very many heretics.

To the south of the city, on the left of the road, is a large *saṅghârâma;* this is where the Arhat Dêvaśarma wrote the *Shih-shin-lun* (*Vijñânakâya Śâstra*), in which he defends the position that there is no "I" as an individual.[71] The Arhat Gôpa (Kiu-po) composed also in this place the *Shing-kiau-iu-shih-lun,* in which he defends the position that there is an "I" as an individual.[72] These doctrines excited much controversial discussion. Again, in this place Dharmapâla Bôdhisattva during seven days defeated a hundred doctors belonging to the Little Vehicle.

By the side of the *saṅghârâma* is a *stûpa* about 200 feet high, which was built by Aśôka-râja. Here Tathâgata in old days preached during six years, and occupied himself whilst so doing in guiding and converting men. By the side of this *stûpa* is a wonderful tree which is 6 or 7 feet high. Through many years it has remained just the same, without increase or decrease. Formerly when Tathâgata had cleansed his teeth, he threw away in this place the small piece of twig he had used. It took root, and produced the exuberant foliage which remains to the present time.[73] The heretics and Brâhmaṇs have frequently come together and cut it down, but it grows again as before.

Not far from this spot are traces where the four past Buddhas sat and walked. There is also a nail and hair *stûpa.* Sacred buildings here follow one another in succession; the woods, and lakes reflecting their shadows, are seen everywhere.

Going from this north-east 500 li or so, we come to the kingdom of *Shi-sah-lo-fu-sih-tai* (*Śrâvastî*).

END OF BOOK V.

---

[72] For many arguments on this question of "no personal self," see the Life of Buddha (*Buddhacharita*) by Aśvaghôsha, *passim;* also *Wong Püh,* § 190.

[73] This tree is also noticed by Fa-hian in his account of Sa-chi, and it is this which has led General Cunningham to identify Viśâkhâ with Sâkêta or Ayôdhyâ.

ADDITIONS AND CORRECTIONS.

VOL. I.

———◆———

NOTE 1.—There is an important work called the *Shih-kia-fang-chi*, or "An Account of Buddhist Regions," written by Tao-Sün, who lived A.D. 595–667, in which the three routes from China to India are named (part i. fol. 10 b.) The first is to the south-west of Lake Lop to Tibet and Nêpâl; the second or middle route is from Shen-shen or Leu-lan or Na-fo-po (Tao-Sün speaks of these as one place) to Khotan and so on; the third route is the outward one followed by Hiuen Tsiang. Tao-Sün, in speaking of the Po-lo-mo-lo Moun-tain (vide *infra*, vol. ii. p. 214), renders it "the *black bee* Moun-tain." Perhaps the Temple of Boram Deo, "in a secluded valley at the foot of the Mekhala Hills, near Kamarda," is connected with the worship of Durgâ under this name (Cunningham, *Arch. Surv.*, vol. xvii. p. iv.)

Page xv. *line* 21.—For *Hwui Sâng*, read *Hwei Sâng.*

Page xxxiv.—The custom of putting a sacred object on the head in token of reverence, is still observed in the Greek Church; *conf.* the Liturgy of St. Chrysostom (Neale's *Greek Liturgies*, p. 127) where the sacred vessel is carried on the head of the deacon.

Page xxxv.—The idea of a *square* vihâra being indestructible would con-firm the opinion given (p. 62, vol. i. n. 215) that Svetavâras is the Tetragonis of Pliny; the treasure city of Rameses is also described as "solid upon the earth, like the four pillars of the firmament" (*Funeral Tent of an Egyptian Queen*, p. 18).

VOL. I.   Q

Page xl.—The " yellow spring " may be compared with the Pâli *odakantiko.*

Page xli.—The "marks and impressions" are probably the *wheel marks,* &c., on the bottom of a Buddha's foot ; *cf.* p. 204 *infra.*

Page xlii. *line* 9.—The phrase *shang-tso* refers to the chief of the Sthaviras or priests.

Page xliii.—The symbol *ku* which I here (*last line*) translate by "ruins," is so used throughout Fa-hian ; Huien Tsiang uses the full phrase *ku ke; cf.* K. II. fol. 12, of the *Si-yu-ki,* also *infra,* p. 92.

Page li.—The charioteer called Chhandaka is elsewhere called Kaṇṭaka (*Chung-hu-mo-ho-ti-king,* passim).

Page lxi. *line* 10.—I have taken the phrase *"peh tung hia"* (north, east, below) to be an error for *tung peh hing* (going north-east).

Page lxiv. *line* 10.—The Lôkántarika hells are described as being outside the iron girdle that surrounds a Sakwala.

Page lxix.—With the "one-footed men," compare the Sansc. *Ékacharaṇâs.*

Page lxxxi. *line* 18.—The phrase for "rested" is not to be confined to the "summer rest" of the Buddhists ; it frequently means "remained at rest," or "in quiet ;" *cf.* "the daily use of the Shamans," p. 15.

Page lxxxiii. *line* 4.—Read *Liu* for *Lin.*

Page lxxxiii. *line* 21.—For *fire* read *six.*

Page 17, *n.* 52.—For *Bagarach* read *Bagarash.*

Page 25, *n.* 79.—Red garments are the badge of those condemned to death : vide *the Nâgânanda,* Boyd's translation, p. 62, 63, 67.

Page 105, *n.* 77.—Vasubandhu is sometimes called the twentieth patriarch, *cf.* p. 120, n. 2.

Page 135, *last line.*—For note 4 read 41.

Page 146, *n.* 80.—For Manîkvâla read Manîkyâla.

Page 176, *n.* 30.—The expression, the *"Mung"* king, is frequently used by I-tsing. Perhaps he is the same as the *Balâ-râi,* or the Great King or Lord Paramount of the Muslims (vide Thomas, *The Indian Balhará,* p. 11).

Page 237, *line* 17.—Omit the comma after *li,* and insert one after *"which."*

PRINTED BY BALLANTYNE HANSON AND CO.
EDINBURGH AND LONDON.